Sophia Money-Coutts ~~~~~~~~~~ who has worked as Features Director at *Tatler* for the past five years. Prior to that she worked as a writer an~~~~~~~~~~~~~ *St*~~~~~ and the *Daily Mail* i~~~~~~~~~ ~~~~~Dhabi. She writes a w~~~~~~~~~~~~ ~~~~~' for *The Sunday Teleg*~~~~~~~~ ~~~~~~o and television ch~~~~~~~ ~~~~~~~~~arry's wedding and ~~e etiquette of the threesome. ~~~ *One* is her debut novel.

Twitter: @sophiamcoutts
Instagram: sophiamcoutts
www.sophiamoneycoutts.com

The Plus One

Sophia Money-Coutts

ONE PLACE. MANY STORIES

HQ
An imprint of HarperCollinsPublishers Ltd.
1 London Bridge Street
London SE1 9GF

This edition 2019

3
First published in Great Britain by
HQ, an imprint of HarperCollinsPublishers Ltd. 2018

ISBN: 978-0-00-828850-1

MIX
Paper from
responsible sources
FSC™ C007454

This book is set in 11.6/16 pt. Bembo

Printed and bound by
CPI Group, Croydon CR0 4YY

To my family, who are madder than any
of the characters in this book.
But that's why I love you all so much.

I BLAME SENSE AND SENSIBILITY. I saw the film when I was twelve. A very impressionable age. And more specifically, I blame Kate Winslet. She, Marianne, the second sister, nearly dies for love. That bit where she goes walking in a storm to look at Willoughby's house and is rescued by Colonel Brandon but spends the next few days sweating with a life-threatening fever? That, I decided, was the appropriate level of drama in a relationship.

I consequently set about trying to be as like Marianne as I could. She was into poetry, which seemed a sign because I also liked reading. I bought a little book of Shakespeare's sonnets in homage, which I carried in my school bag at all times in case I had a moment between lessons when I could whip it out and whisper lines to myself in a suitably dramatic manner. I also learned Sonnet 116, Marianne and Willoughby's favourite, off by heart.

'*Let me not to the marriage of true minds admit impediments. Love is not love, which alters when it alteration finds…*'

Imagine a tubby 12-year-old wandering the streets of Battersea in rainbow-coloured leggings muttering that to herself. I was ripe for a kicking. So, yes, I blame *Sense and Sensibility* for making me think I had to find someone. It set me on the wrong path entirely.

I

IF I'D KNOWN THAT the week was going to end in such disaster, I might not have bothered with it. I might just have stayed in bed and slept like some sort of hibernating bear for the rest of the winter.

Not that it started terribly well either. It was Tuesday, 2nd January, the most depressing day of the year, when everyone trudges back to work feeling depressed, overweight and broke. It also just happened to be my birthday. My *thirtieth* birthday. So, I was gloomier than anyone else that morning. Not only had I turned a decade older overnight, but I was still single, living with Joe, a gay oboist, in a damp flat in Shepherd's Bush and starting to think that those terrifying *Daily Mail* articles about dwindling fertility levels were aimed directly at me.

I cycled from my flat to the *Posh!* magazine offices in Notting Hill trying not to be sick. The hangover was entirely my own fault; I'd stayed up late the night before drinking red wine on the sofa with Joe. Dry January could get stuffed. Joe had called it an early birthday celebration; I'd called it a wake for my youth. Either way, we'd made our way through three bottles of wine from the corner shop underneath our flat and I'd woken up feeling like my brain had been replaced with jelly.

Wobbling along Notting Hill Gate, I locked my bike beside the *Posh!* office, then dipped into Pret to order: one white Americano, one egg and bacon breakfast baguette and one berry muffin. According to Pret's nutritional page (book-marked on my work computer), this came to 950 calories, but as I hadn't actually eaten anything with Joe the night before I decided the calories could get stuffed too.

★

'Morning, Enid,' I said over my computer screen, putting the Pret bag on my desk. Enid was the PA to Peregrine Monmouth, the editor for *Posh!* magazine, and a woman as wide as she was tall. She was loved in the office on the basis that she put through everyone's expenses and approved holidays.

'Polly, my angel! Happy Birthday!' She waddled around the desk and enveloped me in a hug. 'And Happy New Year,' she said, crushing my face to her gigantic bosom. Her breath smelled of coffee.

'Happy New Year,' I mumbled into Enid's cardigan, before pulling back and standing up straight again, putting a hand to my forehead as it throbbed. I needed some painkillers.

'Did you have a nice break?' she asked.

'Mmm,' I replied vaguely, leaning to turn on my computer. What was my password again?

'Were you with your mum then?' Enid returned to her desk and started rustling in a bag beside it.

'Mmmm.' It was some variation of my mum's dog's name and a number. *Bertie123*? It didn't work. Shit. I'd have to call that woman in IT whose name I could never remember.

'And did you get any nice presents?'

Bertie19. That was it. Bingo.

Emails started spilling into my inbox and disappearing off the screen. I watched as the counter spiralled up to 632. They were mostly press releases about diets, I observed, scrolling through them. Sugar-free, gluten-free, dairy-free, fat-free. Something new designed by a Californian doctor called the 'Raisin Diet', on which you were only allowed to eat thirty raisins a day.

'Sorry, Enid,' I said, shaking my head and reaching for my baguette. 'I'm concentrating. Any nice presents? You know, some books from Mum. How was your Christmas?'

'Lovely, thanks. Just me and Dave and the kids at home. And Dave's mum, who's losing her marbles a bit, but we managed. I overdid it on the Baileys though so I'm on a new diet I read about.'

'Oh yeah?'

'It's called the Raisin Diet, it's supposed to be ever so good. You eat ten raisins for breakfast, ten raisins for lunch and ten raisins for supper and they say you can lose a stone in a week.'

I watched over my computer screen as Enid counted out raisins from a little Tupperware box.

'Morning, all, Happy New Year and all that nonsense.

Meeting in my office in fifteen minutes please,' boomed Peregrine's voice, as he swept through the door in a navy overcoat and trilby.

Peregrine was a 55-year-old social climber who launched *Posh!* in the Nineties in an attempt to mix with the sort of people he thought should be his friends. Dukes, earls, lords, the odd Ukrainian oligarch. He applied the same principal to his wives. First, an Italian jewellery heiress. Second, the daughter of a Venezuelan oil baron. He was currently married to a French stick insect who was, as Peregrine told anyone he ever met, a distant relation to the Monaco Royals.

'Where is everyone?' he said, reappearing from his office, coat and hat now removed.

I looked around at the empty desks. 'Not sure. It's just me and Enid so far.'

'Well, I want a meeting with you and Lala as soon as she's in. I've got a major story we need to get going with.'

'Sure. What is it?'

'Top secret. Just us three in the meeting. Need-to-know basis,' he said, glancing at Enid. 'You all right?' he added.

Enid was poking the inside of her mouth with a finger. 'Just got a bit of raisin stuck,' she replied.

Peregrine grimaced, then looked back at me. 'Right. Well. Will you let me know as soon as Lala is in?'

I nodded.

'Got it,' said Enid, waving a finger.

★

An hour later, Lala, the magazine's party editor, and I were sitting in Peregrine's office. I'd drunk my coffee and eaten both the baguette and the muffin but still felt perilously close to death.

'So, there's yet another Royal baby on the way,' said Peregrine, 'the Countess of Hartlepool told me at lunch yesterday. They have the same gynaecologist, apparently.'

'Due when?' I asked.

'July,' he said. 'So I want us to get cracking with a quick piece which we can squeeze into the next issue.'

I wondered if I'd live as far as July given how I felt today. Some birthday this was. 'What about something on the Royal playmates?' I said.

Peregrine nodded while scratching his belly, which rolled over his waistband and rested on the tops of his legs. 'Yes. That sort of thing. The Fotheringham-Montagues are having their second too, I think.'

'And my friend Octavia de Flamingo is having her first baby,' said Lala, chewing on her pen. 'They've already reserved a place at Eton in case it's a boy.'

'Well, we need at least ten others so can you both ask around and find more posh babies,' said Peregrine. 'I want it on my desk first thing on Friday, Polly. And can you get the pictures of them all too.'

'Of the parents?' I checked.

'No, no, no!' he roared. 'Of the babies! I want all the women's scan pictures. The sort of thing that no one else will have seen. You know, real, insidery stuff.'

I sighed as I walked back to my desk. *Posh!* was now so insidery it was going to print pictures of the aristocracy's wombs.

★

My Tuesday evenings were traditionally spent having supper with my mum in her Battersea flat and tonight, as a birthday treat, I was doing exactly the same thing.

It was a chaotic and mummified flat. Mum had lived there for nearly twenty years, ever since Dad died and we'd moved to London from Surrey. She worked in a curtain shop nearby because her boss allowed her to bring her 9-year-old Jack Russell to the shop so long as he stayed behind the counter and didn't wee on any of the damask that lay around the place in giant rolls. Bertie largely obliged, only cocking his leg discreetly on the very darkest rolls he could find if Mum got distracted by talking to a customer for too long.

It was the curtain shop that had landed me a job at *Posh!*. Peregrine's second wife – the Venezuelan one – had come in to discuss pelmets for their new house in Chelsea while I was in there talking to Mum one Saturday. And even though Alejandra had all the charm and warmth of a South American despot, I plucked up the courage to mention that I wanted to be a journalist. So, because I was desperate and Peregrine was miserly, he offered me the job as his assistant a few months later. I started by replying to his party invitations and buying his coffees, but after a year or so I'd started writing small pieces for the magazine. Nothing serious. Short articles I mostly made up about the latest trend in fancy dress or the most fashionable canapé to serve at a drinks party. But I worked my way up from there until Peregrine let me write a few longer pieces and interviews with various mad members of the British aristocracy. It wasn't the dream role. I was hardly Kate Adie reporting from the Gaza Strip in a flak jacket. But it was a writing job, and, even though back when I started I didn't know anything about the upper classes (I thought a viscount was a type of biscuit), it seemed a good start.

'Happy birthday, darling, kick my boots out of the way,' Mum shouted from upstairs when I pushed her front door open that night to the sound of Bertie barking. There was a pile of brown envelopes on the radiator grille in the hall, two marked 'Urgent'.

'Mums, do you ever open your post?' I asked, walking upstairs and into the sitting room.

'Oh yes, yes, yes, don't fuss,' she said, taking the envelopes and putting them down on her desk, where magazines and old papers covered every spare chink of surface. 'I've made a cake for pudding,' she went on, 'but I've got some prawns in the fridge that need eating, so we're having them first. I thought I might make a risotto?'

'Mmm, lovely, thank you,' I replied, wondering whether Peregrine would believe me if I called in sick because my mother had poisoned me with prawns so old they had tap-danced their way into the risotto.

'Have you had a nice birthday?' Mum asked. 'How was work?'

'Oh, you know, Peregrine's Napoleonic tendencies are as rampant as ever. I've got to write a piece on Royal babies and their playmates.'

'Oh dear,' said Mum vaguely, as she walked towards the kitchen, opened the fridge and took out a bottle of wine. In the four years I'd worked at *Posh!*, I'd learned more about the upper classes than I'd ever expected to. A duke was higher than an earl in the pecking order and they were all obsessed with their Labradors. But Mum, a librarian's daughter from Surrey, while supportive of my job, wasn't much interested in the details.

She poured two glasses of white wine and handed me one. 'Now, let's sit down and then I can give you your present.'

I collapsed on the sofa whereupon Bertie instantly jumped on my lap and white wine sloshed over the rim of my glass and into my crotch.

'Bertie, get down,' said Mum, handing me a small jewellery box and sitting down beside me. She stared at Bertie and pointed at the floor, as he slowly and reluctantly climbed off the sofa. I opened the box. It was a ring. A thin, delicate gold band with a knot twisted into the metal.

'Your dad gave it to me when you were born. So, I thought, to mark a big birthday, you should have it.'

'Oh, Mum...' I felt choked. She hardly ever mentioned Dad. He'd had a heart attack and died at forty-five when I was just ten years old. Our lives changed forever in that moment. We had to sell our pretty, Victorian house in Surrey and Mum and I moved to this flat in Battersea. We were both in shock. But we got on with our new life in London because there was no alternative. And we'd been a small, but intensely close, unit ever since. Just us two. And then Bertie, when I left for university and Mum decided she needed a small, hairy substitute child.

I slipped the ring on my finger. It was a bit tight over the knuckle, but it went on easily enough. 'I love it,' I said, looking at my hand, then looking up at Mum. 'Thank you.'

'Good, I'm glad it fits. And now, listen, I have something I need to chat to you about.'

'Hmmm?' I was trying to turn the ring on my finger. A bout of dysentery from prawn-related food poisoning might not be the worst thing, actually. I could probably lose half a stone.

'Polly?'

'Yes, yes, sorry, am listening.' I stopped fiddling with the ring and sat back against the sofa.

'So,' started Mum. 'I went to see Dr Young last week. You know this chest pain that's been worrying me? Well, I've been taking my blood pressure pills but they haven't been doing any good so I went back on Thursday. Terrible this week because the place was full of people sneezing everywhere. But I went back and, well, he wants me to have a scan.'

'A scan?' I frowned at her.

'Yes. And he says it may be nothing but it's just to be sure that it is nothing.'

'OK… But what would it be if it wasn't nothing?'

'Well, you know, it could be a little something,' said Mum, breezily. 'But he wants me to have a scan to check.'

'When is it?' I felt sick. Panicky. Only two minutes ago I'd been worrying about the sell-by date on a packet of prawns. It suddenly seemed very silly.

'I'm waiting for the letter to confirm the date. Dr Young said I'll hear in the next couple of weeks but the post is so slow these days, so we'll see.'

'It might help if you looked at the pile of post downstairs every now and then, Mum,' I said, as gently as I could. 'You don't want to miss it.'

'No. No, I know.'

I'd always told myself that Mum and I had done all right on our own over the years. Better, even, than all right. We were way closer than some of my friends were with their parents. But every now and then I wished Mum had a husband to look after her. This was one of those moments. For support. For help. For another person to talk to. She could hardly discuss the appointment with Bertie.

'Well, will you let me know when you get the letter and I'll come with you? Where will it be?' I asked.

'Oh there's no need, darling. You've got work. Don't fuss.'

'Don't be silly, obviously I'm coming. I work for a magazine, not MI6. No one will mind if I take a few hours off.'

'What about Peregrine?'

'He'll manage.'

'OK. If you're sure, that would be lovely. The appointment will be at St Thomas'.'

'Good, that's sorted,' I said, trying to sound confident, as

if the scan was a routine check-up and there was nothing to
worry about. 'Now let's have a sniff of those prawns.'

★

By Friday afternoon, I had six posh babies and their scan pictures. Where the hell were another four going to come from?
My phone vibrated beside my keyboard and a text popped up
from Bill, an old friend who always threw a dinner party at
the end of the first week of January to celebrate the fact the
most cheerless week of the year was over.

Come over any time from 7! X

I looked back at my screen full of baby scans. Jesus. A baby.
That seemed a long way off. I hadn't had a proper boyfriend
since university when I went out with a law student called
Harry for a year, but then Harry decided to move to Dubai
and I cried for about a week before my best friend, Lex, told
me I needed to 'get back out there'. My love life, ever since,
had been drier than a Weetabix. The odd date, the odd fumble,
the odd shag which I'd get overexcited about before realizing
that, actually, the shag had been terrible and what was I getting
so overexcited about anyway?

Last year, I'd had sex twice, both times with a Norwegian
banker called Fred who I met through a mutual friend at a
picnic in Green Park in the summer. If you can call several
bottles of rosé and some olives from M&S a picnic. Lex and
I drank so much wine that we decided to pee under a low-
hanging tree in the park as it got dark. This had apparently

impressed Fred, who moved to sit closer to me when Lex and I returned to the circle.

We'd all ended up in the Tiki bar of the London Hilton on Park Lane, where Fred ordered me a drink which came served in a coconut. He'd lunged in the car park and then I'd waited until I was safely inside my cab home before wiping off the wetness around my mouth with the back of my hand. We'd gone on a couple of dates and I'd slept with him on both those dates – possibly a mistake – and then he'd gone quiet. After a week, I texted him breezily asking if he was around for a drink. He replied a few days later.

Oh, sorry been travelling so much for work and not sure that's going to change any time soon. F

'F for fucking nobody, that's who,' said Lex, loyally, when I told her.

So, that, for me, was the total of last year's romantic adventures. Depressing. Other people seemed to have sex all the time. And yet here I was, sitting in my office like an asexual plant, hunting for scan pictures, evidence that other people had had sex.

I squinted through the window up the alleyway towards Notting Hill Gate. It was the kind of grey January day that couldn't be bothered to get properly light, when people hurried along pavements with their shoulders hunched, as if warding off the gloom.

Whatever. It would be six o' clock soon and I could escape it all for Bill's flat and a delicious glass of wine. Or several delicious glasses of wine, if I was honest.

★

At one second past six, I left the office, winding my way
through the hordes of tourists at Notting Hill Gate Tube
station. They were dribbling along at that special tourist pace
which makes you want to kick them all in the shins. Then,
emerging at Brixton, I walked to the corner shop at the end
of Bill's street to buy wine. And a big bag of Kettle Chips.
'Let's go mad, it's Friday, isn't it?' I said to the man behind
the till, who ignored me.

Bill lived in the ground-floor flat on a street of white ter-
raced houses. He'd bought it while working as a programmer
at Google, though he'd left them recently to concentrate on
developing an app for the NHS. Something to do with making
appointments. Bill said that it was putting his nerd skills to
good use, finally. He'd never tried to hide his dorkiness. It
was one of the reasons we became friends at a party when we
were teenagers.

Lex had been off snogging some boy upstairs in the bathroom (she was always snogging or being fingered, there was
a lot of fingering back then) and I'd been sitting on a sofa
in the basement, tapping my foot along to Blue so it looked
like I was having a good time when, actually, I was having a
perfectly miserable time because no boy ever wanted to snog
me. And if no boy ever wanted to snog me then how would
I ever be fingered? And if I was never fingered how would I
ever get to have actual sex? It seemed hopeless. And, just at the
moment when I decided I might go all *Sound of Music* and enter

a convent – were there convents in South London? – a boy had sat down on the other end of the sofa. He had messy black hair and glasses that were so thick they looked double-glazed.

'I hate parties,' he'd said, squinting at me from behind his double-glazing. 'Do you hate parties too?'

I'd nodded shyly at him and he'd grinned back.

'They're awful, aren't they? I'm Bill by the way.' He'd stuck out a hand for me to shake, so I shook it. And then we'd started talking over the music about our GCSEs. It was only when Lex surfaced for air an hour or so later, gasping for breath, mouth rubbed as red as a strawberry, that I realized I'd made a friend who was a boy. Not a boyfriend. I didn't want to snog Bill. His glasses really were shocking. But he became a friend who was a boy all the same. And we'd been friends ever since.

'Come in, come in,' Bill said when I arrived. He opened the front door with one hand and held a pair of jeans in the other. 'Sorry, I haven't changed yet.' He grinned. 'You're the first.'

'Go change,' I said. 'Is there anything I can do?'

'No. Leave those bottles on the side and open whatever you want. I'll be two minutes,' he said, walking towards his bedroom.

I opened the fridge. It was rammed. Sausages, packets of bacon, some steaks. Something that might once have been a tomato and would now be of considerable interest to a research scientist. No other discernible vegetables. I reached for a bottle of white wine and fished in a drawer for a corkscrew.

Bill appeared back in the kitchen in his jeans and a t-shirt that said 'I am a computer whisperer' on it. In the years since

I'd met him, he'd discovered contact lenses but developed a questionable line of t-shirts. 'I'll have one of those please. Actually, no I won't. I'll have a beer first. So, how's tricks?' he asked, opening a bottle. 'How was Christmas? How was your birthday and so on? I've got you a card actually.' He picked up an envelope from his kitchen table and gave it to me. 'Here you go.'

'Being single at 30 isn't as bad as it used to be,' the front of the card read. I smiled, 'Thanks, dude. Really helpful.' I put the card down on the side and had a sip of wine. 'And Christmas was lovely, thanks. Quiet, but kind of perfect. I ate, I slept. You know, the usual.' I'd been worrying about Mum and her scan all week, but I didn't want to mention it to anyone else yet. If I didn't talk about it, I could keep a lid on the panic I felt when I woke in the middle of the night and lay in bed thinking about the appointment. I had decided to wait for the results of the scan and then we could go from there. 'Anyway, how was yours?'

'Terrible,' Bill replied. 'I was working for most of it, trying to sort out some investors.' He took a swig of beer and leant on the kitchen counter. 'So, I haven't left the office before midnight this week and I'm doing no exercise apart from walking from my desk to have a pee four times a day. But that's how start-up life is,' he sighed and had another slug of his beer.

'Love life?' I asked.

'I'm still seeing that girl, Willow. I told you about her before Christmas, right?'

I nodded. 'The Tinder one? Who works in… ?' I couldn't

actually remember much about her. I was always, selfishly, slightly peeved when Bill was dating someone because it meant he was less available for cinema trips and pizza.

'Interior design, yeah. She's cool. But everything's so busy at the moment that I keep having to cancel on any plans we make in favour of a "chicken chow mein for one" at my desk.'

'Have you invited her tonight?'

'Yeah. But she couldn't make it.'

'OK. So, who's coming?'

Normally, Lex would be here too, and she and I would spend the night drinking wine while discussing our New Year's resolutions. But Lex had gone away to Italy with her boyfriend, Hamish, this year. So, I was slightly nervous about who Bill had invited. Or not nervous exactly. Just apprehensive about having to talk to strangers all night.

'Er, there's Robin and Sal, who you know. Then a couple I don't think you've met who are friends from home who've just got engaged – Jonny and Olivia. Two friends from business school you haven't met either. Lou, who's in town for a bit from America, who you'll love, she's amazing. And a guy called Callum I haven't seen for years but who knows Lou, too.' He looked at his phone as it buzzed. 'Oh, that's her now,' he said.

'Lou, hi,' he said, answering it. 'No, no, don't worry, just a bottle of something would be great… number fifty-three, yep? Blue door, just ring the bell. See you in a tick.'

★

By 11 p.m., everyone was still sitting around Bill's kitchen table, their wine glasses smeary from sticky fingers. I'd drunk a lot of red wine and was sitting at one end of the table, holed up like a hostage, while Sal and Olivia, sitting either side of me, discussed their weddings. How was it physically possible for two fully grown women to care so much about what font their wedding invitations should be written in? I thought about the countless weddings I'd been to in the past couple of years. Lace dress after lace dress (since these days everyone wanted to look as demure as Kate Middleton on her wedding day), fistfuls of confetti outside the church, a race back to the reception for ninety-four glasses of champagne and three canapés. Dinner was usually a bit of a blur if I was honest. Some sort of dry chicken, probably. Then thirty-eight cocktails after dinner, which I typically spilled all over myself and the dance floor. Bed shortly after midnight with a blistered foot from the inappropriate heels I'd worn. I couldn't recall what font any of the invitations were written in.

'Polly,' they said simply at the top. Just 'Polly' on its own. Never 'Polly and so-and-so' since I never had a boyfriend. Sometimes an invitation said 'Polly and plus one'. But that was similarly hopeless since I never had one of those either. I reached for the wine bottle, telling myself to stop being so morose.

'Who's for coffee?' asked Bill, standing up.

'I'm OK on red.'

'You're not on your bike tonight?' asked Bill.

'Nope, I'll Uber. But touched by your concern.'

'Just checking. Right, everyone next door. I'm going to put the kettle on.'

There were murmurs of approval and everyone stood and started to gather up plates and paper napkins from the floor. 'Don't do any of that,' said Bill. 'I'll do it later.'

I picked up the wine bottle and my glass and walked through the doors into the sitting room, collapsing onto a sofa and yawning. Definitely a bit pissed.

Sal and Olivia followed after me and sat on the opposite sofa, still quacking on about weddings. 'We're having a photo booth but not a cheese table because I don't think it ever gets eaten. What do you think?' I heard Sal say.

As if she'd been asked her opinion on Palestine, Olivia solemnly replied, 'It's so hard, isn't it? We're not having a photo booth but we are going to have a videographer there all day, so…'

I yawned again. I'd been at uni with Sal. She once stripped naked and ran across a football pitch to protest against tuition fees. But here, discussing cheese tables and photo booths, she seemed a different person. An alien from Planet Wedding.

'So, you're a fellow cyclist?' said Bill's friend from business school, sitting down beside me on the sofa.

'Yup. Most of the time. Just not when I've drunk ten bottles of wine.'

'Very sensible. Sorry, I'm Callum by the way.' He stuck his hand out for me to shake.

Stuck, as I had been, between two wedding fetishists, I hadn't noticed Callum much. He had a shaved head and was wearing a light grey t-shirt, which showed off a pair of muscly upper arms, and excellent trainers. Navy blue Nike Airs. I always looked at men's shoes. Pointy black lace-ups: bad. The correct pair of trainers: aphrodisiac. Lex always criticized me for being too picky about men's shoes. But what if you started dating someone who wore pointy black lace-ups, or, worse, shiny brown shoes with square ends, and then fell in love with them? You'd be looking at spending the rest of your life with someone who wore bad shoes.

'I'm Polly,' I replied, looking up from Callum's trainers.

'So you're an old mate of Bill's?'

'Yep, for years. Since we were teenagers.'

He nodded.

'And you met him at business school?'

He nodded again. 'Yeah, at LBS.'

'So what do you do now?' I asked.

'Deeply boring. I work in insurance, although I'm trying to move into K&R.'

'What's that?'

'Kidnap and ransom. So more the security world really.' He leant back against the sofa and propped one of his muscly arms on it.

'How very James Bond.'

He laughed. 'We'll see.'

'Do you travel a lot?'

'A bit. I'd like to do more. To see more. What about you?'

'I work for a magazine. It's called *Posh!*' I said, as if it was a question, wondering if he'd heard of it.

He laughed again and nodded. 'I know. Sort of... society stuff?'

'Exactly. Castles. Labradors. That sort of thing.'

He grinned at me. 'I like Labradors. Fun?'

'Yup. Mad, but fun.'

'Do you get to travel much?'

'Sometimes. To cold, draughty piles in Scotland if I'm very lucky.'

'How glamorous,' he said, grinning again.

Was this flirting? I wasn't sure. I was never sure. At school, we'd learned about flirting by reading *Cosmopolitan*, which said that it meant brushing the other person with your hand lightly. Also, that girls should bite their lips in front of boys, or was it lick their lips? They should do something to attract attention to their mouths, anyway. My flirting skills hadn't progressed much since and, sometimes, when trying to cack-handedly flirt with someone, I'd simultaneously touch a man's arm or knee *and* lick my lips and end up looking like I was having some kind of stroke.

'Hang on, hold your glass for a moment,' he said, leaning across me.

My stomach flipped. Was he lunging? Here? Already? In Bill's flat? Blimey. Maybe I didn't give myself enough credit. Maybe I was better at flirting than I realized.

He wasn't lunging. He was reaching for a book. Underneath my glass, on the coffee table, was a huge, heavy coffee table book. Callum picked it up and laid it across both our laps.

He leant back and started flicking through the pages. They

were exquisite travel photos – reindeer in the snow around a Swedish lake, an old man washing himself on some steps in Delhi, a volcano in Indonesia belching out great clouds of orange smoke.

'I want to go here,' he said, pointing at a photo of a chalky landscape, a salt flat in Ethiopia.

'Go on then. And then… let's go here,' I replied, turning the page. It was Venice.

'Venice? Have you ever been?' He turned to look at me.

'No.' Was now a good moment to touch his arm? I quite wanted to touch his arm.

'Then I will take you.'

'Ha!' I laughed nervously and clapped my hand on his forearm.

We carried on turning the pages and laughing for a while, discussing where we wanted to go until the photos were becoming quite blurry. I wasn't really concentrating anyway, because Callum had moved his leg underneath the book so it was touching mine. I glanced across at him. How tall was he? Hard to tell sitting down.

'Right, team,' said Bill, sometime later from across the room, draining his coffee cup. 'I think it might be home time. Sorry to end the party but I've got to go into the office tomorrow.'

Callum closed the book and moved his leg, stretching out on the sofa and yawning. 'Fun sponge.'

'I know, mate, but some of us can't just drink for a living. We've got real jobs.'

'Talk to me when I'm in Peshawar.' He stood up and clapped Bill on the back in a man hug. 'Good to see you after so long, mate. Thanks for dinner.' He was the same height as Bill, I noted. Sort of six foot-ish. A good height. The size I always wanted a man to be so I didn't feel like a giraffe in bed next to him. That thing about everybody being the same size lying down is rubbish.

Around us, everyone else was saying goodbye to one another. 'Thanks, love,' I said, hugging Bill. 'Don't work too hard tomorrow.'

'Welcome,' he said back, into my shoulder. 'And I won't. I should be around on Sunday if you are? Cinema or something? Is Lex back?'

'Yup, she gets back tomorrow so said I'd see her for lunch on Sunday. Wanna join?'

'Maybe, speak tomorrow?'

I nodded and Bill turned to say goodbye to Lou behind us.

'Where you heading back to?' Callum asked as we stood by the open front door. I was squinting at my phone, trying to find Uber.

'Shepherd's Bush.'

'Perfect. As you're not cycling I will escort you home.'

'Why, where are you?'

'Nearby,' he replied. 'What's your postcode?'

This never happened. Sightings of the Loch Ness Monster were more common than me going home with anyone. I frowned as I tried to remember what state my bikini line was in. I probably shouldn't sleep with him; I had an awful feeling it looked like the Hanging Gardens of Babylon.

'What's wrong?' he said, looking at my face.

'Nothing, all good,' I replied quickly. Also, I knew I hadn't shaved my legs for weeks. Or months, maybe. So, a few minutes later, in the back of the Uber, I reached down and tried to surreptitiously stick two fingers underneath the ankle of my jeans to check how bristly my legs were. They felt like a scouring brush.

'What you doing?' asked Callum, looking at me quizzically.

'Just an itch.' I sat back in the taxi.

'You're not coming in,' I said, in my sternest voice, when the car pulled up outside my flat.

''Course I am. I need to make sure you get in safely,' he replied, opening his door and getting out.

So, as alarmed as I was about my ape-like levels of hairiness, I let him in, whereupon he immediately started looking through my kitchen cupboards. I kicked off my shoes and sat at the kitchen table, watching him, still hiccupping.

'Shhhhhh, my flatmate's asleep,' I said to his back, as he inspected the labels of five or six half-empty bottles he'd discovered in one cupboard.

'This'll do.' It was a bottle of cheap vodka, the sort that turns you blind. 'Where are your glasses?'

I pointed at a cupboard above his head.

'I can't drink all that,' I said, as he handed me a glass.

'Yes you can, just knock it back.' He swallowed his in one and looked at me expectantly.

I lifted my glass, nearly gagged at the vapours, then opened my mouth and took three slugs.

'Good work.' He took the glass back as I shivered and put it down on the table. 'I mean, why do the Russians like this so much? It's disgusting, swallowing it makes me—'

He interrupted me by cupping my face with his hands and kissing me. His tongue tasted of vodka.

'Which one's your room?'

I pointed at a door, and he took my hand, pulled me off the kitchen table and into my room, where I froze. There were two embarrassing things I needed to hide: my slightly shrivelled, browning earplugs on the bedside table, and my ancient bunny rabbit, a childhood comforter, which was lying between the pillows, his glass eyes glaring at me with an accusatory air.

I reached for both, opened my knicker drawer and stuffed them in there. I felt briefly guilty about my rabbit and then thought, *You are about to have sex for the first time in five hundred months, Polly, now is not the time to be sentimental about your stuffed toy.*

Callum sat down at the end of the bed and started unlacing his shoes.

'Hang on, I'm just going to do something.' I picked up a box of matches on the bedside table and lit a candle next to it.

And here is a list of the things that happened next, which illustrates why I should never, ever be allowed to even think about having sex with anyone.

Having lit the candle, I sat next to Callum and he started unbuttoning my shirt. But then I panicked about him doing this while I was sitting because of the fat rolls on my stomach, so I lay down instead, pulling him back onto the bed. He then undid the rest of my shirt buttons and there were a few undignified moments where I flailed around like a beached seal trying to get my arms out of it.

The tussle of the bra strap. Callum reached for it, clearly wanting to be one of those nimble-fingered men who just have to blink at a bra strap – any bra strap – for it to ping free. 'I've nearly got it,' he said, after several seconds of fiddling while I arched my back.

Getting my knickers off. This required me to waggle my legs in the air like an upturned beetle.

Callum then moved his way down my stomach until he was kneeling on the floor, his head between my legs. I wondered whether to make a joke about needing some sort of Black & Decker machinery to get through the hair and then decided it would kill the vibe. So, I started worrying about my breathing instead. It's awkward to just lie there in silence, so I decided to start panting a bit as he used his tongue on me. But it's quite hard to pant when, after a promising beginning, Callum – perhaps encouraged by my erratic breathing – started working harder with his tongue, like a dog at a water bowl. So, then it started hurting, as opposed to feeling remotely pleasurable, and I decided I'd lost sensation in my entire vagina and instead lay there wondering when to suggest that he came back up again. And how do you do that, anyway, without causing offence?

The worst bit of all. I tapped him on the head and he looked up. 'Come up,' I said, in what I hoped was a seductive, come-hither way.

He looked up from between my legs and frowned. 'Why? Aren't you enjoying it?'

Oh, GOD, why is sex this embarrassing? Does it always have to be this embarrassing?

'No, no, I just want to, erm, return the favour.'

CRINGE. I thought I might die. I might actually die from cringing.

So Callum crawled back up and rolled over, lying on his back, still with his boxers on. I then climbed on top of him, trying not to slouch again so that my stomach didn't crease into rolls of fat. Then I noticed that I hadn't plucked my nipple hairs recently either. Too late. I wriggled backwards so that I was kneeling between his legs and started pulling his boxers off. Another difficult move because I had to stand up to pull them out from underneath him.

Callum's penis wasn't quite hard, so I opened my mouth and gently started sucking the head of it. He groaned. I ran my mouth slowly down it, trying to ignore the musty smell. After a few minutes, my thigh muscles started to burn. For God's sake. How much longer was this going to go on for? I wriggled my knees in a bit closer, then opened one eye and squinted at his penis. Why do they look like giant earthworms? Then his moaning started getting louder and I felt one of his hands on my head, pressing my mouth down. I'd read magazine articles before that said you should suck their balls as well, but I'd never been sure I could fit everything in my mouth at once. It would be like tackling a foot-long Subway. Or were you supposed to suck just one ball at a time?

I gagged as his penis hit the back of my throat, then he gave a sudden shout and my mouth filled with warm semen. Slightly salty, slightly sweet. I swallowed as quickly as possible. The thought of that swimming around in my stomach with the vodka was ungodly.

'Just going to get a glass of water,' I said through a sticky mouth, climbing over him and picking up an empty glass from the bedside table. In the bathroom, I wiped my mouth with some tissue and looked in the mirror. Well, that bit's done so that's something. And it's always quite gratifying to get there, isn't it? Mostly because then your thighs get a break, but also because it means that you've done something right and your teeth didn't get in the way. And anyway, I decided, filling up the glass from the tap again in case he wanted a drink, it's my turn. That's the rule. He should possibly have tried harder to sort me out first. But never mind. He could make up for it now.

'D'you want some water?' I whispered, walking back into the bedroom and holding out the glass. Callum was standing up with his jeans back on and his phone in his hand.

'No, I'm good, thanks. I'm actually going to get an Uber. Got golf in the morning so I need to get home.'

'Oh. OK. Cool. No problem,' I stuttered.

WHAT?

'Thanks though, that was great.' He reached down for his t-shirt, pulled it over his head, patted his jean pockets, then – while I was still standing there, naked, cold, holding the glass of water – leant in and kissed me on the cheek.

'Good to meet you.'

'Er, yeah. You too. Hang on, I'll let you out.'

'Nah, don't worry. I can let myself out. See you soon.'

'Oh… Sure. OK… Bye,' I said, still holding the glass of water, as he walked out.

I heard the front door close, put the glass down and stood naked in my bedroom thinking. Was that now a thing? Can men just Uber at – I looked at my phone – 2.54 a.m. after a blow job, having not returned the favour, and think that's acceptable?

2

WHEN I EMERGED FROM my bedroom in the morning, Joe was in the kitchen making toast. He was wearing threadbare boxers and an old rugby shirt, both of which were too small for his sixteen-stone frame.

'Morning, my little *chou fleur*, want some breakfast?'

I'd met Joe via a Gumtree advert three years earlier, when I moved out of my mum's place. I was too old to have my knickers ironed for me, I'd decided back then. And Joe had since become a sort of surrogate boyfriend-slash-brother figure, a proper friend to both me and my mates. Our flat was above a corner shop run by a large Jamaican lady called Barbara who was obsessed with horoscopes. I'd go in there to buy bacon on a Saturday morning and come out half an hour later, having been told how my weekend would pan out. It was always bad news. Barbara would suck in her cheeks and say that Mars was doing something weird with Jupiter and that Saturn was all over the shop, and so I should be very careful about any mysterious men that crossed my path.

'No. I'm feeling a bit delicate this morning. Can you put the kettle on?'

'How was last night?'

'Oh, you know. Dinner at Bill's. Brought someone back here to have sex for the first time in nine hundred years, nearly choked to death giving him a blow job before he Ubered straight out of here.'

'Polly, my darling, how dramatic. Why didn't he stay?'

'Beats me.' I collapsed on the sofa and caught sight of the vodka bottle on the kitchen counter. 'I don't know how I manage it.'

'Who was he?'

'A mate of Bill's. Kind of handsome. Lives around here somewhere.'

'So, is this grand romance going to continue?' Joe sat down in the armchair opposite me with his plate of toast.

'I doubt it. And anyway he plays golf.'

Joe shuddered. 'Revolting.'

I sighed. 'Why can't I be a normal person and have any kind of normal, functioning relationship? Or not even a relationship, just normal, straightforward sex? The only thing I've had in my vagina recently is a speculum.'

'More *poisson* in the *mer*, my darling. Beating ourselves up won't help. What plans for the weekend?'

'Well, first I'd quite like you to close that gaping hole in your boxers,' I said, my gaze accidentally dropping to his crotch. 'Then I might kill myself. And not much else really. Going over to Lex's tomorrow. And seeing Bill maybe. What about you?'

'The usual, just a bit of light pillaging. Got a date this afternoon.'

'Who with?'

'Lovely chap called Marcus, he plays the French horn.'

'Does he indeed. Where did we find him?'

'Teaches at the academy. He's got an arse like Tom Daley's. It might be love.'

It was 'love' quite often with Joe. In the past few months, various of these loves had passed through the front door. There had been Lee, a waiter from a pub in Kilburn; Josh, who Joe had picked up in the Apple Store buying a new iPhone; Paddington, a footman from Buckingham Palace, and Tomas, an Argentine polo player who insisted he was straight, but liked Joe to do unmentionable things to him with various leather props that he kept under his bed in a box. I tried never to go into Joe's room in case this box was lying open.

The thought of Joe's box made me feel a bit weak again.

'I'm going to go back to bed actually, forget the tea.'

'Okey-dokey, my petal, I'll be quiet later. It's only a first date, don't want to scare the poor boy. And don't worry about your boyfriend running off like that, happens to the best of us.'

'Does it?'

He paused. 'Well, not me, no.'

'Great, that's very helpful, thanks.' I plodded back to my bed and put my earplugs in.

★

By 3 p.m., I'd had a bath, eaten seven pieces of toast and honey, drunk three cups of tea and I was lying on the sofa watching an old DVD of *Three Men and a Little Lady*. I'd also carefully stalked Callum on Instagram and spent two hours wondering idly whether I could follow him. Then my phone vibrated with a WhatsApp from Bill.

You get home safely?

I typed out my reply, unsure whether he knew anything about Callum. I could tell him tomorrow. Didn't feel up to it now.

Yes! Thank you for dinner! How's the office?

Alright. But listen, do you mind if I don't come for lunch tomorrow? I'm seeing Willow for a drink.

COURSE, don't be silly. Where you guys going?

Dunno. Southbank maybe. Good date place, right?

I sent back a row of thumbs-up emojis and then flicked back to Callum's Instagram again. Mostly pictures of rugby games and foreign beaches. Bit boring, if I was honest. Why was I obsessing over it?

*

I woke the following day feeling human again after spending the evening horizontal on my sofa, spooning Thai green curry and sweet clumps of coconut rice into my mouth. Lex had changed our lunch date to brunch, which seemed unlike her because she wasn't much of a morning person. Eggstacy was a café in Notting Hill which, as its ludicrous name suggested, specialized in breakfast. Great folds of buttery scrambled eggs with Gruyère cheese grated over the top, creamed mushrooms, ramekins of smoky beans, thick slabs of white bread. Butter by the bucketful. I made myself walk there from the flat in preparation, given my supper the night before. It had not been a good weekend for calories.

Lex and I had known one another since we were eleven, when Mum and I moved to London. That was the year I left my primary school in the country, where I'd been taught by a teacher like Miss Honey in *Matilda*, and went to a secondary school near Mum's flat in Battersea. The same school as Lex. There were no Miss Honeys there. Instead, I found classmates who were already into boys and eyeshadow and something called Take That. Lex took pity on me in the way that you might take pity on a cowering stray on the street.

'Do you want to look at my sticker book?' she said one lunchtime, which is still the best pick-up line that anyone's ever used on me. And so, in the sweetly uncomplicated way that children do, we became friends. And we stayed friends.

We went on to Leeds together, both reading English, as did Bill, to study Physics. We formed an unlikely trio. The science nerd (Bill), the short, sex-obsessed blonde (Lex) and me, the tall, frizzy-haired romantic who was fixated with *Sense and Sensibility* and on the lookout for my own Willoughby.

Lex was already at a table by the time I got to Eggstacy, sweating from the exertion of walking up Holland Park Avenue. I waved at her from the door and pushed my way through the clusters of tables to the back.

'Hi, love,' I said, as she stood to hug me. 'Welcome home. How was it?'

'It was…' She smiled at me coyly.

'What?'

'It was… Well… This happened.' She thrust her hand towards me.

'Lex, oh my God!' There was a diamond ring on her finger. I took her hand in mine and pulled it towards my face. A diamond the size of a broad bean in the middle of the ring, surrounded by lots of smaller diamonds. 'Are you kidding?'

'No! It would be quite a weird joke, wouldn't it?' she said, smiling at me.

'You're engaged? To Hamish?'

'Yes! Again, it would be quite weird if I'd got engaged to anyone else since I'd last seen you.'

'Right, yes, 'course. Bloody hell. You could blind someone with that thing,' I said, looking at the ring again. 'I mean, congratulations.' We were still both standing up so I reached over the table to hug her again. It felt weird though. Not the hug. The news. Lex was engaged. To Hamish. To someone she'd only been going out with for, what, a year? To someone I wasn't wholly sure about. And I mean what's the deal in this situation? When your best friend gets engaged to someone you're not sure about?

'Could I have a coffee?' I said to a nearby waitress. 'A really strong Americano?'

She nodded and went off.

A quick summary. Hamish was Lex's boyfriend. Fiancé, I suppose I should call him now. He was a former rugby player-turned-banker with lumpy ears who Lex met in a pub in Kennington. I'd never been sure about him because he was the sort of man who made jokes about women staying in the kitchen. But whenever I asked why Lex put up with him, she'd smiled in a pathetic way and said that she liked him. After a couple of months of dating, she'd said that she loved him.

We sat down. 'I mean, blimey,' I went on. 'Sorry. I'm just trying to process it. I had no idea,' I said. 'Did you?'

'No, not really,' she said, holding her hand out in front of her. The broad bean caught the bulb overhead and twinkled as if it was winking at me.

'How did he do it?'

'In bed in the hotel, classic Hammy.'

I nodded slowly. The way that Lex sometimes called Hamish 'Hammy' made me feel ill. Where was my coffee?

'It was just after he tried to strangle me with my own hair actually,' she went on.

'What?' I frowned at her.

'Well, it was New Year's Eve, in the morning. And we were in bed, just indulging in a bit of harmless foreplay, when suddenly he grabbed a handful of hair and pulled it across my neck. I mean, what's up with that?'

A man on the next-door table looked across at us.

'What did you do?' I whispered.

'I kind of pretended to go along with it for a bit. Because you have to, right? And then he came and it was while we were lying there afterwards that he proposed.' She had a sip of her tea and put the cup back down on its saucer. 'Guys are so weird.'

'Did you like it?'

'The proposal?'

'No! The hair thing. But yes, also the proposal.'

'I didn't not like it. It's something a bit different, isn't it, being throttled by your own highlights? And, yes to the proposal.' She paused and looked directly across the table at me. 'I know it's quite quick. But, Pols, lying there, in that hotel room, it felt right. Honestly.'

I nodded again. I felt like there were a million questions I should be asking. Had they set a date? Had she told her parents? Had she thought about a dress? Were they having any sort of engagement party? But I wasn't sure I could ask them genuinely enough. Convincingly enough. Was that bad? It was quite bad, wasn't it? Unsupportive.

'You'll be my maid of honour, right?' she said.

'Yes, of course I will,' I said, smiling back even though I felt alarmed at the prospect, worried that this meant traipsing down the aisle behind Lex like a giant 4-year-old in a hideous dress.

'Great,' she said. 'I'm psyched about dress shopping. I'll send you some dates because appointments get booked up.' Lex works in fashion PR. I suspected she'd have ambitious ideas for her wedding dress.

'Can't wait!' I said. There. Was that convincing? Did that sound enthusiastic? I wasn't sure.

'Anyway, let's not do wedding stuff now, I can't take it all in,' she said, as if reading my mind. 'How's your weekend been?'

Finally, the waitress came back with my coffee. 'Thanks,' I said, as she put it down. 'Well, no proposals,' I said, pouring the thimble of milk into my coffee. 'I went to Bill's on Friday night for that dinner.'

'Oh yeah, how was it? I missed you guys.'

'Good,' I said slowly. 'I, er, I sort of kissed a friend of his actually.'

'Oh excuse me,' said Lex loudly, sitting forward in her seat. 'What?'

'Leaving it until now to drop the news that you got lucky. What's he like? What does he look like? Did you touch his penis?'

'Lex,' I hissed, trying to quieten her.

'Oh my God!' she shrieked, ignoring me. 'You might have a plus one for my wedding!'

The man on the table next to us shifted in his seat again, as if flinching.

'Shhhhh! Lex, I don't think we're hearing wedding bells with this one. And "getting lucky" would be a generous description.'

'Who is he?'

'Just a friend of Bill's. From business school. Called Callum.'

'Aaaaand? Come on.'

'And nothing. He came home with me and there was a bit of a disaster. That's all.'

'What do you mean, disaster?'

'Not much.' I glanced at the man next to us and lowered my voice again. 'I gave him a blow job and then he went home.'

'What do you mean home? Straight home? Straight after he came in your mouth?'

'Shhhhh. Seriously. People can hear. And yes.'

'You didn't actually shag?'

'No,' I hissed.

'Well,' said Lex, leaning back in her seat again. 'He has incredibly bad manners. Now, shall we order some eggs?'

'Do you think I can start following him on Instagram?' I asked. I was still wondering if I could, but also worrying this seemed a bit desperate. A bit keen. And I didn't even know if I liked him. I was just feeling a bit low on excitement and the thing was, even though Callum had left after the blow job, I'd still come within touching distance of a penis. And that was rare. For me.

'Do you want to see him again? Do you actually like him?' she said.

I pulled a face. 'Dunno. Am I just being desperate?'

'Because something's happened with him?'

'Well, kind of. I guess because he's the first heterosexual man to be in my flat for several decades.'

'But he left immediately afterwards. Like, straight afterwards? No quick cuddle? No "we should do this again"?'

'Nope.'

She winced. 'Up to you, love, but I'd probably leave it.'

I'd always been bad at playing it cool. When I was eleven I went to my first disco in a hessian dress that Mum gave me for Christmas. She plaited my hair for the occasion after I showed her a picture from *Just Seventeen* magazine. The result was more

Little House on the Prairie, but I didn't let that stop me, chubby, 11-year-old me, asking handsome Jack – the boy every girl in Year 7 worshipped – for a dance. It was a particularly bold move on my part because handsome Jack was already on the dance floor with his girlfriend (the school bitch, Jenny) when I chose to walk up to him.

'Yeah, maybe I should leave it,' I said.

I looked down at my menu and tried to concentrate on what kind of eggs I wanted, but what I was actually thinking was that my best friend was getting married, and I didn't even have a boyfriend. Which meant I still had to find someone, go out with them long enough for them to fall in love with me – and this could be many years – before he'd even propose. And as I'd just turned thirty, I did a quick calculation in my head, this meant I might not be married for at least five or six more years. And I definitely read something the other day about getting pregnant before you turned thirty-five, otherwise you had, like, a 3 per cent chance of even having children.

'What eggs are you having?' asked Lex.

But I wasn't listening. Because now I was getting really hysterical. Maybe I'd never get married? Maybe I'd just go to all my friends' weddings alone. Maybe all the wedding invitations I'd ever get would have a solitary 'Polly' written at the top of them and I'd go along and people would say 'How's the love life?' and I'd say 'Haven't found one yet!' in a falsely cheery manner and they'd look at me sadly, as if I'd just told them I'd got a terminal disease. And then they'd be dancing in couples after dinner and I'd be dancing on my own and all my friends would have children and I'd just become the weird, asexual old woman – Auntie Polly – who'd come over for lunch every now and then smelling of dust and Rich Tea biscuits. 'Poor old Polly,' friends would say to one another. 'Such a pity, she just never met anyone.' And I'd die alone in my flat and it would be months before anyone found me. Although it probably wouldn't even be my flat since I couldn't afford to buy one and I didn't even know what a pension was either and…

'POLLY?' said Lex.

I looked up. 'Yes?'

'What eggs are you going to have?'

'Oh. Dunno. I was just thinking about pensions.'

'You're so weird,' she said, shaking her head. 'I'm having scrambled with a side of avocado. And another cup of tea.'

I looked down at the menu again. Eggs, I thought. Ha! It was all very well for Lex to bang on about eggs. Her eggs were probably fine. It was mine I was worried about.

*

On Monday morning, I went through my usual routine: arrive at work, drop bag on desk, go to Pret for an Americano, come back to desk, check all forms of social media on phone and computer despite the fact I had been checking them constantly on the bus on the way in. Instagram, Twitter, Facebook, repeat.

My finger hovered over the 'Follow' button again on

Callum's Instagram profile. I was still obsessing over it. Good idea? Bad idea? Should I? Shouldn't I? In the unlikely event that I was ever the President of the United States, I would have to be more decisive than this with any nuclear buttons. I tapped on 'Follow' and quickly put my phone back on my desk again.

'Polly, can you come into my office in ten minutes,' shouted Peregrine from his office. 'We need to be all over this story about Jasper Milton. Lala, too. Where is Lala?'

'Not sure,' I said slowly, frowning at the desk next to me where Lala should have been sitting. 'I'll text her.'

Technically, Lala's job meant that she looked after the party pages in *Posh!*, the pages where terrifically fat, red-faced men danced with terrifically thin, plastic-surgeried women. In reality, it meant Lala emailed her friends every now and then asking if she could photograph their wedding. She was twenty-eight and ravishingly beautiful. Even on a bad day, Lala still looked like a messy Brigitte Bardot, blonde hair piled on top of her head, black eyeliner still on from the night before. The daughter of the fifteenth Earl of Oswestry, she could tell you the difference between a soup spoon and a dessert spoon. On the other hand, she couldn't tell you who the prime minister was, or what one plus three amounted to, or much about anything else. Her love life was similarly chaotic. Men worshipped her for the first few dates, but the last three men she'd dated had all gone silent after she slept with them. 'I think I'm maybe doing it wrong,' Lala had said sadly at her desk a few months ago, before ordering *The Joy of Sex* from Amazon.

Morning, La, he's on the rampage. When you getting in? X

I put my phone back on my desk. Next job: find out what Jasper Milton, the Marquess of Milton and notorious society heart-throb, had been up to now. Lala had once snogged him while at a shooting weekend in Gloucestershire, and they'd gone on a few dates afterwards. Lala's mother was thrilled at the prospect of her daughter dating the country's most eligible bachelor. But he'd ended things with Lala a couple of weeks later by failing to turn up to dinner with her, having spent the day in a Knightsbridge casino gambling on the Cheltenham Races.

'I don't want to go out with someone who prefers horses to me,' Lala said tearfully in the office the next day. I hadn't wanted to tell her that this counted out almost the entire British aristocracy.

Jasper, I knew from working at *Posh!*, was always photographed at parties, drink in one hand, fag in the other, women standing adoringly around him. But I hadn't read any of the papers that weekend so I quickly googled him, to find out what Peregrine was banging on about. Ah, here we go. I clicked on the headline for the *Mail on Sunday*:

EXCLUSIVE: PLAYBOY SINGLE AGAIN!

A picture below showed a handsome blond figure falling through a nightclub door, shirt undone, feet bare. 'Some say it was only a matter of time,' started the story, 'but the *Mail on Sunday* can confirm that Jasper, the Marquess of Milton, has ended his relationship with Lady Caroline Aspidistra after just three months.

'Sources close to the Marquess, pictured here in Kensington on Friday evening, say the couple had an argument over his partying habits and his late-night return from The Potted Shrimp nightclub in Chelsea earlier last week proved the final straw for Lady Caroline.

'It's the latest in a steady stream of break-ups for the 32-year-old playboy, who last year alone was linked to Princess Clara of Denmark, Lady Gwendolyn Sponge and the actress, Ophelia Jenkins. Friends are said to be worrying that he still shows no inclination to settle down.'

Jasper himself was quoted towards the end of it. 'Caz is a wonderful girl. Much too good for me if I'm honest. But we've gone our separate ways. And that's all I'm going to say on the matter, I'm afraid. Now sod off and leave me to my hangover.'

Apart from Jasper's reputation as a dangerous heartbreaker, I didn't know much else about him. I clicked on to his Wikipedia page and scrolled down. He grew up in a castle in Yorkshire, was kicked out of Eton for seducing a matron then went into the Army and did a six-month stint serving in Iraq. It didn't seem very clear what he was doing now, apart from falling out of nightclubs, but his lack of A-levels or job didn't much matter because he was next in line to a whopping fortune.

His father was the Duke of Montgomery, an army sort who had won a military medal for bravery in the Falklands and was worth a rumoured £500 million. Rumour also had it he had an increasingly dicky heart, meaning Jasper would inherit a 120-room castle in Yorkshire, 15,000 acres of the countryside, another 20,000 acres of Scotland, a townhouse in South Kensington and all the art, furniture and silver that the family had accumulated over the centuries.

'I'M HERE!' screamed Lala, bursting through the door. 'So sorry, what an awful morning. I had the most terrible dreams last night and then my hairdryer wouldn't work and then I couldn't find any clean knickers and…'

'Don't worry but you-know-who wants to talk to us about Jasper Milton. Have you heard?'

'Oh dear, poor Jaz, what's he done this time?' said Lala, emptying her pockets onto her desk. Coins, chewing gum wrappers, lighters, lip balms and taxi receipts fluttered everywhere.

'Single again apparently. Split from Lady Caroline Whatshername. There are some photos of him falling out of a club that the *Mail* has.'

Lala peered over my shoulder at my screen. 'Oh, I knew that wouldn't last. Although…' She stood up and counted on her fingers. 'Three months. Not bad for him. Probably a record.'

'CAN YOU BOTH GET INTO MY FUCKING OFFICE THIS FUCKING SECOND. THIS IS A MAJOR FUCKING STORY.'

'Hang on, let me find a hair tie. Where are all my hair ties?' said Lala, leaning over the desk and prodding at the pile of dirty wrappers.

'Never mind your hair. Come on, let's go through before we're flayed.'

'Right, you two,' said Peregrine, not looking up from his computer as we walked in. 'The most eligible chap in the country is up for grabs. Yet again. I want to go big on this so we've got to get a move on.'

'What about a piece on the family as a whole?' I ventured. 'We talk to everyone we can think of who knows the family. How's the Duke? What's the feeling? What's going on with the Duchess? That sort of stuff.'

I glanced at Lala for some input, but she was doodling a flower on her notepad.

'A big profile on the whole family, basically,' I pressed on.

'No, no, no, the papers have all that already, they'll already have people in the village now, trying to dig stuff up on the Duke's health. I want more. I want to know what the Duke has for breakfast, what that bonkers Duchess does all day, what Jasper does all day, kicking about at home. Why can't he find love? Why can't he settle down? What's he really looking for? We need to give our readers more than a few quotes from an unnamed source. I want a proper, insider look at this.'

'I could always ask Jasper if we could have an interview?' said Lala, looking up from her notepad.

'Would he do it?' asked Peregrine, scratching at his scalp. Dandruff floated to the floor like little snowflakes.

'I don't know, but I can ask him,' Lala replied, lowering her head again to her flower.

Peregrine sighed. He struggled with Lala, with her lateness, with the Monday mornings when Lala only appeared in the office at midday. Her list of improbable excuses had previously included lack of sleep due to bed bugs and having to call a handyman round to get rid of a spider in her bath.

But equally, the office needed Lala. Her random musings on British toffs – 'Oh, by the way, I heard this weekend that the Duke of Anchovy is having an affair with his butler' – were vital to the magazine.

'OK, Lala, marvellous, thank you. Could you possibly get in touch with Jasper this morning and see what he says?'

''Course. Could I just go and get a coffee first? I'm desperate for a coffee, didn't get much sleep last night.'

'OK, go and get a coffee and then could you kindly find Jasper for us? If you can possibly manage that teeny-tiny one thing this morning?'

'Yah, yah, I'll track him down, Peregrine, don't you worry. Poor old Jaz.'

'In the meantime, Polly, I want you to be in charge of this. So can you make a start on research. Go through old issues; we did an interview with the Duke five years ago. I think that was when he trod on a gun and accidentally shot one of his Labradors.'

'On it.'

I spent the rest of the day alternating between research on the Montgomerys and obsessively checking Instagram to see if Callum had followed me back. If, at any moment, I had to step away from my desk – to Peregrine's office, to the loo, to Pret at lunchtime – I took my phone and obsessively checked that too. But by 5.30 p.m. Callum still hadn't followed me back and my mood was hovering somewhere between high-risk depression and suicide.

★

'So there's good news,' said Lala, the next morning in Peregrine's office, twirling a strand of hair around her pen. 'Jasper says he will do an interview, an exclusive one because he trusts us, but I don't want to do it. It would be a bit strange, you know, given everything...'

'Terrific, thank you, Lala. Congratulations on the most productive thing you've ever done. When can he do it?'

'Well, he suggested the last weekend in January, at home. Montgomery Castle. They're shooting so everyone's at home, and he said whoever does the interview is very welcome to join them for Saturday, for the shoot, then stay for dinner on Saturday night. If that works?'

'Why are they giving us so much access?' I asked. I was suspicious. Normally, you were given half an hour with an interview subject, you had to email your entirely inoffensive list of questions over beforehand – What's your favourite colour? What's your star sign? What's your favourite animal? – and then a minder would sit in on the interview, like a Rottweiler waiting to tear the journalist apart if they dared deviate from their questions.

'Erm, not sure really. I think the family just really want to set the record straight and feel like we're the ones to do it. I've promised them it'll be a nice piece,' said Lala. 'It will, won't it?'

'Of course!' said Peregrine. 'It'll be excellent. I can see the headline now: PULLING THE TRIGGER WITH BRITAIN'S MOST ELIGIBLE BACHELOR!

'Polly,' he went on, 'I'd like you to do the interview, so cancel whatever you were doing that weekend and start getting ready. I want you to find out everything you can about him. Why can't he keep a girlfriend? Are the Duke and Duchess pressurizing him to get married? Does he think he'll ever find The One? And can you talk to the picture desk about it, I want photos of Jasper through the ages. As a page boy at the King of Lichtenstein's wedding, his first day at Eton, the university years, at the races, out hunting and so on. Everything.'

'Sure,' I said, but I was suddenly nervous. 'La, what should I wear? And dinner, will it be smart?'

'You need tweed for the shooting, a hat and some boots. Oh, and some shooting socks. And then it'll probably just be black tie on Saturday night.'

'*Just* black tie?'

'Well, you know, a dress or skirt. Knee-length or longer. Heels,' said Lala.

'Polly, do stop fussing about the detail,' said Peregrine. 'Lala, take her to the fashion cupboard. Sort it out there.'

Back at my computer, I had a little red Instagram notification: Callum had followed me back. Only twenty-four hours later, I thought to myself, which seems odd when everyone has their phones on them *all* the time. And then I thought: stop being so psycho.

'Lala, look, he's followed me back.'

'Who?'

'That guy Callum I told you about from the weekend.'

'Ohhhhh yes. The one who lives in Brixton?'

'No, no. That's Bill. You've met Bill.'

She frowned at me.

'You know. Dark hair, used to work for Google, now developing his own app.'

'Oh yes. Cute. Dimples?'

I frowned. 'You have weird taste. But no, I don't mean Bill.'

'Who then?'

'Callum.'

'Is he the Instagram one?'

'What do you mean?'

'Is he the one who's just added you on Instagram?'

'YES. Jesus, I feel like we might both die of old age having this conversation.'

'But who is he?'

'A friend of Bill's. I kissed him on Friday night after Bill's dinner party. Do you really not remember me telling you all this yesterday?'

'When?'

'When we went to get coffee after talking to Peregrine about Jasper.'

'Oh, then. Pols, that was eleven o'clock on Monday morning. I can barely remember my own name at eleven o'clock on Monday mornings.'

'So I need to take you through the whole thing again?'

'Yes. Come on. Let's go to the fashion cupboard and you can talk me through it there.'

★

While I repeated the entire sorry story of Friday night, Lala and Allegra, the magazine's French fashion editor (nicknamed Legs on the basis that hers were skinnier than a pair of chopsticks), clicked through websites looking for suitably tweedy clothes. After half an hour of umming and aahing, they decided I needed the following:

1) *One tweed Ralph Lauren coat*
2) *One brown felt hat with a feather sticking out of it ('You must wear a hat, Pols, toffs like everyone wearing hats because it means they can pretend it's still two hundred years ago and they rule everything')*
3) *One pair of Jimmy Choo riding boots*
4) *One three-quarter-length black Dolce & Gabbana dress*
5) *One pair of Charlotte Olympia heels.*

'And not too much make-up, Pols, they don't like too much make-up,' Lala added sternly.

'Why? What's wrong with make-up?'

'It's vulgar. Makes you look like you've tried too hard.'

'OK. And what shall I do with my hair?'

'Mustn't be too perfect, otherwise that suggests that you're vain and have been indoors all day.'

'Instead of running around outside killing things?'

'Exactly. Happy? You never know, you might fall madly in love with Jasper and end up marrying him. Imagine that. Oh, except you don't need a boyfriend any more.'

'Callum is not my boyfriend. Did you not listen to a word of my story?'

'But do you want him to be? You must like him, otherwise you wouldn't have talked on and on about him.'

'I had to keep talking on and on about him because you weren't listening. And I don't really know. I think maybe he's just a distraction. Or maybe it's just my biological clock.'

'What ees thees clock?' interjected Legs. Being French, she disliked most things, but she especially disliked: fat people, most forms of carbohydrate, London buses, flat shoes, any kind of comfortable or functional clothing, Peregrine and rain.

'It's a thing you supposedly get when you turn thirty,' I explained. 'It means you want to have babies.'

'Pfff. You cannot possibly 'ave a baby. Babies are so unchic,' said Legs.

'No, no. Well, I don't mean "no". I want them at some point. But not now. I couldn't afford one anyway. I can barely afford my own lunch.'

'Pffff.' Legs wasn't big on lunch either. She always had an Americano with macadamia nut milk for breakfast, a Diet Coke for lunch, then several Martinis at whatever fashion dinner she had that night while she pushed a piece of fish so tiny you could hardly see it, let alone eat it, around her plate.

*

Later that week, I did my homework on the Montgomerys, which meant Googling them and leafing through old copies of *Posh!*. As far as I could work out, there were four main characters, all of whom would be there for the weekend.

The main focus was obviously Jasper. 33-year-old Jasper, the Marquess of Milton. Suave, sandy-haired playboy, tall and obsessed with horse racing. By all accounts, he had impeccable manners until approximately ten minutes after he'd slept with you, when he would lose all interest and go back to studying the *Racing Post*. After leaving the Army he had moved home and seemingly learnt how to run the family estate.

Then there was his father, Charles, the Duke of Montgomery. Clearly, as a former army major, he was the kind of man who always had toast and marmalade in his 153-room house at 0755 hours and would then take a post-breakfast shit at precisely 0840, before walking his black Labrador and then settling down at 0930 hours to write a letter to the *Telegraph* about the state of the armed services. He had been hospitalized a few times for various heart operations, according to several newspaper reports, and remained as frail as a green bean.

The Duke's wife, Jasper's mother, was a woman called Eleanor, the Duchess of Montgomery. She grew up in a Scottish castle and was mad. Properly, totally mad, according to past *Posh!* interviews in which she only talked about her chickens. She was, as far as I could tell, in love with her chickens. At one point she had thirty-nine of them, all with different names. She had told one interviewer that, when they were born, her trick was to carry the chicks around in her bra so that she bonded with them. 'I've never crushed any of them,' she'd said. 'I love them like they're my own children. Maybe even more.'

Meanwhile, Jasper's sister, Lady Violet, was in love with her horse. Apparently, nobody in this family could form proper human relationships, so instead they made questionably close friends with their animals. Violet was twenty-five and also living at home in Yorkshire, having attempted a cookery course, a secretarial course, an art foundation course and a needlework course. Presumably, she had now run out of courses. No boyfriend, although she had once been linked to Prince Harry. Who hadn't?

So, that was the line-up for the weekend, the family that I had to interview for an eight-page piece in *Posh!* to prove what a normal, upstanding family they were.

Mum sent me a message that same afternoon.

Got the letter, the appointment is at 4.15 on 2nd February at St Thomas' Hospital. Is that all right, darling? X

I checked my diary. It was the week after I was going to Castle Montgomery, so I would make Peregrine give me the afternoon off.

Course, easy-peasy. Will ring later Xxxx

3

ON THE SATURDAY MORNING, I caught the 7.05 from King's Cross, which arrived in York station just before 10 a.m., where an idling taxi driver outside picked me up.

'You're wanting the castle?' said the driver. His car smelt of dogs.

'Yes please,' I said, shutting my eyes and leaning back in the seat to try to denote that I wasn't up for chatting.

'I know that young Lord Jasper,' said the driver, as the car kicked into action.

'Mmmm,' I replied, eyes still closed.

'I've been driving him about since he was a lad.'

'Mmmm.'

'And if you ask me...'

I wasn't.

'... there's something not right about that family. All that money, all them rooms, all them horses. And now Lord Jasper in the newspapers again. Still no wife. And all that carrying on between the Duchess and that gamekeeper, I ask you. It ain't right.'

'The gamekeeper?' I opened one eye.

'Oh yes,' he said, nodding his head. 'If you ask me, it's

disgustin', behaving like that while your husband's heart's playing up. If my Marjorie ever even thought about it, I'd have something to say about it. Not that I've ever given her cause for complaint in that department.'

I decided to gloss over this personal detail. 'Does everyone know about the Duchess?'

'Oh yeah. Everyone up 'ere does anyway. And Tony, he's the chap, braggin' about it in the pub every night.' He shook his head.

'How long's that been going on for?'

'Years, far as I know. I tell you, if my Marjorie…'

Twenty minutes later, he pulled up outside the front door. 'Here you go then, that'll be twenty-five pounds. Will you be wanting a lift back later?'

'Oh no, thanks, I'm here for the night.'

'Right you are. Here's my card anyways, you never know.'

I climbed out and looked up. It made the Disney castle look poky. There were turrets and gargoyles grimacing out on various corners. It was the sort of place from which a treasonous medieval baron would have plotted his march on London. I tugged on a metal pulley by the front door. Nothing. I pulled it again. Nothing. I peered through the glass of the front door into the hall and spied a large fireplace. There was no sign of human activity – just a large stuffed bear standing beside a grand piano.

Feeling awkward, I tiptoed across the lawn at the front of the house to find another door, like a visiting peasant who had come to pay my rent. Then, through a large stone arch to the left-hand side of the castle, I saw a door suddenly swing open and a male figure, clad entirely in tweed, marched out of it, followed by a black Labrador. Tweed hat, tweed coat, tweed trousers. The only thing which wasn't tweed was the man's face: the face was red.

He turned and shouted back behind him, 'I TOLD EVERYONE WE NEEDED TO BE READY AT ELEVEN AND AS USUAL IN THIS FAMILY, YOU'RE ALL LATE. I don't know why we can't ever do anything on time, it's a bloody shambles—'

The tweed-covered man spotted me.

'AND WHO ARE YOU?' he bellowed.

'Um, hello… I'm, um… I've come from *Posh!* magazine. I'm here to see Jasper, it's for an interview?'

He frowned. 'Oh, the journalist,' he roared, in much the same manner in which someone would say 'paedophile'.

'I'm here today… and then staying tonight… and then writing a piece…' I stuttered.

'Nothing to do with me, you want my son Jasper. He's probably up in his room. You'll have to excuse me for a moment, I'm trying to get ready for this damn shoot.' The Duke of Montgomery turned to roar through the open door, 'BUT EVERYONE'S BLOODY LATE THIS MORNING!'

He looked back at me. 'Go through there and find Ian, he'll point you in the right direction. And if you could get any of my family to hurry up that would be marvellous. Where's my bloody dog? Ah, there you are, Inca. Come on, good boy.' He stalked past me under the stone arch, the dog at his heels, leaving the back door open.

Inside was a room that smelled of mud and damp towels and was stuffed with coats, boots, hats, fishing rods and dog beds. No actual humans. So I walked anxiously through the room, feeling like an intruder, worried that an alarm would go off any second, and into a corridor so long I couldn't see the end of it. Huge portraits peered down at me from the walls. I squinted at the closest one, which depicted a plain-looking woman in a green silk dress, white hair piled on her head.

'The Duchess of Montgomery, 1745,' read a plaque beneath it. There were more Montgomerys lining the corridor. Male Montgomerys, female Montgomerys, fat Montgomerys, thin, bearded Montgomerys, baby Montgomerys. A waft of cigarette smoke drifted towards me as I started to walk down the corridor.

'Who's that?' came a shriek from a room on the left. 'Ian, is that you? I can't find my trousers.'

'Er, no, it's not Ian,' I said, sticking my head into a large kitchen to see a woman sitting at the table, cigarette in hand, smoke snaking its way towards the ceiling. She was wearing a dark green polo neck and a pair of white knickers. No trousers.

'Who are you?' she said.

'I'm Polly. I'm sorry to, um, interrupt. It's only that I was told to come and find someone called Ian because I'm here to talk to Jasper. I'm from *Posh!*.' I was gabbling. 'The magazine?'

The woman drew lengthily on her cigarette. 'Yes, I'm trying to find Ian, too. I need my trousers. We're all late this morning and in terrible trouble with my husband. As usual.'

'Oh,' I said, in a manner which I hoped suggested I was

sympathetic and yet relaxed about being granted an audience with the Duchess in her knickers. Who and where was Ian?

A dog that looked like Bertie was curled up and sleeping on the back of a sofa underneath the kitchen window. 'Oh, sweet,' I said, nodding towards it, trying to make conversation so I could stop thinking about the Duchess's knickers. 'Do you have a terrier?'

The Duchess looked over her shoulder. 'He was a terrier, yes. A Yorkie called Toto. But he's dead.'

'Oh.'

'He's dead too,' she said, pointing at an orange guinea pig on a bookshelf beside the Aga.

'Oh, right.'

'I can't bear to bury the pets, you see. So I have them stuffed by a taxidermist in town.' She took another drag of her cigarette. 'I might do the same to my husband one day.'

Thankfully, I heard the sound of footsteps approaching.

'Ian, there you are,' the Duchess exclaimed. 'I can't find my trousers. Have you seen them?'

I turned around. Ian was apparently a sort of giant butler, well over six foot, in a uniform, with his hair neatly brushed to the side. A pair of tweed trousers lay across his arm.

'Are these the ones, madam?'

'Yes. You are a poppet.' The Duchess stubbed out her cigarette and stood up. She was tall, with pale, thin legs. I stared resolutely at the floor.

'This is Holly by the way, she's come to interview Jasper. How long are you here for?'

'Well, today and tonight he said, I think, if that's all right. I mean, I don't have to stay, I just need to—'

'No, do stay,' said the Duchess, taking the tweed trousers from Ian. 'Lovely to have some fresh blood,' she added. It sounded like a threat.

'Are you walking out with us today?'

'I'm not sure,' I replied, confused. 'What does… um, what does that mean?'

'What?'

'What you just said. Walking out?'

'Oh,' she said, surprised. Then, quite slowly, as if she was talking to a small child, 'As in, are you coming shooting with us?'

'With a gun?'

She smiled at me. 'Darling, no, we wouldn't give you a gun. You don't look like a trained killer. Walking out means coming along and watching. Jolly cold, frightfully boring. But you can stand with Jasper.'

I was relieved. 'Oh, right. Then yes, I think so. If that's all right.'

'Have you got any clothes?' she asked, standing up to put her own trousers on. One leg in, then the other. She maintained eye contact with me throughout. It was like some kind of weird, reverse striptease.

'Uhhh, yes. In here.' I jiggled my overnight bag.

'Good, well, we're already all terribly late. Ian, has someone made a room up?'

'Yes, madam.'

'Marvellous, in that case can you show Holly to her room and she can quickly get changed. I can't tell you the row there'll be if we're not at the stables in the next ten minutes. And take her to Jasper's room afterwards, will you?' She stalked out, in the direction of the boot room.

'It's Polly, actually,' I said to Ian, apologetically.

'Welcome, madam,' he replied, holding a giant hand out for my bag.

I followed Ian as he walked slowly out of the kitchen and back into the corridor, past more dead Montgomerys, up a twisting staircase, along another corridor, down some carpeted stairs and then he turned and opened a door.

'Here you are, you're in Nanny's old room. There's a bathroom just through there. I'll give you a few moments to change and then take you to Lord Jasper.'

'Great, thanks. Yes please.'

I stepped into the room as Ian closed the door behind me. It looked like it hadn't been redecorated for fifty years. Flowery wallpaper, a yellowing carpet and a pink quilt on a narrow single bed. I pressed my hand on the mattress and winced as a spring pinged underneath it. There was a stuffed ferret with horrid little pink eyes on the mantelpiece. My phone buzzed from inside the bag. It was Lala.

You there? Keep me posted. Xxx

I chucked the phone down on the quilt. Later was fine, I needed to put on my tweed. A few moments later, I looked like a Victorian lady explorer off to discover the dusty crevices of the empire. Was I supposed to look like this? I fished my lip-gloss out of my bag and added some for effect, then glanced in the mirror again. If Joe could see me, he would die of a heart attack from laughing.

There was a discreet knock at the door and a gentle cough outside.

'Sorry, sorry, just coming.' I threw the lip-gloss on the bed and opened the door.

'Magnificent,' said Ian. 'Follow me.'

Sedate apparently being Ian's preferred pace, I followed him back up the carpeted stairs and along the corridor.

'Lord Jasper,' said Ian, stopping outside a closed door from behind which I could hear Van Morrison playing. 'I've got the journalist from London here.'

Van Morrison stopped. 'Oh, Jesus,' came a groan.

'She's not called Jesus, sir. She's called Polly,' said Ian.

'Good one,' said Jasper, throwing open the door and smiling at me. 'Polly, hello, any friend of Lala's is a friend of mine.'

He was handsome, I had to admit it. And taller than I expected, with blue eyes and dirty blond hair that he swept to the side with one hand. He was also wearing an absurd pair of tweed knickerbockers which gathered just beneath his knees, but his shirt was loose and unbuttoned. He, too, was barefoot. Was nobody in this family able to dress themselves properly?

Jasper held out his hand. 'How do you do?'

But I didn't have a second to answer how I was doing, because he immediately turned to Ian.

'Now, Ian, my good man, I can't seem to find a single pair

of shooting socks. I mean, I don't know what you do with them. Do you eat them? I buy a million pairs every year and then the shooting season rolls around again and they've all gone. It's the bloody end, I tell you.'

'I'll have a look in your father's room, sir.' Ian turned and glided silently back along the passage.

'Right, well, Polly, I'm so sorry. It's a madhouse here, as you've probably already gathered. Did you meet my parents?'

'Yes, your father was outside with his dog, and your mother was in the kitchen, looking for her trousers.'

'And here I am, looking for my socks. What a shambles we all are.' He pushed his hair to the side again. 'You look superb anyway. Have you been out shooting before?'

I looked down at my tweed self-consciously. 'Oh, thanks. And no, I haven't.'

Jasper started doing up his shirt. 'Well, give me two seconds and, socks permitting, we can be on our way. How are you with dogs by the way?'

'With them?'

'Do you mind them? Do you like them?'

'Oh, no… I mean, yes. I love them. I've grown up with them. My mother has a small terrier called Bertie.'

'How sweet. Mine is an abominably badly behaved Labrador called Bovril. Do you mind being in charge of him today while I shoot? I'll tell you where to stand and all that.'

'Sure. No problem. What about the interview though?'

'What interview?'

'Well, I need to sit down with you at some point and chat

about, you know, the pictures in the paper and…' I trail off, nervously.

'Oh, don't worry about that, we'll have acres of time tonight over dinner. Now, let's go and find these socks.'

★

An hour later, I was standing behind Jasper in a field on the side of a steep hill, holding on to Bovril's lead with one hand, and my hat with the other. There were five other men spread out along the field, each holding a gun, each with a woman standing dutifully behind them, also holding some colour of Labrador on a lead. The wind was blowing odd noises towards us from a wood at the bottom of the field, some sort of weird warbling and the sound of crashing footsteps through thick undergrowth.

'What is that?' I asked Jasper.

He didn't reply.

'Jasper?' I tapped him on the shoulder and he looked around. 'What's… that… noise?' I mouthed slowly at him and pointed at the trees.

'Hang on.' He reached into his ear and pulled out an orange earplug. 'What?'

'Sorry. I just wasn't sure what the noise was.'

'It's the beaters. They're…'

'What are beaters?'

'They're the people who flush the birds out. And they're down there, in the woods, walking towards us from the other

side to flush out the birds, to make them fly over us. Then...
bang. See?'

It didn't seem very fair, a load of people hollering in a forest,
trying to make the pheasants fly towards a line of armed men
standing on a hill. Beside me, Bovril yawned and lay down.
I fished in my pocket for my phone, my hands already numb
from the cold. 'Beaters people who chase birds,' I tapped
into my notes with stiff fingers. 'Jasper has dog called Bovril.
Duchess mad, stuffs all family pets.'

A sudden, loud bang to the right made me jump so I slid
my phone back into my pocket and looked up in the air to
see a pheasant whirling in small circles towards the ground.
It hit the grass with a thud. Bovril looked at it, then looked
up at me, then whined.

I jumped again as Jasper's gun went off. The smell of
gunpowder floated through the air and there was another thud
behind us as that pheasant tumbled to the ground.

'Let Bovril off his lead, will you?' instructed Jasper, eyes
still on the sky as if scanning for the Luftwaffe.

Bovril, pleased to be free, bounded towards the dead pheasant, picked it up by the neck, and trotted obediently back,
dropping it on my boot. I looked down at it and inched my foot
away, uncertain of Jimmy Choo's policy on accepting back boots
which had pheasant blood on them. Frowned upon, probably.

The sound of gunshots rang out. Suddenly, dozens of birds
were flying out from the wood. I clapped my hands over my
ears and looked up into the sky. Pheasants poured overhead
as the shooting continued, some tumbling from the sky like

stones, some flying straight on over the hedge behind them. *I'd keep flying if I were you*, I willed them, *keep going until you get to somewhere nice and warm, like Africa.*

Jasper muttered the odd 'fuck' and a small pile of empty red cartridges piled up behind him. Bovril, meanwhile, galloped back and forth, fetching pheasants and proudly creating a pile at my feet. Some were still twitching, which made me grimace. Urgh, what was I doing standing in this cold field? All I wanted was to sit down with Jasper and get the interview done.

A whistle blew and Jasper put down his gun. 'Well, that wasn't too bad, was it? Must have been sixty or so birds that came out of there.'

Poor things, I wanted to say. 'Hmm,' I said instead. 'How long have you been doing it?'

'Since I was six.'

'Six? I was still learning to tell the time when I was six.'

'Dad started me pretty early. Right, come on. Another drive, then it's elevenses.'

'Drive? In a car?' I was hopeful about warming up.

'No, no, you appalling townie. That's what we're on now. A "drive" is this, standing around in a field waiting for birds to be driven towards us. So, we've got one more, then elevenses, then probably another couple, then lunch, then maybe two more drives after that depending on the light.'

The day stretched before me. My fingers had gone white from the cold and my feet were presumably the same colour despite being wrapped in scratchy woollen socks. It would serve Peregrine right if I succumbed to frostbite while shooting in Yorkshire.

★

Lunch was back in the castle, in a room with the heads of dead animals looking down at us. Stag heads staring glassily out in front of them, snarling fox heads, a zebra head, a warthog head, the head of something else that looked like a deer but had curling horns. I stared at them. You never saw zebra heads on *60 Minute Makeover*.

'We killed the last journalist who came to stay with us,' said a voice behind me. I turned around. It was the Duke. 'Only joking,' he said, before I had the chance to reply.

'Now, come on, everybody sit,' he ordered.

I was sitting between a man who was wearing bright yellow socks with his tweed outfit, called Barny, and another guest called Max. Barny, I learned, was actually called Barnaby and he was fifty-first in line to the throne. He didn't have a job, but lived at the family estate in Gloucestershire and spent his time shooting. When he wasn't shooting, he told me, he was fishing or horse racing.

'Oh,' I said, starting to run out of small talk. He seemed obsessed with killing things. 'So do you travel much?'

'No,' he said firmly, 'going abroad is ghastly. Apart from the Alps. I go skiing three or four times a year. I'd like to go hunting tigers in India, but they're making it very tricky to do that these days.'

'Barny, you can't say that sort of thing,' said Max, joining the conversation. 'Polly, I'm so sorry. Barny is completely appalling, but we've all been friends since school and we can't seem to shake him off.'

'How rude,' said Barny. 'No shooting invitation for you this year, Maximillian.'

'You see, Polly? Barny blackmails us into being friends with him. Tragic.'

I looked along to Jasper, positioned at the head of the table, with two blondes sitting either side and smiling at him in an adoring fashion. His ideal habitat, I suspected. He'd loosened the collar around his neck and was leaning forwards on the table, telling them some story. He reached for a bottle in front of him and topped up both their glasses while still talking, then put the bottle back and looked down the table at me. He caught my eye and winked. Please, I thought, I'm not that easy.

I turned to Max, sensing if not an ally then at least someone I might be able to hold a conversation with, and asked him about the others. 'Max,' I began, 'who is everyone else here? I mean, obviously, I know about Jasper and his family. But I'm not sure about anyone else. Do you know them all?'

'I'm so sorry,' he said, folding his napkin and putting it on the table.

'What do you mean?'

'Well, just poor you. Having to come to this. Do we all seem totally absurd?' Max asked.

I wasn't sure how to answer. 'No,' I said after a pause. 'I'm just trying to gauge who everybody is.'

'OK, let me talk you through them all. So, next to Jasper's father is Willy Naseby-Dawson, she's…'

I looked at the blonde girl again. 'Why's she called Willy if she's a girl?'

'Short for Wilhelmina. She's from a German family, she's Barny's wife. Poor thing. And then on her other side is Archie Spiffington, who's married to the girl Barny's talking to now, Jessica. They got married last year because she was pregnant – her father was very upset at that and insisted on them getting hitched. Her family's disgustingly rich. Her great-great-grandfather invented the railway or something. Anyway, big wedding in London, then six months later along comes their son Ludo, who's now about seven months, I think. I'm the godfather.'

'Oh, sweet, where's Ludo?'

'No idea, with the nanny in London probably. And then, on Jessica's other side is Seb – Sebastian, Lord Ullswater. He's a fairly dubious character who used to be in the Army and now sells weapons to anyone who'll buy them. And he's married to that girl on the other side of Jasper, the girl on my right, who's called Muffy.'

'And what about you?' I asked him.

'What do you mean, what about me?'

'Are you married?'

Max threw his head back and laughed. 'I'm gay, my darling. Can you not tell because I'm wearing such manly trousers?'

'Oh, right,' I said, blushing. 'Although, you could still get married.'

'Yes, that's true,' he said, nodding.

'Have you got a boyfriend?'

'No. Not terribly good with boyfriends.'

'Max,' said Barny, from my other side. 'None of us want to hear about your love life over pudding.'

'I wish there was one, Barny, old boy. But it's been slow-going of late.'

'You should meet my flatmate, Joe,' I said to Max. 'You're just his type.'

'Oh really? What's his type?'

'Well, actually, quite wide ranging, I'd say. But dark, handsome and funny. And you're all of those.'

'Right,' bellowed the Duke from the other end of the room, slamming his fists down on the table. 'Finish up your pudding and let's get going.'

'Come on then,' Max said to me. Then he called down the table, 'Jasper, I'm stealing Polly to stand with me this afternoon. Violet, why don't you go with your brother? I need to talk to Polly about her flatmate.'

Jasper's sister. I'd barely noticed the woman sitting three to my left. She seemed much quieter than her talkative brother.

'Fine by me,' said Violet, carefully putting her napkin back on the table. 'If anyone wants to borrow another layer then shout, it looks like rain this afternoon.'

*

It started raining while I stood behind Max waiting for the shooting to start again. Having defrosted enough to handle a knife and fork over lunch, my hands were stiff with cold again. Max stood, gun slung over his arm, cigarette dangling from his lips.

'You all right?' He glanced back at me.

'Yes, yes, fine. Who needs hands anyway?'

'You going back to London after this?'

'No, I'm staying tonight. I haven't had my interview with Jasper yet.'

He exhaled smoke into the air. 'That's brave. Have you talked much to their Graces?'

'Who?'

'The Duke and Duchess.'

'No, not really.' I squinted in the distance to see the Duke standing at the other end of the field. The Duchess had announced after lunch that she wasn't coming out that afternoon because she had work to do in her hen house.

'They're barking,' said Max, grinding his cigarette out in the mud with his boot. 'Truly barking.'

'I've noticed.'

'Which is why Jasper is a bit... complicated sometimes.'

'You've known him for ever?'

He nodded again. 'We were at prep school together. Then the same house at Eton, until he got kicked out. Then Edinburgh University.' He paused. 'He's been a good friend. Stood up for me at school when I came out. Not that my sexuality was a huge surprise to anyone. I mean, darling, look at me!'

I laughed. Max was wearing tweed, but also pink socks, a pink shirt, a yellow tie and a pink beanie.

'So, he's been a good friend,' he carried on. 'And, I know we all get a bit carried away sometimes…'

'Carried away?'

'Those pictures, after he broke up with Caz, are a case in point.' Max raised his eyebrows at me. 'Anyway, Jasper knows exactly who told the papers he'd broken it off with her, who told the photographers where he was that night. But he's not going to say anything. He's too honourable.'

There was a bang down the line and a pheasant dropped through the air towards the ground. 'Right, here we go again. Time to concentrate,' said Max, turning round and lifting his gun.

*

Back at the castle there was tea. The sort of tea you read about in a Dickens novel. Sandwiches, sausage rolls, fruitcake, shortbread, tea in actual teapots. Also, port. Port! In miniature wine glasses! Joe and I put away a couple of cheap bottles of Pinot Grigio from Barbara's shop almost every night, but we didn't drink as much as this lot. The Duke's blood must be 93 per cent alcohol, I reckoned, watching him drain another glass of the syrupy red liquid.

After half an hour or so of standing on the fringes of the drawing room, defrosting my hands yet again on a teacup, Jasper's friends started leaving and I snuck out gratefully to my room. I then ran a hot bath with a good few slugs from an ancient-looking bottle of hyacinth bath oil I found in the bathroom cupboard. Sylvia Plath once said that a hot bath cured everything, which I'd always thought slightly ironic, because poor Sylvia then went and killed herself. But I needed a bath to help collect my thoughts. The evening dinner promised to be a sort of cross between *Downton Abbey* and *Coronation Street*, while everyone politely ate their soup. Or drank their soup. What does one do with soup? Anyway, everyone would be doing something with their soup and discussing the day while bad tempers seethed underneath. Maybe soup would be thrown.

Because nobody in this house, this castle, rather, seemed able to move without some form of alcohol in their hand, Ian had sent me upstairs with something called a 'hot toddy'. A few fingers of whisky, some hot water and a teaspoon or so of honey, he'd explained. 'It'll warm you up,' he'd said.

I swirled it around in its glass, splashing hot, oily water over the side of the bath. It burned my throat going down.

My phone suddenly vibrated on the bed, so I climbed out of the bath, wrapped myself in a scratchy towel, picked it up and lay – steaming – on the narrow little mattress. It was Lala again.

How's it going, Pols? Do you like Jaz? Send my love to everyone. Don't forget the make-up thing Xxxx

I quickly typed out a reply.

All good, don't worry. I'll report back on Monday xxxx

Still hot and damp from the bath, I then stood up to heave myself into the floor-length dress Legs and Lala had insisted

I wear. No tights, because they were common apparently. I looked in the full-length mirror. A ropey Twenties flapper girl looked back at me. But it would have to do. And somehow I needed to walk downstairs in the ridiculous heels they'd given me, so high they looked like they might give me vertigo.

I picked up my phone again and checked the time. Nearly seven o'clock. I needed to find the drawing room where Ian had told me the family gathered for drinks. More drinks! And I still hadn't sat down to interview Jasper yet. I'd scribbled some more notes on my phone – his penchant for Van Morrison, his habit of constantly brushing his hair from his eyes, Max's comment about him being 'honourable' – but I needed Jasper on record about his relationships. I needed him to open up a bit. I couldn't come all this way and report back to Peregrine with so little. Maybe more drinks would help, I thought, as I closed the bedroom door behind me and inched down the stairs like a wobbly drunk, clutching at the banister. A grandfather clock ticked gently from below, but otherwise the house was silent. Ian's instructions for finding the drawing room had been along these lines: 'Come downstairs, turn left and walk fifty yards down the corridor, turn right into another corridor, click your heels three times and the drawing room will be on your right-hand side.'

The sound of smashing glass, followed by a high-pitched scream gave me a clue. It was exactly the sort of high-pitched scream that might come from an angry and potentially violent duchess.

'WE ARE ALL HAVING FUCKING DINNER TOGETHER, ELEANOR, I MEAN IT.'

Another high-pitched scream. I froze outside the door. Rude to walk in on a row. But quite rude to stand out here listening to it, also. I wondered if I should hobble back upstairs again. But I could already feel a blister coming up on my little toe from those wretched heels. I was hovering like this in the hall, as if playing a private game of musical statues, when I heard a small cough behind me.

'Polly, there you are,' said Ian. 'Follow me and let's get you another drink.' He swept past, carrying a silver tray with several Martini glasses on it.

'Really?'

'Absolutely, nothing to worry about,' he said, pushing the door open.

The Duchess was standing beside the fireplace, still in her shooting clothes. The Duke was sitting in a large red armchair. Inca walked towards me and shoved his wet nose into my crotch.

'Do get your bloody dog to behave,' said the Duchess, huffily.

'That's all right,' I said, brushing smears from Inca's wet nose off the three-thousand-pound dress.

'Very kind of you to dress so wonderfully, Polly, but we're terribly relaxed here,' said the Duke, who was wearing a blue shirt and electric red cords with a pair of velvet slippers. 'Ian, what are we having for dinner?'

'I think Chef's doing mushroom soufflé, followed by roast partridge and then rhubarb syllabub, Your Grace. And there's some cheese, if you'd like?'

'Yes, we simply must have cheese,' the Duke said gravely.

'Well, if you'll forgive me,' said the Duchess, 'I'm going to go and get changed and then go out. So, I'm afraid I won't be joining you for dinner, Polly, but my husband and children will look after you.' She glared at the Duke and stalked out, slamming the door behind her.

'Drink, Polly?' asked the Duke. 'I'm going to have another one. A strong one, I think. Bugger the doctors.'

★

After its warlike beginning, dinner was almost disappointingly peaceful. Jasper, the Duke, Violet and I sat at one end of a vast mahogany table in the dining room, the light from several silver candlesticks flickering off the dark green walls and an eight-foot stuffed polar bear casting a long shadow along the room at the other end of the table. It was his grandfather's, the Duke told me, one of forty-six polar bears brought back as a trophy from one of his hunting expeditions in the Arctic in 1906.

There was no shouting. No Duchess. Violet (in jeans and a t-shirt) talked about her horses, the Duke generally talked about the animals he'd killed, Jasper (in jeans and a collared blue shirt) quietly fed Bovril scraps of partridge. I felt excruciatingly out of place given that I was dressed as if I was off to a pre-war nightclub, but I kicked my shoes off under the table. I rubbed my feet together as the Duke asked me questions about London.

'Far too many people in London,' he said, wiping his

mouth with his napkin at the end of dinner and standing up. He then announced he needed to walk Inca and Violet said she wanted to have a bath. Which left Jasper and me sitting at one end of the table, candles still burning and Ian humming while removing bowls and dirty napkins.

'Another bottle?' Ian asked.

'I think so, don't you?' replied Jasper, pushing his chair back from the table and stretching his legs out in front of him. 'OK, Polly, let's get this over with.'

'Get what over with?'

'The interview, our little chat. What do you want to know about me and this madhouse?'

'Oh, I see. OK. You call it a madhouse?'

'What else would you call it? My father is a Victorian whose dearest wish is that he'd fought in the Boer War. My mother is happiest pottering about in the hen house with her friend, the gamekeeper.'

'Ah. So, that's…'

Jasper raised an eyebrow at me.

'… common knowledge?'

'Desperately common. The whole village knows about it. It's been on and off for years. As long as I can remember. I don't mind so much but I think Violet probably does. So, instead, she thinks of horses from morning till night.'

'Hang on, hang on, can I record this?' I pulled my phone out of my pocket and waved it at him.

He smiled at me. 'Ah my inquisitor. I didn't realize I was doing an interview for *Newsnight*.'

'You're not. But I quite need to record it. Can I?' I held my phone up again.

"Course. I will say lots of immensely intelligent things.'

'We'll see about that,' I said, fiddling with my phone to make sure it was recording. 'And what about you?'

'What do you mean "What about me?"'

'Are you as mad as everyone else?'

'No,' he replied. 'I'm the sanest of the lot.' He smiled again and swept his hair out of his eyes.

'What about your break-up? What about those photos?'

'What photos?'

'The ones in the paper.'

He looked straight into my eyes. It was unnerving, as if he could see directly into my brain. A sort of posh Paul McKenna. 'I don't want to talk about Caz,' he replied. 'She's a sweet girl. It just wasn't right. Or I'm not right...' He trailed off. 'And those photos... All right, so occasionally I behave badly and let off a bit of steam. I go out and I behave like an idiot. But I don't think being photographed stumbling out of a club is the worst thing in the world.'

He leant closer, shifting in his chair, still looking into my eyes. 'Forgive me, Polly, for I have sinned.'

I burst out laughing. 'Nice try. But you can't charm your way out that easily.'

'Fine.' He sat back again, reached across the table for the wine and filled our glasses up. 'OK, go on, ask me anything.'

I raised an eyebrow at him. 'I'm trying to work you out.'

'That's not a question.'

'I'm just trying to work out whether the joking is a front.'

'A front?'

'Like a mask. Covering up something more serious. You joke a lot.'

'What did you expect?'

I frowned. 'I'm not sure. You to be more cagey, more defensive.'

'You expected me,' he began, 'to be a cretin in red trousers who couldn't spell his own name?'

'Well, maybe a bit. I mean, er, some of your friends at lunch, for example.' I was thinking about Barny.

'Yes. Most of them are bad, aren't they? But...' He shrugged. 'They're my friends, I've known them since school. And they don't mean to be such thundering morons. They were just born like that.'

'And you weren't?'

'No. I'm different.' He grinned.

'How?'

'OK. I know there's all this...' He threw his arm out in front of him and across the room. 'But sometimes I just want something normal. A normal family which doesn't want to kill each other the whole time. A normal job in London. A normal girlfriend, frankly, who doesn't look like a horse and talk about horses and want to marry me so she can live in a castle and have more horses.'

'Oh, so you do want a girlfriend?' I sensed this was the moment to push him a bit harder, to try to unpick him. 'You want a proper relationship?'

He looked at me again, straight-faced. 'Who's asking?'

'I am,' I persevered. It was tricky, this bit, quizzing someone about their most personal feelings. But Peregrine wanted quotes on Jasper's love life, so I needed him to talk about it. I needed a bit of sensitivity from the most eligible man in the country, a chink in his manly armour.

'So, OK, you're single again,' I pressed on, 'and I know you don't want to talk about Lady Caroline… Caz… but what's the deal with all the women?'

His wine glass froze in mid-air, before he placed it back down on the table. 'Polly, I can't believe it. "All the women" indeed. Who's told you that?'

'OK, so I know you dated Lala, briefly, and I know about a few others. The rumours about you and that Danish princess, last year, for example?'

Jasper grimaced in his seat. 'Clara. I had dinner with her once and that was it. Terrible sense of humour. She didn't laugh at any of my jokes.'

'All right, the photos of you and Lady Gwendolyn Sponge?'

'Nothing to it. Our parents are old friends.'

'Who was that one you went skiing with last year then?'

He frowned at me.

'You were photographed laughing on a chairlift together.'

His face cleared. 'Oh, Ophelia. Yes. She's a darling. But about as bright as my friend Bovril.'

Under the table, Bovril thumped his tail at the sound of his name.

'Fine. But I imagine there have been… many more.'

He sighed. 'Many more. I mean honestly, who makes up this nonsense?'

'So it's rubbish? All those tales about the legendary Jasper Milton are nonsense?'

'You, Little Miss Inquisitor, are teasing me. And anyway, what does my personal life really matter to you?' He looked at me with a straight face. 'Why are you blushing?'

I put my hand up to my cheek. 'I'm not. It's all this wine.'

'Oh. I thought it might be because I'm flirting with you.'

'Is this you flirting? I'm amazed you get anyone into bed at all.'

He laughed. 'Touché.' And then he brushed his hair to the side, out of his eyes, again. And just for a second, literally for a second, I promise, I wondered what it would be like to be in bed with him, my own fingers in his hair. But then I thought about Lala and told myself to have a sip of water. I couldn't go around the place fantasizing about my interview subjects. Kate Adie would never do that. I tried to get back to the point.

'Do you think you'll settle down though? Find someone? Get married? Have children? Do all that?'

He sighed again and sat back in his seat. 'Maybe. I don't know. How does one know? Do you know?'

'This isn't about me.'

He laughed. 'See? You don't know either. It's not that easy, is it?'

'What isn't?'

He shrugged. 'Relationships, life, getting older and realizing things can be more complicated than you thought.'

'You feel hard done by?'

'No,' he said, shaking his head. 'That's not what I'm saying at all. In the great lottery of life, as my father is fond of saying, I know I've done pretty well. But do you know what? Maybe, sometimes, I don't want to take over this whole place. I don't want to be told how lucky I am because I get to devote my whole life to a leaky castle and an estate that needs constant attention and I don't want to be in the papers falling out of a club. But that doesn't mean that I know what I do want.'

I stayed quiet and glanced up at a portrait of the sixth Duchess of Montgomery, a fat, pale lady in a green dress looking impassively at us from the wall. I looked from the painting to Jasper, who suddenly smiled at me.

'What's funny?' I said.

'Oh, I don't know. Me, sitting here, talking to you about how terribly hard my life is. Come on, let's have more wine and you keep asking me all your clever questions.' He reached for the bottle and filled up our glasses again.

'Does it bother you, what other people say? What newspapers say?'

'It would be a lie if I said that it didn't. Sometimes it does. But then you just have to remind yourself that they don't know the real story.'

'Which is?'

He sighed. 'Oh, I suppose that we're a bunch of dysfunctional misfits trying to muddle through like everyone else. Just… in a bigger house. But you can't say that,' he said, inclining his head towards my phone, still recording on the table. 'I'll get in trouble. More trouble. "Poor little rich boy", they'll all say.'

'It's quite a defence plea though.' I said this smiling at him. I couldn't take his sob story that seriously but I still felt a twinge of sympathy. A very tiny one.

'Nope,' he said, 'Sorry. Can't use it. That was just for you to know. Not everyone else. And what about you, anyway?'

'What do you mean?'

'What's your story? Why are you here interviewing me?'

I felt awkward. 'Erm, it's not very exciting. I grew up in Surrey, then my dad died, so Mum and I moved to Battersea where she's lived ever since. I was all right at English at school so my teacher said I should think about becoming a journalist. I think he meant more politics and news than castles and Labradors, though, no offence.'

'None taken.'

'But this is good for now.'

He nodded in silence. 'Have you got a boyfriend?'

I laughed. 'I'm supposed to be asking the questions.'

'You are. I'm just being nosy.'

'No, as it happens. I don't. A bit like you, I guess, relationships aren't my thing.'

'Good,' he said. 'I couldn't imagine you with an Ed or a James, living in some terribly poky flat in Wandsworth.'

'Oh, I see. You're not a man of the people at all. You're a snob?'

'I'm teasing. Some of my closest friends are called Ed and James. But come on, Polly, you really must lighten up or we'll never get anywhere. If we're going to get married one day, you'll need to stop being so stern.'

'You're ridiculous,' I said. But I laughed. I couldn't help myself. He was clearly the boy your mother warned you about but he was also charming. More charming than I'd thought earlier that day. More charming than the papers made out. Or maybe it was the wine?

'Why shouldn't we get married? I think you're terribly sweet. And funny. And you clearly know nothing about horses which is also a bonus.'

And then he leaned forward and kissed me. Briefly. His lips brushed mine for two or three seconds, tops, before I pulled my head back. Slow reflexes, admittedly. But, in my defence, I was very drunk.

'Don't even think about it,' I said in my most matronly voice, pulling away.

'No?'

'No. This is work. For me anyway. And just when I was starting to like you.'

'Have I ruined it?' he said, still leaning forward, still smiling at me.

I ignored the question. 'Your seduction techniques might have worked on Lala, but not me.'

He sighed and sat back in his seat. 'Good old Lala. How is she, anyway?'

'She's very well. Well… kind of. You know Lala.'

'I did like her,' he said, staring at the table as if in a trance. 'It just wasn't the right timing again.' He paused. 'Or it was something else. I don't know.' He looked up at me. 'You won't write about me and her though, will you?'

'You and Lala? No. Don't worry.'

'Good. I don't mind being written about that much but I don't want to cause trouble for anyone else. I mean, I ask for it, I know. Others don't.'

He threw back his wine glass and I tried to think of something to say, but I couldn't. So, we sat for a few moments in silence while ancestors in wigs frowned down from the walls. The mood had changed but I wasn't sure why.

'Bedtime, I think,' he said after a few moments. 'Let me show you the way to your room.'

I followed him in silence back down the long corridor and up the stairs. I felt awkward about things. About the whole day. The entire family should be in an asylum. I knew Peregrine would expect my piece on the family to be glowing, to talk about how upstanding they all were. To put a gloss on life in the castle and be as flattering as I could about the Duke and Duchess. But the truth was they all seemed a bit lost. Trapped. Although, having met Jasper, I could at least write about how much more self-aware he was in real life, as opposed to how he was portrayed in the papers. I could definitely bring myself to do that, I thought, as I reached for the zip on the back of my dress. For God's sake, it was going to take me about five hours to get out of this thing.

4

'GOOD TIME THEN?' ASKED the taxi driver as I got back into his car early the next morning, having fished out his card and decided I would sneak out early before breakfast, before any more awkwardness over bacon and eggs. I didn't want to talk to anyone because I had the kind of hangover that I thought I might die from.

'Mmmm, kind of,' I replied, shutting my eyes.

'See much of the Duke?'

'A bit.' Eyes still closed.

'And the Duchess?'

'I saw a bit more of her actually.' I had to silence this. How could I silence him?

'So you're back to London then?'

'Yup.'

'Back to the Big Smoke. I don't know how you do it. I like the quiet life myself.'

'Mmmm.' Could have fooled me.

'Can't be doing with all the stress of London, do y'know what I mean? People rushin' about all the time. And all that noise. How d'you sleep at night with all that noise? All them buses and cars. And people.'

'I can sort of sleep anywhere,' I muttered. Like right now, I thought to myself, literally right this very second.

'Nope, not for me. I'm happier up here. Just me and my Marjorie. I drive my car, she works in the local library. Loves it there, she does. Says she likes the peace.'

'Mmm. I can imagine.'

'Not much of a reader myself. But she loves it. Always got her head in a book, has my Marjorie.'

'Mmm. Listen, I don't mean to be rude but do you mind if I have a quick doze? I'm just a bit tired.'

'No, no, right you are. You have a doze. I read an article the other day about sleep. What was it called?' He paused. '"The Power of the Nap", I think, something like that. I have trouble sleeping myself, do you ever find that? Not every night, just sometimes. My head hits the pillow and the brain's still going, d'you know what I mean?'

I didn't reply. My brain felt like it was about to dribble out through my nose. I was worrying about whether I was going to say anything to Lala about the kiss. Not that you could even call it a kiss really. But, still, did I have to mention it?

Half an hour later, I'd reached the station, paid off the most talkative taxi driver in Yorkshire and installed myself in the Quiet Carriage with provisions for the journey: one large latte, a Diet Coke, a large bottle of still water, two plain croissants and a packet of salt and vinegar McCoy's crisps.

'Ladies and gentleman, welcome to York. This train is for London King's Cross, calling at all stations to Peterborough, where there is a bus replacement service to…'

Fuck's sake. I scrolled through my phone. Three emails from Peregrine asking how the weekend was going, a text from Mum saying that Jeremy Paxman was very poor on *Celebrity Bake Off* last night and she thought he might get the boot, a message from Bill with the link to a review for a new French restaurant in Shepherd's Bush and a message from Lex saying could I ring her 'immediately'. Some sort of sordid sex story, probably. Strangled with courgetti. Spanked with a spatula. That sort of thing. It could wait. I was in no way strong enough for that discussion, and anyway I was in the Quiet Carriage. I fell asleep before I'd even had a sip of coffee.

★

The flat smelt when I opened the door. It was the sort of smell you know if you've ever ventured into the bedroom of a teenage boy. A musty, stale odour. In the sitting room, Joe lay on the sofa in his boxer shorts and a t-shirt watching *Antiques Roadshow*, empty packets of crisps scattered around him. A large bottle of Lucozade stood propped on his belly like a cairn on top of a hill.

'My angel is home!' he said, swivelling his head towards the door.

'I'm not feeling very angelic, I can tell you that for free.'

'Oh dear. Did it not go well?'

'It went… Erm… How did it go?' I dropped my bags by the kitchen table and flopped on the opposite sofa. 'For starters, I probably shouldn't have kissed my interview subject.'

'You didn't?'

'Not really. I mean he tried to, but I said no.'

'Pols! What on earth? That's unlike you.'

'I know, I know. But I was trying to be professional. Or something.'

'Did you fancy him?'

'No. Not my type. He's kind of hot, but in a very obvious way. Tall. Blond hair, sort of… athletic, you know. Blah blah.'

Joe rolled his eyes. 'Those are the *worst*. The ones who are obviously hot.'

'Don't be mean, I'm not strong enough. I nearly died from my hangover on the train.'

'Here, have some Lucozade. And then sit down and tell me everything.'

'No, no, I'm good. I think I need a hot bath and bed.'

Joe sighed and turned his head back to the telly. 'You're so boring. I tell you everything.'

'Too much sometimes, I'd say. Anyway, what have you been doing all weekend? Apart from marinating on the sofa.'

'Oh, this and that. Went out with a bunch of gays last night in Soho. Got roaringly drunk and ended up in Mr Wong's eating three-headed sweet and sour chicken.'

'Any action?'

'Nope. Chaste weekend for me. Which is why I'm seeking solace in crisps. But I'm terribly cheered that you've had a bit more activity, my darling. Was beginning to worry you'd rust up.'

'It really wasn't activity. But it's good that you have such a clear understanding of how female anatomy works.'

'Isn't it just? Ah, Pols, Fiona Bruce is the only woman for
me anyway. Look at her being nice to that little man about
his hideous clock.'

'I think I'm going to leave you to it and have a bath
and get immediately into bed so I can face you-know-who
tomorrow.'

'Your new boyfriend?'

'Who's my new... Oh... No, I mean Peregrine.'

'Have you rung your mother?' Joe and I had a Sunday
evening pact that we would always ring our parents.

'Shit. And Lex texted me asking me to ring too. Oh, God,
I can't be bothered. Is it terribly bad if I ignore them all?'

'Text them, then your mum won't worry and the others
will know you're alive.'

'OK, thanks, Dad.'

'Welcome. Now go to your room. You've been a very
naughty girl.'

I texted Mum once in bed.

*Just home. Going to crash out. Will ring tomorrow for a gossip.
You OK? XXX*

Then I texted Lex.

*Just home. Going to crash out. Long story. Will ring tomorrow.
You OK or suffering some sort of grievous sex injury? XXX*

Except obviously I got them the wrong way round.

Darling, should I be suffering some sort of sex injury? Glad
you're home safely. Speak tomorrow. X

★

I went into the office early the next morning feeling like a weary First World War soldier on the morning of the Somme. I ordered an extra-strong Americano in Pret. It was going to be One Of Those Days.

On my to-do list:

1) *Write 2,500 words about the Marquess of Milton which Peregrine would like, revealing the 'real' Jasper, the charming, outdoorsy, upstanding young man who would be the fourteenth duke.*

2) *Call Lex, who'd texted last night – ever the dramatist – to say if I didn't call her that morning she'd put a curse on me.*

3) *Call Mum to talk about Bertie, Jeremy Paxman and her hospital appointment.*

4) *Text Bill.*

5) *Decide what I was going to say to Lala about Jasper.*

My phone vibrated on my desk and made me jump. It was a message. From a random number.

Hope you got home to your poky flat in one piece. I'm intrigued about what you're going to write. Dinner this week? J

I looked blankly at my phone for a few seconds. J for Jasper? Jasper had texted me. I texted him back.

How did you get my number, you creep?

I move in mysterious ways. Dinner Friday?

I'll have written the piece by Friday...

Fine. We can discuss it over dinner. The Italian on Kensington Park Road at 8 work for you?

'Morning, Polly.'

I jumped again as the office door crashed open and I dropped my phone. It was Peregrine.

'Morning.'

'How was it? What did you get?' he asked.

'It was… erm… I got… it was…'

'Come on, Polly, you're a journalist not a mute. What did he say?'

'Various things. Lots of pressure, lets off steam every now and then, he knows who sold the pictures, family life a bit tricky and so on. It'll make a piece.'

'Good. Can you file this afternoon? Say five o' clock?'

'I think so. Should be fine.'

'Good.' He paused in his office doorway and squinted at me. 'You all right? You look terrible.'

'Oh no. No, fine, thank you. Probably just caught a cold from the shooting or something.'

'Well, dose yourself up on Lemsip in that case and get cracking. Two thousand five hundred words. My desk. Tea time.'

Which is why I didn't have time to ring Lex or Mum that morning. Although I didn't have to worry about Lala because she was off sick, apparently.

Sorry, Pols, think I've got food poisoning so not coming in today. How was it? Xxxxx

Lala seemed to be incredibly unlucky with food poisoning on Mondays, but at least I had another day to work out what I'd tell her about Jasper, because I agreed to have dinner with him.

Tell you tomorrow, get some sleep, you idiot. X

★

It took me five coffees and untold calories but by 5 p.m. I'd squeezed out 2,500 perfectly all right words on Jasper and his family – the censored version. According to my piece, they were eccentric – naturally – but didn't everyone prefer their aristocrats that way? No point in having a duke who went about life like a dreary geography teacher. As for Jasper, he was a charming and, yes, admittedly quite handsome man who loved his Labrador and liked to forget about the pressure of inheriting such a large chunk of the country.

Given he was inheriting £500 million, I thought this was absurdly generous, but this was *Posh!* not the *Guardian*, and our readers would nod along and sympathize with him from their own castles. The Duchess, I wrote carefully, was in excellent shape and on 'friendly' terms with the estate staff. And Violet was a sweet, quiet girl who generally preferred her pony to people. 'It's lucky,' I wrote, 'that the castle is overseen by Ian, the butler, a modern-day Jeeves, who strolls silently about the corridors finding vital bits of clothing, extra bottles of red wine and the odd lost dog. Should you require it, he also makes a terrific hot toddy.'

'Good,' said Peregrine, walking towards my desk, article in hand. 'Just a few marks. You liked him then?'

'Who?'

'Jasper. You're very nice about him.'

'Oh, well, I mean. Yes, I did like him. He's, you know, fun.'

'Mmm. Can you look at my comments? I think just a few more nice lines about the family as a whole. I don't think we can be too kind to them, useful to keep them onside. Then put it through and talk to the art department about pictures.'

''Course.'

'Keep them onside'. Honestly. I couldn't have been kinder to this mad, addled, gamekeeper-shagging family.

★

'I've made some pasta with fridge droppings, I hope that's OK,' said Mum when I arrived for supper at her flat that night.

'Delicious. How was your day?'

'Oh, fine, fine. There was a tiresome woman who spent four hours deciding what colour toile to have for her bedroom curtains, but other than that it was easy enough. How was yours? How was the piece in the end?'

'All right. I had to be a bit careful with it.'

'Why?'

'Oh, just because the whole family are completely mad, but I can hardly write that. And poor Jasper...'

'Who's Jasper?'

'The son.'

'He can't be that poor if he's the son of a duke.'

'Well no, he's not poor, I just mean he has two parents who are constantly at war so he rattles around that place on his own, trying to avoid them both.'

'Why doesn't he get a job?'

'Well, he kind of does have a job. He's learning how to run the estate.'

'Is he good-looking?'

'Erm, kind of.'

'Kind of?'

'He's tall, blond, very charming. He sort of tried to kiss me, as it happens.' I didn't have many secrets from Mum. And vice versa.

'Darling! How thrilling. What does "sort of" mean though?'

'He tried to kiss me, but I stopped it. It seemed a bit… unprofessional.'

'Oh, you girls these days and all this professionalism,' said Mum, rummaging around in the fridge. 'Where is that cheese? I know there's some buried in here somewhere. Ah, here it is, under the fish paste.' She retrieved a small, quite dry-looking nub of Cheddar. 'Do try and be a bit romantic sometimes, Polly love.'

'Mmm, I will,' I said, peering into the pan on the cooker. It was an unidentifiable brown sauce.

'Do you think you'll see him again?' Mum asked this in her 'casual' voice.

'Well, as it happens, Mrs Bennet, I'm having dinner with him on Friday, to discuss the piece, he says, anyway.'

'A date! That's good news,' she said, before narrowing her eyes at me. 'What are you going to wear?'

'Not a clue.'

'And will you brush your hair?'

'I will.'

'Also,' she went on, 'are you still all right for the doctor's appointment on Friday? At 4.15 at St Thomas'?'

'Yes, yes, 'course.'

'Are you sure? I'd probably be fine on my own. If you need to, you know, get ready for your dinner.'

'No, no, of course I'm coming. I've told Peregrine.'

'I don't think it'll take very long. An hour or so maybe. Which should give you enough time to get home afterwards and wash your hair.'

'Phew. Thank God for that.'

'Don't be sarcastic, Polly. Men don't like sarcasm.'

★

It was only on the bus home that I remembered I still needed to call Lex.

'Finally, where have you been all my life?' she said, picking up.

'Sorry, sorry, sorry, just a mad few days and now I'm just on the way back from dinner at Mum's. What's up?'

'I just wanted to check you were free this Friday for our engagement party?'

'Oh, I see,' I said. 'Exciting. And yes, 'course.' Then I remembered the dinner with Jasper. 'Ah, er, actually, shit, no. Sorry, love. I've said yes to having dinner with… someone on Friday.'

'With who?' Lex sounded indignant.

'That guy I interviewed on the weekend. Jasper Milton.'

'Like a date?'

'No, like a dinner.'

'A dinner on a Friday night sounds suspiciously date-like to me.'

'Honestly it's not. I think he just wants to make sure I've said nice things about him.'

'OK, well, can you come for drinks on Friday before your dinner that isn't a date? One glass of champagne?'

'Yup, probably. Where are you having it?'

'Portobello Road.'

'OK, perfect. I think so.'

After we hung up I wondered again if Lex was doing the right thing, or just caught up with the fripperies of a wedding. The ring, the engagement party, the dress. It seemed so all-consuming I was worried she'd forgotten the actual point of marriage.

★

I met Mum at 4 p.m. on Friday. I spotted her from a distance, sitting on a bench just outside the main entrance to the hospital, hunched in her red coat, and felt a pang of sadness. She looked totally alone. Vulnerable. It wasn't often that I wished Dad was still around because I couldn't remember that much about him. Just sitting beside him in the car listening to Dire Straits while he tapped his fingers on the steering wheel and his soily gardening boots by the kitchen door. I felt guilty, sometimes, that I didn't remember more. But once I'd settled at school in Battersea and Mum had found her job in the shop, our life in London was so radically different from life in a quiet Surrey village that I quite forgot it. Maybe it was a coping mechanism. An expensive shrink might hum and haw and say I'd pushed it out of my head deliberately. Who knows? It didn't bug me very often. But that moment, outside the hospital, I wished Dad was there.

Mum sounded slightly less vulnerable when I reached the bench. 'I mean, look at all these people, smoking on their drips. It's a disgrace,' she said loudly, gesturing with her arm.

'Shhh, Mum, they'll hear you.' I leant down to kiss her.

'And the fat ones. Look at all the fat ones.'

'Never mind them. What bit are we going to?'

'Hang on.' She fumbled in her handbag and retrieved the letter. 'The Bill Browning Wing.'

We set off, into the main entrance, down stairs, up lifts, along corridors with pictures of smiling nurses and posters about washing your hands until we came to the door of the wing.

'Hello, can I help you?' said a receptionist, not looking up from her computer.

'Yes. My name is Susan Spencer and I'm here for my MRI scan. We're a bit early though because the appointment's for 4.15. Does that matter? That we're a bit early?' She was nervous.

The receptionist didn't look up. 'Letter, please.'

I gave Mum what I hoped was a reassuring smile and looked

at the others in the waiting area. It was like a local bridge night, clusters of people, mostly old, with grey hair and grey faces, sitting around looking bored. Looking as if death might even be a welcome distraction.

'Right, Mrs Spencer, let me just get your duty nurse and we'll go from there. OK?' The receptionist's voice went up at the end of 'OK' as if she was talking to a child.

'Shall we sit, Mums?'

'Yes, let's.' She looked at her watch. 'I hope Bertie's OK without me in the shop.'

'He'll be fine. He's the last thing you need to worry about.'

'I know, I know.' She was twisting a crumpled tissue around in her fingers.

I changed the subject. 'What are you up to this weekend?'

'Oh, not much. I think I might be in the shop tomorrow. And then I thought I might go to church on Sunday.'

'Church?'

'Yes, you know. The one on Battersea Park Road. Proper, old-fashioned vicar apparently. Doesn't make everyone kiss each other after prayers. Can't be doing with all that.'

'Oh. Cool. Just because you…' I trailed off. As far as I could remember, the last time Mum went to church was when Dad died.

'I thought it might be a peaceful thing to do,' she said firmly, still twisting the tissue in her fingers. 'Just to go and think about things and have a little pray.'

'Want me to come with you?' As soon as I said it, I regretted it. The thought of getting to Battersea on Sunday morning to sit on a hard pew, in a cold church, surrounded by enthusiastic Christians didn't fill me with the Holy spirit.

But it was too late, because Mum looked so hopeful that I had to say yes. 'Oh, would you? Only I don't know anyone who actually goes there. Although I suppose there might be coffee or something afterwards.'

'Maybe even a biscuit. If we're lucky. 'Course I'll come.'

'Susan Spencer?' A nurse in blue overalls and white Crocs appeared in the waiting area.

'Oh,' said Mum, looking at him with surprise. 'It's a man,' she hissed at me under her breath.

'Hello there, I'm Graham,' said the nurse, holding out a hand. 'I'm going to be your nurse today so if you'd like to follow me then we can get the boring paperwork out of the way.'

'Hi, I'm her daughter,' I said, quickly interjecting before Mum could say anything offensive to Graham. 'I'm Polly. Can I come along too?'

''Course you can. More the merrier. Follow me.'

We walked through the swinging doors behind Graham, down a long corridor with stripped beds lined along one side, and into a small office. Graham's Crocs squeaked on the floor.

'Right now, let's have a look at this,' he said, sitting down and opening a blue folder at the desk. 'So, Susan, you're in for an MRI scan today. I'll give you some robes to put on for this but it shouldn't take long. Once we've done all these forms, it'll be into the robes and then we allow about an hour or so for the whole process. Now, can I just confirm you're not wearing anything metal?'

Mum shook her head.

'And you haven't eaten or drunk anything in the past hour?'

She shook her head again. 'I'm gasping for a cup of tea.'

'Oh, I'm sorry, I'm sure you are,' said Graham, sympatheti-cally.

I looked at a poster on the wall behind the computer that said 'Stand up to Cancer'. A smiling family were holding hands on it; a little blonde girl between her parents. A silly phrase. Of course you stand up to cancer. Nobody invites it. Nobody says, 'Come on in, Cancer, do you fancy a cup of coffee?'

Graham carefully lay four different bits of paper on the desk in front of him, in four different colours. 'They said when we got computers it would be so much easier but, honestly, look at all this paperwork. It's just twice the work now. Dear me. Right, can I just confirm a few more things?'

He ran through Mum's address, birthdate, medical history. 'And you, Polly, are the responsible adult today, is that right?'

'Guess so,' I said brightly.

'I'm sorry there are so many things to ask and get through but we're all about safety. I wouldn't do this job if it was otherwise,' said Graham.

'Quite right,' said Mum.

I nodded and tried to assume the expression of a responsible adult. Strange, feeling as if our roles had reversed like this. What is the age at which you start looking after your parents instead of vice versa? I'd needed Mum from the second I was born and I still needed her now, when there was a rare love life drama or I had cystitis yet again or Peregrine did something dementing. But when do parents start needing you back more than you need them? Maybe it was now, I thought, in this hospital office. Maybe it was right this second.

'I think that's everything,' said Graham, putting four stickers with Mum's name on the four different bits of paper and turning to me. 'Polly, I'm going to take your mum to the ward to get changed. Susan, once we're down there, Dr Singh the radiographer will talk you through it all.'

She nodded.

I wanted to say something comforting. 'I feel like we're in *Casualty*,' I said.

'Will you be OK in the waiting area, Polly?' said Graham, after a slight pause. 'Or there's a coffee shop downstairs if you fancy it?'

'No, no, all good. Don't worry about me. I've got a book so I'll just wait. You OK, Mums?'

'Yes, yes, Graham will look after me.'

''Course I will.'

I watched the pair of them walk down the corridor, Graham's Crocs squeaking back across the lino.

After going back downstairs and through another dozen or so corridors, so many corridors I felt like I was in *The Shining*, I found a Costa with a long queue snaking out of it.

'Excuse me, madam, do you want any coffee?' said the lady behind the till when I reached the front.

'Oh sorry, I was miles away,' I said. 'Yes, could I please have a white Americano?'

'Anything to eat?'

'No. I'm OK, thanks. I've got to get into a dress for a dinner tonight.' I don't know why I felt the need to share this with the Costa lady. A distraction from thinking about Mum lying upstairs having her scan, perhaps.

The tables here were as forlorn as the waiting area upstairs. Old people sitting on their own and reading the *Daily Mail*. Plus a man in a wheelchair, wearing an eye patch, playing cards by himself.

I sat for about an hour alternately reading my book and flicking through Instagram. Lex had put up a picture of her newly manicured nails. She'd picked a filter that made her engagement ring exceptionally shiny. 'Game faces for drinks tonight!' she'd written underneath. Why did people act as if they'd been lobotomized as soon as they got engaged? Then I thought about the dress I'd decided on for tonight. It was a red, sleeveless dress from Topshop, a bit short but I reckoned I could get away with it if I wore black tights and flats. Less slutty somehow with flats. My phone buzzed in my hand half an hour later. It was Mum.

All done, just sitting in ward having a cup of tea X

'It was all right, actually,' she said, when I found her upstairs. 'A bit terrifying when you lie back at first, but they played some nice music while I was in there and I almost fell asleep.'

'So did they say anything?'

'No, just that I'll get a letter with the results.'

I heard Graham squeaking towards us and looked up. 'All right then, Susan? Glad you've got your tea. Now, you should get another letter or a phone call from your GP in a week or so to discuss the results. But otherwise you're free to go.'

'Wonderful, thank you so much.'

'Not at all, just take it easy for the rest of the day. Polly, are you going to be with your mum tonight?'

'No, no, she's got a date!' said Mum.

'Not a date, a dinner,' I said emphatically to them.

'Well,' said Graham, looking confused, 'you both have lovely weekends then.'

★

I took Mum back to Battersea from the hospital in an Uber, ignoring her insistence that this was an extravagance and that we should get the number 77 bus. Then I put the kettle on, nipped round the corner to collect Bertie from the curtain shop and walked him back to Mum's flat.

'Come on, Bertie, hurry up, just do it,' I said, as he sniffed a lamp post and then slowly, as slowly as an old man shuffling to the loo in the middle of the night, lifted his leg and did a wee. I then took him upstairs to Mum and left them both sitting on the sofa watching an old episode of *Morse*.

Next I got the bus home, thinking about my to-do list. I might as well get ready as if I was going on a date, right? Be prepared and all that. No point in going out for dinner with a man as hairy as a woodland creature. Especially after that disaster with Callum. *Callum!* I thought to myself as I got into the shower. Shit, I still hadn't said anything to Bill about him. Not that I necessarily had to, I supposed. I just felt like I ought to. Maybe I should make a joke about it tonight, I thought, reaching for my razor.

I shaved basically everything except for my face; checked the mole under my chin and removed the thick black hair that popped out of it like a beanstalk every few days; applied the special occasion Tom Ford body moisturizer I used for the incredibly rare moments when I might have to take my clothes off as part of a group activity, instead of on my own; layered on so much make-up I looked like Danny La Rue; heaved myself into the small red dress and walked to Lex's drinks. On no account drink too much before dinner, I reminded myself.

The engagement party was in a bar called Bananas on the Portobello Road. It was up three flights of stairs, which made me start sweating in my dress.

'Hi, darling,' said Lex, when I arrived, panting, at the bar.

'Hello, you beautiful soon-to-be-bride,' I said.

'And you!' I said ambiguously to Hamish, who was standing next to Lex at the bar. 'Congratulations. Such good news!' I probably wouldn't win an Oscar for my performance, but it would do.

'Thanks, Pols,' he said. 'Now get a drink. Let's get hammered.' Hamish, a huge, totem pole of a man, reached for a champagne glass from a tray on the bar.

'Have you guys talked about dates yet?' I asked.

'Yes,' said Lex. 'We're thinking the second weekend in July. At home, marquee on the lawn, that sort of thing. I know it's quick but I don't want to wait until next summer.'

'Desperate to marry me, aren't you, darling?' said Hamish.

'But enough about us,' said Lex, ignoring him. 'Can we talk about your date please?'

'You've caught a live one, have you?' said Hamish. 'Well done, Pols, it's been… what? Years? Hasn't it?'

I smiled thinly at him. 'Not a date. A dinner. A work dinner.'

'If it's not a date then why have you worn a dress so short I can see your vagina?' asked Lex.

'I know,' I said. 'Do you think it's too much?'

'No. You look smoking. He'll want to bend you over the table and ravish you before the breadsticks.'

'Lex…'

'And have you used your special moisturizer?'

'Maybe.'

'It's definitely a date,' she said. I'd forgotten Lex knew about my special moisturizer.

'I'm sorry I can only stay for a bit,' I said, making a guilty face at her.

'Don't be silly,' she said. 'It's your first date in decades, go have fun.'

'Who's coming tonight then?' I asked, keen to stop anyone else talking about my love life as if it was a rare historical phenomenon.

'Various. About forty of us. Parents, a few colleagues, uni mates. The usual. And Bill's bringing his new girlfriend.'

'Girlfriend?'

'Yes, the new one who works in interior design or something. Funny name.'

'Ohhhh yes, we talked about her a few weeks ago. Didn't know they were doing the girlfriend-boyfriend thing.' I felt irrationally annoyed that Lex knew this first.

'Well, it's got to be something if he's bringing her tonight. Oh, sweetheart, look, it's your parents,' said Lex, as a middle-aged couple appeared through the door and looked around nervously. 'Sorry, love, do you mind if we go and say hello?'

'No, no, you go,' I said. 'Your night.'

I hovered by the bar watching for someone I knew as a few more people arrived, men giving bear hugs to one another, girls air-kissing, shrieking and handing over cards. How many engagement parties had I been to in bars and pubs across London? I wondered. Five hundred million maybe. I smiled at a waiter who was approaching with a tray of cocktail sausages.

'Yes please,' I said, ignoring the sticks and reaching for one with my fingers.

And then I saw him walk through the door. Callum. I was so surprised I swallowed the cocktail sausage whole and caught his eye just as my throat convulsed. I threw a hand in front of my mouth to stop the sausage reappearing and ejecting itself across the room, then turned around to face the bar and bent over slightly to have a coughing fit as quietly and discreetly as I could.

'You all right?' said Callum's voice behind me, then there was a hand on my back.

I swallowed and turned around. My eyes were watery from the choking. A good look.

'Yup, sorry, just…'

'An allergic reaction to seeing me?'

'Ha, er, I mean no. Just apparently unable to swallow properly.' I smiled at him and then felt annoyed with myself for looking too friendly.

'Oh really?' he said.

I blushed. 'Why are you here anyway?' That was better, I told myself. Cool and detached. That's what I should be going for.

'Oh, thanks very much,' he said, leaning around me and putting his arm on the bar to reach for a glass of champagne from the tray. 'Top up?' He nodded his head towards my empty glass.

'Yes, please. Thanks.' *Why does being English and having manners make it basically IMPOSSIBLE to be aloof?* Legs would never have this problem, I thought. She would just be all French and insouciant.

Callum took my empty glass and passed me a full one.

'What I mean is how do you know these guys?' I went on, trying to sound stern.

'I only know Hamish,' he said.

'How come?'

'From rugby.'

'Ohhhhhh, right.'

'How are you anyway?' he said. 'Actually…' He shook his head. 'Scratch that. Can I start again?'

I frowned at him. 'What d'you mean?'

'I behaved badly, I'm sorry for being a dick.'

He paused and there was an awkward moment where I

wasn't sure what to say. I was worrying that I had sausage breath and he was standing quite close to me. And then we were interrupted.

'There she is!' I looked up to see Bill approaching, and caught sight of a blonde girl behind him.

'Hi, dude, sorry, sausage breath,' I said, leaning in to kiss him hello.

'My favourite,' said Bill, 'and this,' he added, taking the blonde girl's hand, 'is Willow.'

'So good to meet you.' I leant in to kiss Willow hello as she held out a hand for me to shake, so we awkwardly did both at the same time. She, obviously, did not smell of sausage; she had shiny blonde hair which smelt like marshmallow.

'Hi,' she said. 'Billy's told me so much about you.'

Billy?

'Hi, mate,' said Bill to Callum, shaking his hand. 'Didn't know you knew this lot.'

'Only Hamish really, we play for the same rugby club.'

'Hi,' said Willow, flicking her hair at Callum. Oh no. She was a hair flicker.

'So,' said Bill, 'Here we all are. Good news about these two, isn't it?' He inclined his head towards Lex and Hamish.

'Mmm, kind of,' I murmured. I was grateful that he hadn't seemed to notice any awkwardness between me and Callum. I obviously couldn't make any sort of joke about it with him now, with both Willow and Callum hovering. I'd have to save it for another day.

'Oh dear, we're in that sort of mood tonight, are we?' Bill

knew my thoughts about Hamish, that I didn't think he was good enough.

'No, no,' I said, mindful that Callum was listening. 'It's just… a bit quick, that's all.'

'Pols,' warned Bill.

'All right, all right.'

'Anyway, where's Joe?' asked Bill.

'Playing in some concert at Wigmore Hall.'

Bill nodded, then looked down at my legs. 'Why are you wearing such a short dress?'

'I'm having dinner with someone.'

'Oooh. Like a date?' asked Willow. It was a bit annoying, the way she said 'Oooh'. Slightly patronising. Then she flicked her hair again.

'No. Just with someone I interviewed last weekend. I'm a journalist,' I explained to her.

'Oh yes, Billy told me. Is it someone famous?'

'Er, kind of. He's called Jasper. Jasper Milton.'

'Oh my God, him,' said Willow, her eyes widening. 'I know him. I mean, I don't know him. But I know who you mean. Wow! How exciting. That's definitely a date. Although, no offence, doesn't he normally date models?'

None taken, I said to myself in my head. Then I nodded.

'Wow,' repeated Willow, eyes still bulging.

'Never heard of him,' said Bill.

'Oh, Billy, come on, he's always in the news,' said Willow. Billy indeed. I'd never known anyone to call him Billy. Why wasn't he stopping her?

'Not in my news he isn't,' said Bill. 'Why were you interviewing him anyway?'

'He's the son of a duke. So, it's perfect *Posh!* stuff. And he
was in the papers the other day. Again. Falling out of a club.
Photographed, I mean.'

'But if you've already interviewed him why are you having
dinner with him now?' said Bill.

'Jeeeeees, sorry,' I said. 'I didn't know I needed permission
from you and a note from my mum to have dinner with
someone.'

We were interrupted by a tinkling sound across the room.
It was Hamish, tapping on his glass.

'Sorry to interrupt everyone from getting lashed,' he
started, 'but I thought I should say a few, brief words. Firstly,
to thank my parents for the party tonight, so drink up
because it's on Dad.' There were laddy cheers from across
the room.

'But really to thank Lex.' He paused. 'Because I know
some of you think this has been a bit fast. But I know that I
want to spend the rest of my life with her. I just know it. So,
could you all raise your glasses to toast my future wife, and I
can't wait for July when I'll be taking her up the aisle myself.'
More laddy cheers.

I rolled my eyes and then looked at my phone. 'Right,
going to make a move. Bye, guys.' I bent down to grab my
bag and blew them a kiss so I didn't have to go through that
awkward rigmarole of kissing people I'd only just said hello
to all over again. And I was still worrying about breathing

on Callum. I needed to find a bit of old gum rolling around in the bottom of my bag.

'DON'T SLEEP WITH HIM ON THE FIRST DATE, POLS,' Bill shouted across the room as I left, so everyone looked at me.

5

'HELLO,' SAID JASPER, STANDING up from the table to kiss me. I had had visions of slinking into the restaurant in a calm and perhaps even seductive manner, but I was, obviously, immediately flustered.

'Hello, how you doing? Where shall I put my coat? Oh, I can just hang it on the back of my...'

'Madam, can I take your coat?' A waiter appeared at our table.

'Yes please, thank you.' I pulled it off and instantly knocked a full water glass over on the table with my elbow. 'Oh God, I'm so sorry, I'm so sorry.' I pulled my napkin out to mop the water up and a fork clattered to the floor. Other tables, I noted, had paused, forks in air, and were watching. Meanwhile, the water was running in a steady line off the table and started pooling beside my chair.

'Madam is not to worry. I will get a cloth,' said the waiter, 'and a clean fork.'

'Madam maybe needs a drink?' said Jasper, who sat back down again at the table, which was discreetly tucked into the corner of the restaurant. He looked relaxed, good even, in jeans and a pale blue collared shirt, sleeves rolled up to his elbows. He leant forward to hand me his napkin. 'Quite the entrance.'

'Not totally what I planned.' I smiled as the waiter returned.

'Here you go, madam.' He put a new napkin on my lap, laid down a new fork, a new water glass and then crouched down to wipe the floor with a cloth.

'What would you like to drink?' the waiter asked, standing up again.

'Er, not sure. What are you having?' I looked at Jasper.

'I'm just finishing a gin and tonic but I might move on to wine.'

'Red?'

'Whatever you like.'

'Um, probably red.'

'A bottle of your Montepulciano please,' said Jasper.

'The two thousand and four, sir?'

'Exactly.'

'You're a regular?' I asked as the waiter retreated from the table, dripping cloth in hand.

'A sometimes regular. When I'm in London. Excellent veal. Now, how is that piece you've written about me?'

'All done.'

'Have you said lots of terrible things?'

'No. Only a few. Actually, I've been terribly nice and left out all sorts of detail that I could have put in.'

'Such as?'

'Never you mind. What have you achieved this week anyway?'

'Oh, not much. Drove around to see a couple of farmers. Had another row with my mother.'

'About what?'

'You can probably guess.'

'Ah.' I felt awkward.

'Ah, exactly. Presumably there's no mention of that in your piece?'

'Oh no, no. 'Course not. Not really the magazine's thing, that's more… newspaper stuff.'

'And how's my friend Lala?'

'Er, she's good.'

'Have you told her that we're having dinner?'

'No. Not exactly.' I'd wimped out in the end. Lala had been 'sick' on Monday and Tuesday, and by Wednesday I decided I should see what happened over dinner with Jasper before mentioning anything.

'Why not?'

'I thought it wasn't worth mentioning. You know. It's just dinner, no big deal.'

'Polly, how wounding.'

I laughed. 'What do you mean?'

'Well, I like you. I enjoyed talking to you at home very much. Apart from your awkwardness and your clumsiness, and your inability to take a compliment, I think you're funny and clever. And I like those things. Much more amusing than having dinner with yet another Henrietta who talks to me about wallpaper samples.'

'You've known a few Henriettas then?'

He raised his eyebrows. 'Not that again.'

'OK, I promise. I don't need to interrogate you any more anyway.'

'Good. Right, now, what are we going to eat? I'm hungry like a wild beast. I'm going to have two starters.'

It was a long dinner in the end. A two-bottle dinner without any further moments of awkwardness or water spilling or me saying anything embarrassing.

'What's the deal with your parents?' he asked at one point.

'The deal?'

'Yeah, you know. Mine are mad but still together, for whatever reason. But… you said your dad… isn't around, right?'

'Yeah, he died when I was ten, so…'

'Why?'

'Why did he die?'

'Yes.'

'Heart attack. Really sudden. In the garden one day and then, bang, that was it. Mum found him face down in the flower bed.'

'So you don't remember him?'

'Not really. I remember Mum being in bed for a long time afterwards, and I lived off a diet of biscuits.'

'Biscuits?' He frowned.

'Yep. Shortbread and chocolate digestives mostly. And toast. A lot of toast and Marmite went down in our house.'

'Where were you living?'

'A place in the country, in Surrey. But then we had to sell it and Mum moved to London so she could get a job.' Normally, when I told people my father died when I was young, they looked as awkward as a nun in a strip joint and stuttered some sort of apology. I liked that Jasper hadn't. He didn't seem at all awkward. It was refreshing.

'And where's your mother now?'

'Still there. In Battersea. With her dog.'

'Never remarried?'

'Nope. She's about as useless with men as me.' I hadn't meant to say the last bit.

'Oh really?' He smiled at me.

'I mean, no. That came out badly. Just being flippant.'

'So is that why you're so defensive about men?' he said.

'What do you mean?'

'Because your father died when you were younger. So, no man has ever matched up and so on?'

'I didn't realize I was talking to a psychologist,' I teased. 'Why the line of questioning?'

'Well, you know everything about me. I'm just trying to level the playing field.'

'Everything? Surely not?'

He shrugged. 'I haven't got any secrets. Apart from being a sexual deviant. Oh, and also I don't like peas.'

'Now you tell me. That could have been my scoop.'

'Being a sexual deviant?' He grinned from across the table.

'The peas thing.'

Jasper laughed. 'You're funny,' he said.

We carried on chatting, drinking red wine while the tables

around us paid and went, and a waiter started sweeping the floor in an obvious, theatrical fashion.

'Could we have the bill?' said Jasper, sometime later, waving across the room at him.

I reached down into my bag for my wallet and braced myself for the awkward 'I'll pay', 'No you won't', 'Let's split it' game.

'Don't even think about it,' said Jasper.

'No, let me, honestly. At least can we split it?' I said, hoping that he wouldn't say yes because that would mean I'd struggle to cover this month's rent and quite possibly have to sell a kidney.

'No, we cannot.' He put his card down on the table.

We put our coats on and went outside. I had a weird feeling in my stomach. It was either my seafood risotto or nervousness.

'Thank you for dinner,' I said, 'it was great.'

'You are entirely welcome, madam.'

'I think I'm going to jump in a cab home,' I gabbled. It was nervousness. But why was I nervous? I had no idea whether Jasper was necessarily planning or expecting anything. Apart from he had said that thing about the bedroom, and he did buy me dinner. Which was expensive. So was he after anything in return?

'Let me flag you a taxi,' he said, raising his arm as a black cab swung around the corner with its light on. See, I told myself, not planning or expecting anything. And I felt the tiniest bit crushed.

The cab pulled up alongside us.

''Night.' I leant forward and kissed Jasper on one cheek,

and then moved to kiss him on the other. But he was quicker than me, and suddenly his mouth was on mine and we were kissing. Properly kissing. Tongues and everything.

'Sorry,' I said a few seconds later to the cabbie, who had been sitting patiently with an open window.

'In you get,' said Jasper, opening the cab door. 'Text me when you get home.' He closed the door behind me and took £20 from his wallet. 'Thank you very much,' he said to the cabbie, handing him the note.

I leant forward. 'Can we go to Devonport Road, just off Goldhawk?'

As we pulled away, I waved at Jasper like a small child – why did I wave like that? – and then fell back into my seat. I fumbled in my bag for my phone just as it vibrated with a message.

I'd been wanting to do that all night.

In normal circumstances, I would deem this sort of message a bit cringe. Like something Zac Efron would do in a terrible high school movie. But although I tried not to be – I told myself it was the sort of thing he probably messaged women all the time – I was kind of thrilled. It came from Jasper. Handsome Jasper, Marquess of Milton, playboy who normally dated models and It girls. But I was interrupted from my Mills & Boon reverie because we went over a speed bump and I got the hiccups.

★

'Good gracious, Polly!' said Barbara, when I put my basket on the counter the following morning. The basket contained one carton of eggs, one packet of streaky bacon, one packet of ground coffee, one carton of green milk, one loaf of white sliced bread (I wasn't in the mood for brown), one carton of Tropicana (smooth) and one packet of Jamaica ginger cake.

'What do you mean?'

'Polly, my treasure, you look dreadful.' Barbara shook her head and looked mournful, as if standing over a grave at a funeral.

'Oh, right, thanks very much.'

'And all this!' Barbara went on, gesturing at the basket. 'This is enough to feed an army of elephants. You can't be eatin' all this on your own.'

'No, no, I've got Joe upstairs.' I'd left the flat minutes earlier to see Joe disappearing into the bathroom with a musical score in his hand and decided the safest option was to evacuate immediately and spend some time – quite a lot of time – loitering in the aisles of Barbara's shop.

'Out last night then, were you?' asked Barbara, as she lifted the eggs out to scan them.

'I had a date actually.' I'd given up on the dinner/date debate given that Jasper had kissed me. I felt the dinner/date line was crossed if someone put their tongue in your mouth.

Barbara dropped the eggs back in the basket and threw her hands up in the air.

'Oh Polly! Good news. Good, good news. Who with?' She narrowed her eyes at me. 'Was it with a man?'

I looked over my shoulder to check that there was nobody in a hurry for their own breakfast behind me.

'Er, yes, yes, it was a man. Sort of tall, blond, very charming.'

'He sounds nice. Oh dear, I've broken an egg,' she said, opening up the carton. 'Get me another carton of eggs.'

I walked back to the aisle with the eggs and retrieved another carton.

'And where did he take you?' asked my interrogator, as I handed them over.

'Just an Italian in Notting Hill.'

'Very good,' said Barbara, nodding and putting the orange juice in a plastic bag as the door jangled and another customer came through it. 'But why aren't you more excited, Polly? I'm more excited than you.'

'Er.' I looked back again for the other customer, not sure that I wanted a stranger to overhear Barbara's love-life advice. 'No, no, I am excited. I'm just a bit surprised, too, that's all.'

'You Capricorns are never happy,' said Barbara. 'Go and have a bath. You will feel better. Auntie Barbara knows. She knows.'

'I will. Thanks. Five million calories should help too,' I said, picking up the plastic bag from the counter.

'Let me know,' Barbara shouted across the shop, as I reached the door. 'Just think, my angel, you could be married by Christmas!'

Upstairs, Joe had emerged from the bathroom and was filling up the kettle in boxer shorts and his favourite t-shirt, which read 'I'll be Bach' and had a little cartoon of Bach underneath it.

'How was Her Majesty?'

'Oh you know. Being all Mystic Meg about my love life.'

'Eh?'

'I was just telling her about my dinner with Jasper last night.'

Joe theatrically clapped a hand to his forehead. 'Pols, of course. Full debrief please.'

'Hang on.' I put the shopping bag on the side. 'Scrambled or fried?'

'Scrambled. Did you get bacon?'

'Yup. And white bread and Tropicana and more coffee.'

'How do I love thee? Let me count the ways. Right, hand me the bacon and I'll be in charge of that. You make the eggs and tell me everything.'

'So I went to Lex and Hamish's engagement drinks first, which was good because I could warm up with a drink.'

'By which you mean three or four drinks, but yes, go on...' he said, crouching in front of the grill and laying out strips of bacon.

'OK, Clouseau. Anyway, left there after a bit and went to that Italian on Kensington Park Road. And then we sat there for three hours basically, just chatting.'

'And...?'

'And what?'

'Come on, Barbara Cartland. I need a bit more than that. Did you snog him?'

'Well, he sort of snogged me. But it was a bit awkward because he'd flagged a cab so the cabbie just sat there while he lunged at me.'

'And there was no question of him coming back here?'

'No! I wasn't even sure if it was a date in the first place.'

'Please,' said Joe, rolling his eyes.

'Well, anyway,' I said, 'he's a playboy so that'll probably be it and I'll never hear from him again. But it was fun.'

'Oh loosen up, Pols. You don't really know him, do you? You've only heard stories about him, right?'

'Yeah, but no smoke without fire and all that. And Lala says…'

'Lala has all the intelligence and sensitivity of this loaf of bread,' said Joe, dropping two slices in the toaster. 'Lower, possibly.'

'Well, he did text me in the cab on the way home saying he'd wanted to kiss me all night.'

'I think that's rather romantic. What did you reply?'

'Just thank you for dinner.'

He sighed. 'I wish you were better at flirting.'

'That's enough, get the plates out. I'm starving.'

★

There wasn't much space in our sitting room. It was more an offshoot of the kitchen than an actual room. The TV was in a corner on a wobbly Ikea stand that Joe had put together when we'd moved in three years before. Then there were two sagging sofas either side of it, each positioned at a slight flare so both of us had the perfect angle for watching telly while lying down. We each had our own sofa: Joe had the brown one, I had a smaller beige sofa bed. A low coffee table was equally carefully positioned between the two sofas so that it was within arm's reach for both of us. The table was usually covered with at least four mugs of half-drunk tea (me), empty crisp packets (Joe), magazines (me) and music scores (Joe).

After another trip downstairs to Barbara's that afternoon, the coffee table was covered with bottles of Lucozade and empty packets of Monster Munch.

'We've got to do something, Joe,' I said, stretching on the sofa. 'We can't lie here all day.' I was also, annoyingly, phone watching. My phone was lying on my stomach so that the second any message came through I'd know about it. It was 3 p.m. and nothing had. Why did girls go so crazy the second any man showed the slightest interest? This time yesterday, I was a fairly rational human being, having dinner later with an interview subject. Twenty-four hours on, I was watching my phone like Glenn Close in *Fatal Attraction*. What mysterious alchemy made us behave like this? The only two messages I'd got all day had been from:

My mother, checking I was still all right to meet for church tomorrow.

11 a.m. at St Saviour's. Brush your hair won't you, Polly love? X

Bill, asking how dinner with 'Lord Byron' went and did I want to go to the cinema tomorrow afternoon to see the new *Star Wars* film. I'd said no, I'd rather eat my own head, and then roped him into coming to church with Mum instead. Bill could be a soft touch like that.

'Why is he making a soufflé if he's never made it before?'

said Joe, from the other sofa, frowning at *Come Dine With Me*. 'These people are idiots.'

'Joe, seriously. We need to do something.'

'Like what?' He turned his head to face me. 'I could honestly lie here all day.'

'It's too depressing, too sordid. Please can we go and do something?'

'Like what?'

'I don't know, I just need a distraction.'

He looked pointedly at my phone. 'You had dinner with him last night, he texted you in the cab on the way home. Can you not be one of those girls?'

'I'm not, I'm not. I'm just…'

'Being needy.'

'A bit.'

'OK. Well, if you really want to do something, a friend of mine is having a birthday party in Soho we could go to for a bit.'

'Which friend?'

'You haven't met him. Anthony. Another gay in the wind section. Plays the French horn.'

'Has he played your French horn?'

'No, he has not.'

'OK. Where's the party?'

'The Green Carnation.'

I frowned.

'You know, the piano bar. The one on Wardour Street.'

'Right, so a gay friend of yours is having his birthday

party in a piano bar in Soho. Honestly, it's like something out of *The Birdcage*. Oh, by the way, I totally forgot, there's a friend of Jasper's I met who I think you'd like. Called Max. Handsome. Funny.'

'When d'you meet him?'

'When I went to Jasper's…'

'Oh dear, Pols. Jasper this, Jasper that. You've got Mentionitis.'

I threw a cushion at him. 'I have not got Mentionitis. Just trying to help you out. But if you don't want my help then…'

'We can discuss it on the bus. Come on, let's go.'

★

Three hours later, we were in the Green Carnation, gathered around a table, hangovers gone and three rounds in.

'How long have you and Joe lived together then?' asked Anthony, a short Scottish man with a shaved head who was wearing a bow tie and shirt, on to which was pinned a badge reading 'Kiss me quick. It's my birthday'.

'Nearly four years. Which is longer than any relationship I've ever had with another man.'

'Love at first sight?'

I looked at the bar where Joe was gesticulating to the barman, holding up both his hands to demonstrate that he wanted ten Jägerbombs.

'Sort of.'

'Do you have to put up with all sorts of shenanigans?'

'Occasionally. Although it's been quite quiet of late.'

'Has it? The Lothario of the Academy losing his touch?' said Anthony, loudly, as Joe lowered the tray of shots on to the table.

'Anthony, you do talk a load of nonsense,' said Joe. 'I'm just having a little pause. And I've also got my hands full with my flatmate here.'

'Oh really?' said another Scot.

'Shots first. Come on, have one of these.' Joe passed Anthony a Jägerbomb and handed the rest out to various others sitting round the table whose names I had forgotten as soon as I was told them.

Anthony threw his shot glass back and then put it back on the table with a smack. 'What's the gossip then?'

'It's not gossip. Honestly. There's literally nothing to gossip about,' I said.

'Yes, it is. She went on a date with one of the poshest men in England,' said Joe.

'Oh you lucky cow,' said Anthony. 'Who's that then?'

'He's called Jasper.'

''Course he is. Jasper what?'

'Jasper Milton. He has this castle and...'

'I know who you mean, he's the one who was in the papers the other day,' said Anthony.

'Exactly,' replied Joe. 'And it's incredibly unprofessional. She went to stay at their massive pile in Yorkshire to interview him, and ended up giving him a blow job under the dining room table.'

'You didn't?' Anthony looked thrilled.

'Joe! I didn't, sorry to disappoint. He just tried to kiss me at the dining room table.'

'But you're going out with him now?' asked Anthony.

'No. We just had dinner last night.'

'And?'

'And nothing,' I said simply. 'Dinner and we kissed before he put me in a taxi home.'

'And have you heard from him since?'

'Well, he texted when I was in the cab but not today.' I picked up my phone and checked it for the 2,829th time that day. Still nothing.

'Have you texted him?'

'No!'

'Why not?'

'Because I can't. I have to wait for him.'

'Says who?'

'Those are the rules!'

Anthony shook his head.

'I promise you. I can't text him. He'll think that means I want to marry him. All men think that if you text them.'

'And you don't want to marry him?'

I burst out laughing. 'Anthony, this is crazy. This is one of those conversations that if he overheard, I'd have to kill myself. This is why women get a bad name.'

'I just don't understand why you don't text him. You know he likes you. What's the problem?'

'It's just not how it works. Let's have another drink and stop talking about it.'

'But you're going to carry on checking your phone every two and a half seconds?'

'Yes.'

★

Twenty minutes later my phone vibrated. It was him.

I realize this is probably too keen, but you're not around tonight are you? I find myself free and I'd like to see you. J

'He sounds dead posh,' said Anthony, reading the message over my shoulder.

'What shall I say?' I asked them.

'Go home and shave,' Joe insisted. 'Quick.'

Which is how I found myself in an Uber heading home, having texted Jasper back saying I was free and did he want to come to my flat 'for a drink'.

I had an hour so I shaved, then covered myself with my Tom Ford moisturizer again. Shins, arms, stomach, smudge between the thighs. Boobs? No. Quite weird to moisturise your actual nipples.

My underwear drawer looked sadder than a charity clothes bank. Black knickers from M&S, size sixteen because I liked pants to be roomy; greying knickers from M&S, size sixteen, which were white for approximately five minutes when I bought them several years ago; 'fun knickers' with stripes and spots on which I occasionally bought from Topshop in an effort to jazz things up. Anything 'sexy' was right at the back of the drawer, buried beneath old tights.

I retrieved a black, lacy pair of French knickers and held them up to my hips. They looked tiny. When had I ever squeezed my bottom into these? I put one foot through and fell over. God, I was a bit pissed. Must brush teeth, I told myself. So, I did that and then went back through the underwear drawer again, looking for my 'sexy' bra. I knew there was a black lacy one somewhere. My party bra. It was hidden under a pair of old sports socks.

Underwear on, I squinted in the mirror and poked my stomach with an index finger. Not great. My knickers were digging into my hips. But it would have to do. You wouldn't be able to see with a pair of jeans over the top. Black jeans. Black low-cut t-shirt. Bare feet because it seemed relaxed and maybe even a bit come-hither. I looked at my toenails, painted dark red approximately some weeks ago. If you squinted, they hardly looked chipped at all.

I rubbed some tinted moisturizer into my face, added a couple of coats of mascara and dabbed some blusher over my cheeks. Then stood back to scrutinize myself. It was fine. Casual. Relaxed.

The doorbell went. OK, Polly, I told myself as I went downstairs, be calm. Be cool. Be... I tripped on the penultimate stair and fell into the back of the door with a thud.

'Polly?' came Jasper's voice from the other side of the door.

'*Fuck me*,' I said, through gritted teeth. My ankle felt like it had exploded.

'Not the most ladylike invitation I've ever had.' He paused. 'You all right?'

'Yup, fine,' I said, trying to uncurl myself in the tight space between the bottom step and the front door. 'Shit, my ankle hurts.'

'Let me in and I'll have a look. I did a First Aid course once. You may need mouth-to-mouth.'

I stood carefully on my left leg, gripping the banister with my right hand, and reached for the door. 'Hi,' I said, opening it while still on one leg. 'Sorry, it really hurts.'

'Why are you apologizing? Come on,' he replied, bending down and picking me up.

'Don't, Jasper, put me down, I'm too heavy, you can't possibly get upstairs carrying me. Honestly, I can hop, just put me down and...'

'Be quiet,' he said, climbing the stairs. 'I carry farm animals. I can manage you.'

Upstairs, he put me down on Joe's sofa and rolled up my jeans. 'It's pretty swollen. Can you move it?'

I slowly rotated my ankle. 'Yup.'

'Then it's not broken. You just need some ice.' He looked over his shoulder and went to rummage in the freezer. He brought back a bag of diced carrots and gently laid it over my ankle. I winced.

'OK?' he asked.

I nodded.

'Good,' he said. 'Now, that drink.'

'Yes,' I said, 'bottle of wine on the table. Bottle opener in the drawer next to the sink. Glasses on the shelf.'

He uncorked it, reached for two wine glasses and came

back to the sofa holding them. He held one out for me, then scooped underneath my knees with one arm and sat down, my legs over his lap.

'Well,' said Jasper, 'you're clearly one for dramatic entrances.'

I laughed and then winced as my ankle throbbed. 'Ow, don't make me laugh.'

He looked at me, then put his wine back down and lifted my legs again.

'What are you doing?'

He didn't answer. Instead, he knelt on the floor, removed the diced carrots and kissed my ankle.

'Better?'

I nodded.

He kissed it again. Then kissed above it, then higher and higher, working his way up my leg. He reached the top of my thigh and looked up at me. 'I'm glad you were free.'

'Me too. Although I was actually in a bar, but then you messaged so I...'

Jasper put his hand behind my head, pulling it gently towards him. 'That's enough talking.' He ran his hand through my hair and pulled it gently. 'Where's your room?'

I nodded towards the door beside the bathroom.

He stood and picked me up again, carried me into the bedroom, then laid me down on my bed. I laughed nervously.

'What's funny?' he said.

'Nothing, I've just never been picked up like that. It seems quite... erm... it seems like something you'd see in a film.

Because I'm quite tall, so I'm always worried that I'm too heavy for boys to…'

'Are you going to talk throughout this?'

'No, no, sorry.' I pinched my lips together.

'Good,' he said, kneeling over me. 'Arms up.'

'Did your nanny teach you to undress women?'

'What did I just say?' he said.

I put my arms up and he pulled my t-shirt off then tossed it on the floor behind me.

Then he pulled his own shirt off, before leaning down to kiss me. 'How soundproof are your walls?' he said.

'Why?'

'Why do you think? I want to make you groan. But I don't want anyone else to hear.' He reached underneath my bra and circled my nipple with his forefinger.

'Groan? How do you know I groan?' He pinched my nipple harder while kissing my neck. 'Aaaaaah.'

'I suspected.'

'Oh, you're one of those, are you? Into noise?'

What should I do, I worried. I was just lying there. Run my fingers down his back?

'I'm into people enjoying themselves,' he said, arching his back as I lightly ran my nails down it.

'People?'

Jasper leant back and rolled his eyes. 'Right, tell you what, we're going to have a moratorium on talking. Not one more word. The only noises I want to hear from you are murmered expressions of pleasure. Deal?'

I smiled. 'Deal.'

I did make quite a few murmered expressions of pleasure, as it happens. Three fairly loud expressions of pleasure as the night went on. Firstly, when he pulled my knickers off and put his head between my legs. Secondly, when I slid down on top of him, rocking slowly, then faster, while he used his hands to make me come again. And thirdly, finally, when he made me kneel facing my headboard, put my hands on the wall and pushed into me from behind, reaching around with one hand to pinch my nipples. Three times. A personal best. Like having a starter, a main course and a pudding. No man had ever made me come three times in one night before because, well, sex can start to chafe a bit, can't it? I was so pleased I didn't even mind that it was 4 a.m. by the time we fell asleep. And I'd totally forgotten about my ankle.

*

The problem the next morning was that I woke up needing to pee. And my stomach was bubbling and making alarming noises. I looked across at Jasper, still apparently asleep, lying on his front, facing away from me. I had to go to the loo before he woke up. But what if he woke up while I got up and heard me in the loo? Or, worse, what if I got up and made a smell in the loo and then he wanted to pee straight after me? He'd probably leave immediately if that happened. If he went into the bathroom and realized what I'd done. And then I'd never hear from him again. So, I decided just to lie there, stomach growling, bladder full. It was deeply uncomfortable. I rotated my ankle under the duvet. At least that felt all right.

Minutes ticked by. Maybe I should just go and then light a match? But then he still might wake up and realize what I'd done and be repulsed. Before Hamish, Lex always took an Imodium if she knew she'd be staying overnight with someone. Which I always thought would make you bloated. But she insisted that it was better than any sort of embarrassing bathroom incident.

More minutes went by. I looked at my phone: 6.41 a.m. Early. What if I went to the loo and ran all the taps to disguise the noise? Would that work? But then he still might wake up and want to go after me.

Had anyone ever been this pathetic about anything in their whole life?

More minutes. I decided I'd have to go. Just have to. I'd creep out as quietly as a thief, run the taps, open the window, go to the loo, light a match and then sort of fan the air a bit with a towel. Then I'd feel better. Much better. Go to the loo, brush teeth. Creep back into bed. I inched one leg out from under the duvet and put a toe on the floor.

'What are you doing?' said Jasper, turning his face towards me. My plan was foiled.

'Nothing,' I said, retracting my leg and putting it back underneath the duvet. 'Just stretching.'

He ran a hand up my stomach and across my left nipple, which instantly hardened. Then he lifted his head, pulled the duvet back and started slowly sucking it. God. I really, really needed the loo. But I'd just have to try to hold it. I ran a finger back and forwards across my teeth quickly to try to de-fuzz them while Jasper turned his attention to my right nipple. He didn't seem that worried about morning breath.

6

MUM WAS THRILLED TO see Bill, who'd always politely shown far more interest in curtain patterns than I ever had. 'Bill, my darling boy,' she said, throwing her arms around him outside St Saviour's. Her head came to roughly the height of Bill's chest, which made for a sweetly biblical sight. A small, grey-haired woman in a duffle coat clasping her arms around a tall man in jeans and Converse.

'Polly, did you have to wear trainers?' she asked, turning to kiss me.

'They're not trainers, they're Superga. And anyway, Bill's wearing them too.'

'Don't tell tales, Polly love, it's not nice,' Mum said as we walked into the church. 'What will the vicar think, you being so untidy?'

'I would imagine he'd be pretty thrilled even if we were all naked, Mum, we'll probably double his congregation.' There were two rows of pews either side of the aisle, and precisely two people sitting separately at the front. They turned around to look as we walked in.

'Shhh, Polly. You mustn't be vulgar in church.'

'Yes, Pols, come on. Please try and maintain a bit of decorum in the house of God,' said Bill, sticking a finger into my back.

'Ow! Can you not? I'm feeling a bit delicate this morning,' I said.

'Why, what did you do last night?' he said.

'Shhhh, you two,' said Mum, holding a hand up in the air to silence us. 'Look, shall we sit in this one?' She gestured at a pew four rows from the front.

'It doesn't look like there's going to be a sudden rush of punters,' I said, shuffling my way down the pew between prayer cushions.

'Sit quietly please. I'm going to have a little pray.' Mum knelt on a cushion and rested her forehead on her hands in front of her.

I sat back and scrutinized our two fellow worshippers. One was a small Chinese lady; the other was a middle-aged man sitting hunched in his overcoat, reading the sports section of the *Sunday Times*.

'Look,' I whispered to Bill, nodding in the man's direction. 'Not very godly, is it, reading the paper in church?'

'I think God has to be grateful for whoever he can get these days. Put your phone away.'

'All right, Dad.' I put it on silent mode and dropped it into my bag.

From behind us came the sound of footsteps. I turned around to see a family coming down the aisle. A weary-looking man in chinos and loafers clasping a small blond boy by the hand, followed by a woman with a scarlet coat and mass of dark frizzy hair holding hands with a smaller girl, who was clutching a doll.

'Andrew darling, let's sit there,' ordered the woman, pointing at the pew behind us. 'You don't mind, do you?' she asked.

'No, no, not at all,' said Bill, 'the more the merrier.'

'Andrew, you go along first, then Demetrius, there's a good boy. Then Mummy will go between you and Persephone. Persephone, please don't pick your nose in church. Right, are we all in?'

'I've left my colouring book at home,' said the boy.

'Demetrius, you don't need your colouring book. We're going to do lots of lovely singing about Jesus,' replied the woman. 'Persephone, WILL you stop picking your nose?'

I looked sideways at Bill. He was clenching his jaw and had closed his eyes in an effort not to laugh. Mum was still kneeling, head in hands.

Then someone else bowled down the aisle. A woman in a floral coat and a beret. She bustled her way to the front, and busied herself behind a pew to the right of the altar, taking off her coat and laying out sheet music. She waved at the Chinese lady, and then pulled out a tape recorder from her bag. She ceremoniously laid it on the ledge of the pew, before pressing play. Tinny, organ music floated down the aisle. 'All rise!' she instructed, standing up.

We stood as a figure in white walked down the aisle. The vicar had long dark hair.

'It's a woman!' hissed Mum in a stage whisper.

'Mmm,' I murmured as quietly as I could.

'No one told me that. It just says "Reverend E. W. Housely" on the sign outside. It doesn't say anything about it being a woman.'

'*Shhh*, Mums, she'll hear you. Everyone will hear you.'

'I suppose I don't mind that it's a woman,' she went on, ignoring me. 'It's just very modern.'

'We live in modern times, Susan,' whispered Bill.

'I suppose we do,' said Mum, keeping her eyes on Reverend Housely as she came to a halt in front of the altar and nodded at the woman in the beret, who stopped the tape recorder.

'Good morning, everyone,' said the vicar, beaming. 'How lovely it is to see some new faces among us. You are all very welcome to this, the Eucharist service at St Saviour's. To kick things off, let's sing one of my favourites, "Lead Us Heavenly Father, Lead Us".'

'A traditional one,' said Mum, nodding in approval.

The woman in the beret pressed play again, and the organ recording began. Bill, who'd sung in the choir at his school, immediately launched into the hymn, his low voice rumbling out across the pews towards the stained-glass window at the front. Behind me came the high-pitched tone of the frizzy-haired mother. 'O'er the world's tempestuous sea… Andrew, tell Demetrius to stand up properly!'

*

There was coffee after the service in a small, cold room to the left-hand side of the church decorated with abysmal children's paintings.

'Hello… Vicar,' said Mum, shaking her hand. 'I'm Susan.'

'Welcome, Susan!' said the vicar back, beaming in a manner that suggested she'd never been so excited to meet anyone in all her life. 'And who have you got with you?'

'This is my daughter, Polly,' said Mum, so I stepped forward, shook the vicar's hand and was also rewarded with a beatific smile. 'And this is Bill,' she continued.

'Bill, hello, wonderful to meet you. Did you enjoy the service?' asked the vicar.

'Well, it was enthusiastic, wasn't it?' Bill replied. 'And that's the main thing.'

'Quite!' The vicar beamed at us all, thrilled with her new flock. At the same moment, the frizzy-haired woman hurried over, holding a child's hand in each of hers.

'Vicar! What a service that was. Demetrius enjoyed it very much, didn't you?'

Demetrius looked at his shoes.

'And Persephone loved the hymns, didn't you, darling? Tell Vicar which one was your favourite?'

'I didn't love them. I hated them,' said Persephone.

'Oh dear, we'll have to do better next week, won't we?' said the vicar, smiling at Persephone, who was holding her doll upside down with one hand and picking her nose with the other.

'She's only joking,' said the frizzy-haired woman. 'Got her

father's sense of humour. Where is he? Andrew? Andrew?' She scanned the room, her hair bouncing on her shoulders. 'We should go and find him, but thank you so much again, Vicar, and see you next week.'

'Same time as always!' said the vicar, still smiling, until they'd all safely left the room when her face fell and she sighed. 'They only come because they need to get into the local school.'

'Oh,' said Mum.

'Sidney, hello, how are you? Come and meet these nice people,' said the vicar, gesturing at the man who had been reading the *Sunday Times*, and who was now loitering over the biscuit tray in the corner.

Sidney picked up a digestive and walked over.

'This is Susan, and Susan's daughter Polly, and Bill. Are you two married?' she asked, looking questioningly at Bill and me.

'God no!' I replied. 'I mean, sorry, no, we're not. Just friends.'

'How long have you been coming here, Sidney?' said Mum, turning her attention to him.

'Oh, a couple of years I'd say. Is that about right, Vicar?' Sidney, wearing an old Barbour with the paper tucked under his arm, had biscuit crumbs on his chin.

'Yes, I'd say that's about right. About the time that I arrived. One of our regulars, aren't you?'

Sidney smiled. 'I suppose I am by now. Very good sermons because she doesn't go on for hours.'

'So we can all get home for lunch in time?'

'Exactly, Susan,' said the vicar. 'That's what Sundays are for. Small bit of praying, big bit of lunch.'

My kind of vicar.

★

Naturally Lala wasn't at her desk on Monday morning when I arrived, but that gave me more rehearsal time. 'La, I have a confession…' No, that makes me sound guilty. 'La, I need to tell you something…' Bit dramatic. 'La, the most hilarious thing happened this weekend. Jasper took me out for supper on Friday night and I slept with him on Saturday night. Three times. And yesterday morning actually.'

Tricky one.

Lala arrived in a cloud of cigarette smoke half an hour later. 'Morning, Pols, how are you? I…' *Cough, cough, cough.* 'God, I've caught the most horrendous cold, I shouldn't really be in.'

'La…'

'I know it was standing outside all day on Saturday racing. It was bloody freezing in Gloucestershire, I honestly thought I might die several times.'

'La…'

'And that desperate girl Sophia Custard-Hardy was there. God, she's appalling. All over the boys and she got incredibly drunk and…'

'*LaLa.*'

She frowned. 'What?'

'It's nothing really, I just wanted to let you know that Jasper and I had dinner on Friday and…'

'You and Jaz?' Lala stood up and put her hands in her coat pockets. 'Where are all my tissues?'

'Yup.'

'To talk about the piece?' She was still burrowing in her pockets, not looking at me. 'Honestly, what do I do with them all? Why do they always vanish?'

'Well, kind of.'

'I thought you'd written it? Ah look, here's one.' She retrieved a sodden piece of tissue from the bottom of her handbag.

'Well, yes, I had.'

'So why have dinner with him?'

'It was a kind of date.'

'A date? You? With Jaz?' Lala looked up at me, hands frozen in front of her face, damp tissue between her fingers.

'Kind of.'

She blew her nose and frowned again. 'Did anything happen?'

'We sort of kissed on the pavement outside but then I got in a taxi and went home. So not really. But then on Saturday night I saw him again…'

'Jasper?'

'Yes.'

'Again?'

'Yes.'

'Why?'

'Well, he texted me. And asked was I free. And I sort of was… So, he came over to mine and, erm, well, he stayed with me.'

Her damp tissue was still hovering in mid-air. 'Did you sleep with him?'

'Um, well, kind of. I mean yes. I mean, there wasn't actually much sleep.' I smiled at her nervously. 'But, yes. Do you mind? Please don't mind. It sort of just happened.'

She blinked. 'No, I don't mind. I can't mind, can I? Jasper and I happened ages ago. It's just a bit… weird that's all.'

'Good weird?'

'I guess so. Just… how did it all start? At Castle Montgomery?'

'Kind of. But honestly, La, I'm not sure it's going to be a huge deal. You know what he's like.'

'Yeah. Be careful, Pols. Do you like him?'

'I don't know really. I like him as a person way more than I thought I would. But I don't think we're going to get married, don't panic.'

I mean, that's what I said to her, but obviously there was a small part of me – the tiny psycho part that lurks in all of us – which had wondered whether it would be better to get married at Castle Montgomery in the summer or the winter and whether there had ever been a duchess called Polly before. But then the more sensible part of my brain kicked in and told me to stop being absurd and that middle-class girls from Surrey didn't marry future dukes apart from in silly romantic novels.

'God yeah,' said Lala, interrupting me from my reverie. 'You'd have Eleanor as your mother-in-law.'

'Yeah. Can you imagine?' I said quickly.

'I did imagine it once. But lucky, probably, that I escaped it. Right, I'm going to go have a fag and get a coffee. Want one?'

'No. No, I'm good, thanks.'

Phew, I thought, as Lala disappeared to Pret. At least I've told her. And she seemed to be OK. So, that was that.

★

There was less good news that afternoon when Mum rang. I picked my phone up with one hand, clutched it between my ear and my shoulder and carried on scrolling through Twitter.

'Hi, Mums. How you doing?'

'Hello, darling, I just thought I should ring you…' Her voice was wobbly.

'Mums, what's up?' I stopped scrolling.

'It's only that I've got the letter from the doctor.'

'What does it say?'

'Well, they think it's… or they seem to think it is something. That it's a tumour.' She started crying.

'Oh God, Mums. Shit. Am so sorry. OK… hang on… what else does it say in the letter?'

'Just that…' Sob. 'Just that…' Sob. 'Just that it's stage two, whatever that is. I don't know what stage two is, how am I supposed to understand that?' Mum let out a cry and I heard Bertie bark in the background.

'OK.' I couldn't bear my own mother crying on the phone to me. What could I say that was comforting? My brain went into practical mode. 'Do they say anything about what the plan is?'

'Yes.' She sobbed again, Bertie barked harder. 'They say that they'll be in touch about operation dates. And then maybe chemo. Chemo! Polly, I'm going to lose all my hair.'

'Oh, Mums, I'm sorry. But… it'll grow back. And listen, there's a plan. So that's something. A plan to sort all this out.' I was clutching at straws, but I didn't know what else to say. What should you say when your mum calls you crying to say she's been diagnosed with cancer?

'I'm here, Mum,' I said gently.

'I'm sorry to call you at work, darling,' she sobbed back.

'Don't be so ridiculous, I'm here whenever you need. So, OK, let's think, is the next step to wait and hear about operation dates?'

She sniffed. 'Yes, I think so.'

'Right, well let me know the second that happens and I'll book some time off work.'

'You don't have to do that.'

''Course I will. And Joe will be thrilled to come and look after you too. He loves nothing more than sitting on the sofa watching telly. So really, don't worry, Mums. We've got this covered. We're all here. It's all going to be fine.'

It was going to be fine. It had to be fine. But I felt helpless. I didn't know what to say and I didn't know anything about cancer. It's a disease that's all around us, in films, on telly, talked about in Tube adverts, on marathon t-shirts, but I'd never known anyone close to me with it. It was a sick feeling, knowing that a tumour – what a grotesque word – had found its way into my mum's body. But some cancers were worse than others, weren't they? You heard people saying that. 'Oh, liver cancer, poor man, that's a bad one.' As if another form of cancer might be a 'good' one. But where did breast cancer fall on this good/bad continuum? What did stage two even mean? Stage two comes after stage one so it couldn't be that bad, right? But how many stages were there?

'Thank you, darling,' said Mum. 'You get back to work.'

'OK, but I love you. And I'll see you for supper later. Why don't I bring it for once?'

'No, no. There's a bit of salmon that's starting to smell, so we'd better have that.'

Now was not the moment to raise Mum's fridge habits. 'OK. I'll bring a bottle of wine. And probably quite a big bar of chocolate.'

'Wonderful, thank you, darling.' She stopped and blew her nose. 'And then I can tell you all about that nice man at church yesterday.'

'What?'

'You know, Sidney, the one with the paper. We had lunch afterwards in a pub around the corner. He's ever so sweet. Lost his wife a few years ago.'

'Like a date?'

'Well, not really, I wasn't dressed properly for a date. But it was a nice lunch all the same.'

'Wow. But OK, right, we will discuss this tonight.'

A lot to discuss tonight, all of a sudden.

'OK, darling, see you seven-ish.'

I hung up and opened Google. 'Stage two breast cancer,' I typed. 'In stage two, the cancer cells have spread beyond the original location and into the surrounding breast tissue,' said the first site I clicked through to. I felt sick at this thing 'spreading' its way through Mum. How long had it been secretly advancing on her body, a malevolent little worm waiting to ambush? And how did you stop it?

7

MUM WENT INTO HOSPITAL within three weeks for her operation. You hear about waiting lists and people lying on gurneys in hospital corridors, but it was quite quick in the end. The procedure was called a lumpectomy – another grim medical term we'd both read up on – which meant removing the tumour and several infected lymph nodes in her chest.

Before the operation, lying in her hospital bed and shrouded in a white gown, her main concern seemed to be Bertie, who was having a little holiday with Joe and me while she was away. You'd think he was a newborn baby, as opposed to an incontinent 9-year-old terrier given the instructions he came with.

'You will take him out for some fresh air, won't you?' she reminded me, as we waited for the nurses to wheel her down to theatre. 'And remember to buy the right kind of Pedigree Chum, the chicken tins not the beef ones, they disagree with him. And a bit of carrot or some vegetables mixed with it. Not tomatoes though, he doesn't like those. And remember to fill his water bowl.'

I nodded. 'He's absolutely fine. Joe's taken him for a walk

already today. Don't panic.' Joe had sent me a message earlier about this walk: *Took Bertie to the park next to the conservatory. He did a dinosaur-sized dump. I am never having children.* But I didn't think Mum needed that level of detail right before surgery.

Two nurses in blue overalls came to collect her half an hour or so later. 'I'll see you in a bit,' she said, reaching for my hand to squeeze it. And I nodded and clenched my jaw so she didn't see me cry as she was wheeled off. I'd felt constant pangs of terror in the past three weeks. What if it didn't work? What if the malevolent little worm in her body carried on marching? What if it couldn't be stopped?

I sat in the family waiting room for two hours, trying to read my book but failing because I kept getting to the end of a sentence and found I'd forgotten the beginning of it. Then I tried to read a magazine but I didn't much care about Kim Kardashian's new knee-lift. I flicked through Instagram and felt annoyed at the pictures of dogs and eggs. Then Bill texted asking me to let him know when Mum was out. I sent him back a thumbs up emoji and wondered whether I'd see Jasper that week. We'd made a vague plan to do something on Saturday, but I'd said it would depend on Mum.

I'd seen him three times since the night of the twisted ankle. Each time he'd come over late to the flat, each time we'd fallen straight into bed and spent most of the night making the sort of shapes you normally see in Cirque du Soleil. I looked up at a poster on the wall opposite me. 'HOW MUCH DO YOU KNOW ABOUT PROSTATE CANCER?' it asked in shouty capitals. I probably shouldn't be thinking about sexual positions in a hospital waiting room while my mother was being operated on.

It was about an hour later that she was wheeled back from the recovery room, pale and asleep. 'She's all right,' said the nurse, 'just dozy. She'll be woozy for a few hours.'

I nodded and reached for Mum's hand, squeezing it so she knew I was there.

★

I went back to hospital the following morning to find she was quite perky. Almost back to normal.

'I'd like a cup of tea,' she said, still lying in her hospital bed. The quiet droning of a morning talk show drifted across the ward from a TV in the corner.

'I'm sure that's doable,' I said, looking over my shoulder for a nurse. 'Hang on, let me go and find someone.'

The operation had been a success, according to Dr Ross, a Scottish doctor who had studied medicine at Edinburgh, which made Mum happy because she deemed it a 'proper' university.

'Not like those made-up universities in places like Bournemouth,' she said to him, when he did his rounds along the ward that morning.

She would spend one more night in the ward, Dr Ross said, but then she'd probably be allowed to go home, where she'd need to rest properly for two weeks for the stitches to heal.

I couldn't find a nurse to ask for a cup of tea so I walked

to the coffee shop downstairs, a coffee shop I was becoming quite familiar with.

'Hiya, love,' said the enormous woman who manned the till. She had, at some unfortunate juncture in her life, decided to tattoo her eyebrows.

'Hi,' I said, smiling. 'Back again. Could I just have a cup of tea?'

'Nothing to eat? You look shattered, love. Here, why don't I just give you one of these? Best before date's today anyway,' she said, picking up a brownie with a pair of tongs and sliding it into a paper bag.

'Oh, go on then, thank you.'

'Got to keep your strength up, a big girl like you,' she said, handing over the bag.

Too kind, I thought to myself, taking the bag and smiling at her.

While waiting for the tea, I looked at my phone. Lex had messaged sending love to Mum and asking if I was around later that week to discuss my maid of honour dress. I felt annoyed that she was quacking on about her wedding while I was at the hospital with Mum so ignored her, slid my phone back into my jeans and walked back upstairs to find that my chair had been taken by a man in a grey suit with neatly brushed hair.

'Polly, you remember Sidney, don't you?' said Mum, who had propped herself up in bed and fanned her hair out behind her on the pillows like a slightly ropey Botticelli figure. The curtain was now drawn around her bed.

'Yes, 'course. Hi, Sidney,' I said, putting the tea down on

the bedside table, unsure of how to greet him. Handshake? Hug? I held out the bag with the brownie in it. 'Want a bit of brownie? The lady downstairs gave it to me for free.'

'Oh how kind,' said Sidney standing up. 'Here, Polly, you have this seat.'

'No, no, Polly's been here all morning,' said Mum. 'Sidney, you sit down.'

'I can perch on the bed. No problem,' I said. 'Brownie?'

'No, no, I'm quite all right. Thank you, Polly. I don't want to ruin my lunch.' Sidney, in a tweed suit, shiny brown lace-up brogues and with a neat side parting, didn't look like a man who ever dared do anything as outrageous as ruin his lunch.

I stuck my hand in the bag and started eating. 'So, what do you do then, Sidney?'

'He's retired now,' said Mum, as Sidney opened his mouth.

'Oh, what did you do?'

'He was a property solicitor,' said Mum, whose energy was seemingly undiminished despite a major operation less than twenty-four hours ago.

'Terribly boring, I'm afraid,' said Sidney. 'Not an exciting job like yours. Susan's told me all about it.'

'Oh, has she?'

'Well, a bit,' he said. 'And of course all about going and staying with your young man.'

'Ah.'

'He sounds terribly exciting,' said Sidney.

'Ha. Maybe. We'll see.' I wondered for the eighty-sixth

time whether I could text Jasper about Saturday evening, and, for the eighty-sixth time, decided I should wait for him to text me. I was trying to play it cooler than I ever had before. Never texting him first. Never being the last to send a message. But my phone was never more than three or four inches from me and the second my screen flashed I was on it like a greyhound after a rabbit. 'We'll see,' I repeated vaguely to Sidney.

'Polly is terribly cynical about men,' said Mum.

'Ah,' said Sidney, looking down at his lap and fiddling with his shirt cuffs.

I scrunched up the paper bag and dusted the crumbs off my jeans. 'Right, Mums, if you're feeling all right I might peel off and go home, leave you two to it?' I was suddenly desperate for some fresh air and the solitude of my flat.

'Yes, yes, thank you, darling, of course. You will remember to walk Bertie, won't you?'

'Yes.'

'And the thing about his food?'

'Yes, I promise. He's fine. He's having a lovely time watching *Eggheads* with Joe.' I kissed the top of her head and waved awkwardly at Sidney. 'Good to see you again. See you soon.'

'Absolutely,' said Sidney, waving at me before he turned back to Mum. 'I thought we might do the crossword, Susan, if you feel up to it?'

'Oh yes,' said Mum, beaming. I left Sidney fumbling in his Daunt Books bag for his copy of the *Telegraph*.

Bertie slept on my bed that night, which I'd forbidden the night before because of his snoring. But he whined and pawed

at my door when I turned my bedside lamp off so I relented
and let him in.

'You are not sleeping under the duvet though. That is the
absolute limit. Only on top of it,' I said as Bertie jumped on
to the bed. He lay down and sighed before – and I genuinely
heard this – he did a little fart.

*

I was back at *Posh!* the next morning when Peregrine sum-
moned me into his office.

'You got much on, Polly?'

'I'm just writing that piece about the most fashionable
colonic irrigation clinics in London.'

'Finish that first. And then I've got something else for you.'

'Oh?' I said this in a hopeful way. My piece about Jasper
was out this week and I was hoping that Peregrine would start
giving me bigger stories off the back of it. More interviews.
I was sick of interviewing celebrity Labradors.

'I had lunch with the Countess of Stow-on-the-Wold yesterday, and she told me that we should be looking at Sheikh…
Hang on, I've written it down somewhere. Funny name.'

He tapped at his computer. 'Yes, that's it. Sheikh Khaled bin
Abdullah. He's just bought a house near them in Gloucestershire
apparently. He's from… how do you pronounce it, Cutter?'

'Qatar?'

'Yes, that's the one. Wherever that is.'

'Middle East.'

'Wherever. He's causing all sorts of fuss in Gloucestershire apparently because he wants to dig up his estate to put a runway in for his private jet. And he's stealing everybody's staff. The poor Countess has just lost her second gardener apparently.'

'Careless of her.'

'What?'

'Nothing, nothing. Right, I'll just do some digging, shall I?'

'Yes please. He's very into his racing, she told me.'

'Oh, I'll ask Jasper then. He might know something.'

'Jasper? Jasper Milton?'

I'd said his name without thinking. I hadn't actually mentioned the fact that I'd been seeing Jasper to Peregrine for fear of interrogation.

'Oh. Yeah. I've sort of… seen him a few times recently.' I wanted to keep it as vague as possible.

'Is he courting you?'

I reflected on the last time Jasper and I had sex, when he'd pushed me face down on my bed, put his hands on my bottom, buried his face between my arse cheeks and used his tongue to make me come. I'd been incredibly worried about his face being that close to, well, my bottom, but eventually I'd relaxed and screamed into my pillow.

'Er, kind of courting, I suppose,' I said to Peregrine.

'Polly, what tremendous news! Let me know when to buy a hat.'

★

According to Google, the Sheikh was a 29-year-old billionaire who'd been to school in America but had recently moved to London. Big house in Mayfair, bigger one in Gloucestershire. Moustache like a Mexican drug lord, eyelashes like a baby lemur. I texted Jasper.

Do you know anything about Sheikh Khaled bin Abdullah? X

He called instantly.

'I might do. Who's asking?'

'Me, obviously. I've got to try and get an interview with him. Or write a profile on him.'

'I can ask him if you like.'

'Seriously? Do you actually know him?'

'A bit. Met him at Ascot last year. He's a friend of Barny's.'

'Who's Barny?'

'The one you sat next to at lunch that day at home.'

'Oh, yeah. Him. How are they friends?'

'Neighbouring estates in Gloucestershire, although Barny's is bigger. Much to the Sheikh's irritation. He's forever trying to buy more land from him but Barny always says no and that immigrants shouldn't be allowed to own property here anyway.'

'Jesus, that guy! But OK, if you don't mind asking him that would be amazing.'

'Your wish is my command. I shall say that the devastatingly clever and amusing girl I'm seeing wants to ask him all sorts of dastardly questions.'

'Seeing?' I smiled at my desk and looked sideways at Lala, who had Bertie on her lap. She was feeding him Haribo sweets.

'I don't like the word "dating". Too American.'

'You sound like your friend Barny.'

'Come on, you have to admit, "dating" is a dreadful word.'
I laughed. 'Don't be so pompous. Where are you anyway?'

'I'm driving to London, as it happens. Trustee meeting
tomorrow. I'd say can I see you but Dad wants to go through
a few things tonight.'

'No, no, don't worry. I should probably concentrate on the
Sheikh for a bit. Plus, Mum's getting home later so I need to
go over there.'

'Righto. Let me bell him now and I'll come back to you.
And you're still on for dinner on Saturday?'

'Oh, yes, I wasn't sure if you were still free and everything
with Mum and…' I stammered, feeling awkward.

'No, no, I'm absolutely free,' he said. 'I feel like you need
scooping up and taking out.'

I smiled down the phone. 'OK. Thank you.'

'How's your lover?' Lala asked, giving Bertie another
Haribo as I hung up.

'He's fine. Knows this sheikh who Peregrine wants me to
write about. Should he be eating those, La?'

'He loves them. Look …' She fished in the sweet packet
and gave Bertie a fried egg. Bertie chewed it briefly, then
swallowed it, before looking at Lala with his ears pricked,
asking for another one. 'And I know who you mean. The
racing sheikh. I've seen him at various things. Looks quite
sweet. Like a sort of teddy bear.'

'Quite a rich teddy bear,' I said, relieved to have got off the topic of Jasper. I still felt awkward discussing him with Lala, especially because recently she had started saying she hadn't been on a date 'for years' and that she was going to die alone and be exhibited in the Natural History Museum as a fossil.

An email from Bill popped up on my computer screen.

Wotcha. Fancy supper? I'm going to be finished early for once. Our usual?

He meant an Italian on Pimlico Road which Bill liked because they gave you as many packets of breadsticks as you wanted. I quickly typed back my reply.

I wish. But I need to go to Mum's. She's getting home from her op tonight. Xxx

I'd been planning on going back to hospital to take her home in a taxi, but Sidney had apparently volunteered to take her home. Quite the Romeo, it seemed.

Bill emailed back instantly.

Course. Do you want alone time or is the patient up for visitors? Takeaway on me, if it's not intruding? Just guessing you may want moral support?

I emailed back saying I'd love that. As would Mum.

★

Bertie was offensively pleased to get home to Mum's that evening. As soon as I put him down in her flat, he raced into the sitting room and jumped on the sofa where she was lying.

'Oh God! Bertie, get down. Mum, are you all right?' She was almost entirely obscured by a pile of duvets.

'I'm quite all right, thank you, darling. Hello, Bertie, have you had a nice holiday? Did she look after you?'

'Yes I did, he's been thoroughly fussed over in the office,' I said. She didn't need to know about the Haribo. Bertie had a terrible stomach afterwards and ruined a corner of Kensington Park Gardens. 'Where's Sidney?'

'He has bridge club tonight and I didn't want him to miss that. What time's Bill getting here?'

'About seven, he said.'

'Perfect. Now, I'm on boring old water but open the bottle of wine that's in the fridge and pour yourself a glass.'

'Yep, will do.'

'And are you sure about a takeaway? There are some chicken breasts in the fridge I bought a few days ago.'

'Yes,' I said firmly, pouring the wine. 'Bill actually suggested it. Easier. Less washing up.'

'Fine,' said Mums. 'I'll have the chicken later in the week.'

Bill arrived half an hour later, and I opened the door to find him standing on the doorstep holding his briefcase, a carrier bag and a bunch of lilies. 'Hello, hello. I've gone a bit overboard on the wine side of things. And possibly the crisp side of things. And the chocolate side of things to be honest.'

'You're an idiot,' I said, taking the carrier bag. 'But a sweet idiot. Come in before you're savaged to death by the least menacing guard dog in Battersea.'

'Hello, Bertie,' said Bill, bending down to scratch him on the head.

'Susan, I want a big hug,' said Bill, once inside. 'I'm not going to ask how you're feeling because I imagine you're bored of being asked that. But I have come armed with wine and crisps and a slightly weird and luminous flavour of hummus that I found in a corner shop around the corner. And these.' He held the lilies out in front of him.

Mum, still lying on the sofa, clutched Bill in a hug while I unpacked the carrier bag in the kitchen. 'Oh, Bill, you heavenly boy, I'm fine,' she said. 'All the better for seeing you. Polly, will you put these in water and Bill, will you tell me all about this new girlfriend of yours?'

'Ah. News travels fast in this part of town.' He raised one eyebrow at me as I handed him a glass of wine.

'I haven't told her very much,' I said.

'Well,' Bill said, sitting on the sofa opposite Mum. 'She's called Willow and she's lovely.'

'And how did you two meet?'

'Tinder, the app, you know, has Pols told you about it?'

'Yes, thank you, William, I'm sixty-one not a hundred and sixty-one. I have heard of it. It was just very different in my day.'

'Letters by carrier pigeon?' said Bill.

She hit him on the arm. 'No. You met at parties, that sort of thing. But then I met Mike and that was that really.'

'You never looked back?' he asked through a mouthful of crisps.

'I never looked back, no.'

'But how did you know, Mum?' I asked from the kitchen sink, where I was cutting the lily stems. 'I mean people are always saying "You know when you know". But what if you don't know? Or what if you think you know when you know, but actually you don't know at all?'

I was still trying to stay calm about Jasper. Not run away with myself. Not imagine what we'd call our children (Olive? I'd always quite liked Olive for a girl), because I still didn't quite believe we were 'dating'. Each time Jasper had stayed with me (all right, it was only three times, but STILL), I'd woken up in the morning and been surprised to find him in my bed. What was a handsome marquess doing in my bed? I was convinced he would tire of my damp flat and it would end any second. But then... but then he'd said on the phone earlier he wanted to 'scoop me up' – I'd replayed the words in my head over and over again – so maybe I needed to have a little more faith.

Mum frowned. 'What do you mean, how did you know? Are you talking about Jasper?'

'Oh Christ, not him,' said Bill, through a mouthful of crisps.

'Bill,' I warned.

'What?'

'Watch it. You haven't even met him.'

'Pols, come on. He's a playboy, you told me so yourself. Susan, you must be on my side. I'm not sure about him.'

I looked at Mum, who opened her mouth and then shut it again.

'And anyway,' I went on, 'I was very nice to Willow at Lex's engagement.'

'Why wouldn't you be?' said Bill, through another mouthful of crisps.

'No reason. She's fine.'

'Fine?'

'Yes. Fine. Perfectly sweet. I mean she's probably not going to find a cure for cancer, but if that's what you want then fine,' I said, putting the flowers on the kitchen table before clapping a hand over my mouth. 'Oh God, Mums, sorry. I didn't really think.'

'Polly darling, don't be silly, but can you both stop bickering. I'm the one with cancer right now so what I say goes, and what I say is we should order from the Indian.'

'Good idea,' said Bill, glaring at me. I unpinned the menu from the fridge and handed it to Mum. 'I'm not that hungry, I'll just pick at something. You order for me.' She handed the menu to Bill.

'I'm famished,' he said, holding the menu with one hand while using a crisp to scoop up the hummus like a spoon with the other. 'So let's get some onion bhajis to start. And then I'm going to have a butter chicken. And it comes with popadoms, right?'

'Yes,' I said, taking the menu from him. 'And I'll get the chicken jalfrezi. And plain rice. Mums, do we have any chutney?'

'Probably, buried in the back of the cupboard.'

'I might get some extra mango chutney, just to be on the safe side,' I said, not relishing the prospect of sticking my hand in the back of Mum's cupboard. 'So, one plain rice and, Bill, what kind do you want?'

'Plain is good for me. Lots of it please. And I'm paying.'

'Lovely boy,' said Mums.

8

AT AROUND NOON THE next day, Lala swept into the office and threw her bag down on the desk in a dramatic fashion.

'Pols, I think my coil's fallen out.'

'What do you mean, fallen out? It's presumably pretty wedged up there.'

'Yes, I know. They're *supposed* to be. But you're supposed to check for the strings every now and then and I can't feel them.' She pulled off her coat and signed into her computer.

'La, I'm not sure I can deal with this just before lunch,' I said, trying to distract myself by reading the email that had just arrived in my inbox from Lex.

Are you happy to wear pink as a maid of honour? And I'm thinking matching shoes. And hair half up, half down. Xxx

I really wasn't sure pink was my colour.

Yes, 'course. What kind of pink? X

She replied instantly.

A sort of labia pink. And also, do you want to bring Jasper as your plus one? Mum will EXPLODE with joy if there's a real-life marquess on the seating plan. Xxx

I sat back in my chair and thought. It was an unfamiliar but warm thought, the thought of having someone with me at a wedding. And not just someone. At having Jasper with me at a wedding, standing beside me, like a normal couple. Instead of standing there like a lemon in a hat and scanning the church for handsome single men. But it still felt quite early to ask him.

La's voice interrupted my reverie. 'What if it's floating about in my body somewhere? What if it's prodding a kidney? Or my lungs?'

'Hold that thought, La. My phone's going.' It was Jasper. Oh shit, the piece, presumably he was ringing me about the *Posh!* piece. It was out today.

I grabbed my phone from my desk and stepped into the hallway.

'Hello,' I said as breezily as I could.

'Good morning,' he said back. Did he sound stern? Quite stern maybe? What if he hated it? What if his parents hated it?

'Listen,' he said, 'I've got something to tell you.'

OH GOD, THIS WAS IT, WASN'T IT? HE WAS ENDING IT. I told myself to take a deep breath. Calm down, Polly, you've only been on a few dates. You were never going to marry him anyway. Your career is more important than a man.

'Yes?' I squeaked.

'So I spoke to Sheikh Khaled and he's asked us to stay.'

'What? What do you mean, to stay?'

'Yes, you know, stay. As in we both go to his house in Gloucestershire and sleep in one of his bedrooms.'

'Right.' I felt relief throb through my body. 'I mean amazing, thank you. I thought you'd be ringing about the piece.'

'What piece?'

'The piece about you!'

'Oh, is it out?'

'Yes!'

'Terrific, I'll ask Ian to go and fetch a copy the moment I've put my phone down. But listen, Khaled wants us to go and stay this weekend.'

'This weekend? As in two days from now?'

'Mmm,' said Jasper, 'so what I was thinking was I could pick you up on Saturday morning, we drive down there and arrive in time for drinks.'

'Um, yeah, I guess,' I said. 'I should just check with Mum, that she'll be all right.'

'It's just for Saturday night,' said Jasper. 'I can have you back by Sunday.'

'I'm sure it'll be fine,' I said quickly, hoping that Sidney could be on crossword duty on Saturday night. 'I'll check with her but otherwise sounds great. Thank you. Can I interview him?'

'I'm sure there'll be half an hour or so when you can sit down and talk to him. I think he's quite excited about being in *Posh!,* to be honest. Sort of sees it as his acceptance into British society, being pictured alongside dukes and so on. He said did you want to take any photos?'

'Er, not sure.'

'And then he said he wanted to talk to me about a couple of horses. So, it could be mutually beneficial.'

'OK, amazing, thank you again. Peregrine will be beside himself.'

'Good. OK, well, you go and tell him and I'll go and read all the terrible things you've said about me.'

'Not terrible,' I said, 'I promise. Well, I think I promise. I hope you like it. I hope your parents like it.'

'Oh God, don't worry about them, they never read anything.'

I hung up and went back to my desk, where Lala looked questioningly at me. 'Are you in love with him?'

'What? La, no. Come on. It's been, like, a few weeks. I'm not in love with him. I just… quite like him.' I smiled. It was actually five weeks and six days exactly since I'd gone to Castle Montgomery. But Lala didn't need to know I was doing anything so pathetic as counting.

'Oh dear. You're definitely in love with him,' she said, turning back to her computer and shaking her head. 'This is a disaster. Anyway, I'm going to google missing coils.'

Jasper texted me an hour or so later.

It's brilliant. You have been much too kind to me and my family. Thank you. You are quite something X

My stomach did a cartwheel and I felt giddy. I couldn't help it. Even though I told myself to be sensible, I stared at his text message for a long time at my desk. 'You are quite something'. Four little words but they felt big to me.

Jesus, it was exhausting being a woman sometimes.

★

I found Legs in the fashion cupboard on Thursday morning clutching her Americano, frowning at the rail of clothes in front of her. I had asked for her help again with clothes for the weekend.

'Morning, Legs.'

She sighed. 'Well, I don't know how thees ees going to work. Chanel have sent a few things but they are sample sizes and—' she looked at the coffee in my hand (a full-fat latte) '—you're a fourteen?'

'More like a twelve.'

She sighed again. 'Eet's going to be difficult. But I will 'ave a go.'

'If you wouldn't mind.'

'So you need something for a dinner on Saturday night, *oui*?'

'Yes.'

'Mmmm.' She glanced at my hips. 'OK. Take thees and try them on.' She handed me several clothes hangers and removed the latte from my hands.

'OK, I'll just nip to the bathroom and try them on.'

'*Non*, do it in here. Faster, then I can see what you look

like. Just go behind there.' She pushed me behind another rail sagging with clothes.

I peeled off my jeans and shirt in a self-conscious fashion, my back to Legs.

'Polly!' she suddenly said in horror. 'What are you doing?'

'What?' I asked, looking over my shoulder, embarrassed. 'You told me to get dressed in here.'

'*Non*. I mean your bra! Your pants! You can't wear thees things. Honestly, it ees some kind of joke, *non*?'

'What do you mean?'

'Polly, I have seen sexier underwear on my grandmother. I am going to ring up my friend at Rigby & Peller and you will go there at lunchtime.'

'And spend a million pounds on a bit of lace that's going to itch and scratch and quite possibly ride so far up my bottom it causes me serious internal injuries? No thanks.'

'No, no, not a million pounds. She will give you a discount. You cannot wear thees peasant underwear, Polly. Now, how is that dress?'

I had wriggled into a short black woollen dress, with a leather trim and a zip right up the back. 'I can't quite get the zip done up.'

'Come here.'

I shuffled in front of her.

'Breathe in.'

'I am breathing in. Can you just watch…'

Legs, with the tenderness of a Nazi prison guard, wrenched the zip up, catching a little bit of my neck flesh at the top.

She stood back and scrutinized me. 'Eet will work. When you 'ave a better bra.'

★

'Hello, I'm Polly,' I said to a middle-aged lady wearing a vibrant shade of pink lipstick behind the counter of Rigby & Peller that lunchtime. 'I think Allegra might have called? From *Posh!* magazine?'

'Oh, Polly, hello! Yes, it's all sorted. I'm Carol. Now, what I want you to do is wander around and have a look at what you think might work. And then I'll measure you and we'll go from there.'

I nodded and looked around her. Maroon bras, peach-coloured bras, black bras. All vast. Legs said it was once the Queen's lingerie maker. But was Her Majesty really that enormous? I supposed she needed something comfortable for all that travelling, for all those boring factory openings she has to go to. To stop her back from hurting. Then I thought to myself, what are you even doing thinking about the Queen's breasts? I spied a white corseted bodice, which did up with little eye hooks at the front, and reached out and touched it.

'Are you after anything special?' said Carol from the till.

'Er, I think just a couple of new bras and some matching knickers,' I said, still looking at the corset. 'This is probably a bit full-on for me.'

'Tell you what, darling, why don't you find a changing

room and I'll bring a few pieces through? What colours are we thinking?'

'Oh. Black really. Maybe white. Except white always seems to go...'

'A bit yellow in the gusset?' said Carol, lowering her voice in a conspiratorial fashion.

'I was going to say grey.'

'That too,' she said, unhooking one of the changing room curtains. 'Right, in you pop. What size are you? I reckon...' She stood back and eyeballed my chest. 'A 36C.'

'A 34C, mostly. But it sort of seems to depend.'

'You don't want any bulges in the back though, darling. Hang on, I'll be two minutes.'

Carol reappeared shortly afterwards with an armful of lace. Peach lace, yellow lace, baby blue lace, orange lace, black lace and a sort of hideous maroon lace, the colour of varicose veins. I tried on so many bras I thought I might have whiplash, but by the end we narrowed it down to a new black bra, a new baby blue bra and matching 'panties' as Carol insisted on calling them. Plus the corset. I'd tried it on at Carol's suggestion, despite my misgivings that it would make me look like something that was auditioning for Sea World, and – actually – it felt pretty freaking amazing. Hot, even, which was never an adjective I'd considered using about myself. It nipped in at the waist and gave me the heaving chest of an Austen heroine. Less performing orca, more Beyoncé.

'So,' said Carol at the till, having folded everything up in tissue paper with the reverence of a bishop. 'Altogether that comes to... two hundred and forty-one pounds please.'

'Oh, Carol, sorry, Allegra said something about a discount?' I cringed at having to ask but I couldn't spend the GDP of Belgium on doilies for my nipples.

'Yes, I've added it, duck. Forty per cent is the press discount. I hope that's all right?'

''Course,' I said, beaming back and rummaging in my wallet for my credit card. 'Just wanted to check. And thank you.'

The underwear would have to become a family heirloom. I would pass them down to my daughters. If they'd gone yellow in the gusset it was too bad.

★

Jasper picked me up outside the flat on Saturday afternoon.

'Quick, go, go, go, otherwise we'll be stuck with her for years,' I said, closing the door to his Range Rover as Barbara peered out from the shop door. I immediately worried about how to sit so my thighs didn't splay all over his smart leather seats and look fat.

'I've been in already to buy some cigarettes,' said Jasper, waving back at Barbara. 'She told me that you were a Capricorn so I had to look out for your mood swings.'

'Oh, I wish she wouldn't! She's a danger to the public.'

'Anyway,' he said, starting the car. 'All ready?'

'Yup,' I said. 'First weekend away.'

'First?'

'I mean. No. Not first necessarily. I don't mean there will

be more.' I blushed. 'I just mean we're going away. Together. For the first time.'

Jasper burst out laughing.

'Oh, for fuck's sake, don't be mean,' I said.

'You are the easiest person in Britain to tease, Polly Spencer. Right, come on, let's get going so we arrive there before midnight.'

★

Little Swinbrook was one of those villages that a visiting American would describe as 'quaint'. There was a lake with a few ducks waddling beside it, neatly clipped grass verges and a thatched pub called The Duck & Doorknob.

'That's the Earl and Countess of Stow-on-the-Wold's place,' said Jasper, pointing out a big wooden gate to the left of the car. 'Swinbrook Hall', said a sign on it. I sat up and tried to peer beyond it, but the driveway was annoyingly discreet, with big box hedges planted either side of the gate.

'And I think this is Khaled,' he said, slowing down and pulling on to a gravel drive a hundred yards down on the other side of the road. This was a metal gate, which slowly started opening in front of us, revealing another thick metal gate behind it. 'Takes his security quite seriously then,' said Jasper, pulling forward until we were sandwiched between the two gates. He opened his window and leant out towards a keypad on the wall.

'Hello, Jasper Milton here.'

There was a muffled reply from the keypad and the sudden whirr as the gate behind us started closing again. Then a clunk when it finally closed, before the gate in front started sliding sideways.

'Open sesame,' said Jasper.

'What happens if he wants to pop to the village for some milk? It would take days.'

'He probably has someone else who worries about the milk,' replied Jasper, driving slowly down a tarmac drive with neatly fenced fields either side of it.

And then the house came into view. It was enormous. Like Buckingham Palace, with steps leading up to the main entrance, stone pillars either side, and a big sweep of gravel in front of it. But Jasper carried on along the tarmac road, past a clump of rhododendrons.

'Where are we going?' I asked, looking behind me at the house.

'Back entrance. You never go to the front. He said to come to the courtyard behind the house.'

'So why do they even have a front door?'

'To look pretty. And for events. Parties. That sort of thing.'

'I went to the front when I came to Castle Montgomery.'

'I know. I was watching you from my bedroom, laughing as you tiptoed across the grass.'

'You weren't?'

''Course I was. I was thrilled, actually. I was expecting some sort of middle-aged frump and then I saw you and...'

'And?'

'I was intrigued.'

'Intrigued because you saw me sneaking across your lawn like a burglar?'

'Exactly. There was something endearing about it.' He stopped the car and leant across, putting his hand underneath my chin and pulling my face in to kiss me. 'Right, come on. Let's go in.'

He jumped out and opened the boot, then swung his bag over his shoulder and picked up mine. I checked my face in the rear-view mirror and got out just as the back door swung open.

It was a man dressed in black tailcoat and grey pinstripe trousers. 'Hello, sir. I'm Edmund. Can I take your bags?'

'Very kind, thank you.'

I walked up the stone steps behind Jasper. 'Hi,' I said, waving awkwardly at the butler. Do you shake hands with butlers? I wasn't sure. Butlers had not loomed large in my life until a couple of months ago and now I knew two. Two butlers! Presumably I'd need someone to put toothpaste on my toothbrush soon.

'Hello, madam. Let me take you to your room.'

Edmund silently led us through the house. Gold chandeliers, gold mirrors, gold side tables, gold chairs and golden banisters on the stairs. It was like walking through the house of a deranged French king. He then stopped in front of a door on the first floor. 'The Marquess of Milton and Miss Polly Spencer,' said a small handwritten card on it.

'Here you go, sir,' said Edmund, gliding in and putting our bags down by a window that looked out from the front of the house and down the drive and the line of trees.

'Very kind, Edmund, thank you. And where's Sheikh Khaled?'

'He's at the stables, sir. He said to make yourselves comfortable and come down for drinks at seven.'

'Marvellous.'

'And can I get you anything now?'

'I wouldn't say no to a whisky if there's one going?' said Jasper. 'Pols, do you want a drink?'

I was inspecting the bathroom. A gold bath. Even a gold bidet and a gold loo seat. Could I put a photo of the gold loo on Instagram or would I get in trouble?

'Polly?'

'Mmm?' I stuck my head out from the bathroom.

'Do you want a drink now? We've got an hour or so before drinks downstairs, so I'm having a whisky.'

'Oh, well in that case, erm, a vodka and tonic would be great, if possible?'

'Of course, madam.' Edmund inclined his head a few millimetres again and walked out.

'That's better,' said Jasper, loosening his tie and taking it off, along with his jacket and throwing them over the sofa at the end of the bed. A gold four-poster with approximately fifteen pillows on it. 'An hour to kill,' he said, looking up at me and smiling. 'What shall we do?'

'Won't Jeeves be back any second with our drinks?'

'Yes.'

'Then I might just jump in the shower and wash my hair first.'

I stripped off in the bathroom and spent the obligatory few minutes when tackling a new shower, trying to work out which way was cold, which way was hot, and got in. Big bottles of Guerlain shampoo and conditioner. I wondered if I could take them home with me. Probably not. I lifted up an armpit to check the stubble situation.

And then suddenly the shower door opened and before I could turn around, Jasper's arm had snaked around my stomach and he was pressing into me from behind.

'Hi,' I said, worrying instantly that mascara had run down my face and I looked like some sort of sad goth.

'Hello,' he said, lifting my wet hair and kissing my shoulder.

I always worry about having sex in the shower. You're generally standing up, right? Unless you're in one of those showers for old people where there's a ledge. If there *isn't* a ledge, it's physically awkward.

Take face-to-face sex in the shower, for example. I have never been one of those doll-sized girls who men can pick up with one arm and hold up against the shower tiles. Never going to happen. He'd put his back out.

So instead, a man had to approach me as if doing a limbo dance, bending his knees a little so his hips were lower than mine. And then I'd have to crane one leg in the air, possibly pressing my foot up against the opposite shower wall for support, or perhaps he's holding the other foot up. It all gets a bit *Strictly Come Dancing*.

Alternatively, I would be in front facing the shower wall and he would be behind me. As Jasper was now. 'Put your hands against the wall,' he said. So, I leant forward, put my hands on the marble and wondered what the cellulite on the backs of my thighs looked like. But I didn't have long to worry about that, because Jasper reached forward and pinched my right nipple hard. Hard.

'Aaaah,' I said, a noise I was hedging my bets with a bit. I didn't want to suggest that I wasn't into this because that felt uptight. Unsexy. So, my noise could also mean 'How lovely, please do it harder.' Even though Jasper was being quite rough. The noise was also meant to suggest 'Would you mind pinching less hard?'

He reached for the shower head, unhooked it and turned it towards me, positioning it so the water was basically shooting straight into my vagina. I wasn't totally into that, either, but I made a more encouraging 'Aaah' sound, and Jasper thrust himself into me.

'That… feels… sensational,' he said in my ear, before kissing my shoulder again.

'Does it? Aaaah.' He'd moved the shower head closer to me, so the jets of water were now really quite sharp on my clitoris. Lucy Hastings had always talked about getting herself off on the showers at school, but I never really understood how because the water pressure was so pathetic. The only thing I ever got from a school shower was a verruca.

'Aaaah,' I said again, putting my hand over Jasper's on the shower head and moving it away a fraction.

Jasper pushed harder into me. Again and again, but quite slowly, holding the shower head with one hand and gripping

my hip with the other. It did feel better than the school showers after a while. Much better. So good that I forgot about the
cellulite on the backs of my thighs and after a few minutes I
came, with louder, more urgent 'aaaahs', followed by Jasper,
seconds later.

'Christ,' he said afterwards, still inside me, putting one of
his hands over mine on the shower wall. We stood for a few
moments, heavy breathing, the water from the shower head
shooting out around our feet. 'Come on,' he said, when I was
getting cold. 'Let's have that drink.' He opened the shower
door and stepped on to the bathmat.

'Two seconds,' I said, not wanting to bend over and pick
up the shower head while he was standing there watching my
bottom. 'I've just got to condition my hair.'

*

The drawing room was full when Jasper and I arrived downstairs for drinks. I felt self-conscious walking in. I'd put the
corset on underneath the Chanel dress and I was worried it
was cutting off circulation to my head. How did those poor
old Victorians do it? No wonder they were always fainting all
over the place and calling for smelling salts.

'Aaah, Jasper!' said a man I recognized as the Sheikh, hur-
rying towards us. He smothered Jasper in a hug.

'Great to see you again, Khaled,' said Jasper, slapping him
on the back. 'And this is my girlfriend, Polly.'

The Sheikh released Jasper, stepped back and looked at

me. 'How do you do, Polly,' he said, holding his hand out. It was soft, like shaking hands with a koala. And he was shorter than I expected, with neatly clipped, dark hair slicked into a side parting and a moustache that perched on his upper lip like a slug.

'I'm very well, thank you. And thank you for having us.'

'Not at all, not at all. Now, what would you like to drink? I am afraid I won't allow alcohol here. So you can have pomegranate juice or a mineral water, if you like?'

He looked enquiringly at me.

'Oh. Um. Pomegranate juice would be delicious, thank you.'

He burst out laughing and clapped one of his freakishly soft hands over his moustache. 'I am just making a little joke with you, Polly. What nonsense is this, no alcohol? Of course there is alcohol. Now you would like a glass of champagne, yes?'

I smiled and breathed out, as much as I could in the corset. 'Yes. Perfect.'

'Jasper?' asked the Sheikh.

'Champagne would be excellent, Khaled, thank you.'

The Sheikh raised his hand in the air and clicked his fingers: 'Two glasses of champagne please.' In the corner, underneath a life-size oil painting of the Sheikh in military uniform, a waiter in white tie leapt as if electrocuted sharply in the buttocks, poured two glasses and carried them over on a gold tray.

'Yes, yes, thank you, thank you, thank you,' said the Sheikh, batting the waiter away again with his hand. 'Now you must meet the other guests.' He turned around to a sofa behind him, where a blonde woman was sitting, legs tucked underneath her, beside a red-faced man in a tweed jacket. A small, yellow-coloured dog was sleeping between them.

'Barny!' said Jasper. 'I didn't know you were coming.'

Barny dragged his eyes from the woman's legs and stood up to shake Jasper's hand.

'Wotcha, old bean.' Of course, I realized, Jasper had mentioned that Barny was friends with the Sheikh.

'And Holly, wasn't it? Terrific to see you again.' Barny leant in to kiss me on the cheek.

'Polly. But close,' I said. He stank of whisky.

'And this is Emile,' said the Sheikh, pointing at the blonde on the sofa.

Emile slowly uncurled her legs, picked up the sleeping dog and stood. She was barefooted, a pair of gold heels discarded beside the sofa. ''Ello,' she said, kissing Jasper first, then turning to kiss me. 'A pleasure. Thees is Frank.' She was cradling him in her arms like a baby.

'Oh sweet,' I said. 'What is he?'

'Ee is a dog,' she said.

'No. No, sorry, I mean what breed is he?'

'Ee is a Pekinese.'

'Oh, 'course. Sweet. PG Wodehouse liked Pekinese dogs, he had several.'

'Oh, I must meet him! Where does ee live?' said Emile.

Fortunately, the Sheikh interrupted at this point.

'Jasper, tomorrow you must come and see my stables,' he said.

'Yes absolutely, I'd love that,' he replied.

'You see, Polly, my horses are like my babies,' said the Sheikh. 'I love them.'

''Course,' I said. 'My mother has a terrier called Bertie so I totally get it.'

The Sheikh looked confused. 'What kind of horse is this?'

'Oh no. No, sorry, not a horse. A dog. A little dog.'

'And your mother, she races this little dog?'

'No. No, it's just that she has a pet. So, I understand how you love your horses.'

'I see,' said the Sheikh, who looked like he didn't see at all. Then another couple appeared in the drawing room.

'Ah, Ralph! Hello, hello. Welcome. Come in. Have a drink!' The Sheikh waved them in.

The couple stepped forward. She was ravishing, dressed like a Forties film star, in a velvet dress, her blonde hair in a chignon and lips painted perfectly scarlet.

'Ah, wotcha!' cried Jasper, spotting him.

Ralph smiled. 'There he is, the old scoundrel. Good to see you,' he said, walking forwards to shake Jasper's hand. Then Jasper gave the blonde a kiss on both cheeks. 'Wonderful to see you both.'

'This is Polly,' he added, as I sidled up beside him.

'Hi,' I said shyly, because Ralph was so handsome I felt like I couldn't look directly at him. Tall with brown hair and proper, white, all-American teeth.

'And I'm Flappy,' said the woman beside Ralph. 'An old school thing,' she added quickly. 'Don't ask.'

'I won't,' I said, 'but why are you a scoundrel? I'm intrigued.'
I raised my eyebrows at Jasper.

'Oh you know, Jasper Milton,' said Ralph, blinding me
with his teeth. 'Blond god of Eton, devil on the cricket field,
devil off the cricket field. Breaking windows and hearts all
over the place. We worshipped him.'

'Such nonsense,' said Jasper. 'I hardly broke any windows
and—' he put his arm around my waist '—even fewer hearts.
They were always breaking mine, if I recall it correctly.' He
kissed the top of my head and my stomach flipped.

The Sheikh waved one of his small hands in the air.
'Everybody, please sit.'

Flappy and I moved to sit on a sofa near the fireplace
together. I sat down carefully in case my corset gave up
under the strain, pinged loose and a rogue button shot into
someone's eye.

'Have you known Jasper long?' Flappy asked.

'No,' I said, 'couple of months. I went to interview him at
Castle Montgomery, I work for *Posh!* magazine?'

Flappy nodded. 'Oh, of course, you wrote that piece. I read
that.' She grinned at me. 'You were very nice about him.'

'Too nice?'

'No.' She sipped from her champagne glass and then shook
her head. 'You got it all spot on.'

'You know them?'

'Not that well. We've been to stay a few times. But Ralph
and Jasper sort of grew up together so I know him a bit better
than the rest of his family. He's a good one, you know.'

I smiled back at her. 'I think so.'

She lowered her voice and leaned towards me. 'And have you met the Sheikh before?'

I shook my head.

'Neither have I. Funny chap, isn't he?'

'Mmm.'

'Everyone's falling over themselves to try and make friends with him because he's got so much money. But it'll be someone else next week. A new Arab. Or a Russian. Or I hear the Chinese are doing very well at the moment.'

'Er, yes, they do seem to be,' I said, having another sip of champagne. I thought about the sort of conversations I had in the pub with Bill and Lex, where we'd spent hours discussing whether you'd rather have arms for legs or legs for arms.

Flappy sighed and sat back on the sofa, then screamed, leapt into the air and dropped her champagne glass.

'Darling,' said Ralph, rushing over. 'What's the matter?'

'It's… there's a mouse under this cushion,' she said.

'A mouse?'

'A dead mouse,' she said. 'Or it might be a vole.'

The Sheikh clicked his fingers again and the waiter hurried over, leant down and carefully picked up what was clearly a mouse by its tail. He placed the mouse on his gold tray, then picked up the cushion from the floor and placed it back on the sofa, patting it a couple of times.

'There you go, madam,' he said.

Flappy lowered herself slowly back on to the sofa. 'Thank you.'

Emile piped up from the other side of the room. 'I think eet must 'ave been Frank. Ee brings them inside sometimes and leaves them for me as a sort of, 'ow do you say, *cadeau*?'

'A present,' said Jasper.

'Yes, exactly. A present. You naughty boy,' said Emile, laughing and stroking Frank, who had raised his head at Flappy's scream but since closed his eyes again.

Then a gong went off in the hall. 'Everyone, please, through to the dinner room, it is time for eatings,' said the Sheikh.

★

'Ask me any questionings you like, Polly, any questionings,' said the Sheikh, when everyone had sat down in the dining room. We were sitting on the sort of gold thrones that Tudor monarchs had been crowned upon. Several gold candlesticks ran along the table.

I debated asking him whether he'd rather have legs for arms or arms for legs, then decided against it. 'Erm, OK. Why did you move here, to Little Swinbrook? What brought you from America?'

'Because I love the English weather so much,' he said, popping a bit of bread roll in his mouth.

'Really?'

He roared with laughter and revealed his gummy bit of bread roll again. 'No, Polly, I make another little joke.'

'Oh, I see,' I said, laughing nervously then picking up my wine glass and taking a big gulp. It felt like it might be a long dinner. 'But why do you love England so much?'

'It is your ways,' he said. 'All the English ways. Like the shooting and the hunting and the obsession with those big black dogs.'

'Labradors.'

'Yes, exactly,' he said. 'I have ten.'

'Ten Labradors?'

'Yes, they are all outside. You can see them tomorrow if you like?'

'Sure.'

He nodded approvingly. 'And your big houses, like this,' he said, sitting back and flinging his arms open. 'They are magnificent. We have nothing like it in my country.'

'Do you have to go home much though? Do you not have official duties there?'

He waved his hand airily. 'My brother, he can do all these things. It is too hot for me in Doha.'

'So you don't go back much?'

'Sometimes. I have a plane. So, if I like, I go. If not, I stay here with my Labradogs. *Labradogs*?' He looked questioningly at me.

'Labradors.'

'Ah yes, Labradors.'

'I've heard about this plane, Sheikh Khaled. You want to build a runway here?'

'Yes, but just a little runway and all my neighbours, they make such noises about it.'

'Mmm.' I nodded in what I hoped was a sympathetic way.

'And,' he went on, 'my plane is not a big plane. It is not like Air Force One, Polly. It has only one bedroom.' The Sheikh shifted in his seat, then looked at me again. 'But I do have another idea I need your advices on.'

'OK.'

'How do I become a duke?'

'Erm...'

'Because,' he went on, 'I have bought this big house and I have all these dogs and horses and now I would like very much to be a duke. But how?' His eyebrows wrinkled as he frowned at me.

'Well,' I began, 'I don't think you can just be made a duke.'

'But what about Prince William? He is a duke.'

'Yes, that's... true,' I said slowly, looking down the table in Jasper's direction, but he was busy chatting to Flappy. 'But he's royal, so it's a bit... different.'

'I am royal too,' said the Sheikh, looking affronted.

'Of course you are,' I said, quickly. 'It's just... a funny system here.'

'You English and your systems, Polly. It is so confusing. Can I just pay moneys to be a duke?'

'I don't think you can buy one. You have to be made one.'

'But you just said they don't make them any more.'

'No, they don't,' I said, looking towards Jasper again.

'Would it help if I am making friends with the Queen?' he asked.

'Er, you could try.'

'OK, in that case, what if I invite the Queen to come to my house to see my horses? She can come for some dinings and I will show her my stables. And then she can even stay if she likes. It is no problem for me.'

'Good idea,' I said, feeling weak.

★

After dinner, we moved back to the drawing room, where I ended up on the sofa next to Barny, another tumbler of whisky in his hand. A waiter was circling the room with a gold tray and a box of cigars on it.

'You enjoying all this then?' said Barny, leaning forward and taking a cigar from the box.

'All this?'

'The trappings. The luxury. The splendour of dating a marquess.' He took what looked like a pair of nail scissors from the tray and cut off the end of his cigar, then put them back on the gold tray and the waiter slunk off.

I looked across the room. Jasper was out of earshot, standing beside the gold fireplace with Ralph.

'Yeah, it's been, um, an eye-opener, I suppose,' I said, deciding to play it cool. Rise above it, I heard Mum say in my head. Her other favourite was 'turn the other cheek'. Either mantra would work in this situation. Although I couldn't really turn my cheek right now because I wouldn't have anyone to talk to.

'How long do you give it then?' Barny asked.

'Give what?'

'You and my friend Jasper?'

'You tell me, Barny, as you're so interested.'

He sat back on the sofa and laughed, whisky spilling over the lip of his glass. 'Very good. Very cool. Cooler than all the others.'

'I'm not trying to be cool. I just don't know what will happen between Jasper and me because I'm not a fortune teller.'

'Oh? Fortune hunting more your thing then, is it?'

The rising above it thing fell down a bit here. 'Don't be a dickhead,' I said, annoyed that I couldn't think of anything more articulate.

Barny remained calm, sitting back against the sofa, one leg crossed over the other. 'Darling, I'm just being honest. I've seen various girls come and go over the years. He promises them the world. They all think they're going to end up in the castle. None lasts longer than a few months.' He puffed on his cigar, exhaling smoke towards the ceiling. 'In a way, you could say I'm just looking out for you.'

'Oh, I see, that's what you're doing. So kind, thank you.'

'Not at all,' he said.

'Where's your wife, anyway, given your concern about other people's relationships?'

He had another sip of whisky, the ice clinking in his glass as he lowered it down again. 'London, I think. Not totally sure, to be honest.'

'Everything all right?' said Jasper, suddenly at my shoulder.

'Fine,' I said quickly.

'Barny behaving himself?'

'Kind of,' I said, forcing myself to laugh.

'I thought we might go up, if you feel like it?' he said to me. 'I'm shattered.'

'Good idea,' I said, standing up.

'Night, Barny old chap,' said Jasper. 'See you in the morning.'

'Night, Jaz,' he said. 'And goodnight, Holly.'

'Polly,' I said.

'Sorry,' he said, 'I'm terribly bad at remembering the names of Jasper's girlfriends.' He smirked from the sofa.

'That's enough, thank you, Barnaby,' said Jasper, taking my hand and leading me away from the sofa. 'Come on, let's say goodnight to Khaled and go to bed.'

★

Upstairs, I felt relieved. Relieved chiefly to have got away from the drawing room and Barny. But also relieved at unpicking my corset so my internal organs could rearrange themselves in all the right places. I brushed my teeth but left my make-up on. It was too early for Jasper to see my natural face. Terrible for your skin to sleep overnight in it, but too bad. I walked back into the bedroom self-consciously, French knickers still on, Jasper watching me from the bed, as he'd simply stripped and dropped his jacket, trousers, shirt and socks on the floor.

'Was he a nightmare?' he said as I put my head on his chest.

'Who?'

'Barny.'

'Oh. No. Not at all. I can handle him.'

'That's my girl,' he said, kissing my head.

Jasper fell asleep within minutes. I lay there awake for about an hour, feeling strange in this big gold house. Feeling almost homesick. His friends thought this was a fling. Fair enough, so did I still. A bit. It felt like a fantasy, all these weekends in big houses and butlers. But say things did get more serious, would they ever accept me? And could weekends like this ever feel normal? I drifted off to sleep and dreamt about having arms for legs.

*

After breakfast the next morning (eggs and bacon laid out on the side in the dining room in gold bowls, uniformed waiters scurrying around us with coffee and orange juice) the Sheikh took Jasper and me for the promised tour of the stables. And to see his pack of Labradors.

'This way, this way,' he said, crunching down the gravel drive in front of us. He had dressed like Sherlock Holmes for the occasion. Leather boots, tweed trousers, tweed coat, peculiar deerstalker hat.

The stables were set in a large stone quad towards the end of the drive. We walked through an archway into a cobbled courtyard, the heads of various horses poking out from doors on each side. I zoned out while Jasper and Khaled discussed them because I wasn't sure what a gelding was and I wasn't much interested in hearing about stallion sperm. I've never understood why posh people are so in love with horses. Most of Khaled's looked bored, standing in their boxes, chewing hay in an idle manner. I know they're majestic, but a horse is a horse. Four legs and a tail. Like a big dog. Except more expensive and more labour intensive than a dog. And less practical. You can't take a horse on the Tube. And yet, if possible, the aristocracy were almost more obsessed with horses than they were with dogs. Hours could be spent discussing their bloodlines. Bloodlines! Of an animal! If you ever get to the point of worrying about the ancestry of your horse, you need more going on in your life.

'Polly, you are OK?' said Khaled as we strolled around the courtyard, shaking me from my thoughts.

'Mmm.'

'You want to come and see my dogs, I know,' he said, smiling at me.

''Course I do,' I said, enthusiastically.

So, we went back through the archway and off to the right, where there was a large kennel. Having seen us, the Labradors bounded up to the metal gate, tails wagging. Khaled opened it and let them all out.

'What are they all called?' I said, trying to stop them sniffing my crotch.

'They are all called after English kings,' he said. 'So that is Albert, that one is Edward, that one is Alfred. Then we have Henry over here and…' He carried on. 'And I am going to breed from James, this one, and then have puppies and keep a few girls so I can name them after the English queens.'

An hour or so later, we'd said our goodbyes and Jasper dropped me off at Swindon station because he had to drive back to Yorkshire. It was a toss-up, I decided on the train, as to who was more mad – the Montgomery family or Sheikh Khaled.

9

A FEW DAYS LATER I was sitting at my computer googling how many calories were in an almond croissant when Enid's phone rang.

'Oh dear,' she was saying, clearly placating the person on the other end of the line. 'Oh dear. Yes, don't worry, I'll send her straight down.'

'Pols,' she said, hanging up the phone and peering around at my desk. 'Alan's in a right old state. He says can you go down to reception immediately.'

'What? Why?'

'Didn't say. Just said it was urgent.'

I took the lift downstairs, wondering what on earth was so urgent that Alan, the building's caretaker, wanted me so immediately for. A PR dropping off some useless new product probably. A bottle of dandelion-flavoured milk. A chocolate hat.

The lift doors opened and I stepped out, except I could barely move because there were so many bouquets of white roses everywhere – leading from the lift to the reception desk and covering the floor to the building's entrance.

'What's going on?' I asked, tiptoeing carefully between floral bouquets to the desk.

'You bloody tell me,' said Alan, as another man stuck his head through the entrance door. 'That's your lot then. Fifty bouquets,' said the man. 'Can you sign here?' He waved a clipboard at us from the door.

'No, I bloody can't. Get Polly here to sign as they're all for her.'

'For *me*?'

'Yes. This place, deary me, I mean I've seen some things in my time but never fifty bouquets of roses.'

'Who the hell from?'

'You tell me. You must have a secret admirer.'

Fifty bouquets. An unhinged number of flowers. I mean that's like... I tried to do the sums in my head... thousands of pounds' worth of roses. I reached out for the delivery man's clipboard. It could only be Jasper. What a nutter, I thought, shaking my head and smiling as I handed back the clipboard. But I was ecstatic, obviously. It was the most romantic, most fairy-tale thing anyone had ever done for me.

'Sorry, Alan. Chaos, I know, but I think it's just a friend of mine. Making a grand gesture.'

He grunted. 'Some friends you have.'

'Mmm,' I murmured back, crouching down to look at one of them. 'Is there a card?' I said, looking up at the delivery man.

'Dunno, love, I just drive the van.'

'Polly, you know how fond of you I am,' Alan went on, 'but this lot is a fire hazard and it all needs to be cleared.'

'Sure, fifty bunches of flowers in water, a fire hazard,' I said, inspecting another bunch. No card. And another. No card. And another five. Nope, no cards on them either.

'Shall I ring up to your office and get someone to come down and help remove them?' Alan asked.

'Er. Yes. Do you mind?' I said, crossing the reception like a frog, crouching down, inspecting one bunch for a card, standing up again and trying another bunch.

Moments later the lift pinged open and Lala and Legs appeared. '*Mon dieu*,' said Legs.

'Are they from Jaz?' said Lala.

'I think so,' I said, still crouching down. 'Do you guys mind helping me shift them upstairs?'

It took five trips between us to shuffle them all into the office.

'Here's a card, Pols,' said Lala, on the last run. I tore it off the cellophane and opened it.

Polly,

Thank you for all your advices on the Queen and I look forward to reading your interview.

My best respects,

HRH Sheikh Khaled

'Oh. They're from the Sheikh!' I said, feeling deflated. I mean, very kind of him, but I still wished they were from Jasper. I'd

assumed that he must be serious about this, about 'us', if he'd
not only taken me away for a weekend but then sent me fifty
bunches of roses.

'Is he in love with you?' asked Lala.

'The Sheikh? No, definitely not,' I said. 'He probably just
thinks it's what he should do. Like buying ten Labradors.'

'*Non*. Eet's the Rigby & Peller bra,' said Legs. 'I told you,
they are magic.'

★

The flowers weren't the only thing that arrived for me that
day. So did a cardboard box from the House of Fraser: my
maid of honour dress. I opened the box at my desk, watched
by Lala and Legs.

'Oh *non*!' said Legs, clapping her hand over her mouth as
soon as she saw the colour. It wasn't really pink at all. It was
purple and made from crêpe-like material, which fell to the
floor, with a big maroon sash that tied in the front with a
diamanté clip.

I held it up in front of me and looked at them for support.

'You know in American high school movies, there's always
some sort of tragic loser who gets it wrong when she goes
to the prom?' said Lala. 'That is the sort of dress she would
wear. No offence.'

'None taken,' I replied.

'Eet ees so uncool,' added Legs.

'Well, guys, I've got to wear it because Lex has picked it.'

They looked at me in stupefied silence. 'Maybe I can make it better with some accessories, or my hair or something,' I ventured, looking at Legs. 'Or with some nice shoes?'

'Polly, nothing will make thees dress better. Eet ees the worst thing my eyes have ever heard.'

'Seen,' I corrected, folding the bad dress and putting it back in the box.

'Is Jaz your plus one for the wedding?' said Lala.

'I'm not sure yet,' I said, looking up at her. I still hadn't been brave enough to ask him, although maybe I could, after the weekend. Since we'd now been away together. But the thought of him seeing me dressed like the aubergine emoji made me cringe.

'Ee should not see you in that,' said Legs. 'Ee will never make sex with you again.'

*

I had another, more pressing invitation for Jasper anyway: lunch with Mum. She wanted to have a big Sunday lunch at her flat the following weekend, the day before her first chemo session.

'I want to be surrounded by youth. Beautiful youthful faces,' she told me. 'And Sidney of course. And I want to meet Jasper before I lose all my hair. What will he think if he meets me looking like a bald eagle?'

So, I said I'd text everyone and see who was free. Jasper was invited, as were Joe and Bill. Lex and Hamish couldn't come because they were staying with her parents in the country – 'wed-min,' she explained via email that week. When I am a duchess, I thought, tapping out a reply to her, I will ban that word.

I'd been nervous about asking Jasper. Meeting the family. Well, Mum and Bertie. But also hanging out properly with my friends. A big step. But turns out I didn't have to be nervous. Jasper said he would be delighted and what wine should he bring.

I was distracted from his question, however, by a different question from Bill.

Can I bring Willow? X

It annoyed me a bit. I wasn't sure I wanted Willow there, flicking her hair about the place like a human unicorn. I texted back anyway.

Course! X

★

When Jasper, Joe and I arrived in Battersea that Sunday, the flat smelled of beef and there was a discussion going on over potatoes. Bill was already there, as was Willow, sitting on the floor, legs crossed, talking to Mum, who was lying on the sofa in her yellow dressing gown.

'You're here early,' I said, kissing Bill hello. He had a tea towel flung over one shoulder. I waved at Willow on the floor. 'Hi, hi,' I said. 'Don't get up. Honestly.' She didn't.

'I thought your mum might need some help,' said Bill, 'although Sidney here seems to have it covered.'

Sidney, wearing a pink apron, was holding up a bag of potatoes by the oven. 'We'll boil them first,' he said, looking at Bill. 'That is how I've been doing potatoes for forty years.'

'Honestly if we peel them and just lob them in the oven I don't think it makes any difference,' replied Bill.

'They're undoubtedly crispier my way,' said Sidney.

'I'm not sure I've ever cooked a potato,' said Jasper, as he came into the kitchen, followed by Joe. He placed two bottles of red wine on the table, then immediately turned to Mum on the sofa.

'You must be Susan,' he said, leaning down to kiss her on both cheeks. 'I can tell because you are just as ravishing as your daughter.'

'Tosh,' said Mum, blushing.

'And what a magnificent flat,' Jasper added. I thought he was laying it on a bit thick here and I saw Joe smirk out of the corner of my eye. There were spider webs in the corners and clouds of condensation clogged the windows. But Mum beamed again. 'Oh, you sweetheart.'

'Hi, I'm Willow,' said Willow, who managed to get up to kiss Jasper hello, I noticed.

'What kind of man hasn't cooked a potato?' said Bill.

'Not one of my strong points, cooking,' said Jasper. 'I'm Jasper, by the way.' He held his hand out for Bill to shake.

Bill removed the tea towel from his shoulder slowly, wiped his hands on it, threw the tea towel back over his shoulder and shook Jasper's hand. I felt like Attenborough, watching two gorillas square up to one another in the jungle.

'Good to meet you,' Bill said, looking at Jasper. And I might have imagined it but I think his nostrils flared briefly.

'Do you mind if I take my hand back, old chap?' Jasper replied, pulling it away from Bill and rubbing it with his other hand. 'It's like shaking hands with Goliath.'

'That's enough,' I interrupted. 'The testosterone in this house is enough to make someone pregnant. Who wants a drink?'

'Who's pregnant?' asked Mums from the sofa.

Sidney turned back to the oven. 'I'm going to get on with the potatoes.'

An hour or so later, two bottles were already in the recycling bin and the kitchen was calmer. I was stirring the peas, watching Willow and Jasper chatting together in the corner of the sitting room. It was as I feared, she was flicking her hair all over the place. She could win a gold medal at the Olympics for hair flicking, I thought, narrowing my eyes at her.

'I think we need another twenty minutes or so,' said Sidney, crouching down and peering into the oven at his potatoes.

'I'll take the beef out,' said Bill. 'Pols, where would I find tinfoil?'

'In here.' I opened a drawer and handed Bill a roll of it, then lowered my voice. 'How are things with… ?' I nodded my head in Willow's direction.

'Oh good, good. Great, actually. She's sort of living with me at the moment.'

'What? What does "sort of living with me" mean?' Bill had never lived with a girl, as far as I could remember.

'She's technically between flats, so she's staying with me. It's nice, I like it.'

'Wow. Will it… I mean… do you think it'll be permanent?'

'Dunno. It's just quite nice to come home to someone and eat something warm instead of a cold bed and a wank.'

I hit him on the arm.

'I'm joking! Kind of.'

We both looked over at the sofa, Willow and Jasper ensconced deep in some conversation. She'd curled her knees underneath her and was leaning in towards him, but Bertie had wedged himself between them. Good boy.

★

'Can I just say,' said Mums, after we'd all finished eating, 'That was the most delicious lunch with all my favourite people. And I don't know how I'll be feeling over the next couple of months, but I'm very grateful that you're here now.' She raised her glass from the end of the table.

'Hear, hear,' said Joe, who, at a conservative estimate, had polished off two bottles of red wine by himself.

'Excellent potatoes,' said Jasper, raising his glass in Sidney's direction.

Sidney blushed. 'Oh well, thank you, Jasper. And very good beef,' he added quickly, looking at Bill.

'Team effort,' said Bill. 'Important that a man knows how to cook, I feel.'

I tried to kick him under the table.

'Ouch,' said Willow, opposite me.

'Sorry,' I said quickly. 'Cramp.'

'I think you should all go for a walk,' announced Susan, 'take Bertie.'

'I'm up for that,' said Jasper.

'What about the washing up?' I said.

'Leave it,' said Sidney. 'Your mother and I will do the crossword and then I'll sort it out later.'

'Love's young dream,' said Joe.

'Outside,' Mum repeated.

At the scraping back of chairs, Bertie started barking. 'His lead is on the banister,' Mum shouted as we traipsed down the stairs and out into the hazy April afternoon. At the gates of Battersea Park, Joe started singing 'Jerusalem'.

I fell into step next to Willow, feeling like I should make some sort of effort conversationally rather than just physically assaulting her. 'So... how's work?' I asked.

'Fine, fine,' said Willow. 'Well, actually, you know. Bit boring. But it pays the bills and, well, I don't suppose I'll be doing it for ever.'

'How come?'

She looked at me in surprise. 'Well, I'll work for a bit, obviously, but then I'll have children. I mean, I'm not saying it'll happen tomorrow. But, at some point. I've never been much of a career girl.' She made little quotation marks with her fingers around 'career girl'.

'I know that's not very modern or feminist of me,' she

added, doing quotation marks around 'modern' and 'feminist' in the air with her fingers, too.

'Mmm,' I murmured back. She sounded like Lala, who said she was only working at *Posh!* until she met her husband. Then she wanted to move to the country, buy a few dogs and have babies. Every now and then I tried to remonstrate, gently, and suggest she think about her career. But Lala would generally ignore this and ask what I thought of the name Algernon for a boy. I looked towards Jasper and Bill walking in front of us, Joe ahead, still rumbling through 'Jerusalem'. 'So have you guys talked about it?'

'About having children? Not really,' said Willow.

'Mmm,' I murmured again, noncommittally. Bill, I knew, wanted to have his business up and running before even thinking about a family. I wondered if I should warn him: 'Hey, pal, just a heads up. I know you've only been dating for a few months but Willow's already thinking about babies.' Men could be quite thick about this kind of thing.

'What about you and Jasper?' she said.

'What do you mean?'

'Do you think you'll marry him?'

I burst out laughing. 'No idea.' I wasn't about to admit to having thought about it to Willow.

'So you haven't talked about it?'

'No! We've only been seeing each other for, like, two months.' The question reminded me I still needed to pluck up the courage to ask him about coming to Lex's wedding. 'He would freak and run a million miles,' I told her.

'I wouldn't be so sure given our conversation before lunch.'

'Why? What did he say?'

'Oh, just that he liked you a lot and how different you were to anyone else he's dated.'

'Did he?' I grinned and felt a wave of relief. Like the weekend away to Sheikh Khaled's, the fact that he'd actually said something like that felt an indication that Jasper was serious about this. Well, perhaps serious was too strong a word. But it reassured me that this was – hopefully – more than one of his flings.

'Yes!' said Willow. 'So you don't have to pretend.'

'Pretend what?'

'That you're so breezy and relaxed about it.'

'I am relaxed and breezy!'

'Sure,' she said, rolling her eyes at me. 'Oh, can I ask you something?'

''Course.'

'I want to throw Bill a surprise birthday party. In a few weeks. His birthday's on a Friday so I thought we should definitely do something but he keeps saying he hates his birthday.'

'Yeah, he's not a massive fan of it. Childhood thing,' I said vaguely.

I knew the real reason. Bill told me years ago. He'd been bullied at school as a nerdy kid, long before we met. And one year in particular, his eighth birthday, he was all excited because his mum had made him a robot cake. But only one person showed up at his party, the other class nerd. And so they'd played Pass the Parcel just the two of them, sitting there, opposite one another on the floor, handing the parcel to the other one and then back again. Bill had never thrown a birthday party since. But I didn't know if he wanted Willow to know all this, so I kept quiet.

'I just really want to do something proper to celebrate,' she went on. 'But it's a secret. So can you send me a list of names to invite? Just in case I miss people off?'

'Sure,' I said, wondering if I should warn Bill about this too. It was the kind of thing he'd hate.

Up ahead, Joe stopped and shouted back towards us: 'Pols, have you got a plastic bag? Bertie's done a shit.'

*

Jasper drove home to Yorkshire after our walk, so Joe and I went back to the flat in Shepherd's Bush, sat on the sofa and sang along to *Songs of Praise* while sharing a family-sized bar of Dairy Milk. Mum sent me a text message with her verdict later that evening.

Jasper lovely. V. good with Bertie. Excellent sign. Do you think Bill's OK? X

Strange question. I texted back.

Fine, why wouldn't he be? X

She didn't reply. Rinsed by my own mother. Probably playing Scrabble or something with Sidney.

*

Enid was filing her nails at her desk when I arrived at the office the next day. *Rasp, rasp, rasp.* I could see little clouds of nail filings floating on to the carpet.

'Morning, Enid, everything all right?'

'Just broke a nail.'

'Oh, right. I hope it's not serious?'

'Nah, I'll live,' said Enid, not looking up. 'He wants to have a meeting with everyone though.' She nodded her head towards Peregrine's office.

'Why?'

'I dunno. Muttering something about a cover shoot.' *Rasp, rasp, rasp.*

'When?'

'Ten.'

'So I've got time for a coffee?'

'Yes, if you're quick.' She looked up and frowned. 'You all right?'

'Me? Yes, never better. Why?'

'You look awful.' She paused and scrutinized my face. 'Have you ever tried anything for those dark circles?' She waggled one of her scarlet fingers in front of her own eyes.

'Oh thanks very much.'

'Just saying, my love. Don't go exhausting yourself.'

'I'm going to get a coffee. Back in five.'

'All right, my darling.'

The meeting, it turned out, was to discuss a new cover shoot and to discuss it the following assembled around Peregrine's desk:

1) *Legs, in a pair of black jeans and a minute black vest top. No discernible bra.*

2) *Lala, quite the revolutionary today in a skin-tight pair of leather trousers and a Che Guevara t-shirt with her hair piled up on her head and secured by a thick strip of red ribbon.*

3) *Jeffrey, the magazine's art director, a 45-year-old moustachioed man who always dressed in a three-piece suit, paired with a pocket watch, and brought his French bulldog called Bertrand to work every day.*

4) *Me, quite cross at having had to abandon the blueberry muffin on my desk.*

'*Achtung,* everyone,' said Peregrine, as we settled into our chairs. 'We've got to put our heads together and come up for an idea to shoot the Honourable Celestia Smythe.'

'Who ees she?' said Legs.

'She's the daughter of Lord Smythe,' said Peregrine, to blank faces. 'Oh, come on you lot. You know. Former banker turned adviser to the Prime Minister. Polly, come on, you've got half a brain cell. You must know who I mean?'

I nodded. I vaguely remembered his name from some scandal a few years back. He'd left one of the big banks with an enormous payout after a management disaster, yet somehow ended up as a senior member of the Tory Party.

'Anyway,' Peregrine went on, 'she's eighteen and she's got an avocado cookery book coming out so I said she could have the June cover. Which means we need to come up with a brilliant idea.'

Legs snorted in disgust.

Peregrine swivelled his Mac around so we could see a picture of her. She looked much as you might expect someone who wrote an avocado cookery book to look. Pretty, I grudgingly accepted, and shiny with health. Long brown hair, huge green eyes and lashes like a dairy cow.

'If we want to shoot 'er for June we need to dress 'er in Chanel,' said Legs. 'We 'ave promised them that cover.'

'Fine,' said Peregrine, 'but we need to come up with a clever idea. With a concept. I don't want to run another picture of a Sloaney stick-insect grimacing at the camera. We need to try harder than that. Jeffrey, any thoughts on photographers?'

'Well, there's a young Japanese photographer I'd love to try before she gets snapped up by *Vogue*,' he said. 'Big on flowers. Does shoots with flowers sort of scattered everywhere.'

Jeffrey waved his arm in front of him as if to demonstrate the scattering, and then he shrieked. 'Oh! I tell you what, why don't we use avocados instead of flowers?'

Peregrine frowned. 'What?'

'Or, what about a bath of avocados?' Jeffrey continued, excitedly. 'Like in *American Beauty*. You know, where she's lying on the bed with petals? Except, instead of petals, we use avocados?'

'But, Jeffrey, she has to be wearing couture. Chanel couture,' stressed Legs.

'I know,' said Jeffrey, nodding, 'but we can still have her in couture lying on a bed of avocados. Or,' he carried on, his voice getting even higher, 'what about shooting her in couture with an avocado face mask on? That could be frightfully jolly.'

'I like it,' said Peregrine. 'It's bold. It's different.'

'Why not go the whole hog and put her in one of those avocado fancy dress costumes?' I joked.

'Polly,' said Peregrine. 'That's brilliant! I can see it now, dressed as an avocado but in a pair of heels and some Chanel jewellery.'

Oh *crap*, he'd taken it seriously.

'And I want you to do the interview too, please,' he said, looking at me.

'About avocados, I'm guessing?'

'Yes please. It's pegged to the book but cover everything else too. Family life, love life. The usual.'

'No problem,' I said, wondering whether George Orwell had ever interviewed anyone about avocados.

'It's going to be tremendous, I can feel it,' he said, rubbing his hands together. 'Let's make Celestia the new Cara.'

Legs snorted again.

'Right, thanks, everyone. Let's crack on with the day then, shall we?'

It was Peregrine's signal for everyone to leave, but as we all stood he said: 'Polly, can you stay behind for one tick?'

'Sure.'

Everyone else filed out while I remained in my seat.

'I just wanted to say, Polly, that I liked your Sheikh Khaled interview very much. You've got a real eye for detail, keep it up. I liked the line about the gold lavatory especially.'

'Oh,' I replied, surprised. 'Thanks.'

'And I was also wondering how are things with Jasper?' he continued.

'I'm going to have to give you, my boss, a blow-by-blow account of this relationship, am I?'

'Not at all,' he said, hunting around in his right nostril with an index finger. 'You know me, Polly, I merely take a keen interest in the well-being of my team.'

'Well, I'm very touched by your interest and it's all going fine. Great, even. Happy with that?'

'Smashing. We'll make a duchess of you yet.' He retrieved his finger from his nostril and wiped it on his mouse mat. 'Remind me to give you a raise at your next evaluation.'

'Really?'

'No, not really. There's no money obviously. But well done anyway. And for the avocado idea. Terrific stuff. Inspired.'

'You're... welcome,' I said. 'And, in that case, do you mind if I leave a bit early today?'

'Why?'

'It's Mum's first chemo appointment, so I'm taking her to St Thomas'.'

'My dear girl, of course. You don't have to ask for that kind of thing, Polly, go whenever you like. Take as much time as you need. And send your mother my best.'

'Will do.'

★

I caught the Tube to the hospital that afternoon feeling, if I was honest, a bit sorry for myself. I was wallowing in an Eighties ballad Spotify playlist which wasn't helping. I glanced around the carriage at everyone else. Probably, all these people knew others who'd had cancer. Maybe they'd had it themselves. And they all looked all right, didn't they? Life carried on for them. I caught the eye of a man sitting across from me wearing a t-shirt that said 'This isn't a bald patch, it's a solar panel for a sex machine'. So, nearly everyone on here looked all right.

I found Mum sitting in the reception area of St Thomas'. 'How are we feeling?' I asked.

'I'm a bit tired. I didn't sleep terribly well last night.'

'Oh, Mum, sorry.'

'It wasn't me. It was Sidney. Up all night. Trouble with his prostate.'

'Right.' I wasn't sure I knew Sidney well enough to be discussing his prostate. 'Now, where are we going?'

Mum opened her handbag. 'The oncology ward,' she said. 'It's got a name, hang on… the Farber Ward.'

'Right, let's go. It's going to be in, out and you'll be home on the sofa with a cup of tea before you know it.'

'Good afternoon, my darlings,' trilled the nurse at the reception desk of the ward.

'Er, hello,' said Mum. 'I'm Susan Spencer.'

'Susan, you are very welcome. And is this your sister with you?' The receptionist beamed at me.

'I'm her daughter,' I replied. I couldn't tell if the receptionist was joking or not.

The nurse laughed and her bosoms shook. 'I know, my darling, I guessed that. Now, Susan, what time are you booked in for?'

'Three o'clock,' said Mum.

'So there will be a nurse along to collect you any... Ah, here she comes. This is Beatriz.'

'Hello,' said Beatriz, a small woman in a dark blue nurse's dress. 'Which one of you is Susan?'

'I am,' said Mum.

'But can I stay with her?' I asked.

''Course you can,' said Beatriz, 'if you both follow me. Susan, we'll get you started.' She ushered Mum to a big chair in one corner. 'Now, you had your blood taken on Friday, I see. And that was all fine.'

'Yes,' said Mum, 'Dr Ross said the levels were quite all right.'

'That's what we like,' said Beatriz. 'So what I'm going to do now is take your blood pressure and temperature. And then if that's all fine, we'll get you started.'

Mum nodded and started rolling a sleeve up. I looked around at the rest of the ward. A dozen or so patients sitting in uniform green armchairs, all hooked up to drips. An elderly lady, her face as wrinkled as a raisin, sat in one chair with a pillow across her lap, a newspaper on top of the pillow. In another green chair there was a younger, middle-aged woman wearing a pink headscarf, watching an iPad. Close to Mum's chair was an old man in slippers asleep. Or, at least, I hoped he was asleep. Maybe he'd died? What if he had died? Did people die in this ward? I looked at his chest to see if he was still breathing.

'He's all right,' said Beatriz, seeing my face. 'Just dozing. He's been here since ten, poor Martin.'

'Has he got anyone with him?'

'No,' said Beatriz, 'gets the bus on his own from Norwood. Bless him.'

I looked at my hands, trying not to think of Martin finishing his treatment and going home on his own again.

'That all looks all right,' she said to Mum a few minutes later. 'So I think we'll get you started.' She looped a tourniquet over Mum's arm and tightened it. Then she picked up a little plastic packet from her trolley and opened it. It was a needle. I gritted my teeth and looked towards the woman in the pink headscarf. I'd loved nothing more than a good knee scab to pick when I was little, but these days the sight of a needle made my stomach lurch.

'I just have to find a vein, Susan, then I'll hook you up to the carboplatin.'

'OK,' said Mum, her voice wobbling. I took her other hand and squeezed it.

'Come on,' said Beatriz to herself, frowning at the needle, then, a few moments later, 'Nope, that's not going to work. Sorry, Susan, bear with me.'

'Polly, my darling, it's all right, you don't have to grip my hand quite so hard,' said Mum.

'Sorry.' I loosened my grip. My hands were all sweaty. 'Not much of a Florence Nightingale, am I?' I said.

'Let's have another go,' said Beatriz.

I turned my head in the other direction again, feeling sick.

'That's better, all in,' she said, having found a vein. 'So what I'm going to do is link this up to the infusion bag, and then it'll take ninety minutes. Then you need to stay sitting for half an hour, Susan, just to check it's all right. You'll be able to go home after that.'

'Thank you,' said Mum, her voice still wobbling.

I squinted at the bag of chemicals hanging on a drip above Mum's head. It didn't look very poisonous. It was clear, like a bag of water.

'Watch the level of that,' Beatriz said, nodding her head towards the bag as she linked Mum's arm to a tube dangling from it. 'It'll slowly go down, so you can tell when your mum is halfway. Now then—' she stood up '—you're all set. There's a timer that will go off when you're finished.'

'Thank you,' said Mum again.

'You're very welcome. I'll be pottering about the ward so let me know if there are any problems.'

There was a sudden beeping from Martin's chair. 'I'll just see to him,' said Beatriz, moving towards the chair.

'Do you want your paper, Mum?'

'No,' said Mum. 'I want to talk about Jasper.'

'What? Now?'

'Yes, now. We've got a whole hour and a half.'

'You liked him, right?'

'Of course I liked him. He was charming. His manners are ever so good. And he ate all his lunch,' she said. 'Lovely boy. I was pleasantly surprised, if I'm honest. He doesn't seem too posh at all.'

I frowned. 'What do you mean?'

'Well, I just… I don't know… I suppose I expected him to

be all "How do you do?" and to talk like Prince Charles. But he seemed quite normal.'

I laughed. 'Yeah. Kind of. For someone who grew up in a castle.'

'And he helped clear the table and was ever so sweet with Bertie.' She nodded to herself. 'I liked him very much. More than I thought I would.'

'Good,' I replied. 'Me too. That's what I thought when I first met him.'

'But I did think Bill was a bit quiet,' she went on. 'Or on edge. Is he all right? How's his work going?'

'Did you? I think he's all right. Busy trying to get the app off the ground and trying to get investment for it, but I think he's loving being his own boss, running his own thing.' I paused. 'What did you think of Willow?'

'Oh, I thought she was nice too,' said Mum, 'and ever so pretty, isn't she? Such lovely hair. I wish I had that hair.'

'Mmm,' I replied. I was hoping Mum would say she also found her the teeniest, tiniest bit annoying, then I'd feel less of a bitch about thinking the same. On the way home from lunch on Sunday, I'd made a joke to Joe about Willow organizing Bill's surprise party and even he'd told me that I was being unfair. Maybe I just needed to stop being so protective.

★

Mum was much quieter a couple of hours later, when we were finally on our way home in an Uber.

'You all right?' I asked.

'Fine, just tired. But that could be more to do with last night's comings and goings than the medicine.' She refused to use the word 'chemo' I'd noticed.

'Nearly home. Then you can have a cup of tea. Or a drink even. If that's allowed?'

'No, no, I think tea and a bath. And then my bed,' said Mum.

'Is Sidney staying tonight?'

'No. He's got Bertie with him tonight. He wanted to stay but I said I wasn't sure how I'd be feeling so best off him staying home.'

'Oh. I don't want you to be on your own tonight. Do you want me to stay?'

'No, love. I'll be fine. Tea and bed. I'm ever so sleepy.'

'Do you feel sick?'

'No, no. Just sleepy.'

She went to bed as soon as I got her home and I made a mental note to google Mum's chemo medicine. We knew her hair would fall out, Dr Ross had told her that. But I'd tried to avoid googling anything else about the cancer. About the stage of her cancer. About the treatment. About, dreaded phrase, 'survival rates'. It all seemed too bleak. But here, taking my tired mum home from her first chemo appointment, I felt pretty bleak. Other people had big families. Big families who all gathered for Christmases at home. Or gathered at big tables in restaurants for birthdays and they'd all sing loudly when a cake appeared and then everyone around the table would clap for their mum or their dad. Or brother or sister. Or uncle or niece. Or cousin or brother-in-law. I always felt a twinge of jealousy when anybody ever grumbled about an 'in-law'. *Lucky you*, I'd think. *To have someone you could call an in-law. To have such a big family.*

Because I had a little family. Mum. She was my family. My whole family. And I was hers. Bertie, I suppose, was a sort of honorary member. A more human dog than any other dog I'd come across. But even with Bertie we were a small unit. A small family. And I couldn't fathom the idea that my family would disappear. That it would be just me left. And Bertie. One person and one dog doesn't make a family, does it? You can't sit in a restaurant on your birthday with your dog on a seat beside you. Bertie couldn't sing my 'Happy Birthday' or pull a cracker at Christmas. So, the only alternative, I decided, sitting on the bus on the way home, was for Mum to get better again and our small family unit to stay intact. It just had to.

10

I MET LEX FOR drinks in the Windsor Castle pub, just behind Notting Hill Gate Tube station, later that week. She'd emailed a few days before saying we needed a 'wed-min' meeting. I'd replied saying I would come so long as she never used that word again.

'I've got us a bottle of white,' said Lex, when I found her in the pub garden. I sat down and tried to fold my legs underneath the wooden table. Why did they make these tables for gnomes?

'Great, thank you. And crisps. I'm starving. I need about ten bags of crisps.'

Lex didn't look up from a notepad in front of her. 'Not for me. Wedding diet has started. Or "wed-shred", as they call it.'

I did a quick calculation with my fingers. It was now April. The wedding was in July. That was in… three months' time.

'What are you doing?' Lex asked, as I tapped on my fingers, counting the months.

'Nothing, just, er, checking they all still work.'

'You're getting weirder. But listen, I've made a list of everything we need to do.' She waved the notepad at me. 'Bride-to-be' was written on the front of it. *Puh-lease.*

'You and Hamish?'

'No, no. Me and you.'

'So exciting!' I said, with all the enthusiasm of someone who's just been told there's a meteorite hurtling its way towards Earth and everyone will die in the morning.

'So you're on hen duty. Have you had any thoughts about that?'

'Er…'

'I don't want you to go to too much trouble. Just a weekend somewhere, I was thinking Ibiza but that may not work in June. Too busy. Or Lake Como. Laura in my office says Lake Como is lovely in June.'

Laura was a tit, I decided swiftly.

'And I've made a list of people,' Lex went on, 'and we're ten altogether.'

'Okey-dokes.'

'There are just some that I can't ignore. If I invite Rachel from work, I need to have Laura. It's just going to be Sal from uni. And I can't not have my cousin and I need to ask various school friends as well. Or at least I have asked them, they may not all come. So I'll send you all their email addresses. And maybe set up a WhatsApp group, so everyone can get to know one another beforehand. What do you think?'

'Mmm,' I murmured. 'What's Hamish doing for his stag?'

'Going to Prague. I don't want to know the details. So I'll do the WhatsApp group and then you'll sort the hen. But I thought I could split some of the duties between you and Sal as she's good at all this stuff.'

Phew, I thought. Sal was a party planner. I hadn't seen her

since Bill's dinner party in January but I figured since she was also engaged she'd be into all this.

Lex carried on wittering as my phone lit up with a message from Jasper, who was driving down from Castle Montgomery for the night.

I'll be with you by about 10 X

'Sure, sure,' I said vaguely to Lex, as I replied to Jasper.

Can't wait to see you. If I live that long. Long wedding discussions with Lex here... Xxx

'And do you know whether Jasper will be your plus one yet? Only because the wedding planner needs to know for the seating arrangements.'

'Yes, sorry, I keep meaning to ask him. When do you need to know by?'

'Next couple of weeks?'

'OK, ace. I'll let you know.'

Lex ran a line through something in her notepad and nodded. 'Hammy says Callum's coming too by the way,' she said. 'So if Jasper can't come at least you'll have someone to flirt with.'

'Lex, I think that ship—'

But she interrupted me and carried on. 'And then we need to chat about the wedding weekend itself. I'm going home on the Tuesday from work. So when do you want to come? I realize it means taking time off work but I think there'll be so much to do. I was thinking Thursday for you, maybe?'

'Sure.'

Half an hour later, having discussed whether Lex should

have her hair up or down, their honeymoon (to Bora Bora although Lex was worried about Zika) and whether she should buy white or pale blue bridal underwear, she sighed and put her pen down. 'Just so much to do. I think I'm getting stress lines from it all, look at my forehead, look, here.' She pointed to a place just above her right eyebrow. 'Can you see that line? It's new. I spotted it this morning while I was brushing my teeth. I think I might have Botox.'

I scrutinized her forehead. 'Lex, there are 7-year-olds with more wrinkles than you. Don't worry, everything will get done.'

She sighed again. 'I hope so. How are you anyway? What's happening?'

'All good,' I said. 'Apart from taking Mum to her first chemo on Monday.'

'Fuck,' said Lex. 'Fuck, fuck, fuck. I'm the world's worst friend. So sorry. How was it? How is she? How are you?'

'Kind of grim. A room full of people hooked up to bags of poison, so I've been to cheerier places. But Mum was amazing. Didn't stop talking throughout. Well, until I took her home, when she was pretty tired. So… yeah, now we just have to wait and see. Another chemo in a few weeks.'

'How many has she got to have?'

'Three in total, three weeks apart.'

Lex nodded.

I'd spoken to Mum earlier that day and she was fine. Surprisingly fine. Sleeping. Not sick. Checking her hairbrush every day for clumps but nothing yet.

'How did we get to the point where we're discussing your wedding and my mum's chemo appointments?' I said to Lex. 'When did that happen? I mean, literally, when did that happen? Like, are we old enough?'

'God knows,' she replied. 'Although we spent most of our twenties drunk, right? So it was probably around then.'

'Mmm.'

'Another bottle?'

'Yeah, why not?'

★

Why did this feel like a big deal, I thought, lying on Jasper's chest in my bed later that night. It's not a big deal. It's just someone asking someone else to a wedding. Not your own wedding. Someone else's wedding. Get a grip.

'I have a question,' I said, tentatively.

'Uh-oh,' he replied. 'Am I in trouble?'

'No, but someone has a guilty conscience. Do you think you should be in trouble?'

'Why do you think that I think that I'm in trouble?'

'OK, stop it, forget the trouble thing,' I said, laughing. 'You're not in trouble. I have a question.'

'Which is?'

'So you know I was talking to Lex this week about her wedding…'

'Polly Spencer, are you about to propose to me?'

'No!' I slapped him on the chest. 'Stop it. Concentrate.'

'Good. Because when that moment comes I plan on doing the asking.'

I was momentarily stumped. 'OKKKK, now I feel awkward. I'm going to pretend you didn't just say that...'

'I don't mean propose to you.'

'Oh thanks! I mean... never mind... God, this is making it worse.'

'Well, maybe I'll propose to you.'

'Stop it. Literally, stop it.'

'You're so easy to tease.'

'Can we get back to the question?'

'Instead of me talking about us getting married?'

'Yes.'

'You know you're incredibly sexy when you get flustered,' said Jasper, rolling over and pinning me underneath him.

I narrowed my eyes at him. 'OK. The question is, do you want to be my plus one for Lex's wedding?'

He laughed. 'That's it?'

'Yes!'

'I'm quite disappointed you didn't ask me to marry you now,' he said, burying his head in my neck and kissing it.

'Stop it. Honestly, it's making me feel awkward.'

He looked up again and smiled. ''Course I will. I'd love to.'

'Really?'

'Really, truly, honestly,' he said. 'I do hope you're wearing some sort of sensational bridesmaid dress.'

★

A couple of weeks later, I arrived at the studios in East London for the Celestia Smythe cover shoot and buzzed the intercom on a big black door beneath the railway arch.

'Hi, I'm from *Posh!*,' I said.

The door clicked and I pushed it open. There was a woman with a tattoo of the word 'LIFE' on her neck sitting at the reception desk.

'Hiya,' she said. 'Studio three, up the stairs and along to the end.'

Upstairs in the studio, I found the photographer crouching down over her camera bags, then spotted Legs and Jeffrey, both standing near a rail of clothes. Another woman with bright red hair stood beside a nearby table, arranging make-up brushes and sponges. Rock music was playing in the background.

'Morning,' I said to no one in particular, heading immediately to pour myself a coffee from the table that was covered with croissants, fruit and juice.

'Hello,' said the photographer, standing up and coming over. She was wearing a tweed flat cap, with a tweed waistcoat over a black t-shirt. Black jeans. Doc Marten boots. Classic photographer.

'Hi, I'm Polly,' I said, shaking her hand. 'The writer.'

'Kimiko,' she said. 'Great to meet you, I think this is going to be fab.'

'Mmm,' I said, my eyes falling on several stacked crates in the corner. Avocados. Five hundred avocados, which Enid had spent all week moaning about in the office. 'Where am

I going to get five hundred avocados? I can hardly nip down to Tesco and get them all there, can I? I ask you,' and so on and so on.

'Hi, I'm Rachel,' said the lady arranging make-up brushes, walking over.

'Rachel, hi, good to meet you,' I said, shaking her hand. 'I'm just going to go and have a word with Legs. You've met her and Jeffrey?' I asked, nodding in their direction.

'Yes, absolutely. All friends.'

'Great,' I said again.

Legs, as usual, looked less cheerful than a thundercloud. 'I do not think Chanel will be 'appy with this,' she said, gesturing at the rail of clothes.

There were a dozen or so dresses strung along it. I reached out and touched a silver minidress with hundreds of feathers embroidered around the bottom. It looked like something a dancer would wear in *Swan Lake*.

'Beautiful, eesn't it?' said Legs.

'Mmm.' I was trying to imagine wearing it. To the office? To nip to Barbara's in the morning for some Special K?

'Polly, good morning,' said Jeffrey.

'Hi, Jeff. How we doing?'

'I think we'll be all right. Look, what do you reckon?'

He unfurled a green bit of felt lying at his feet. It was the avocado fancy dress costume.

'It's going to look fabulous on the cover,' he said.

Luckily I didn't have a second to reply, because there was a sudden bang behind us as the door flung open and a woman in an enormous trilby walked in. The Honourable Celestia Smythe, I guessed.

'Morning,' came a rather high-pitched voice from underneath the hat.

'Hello,' I replied. 'You must be Celestia?'

'Yah, how do you do?' she said, extending a small, pale hand for me to shake. She then took back the hand and removed the hat, shaking her head about as if auditioning for a shampoo advert. Her hair was as thick and shiny as Kate Middleton's. Presumably all those avocados.

'Let me introduce you to everyone,' I said, waving my hand around the room.

'This is Legs, our fashion director, who will be dressing you.' Celestia stuck out her hand again. 'How do you do?' she repeated to Legs, who wordlessly shook Celestia's hand.

'And this is Jeffrey, our picture editor. He's had a... brilliant, er, idea for today's concept.'

'Jeffrey, hi, how do you do?' said Celestia.

'I'm exceptionally well, thank you, Miss Smythe,' said Jeffrey, before doing a little bow at her. 'It is an honour to meet you.'

'And this is Kimiko the photographer and Rachel the make-up artist.'

'So exciting to meet you all,' said Celestia, smiling around the room. She was even prettier in person, I had to admit. Lime-coloured eyes and the size of a woodland sprite. I could fit my hands around her waist, probably.

'Shall we get going with hair and make-up?' I said. 'I

thought I'd interview you while that was happening if you don't mind?'

'Sure,' she said, eyelashes fluttering at me.

'Oh sorry, do you want a coffee or anything? Or a croissant?'

She shuddered as if I'd asked whether she wanted to go Morris dancing. 'Oh no, thank you. I've brought one of my avocado shakes with me.'

'No probs,' I said brightly. 'I might just top my coffee up and then let's get cracking.'

A few minutes later, she was sitting, eyes closed, on a swivel chair in front of Rachel, who was dabbing at her face with a sponge. I was sitting cross-legged on the floor, phone beside me, recording.

'You have lovely skin,' Rachel said to Celestia.

'Oh that's kind of you,' she replied. 'It's all the vitamin E.'

'So, avocados,' I said. 'Tell me about them.' It wasn't much of an opening gambit but I reckoned if I warmed her up on avocados then I could go in and start asking about her love life.

'Oh, well, I've always been a massive fan of them,' said Celestia, 'I'd always order them with my breakfast. Like, with poached eggs. You know?'

I nodded. 'In cafés?'

'Exactly!' she said brightly.

'But how did you come up with the idea for the book?' I asked.

'So I was in my favourite café on the King's Road a few months ago talking to my friends about what I wanted to do once I'd left Edinburgh...'

'Uni, right?' I said. 'Studying History of Art?'

'Yes,' she said. 'I love Dandy Warhol. But, anyway, I was in that café and I'd just eaten some eggs and avocados, and then I was scrolling through Instagram looking at loads of other pictures of eggs and avocados, and I just thought there was something in avocados. Like, they're so popular nowadays, aren't they?'

'Mmm,' I said, 'Were you always good at cooking?'

'God no,' she said, waving a hand in the air. 'The nanny always did that at home. But cooking with avocados is so easy. You literally just cut around them and remove the stone and then you can do all sorts with them.'

'*Right*. So, what kind of recipes will be in the book? And, sorry, what's it called?'

'It's called *Green Goddess*,' Celestia replied. 'Isn't that clever? And there are all sorts of recipes I've made up in there. Avocado mousse, avocado tostadas, plain avocado and vinaigrette, stuffed avocado. Avocado brownies, avocado face masks...'

Rachel drew liner across one of her eyelids. 'I'll send you a signed copy when it's out,' she continued.

'Oh, wonderful, thank you,' I replied. Although I was fairly dubious about how wonderful this book would be. 'Now, can I ask about what you do when you're not thinking about avocados? Where you live, what you like doing in your spare time?'

'OK, so I live at home still in Chelsea while I'm working on the book. It was just too much to move out and find my own place at the same time.'

'Mmm…'

'And I love spending time with my dog, he's a pug. Called Pasta. And shopping. I *love* shopping. And breakfasts on the King's Road obviously,' she said.

'And friends and…' I paused '… maybe a boyfriend?'

'So I hang out mostly with Gussy Mountbatten and Sally Battenberg, if you know them?' She opened one eye and squinted at me. I knew them from our party pages, both daughters of dukes, both in line to the throne somehow. 'And no boyfriend, no. I was dating Frank von Trapsburg at Edinburgh but he wasn't The One.'

Kimiko interrupted at this point from across the studio, where she had been loading avocados into a free standing bath. 'Rachel, how long do you reckon?'

Rachel stood up and looked at Celestia's face. 'Erm, ten minutes?'

'And I need, maybe, fifteen to try some of thees dresses,' said Legs, sitting beside the clothes rail.

'Fab,' said Kimiko.

*

Celestia was game when it came to lying in a bath of avocados, I had to admit. She stripped down to her knickers in front of us all – milky skin like Cleopatra, pert bottom like a peach – and happily stepped into the bath.

'Oh my God, this is *hilaaaaarious*,' she said, lying back as Kimiko and Jeffrey strategically placed more avocados around her, before Kimiko started taking shots of her while standing on a stepladder.

'Chin up a bit, Celestia, that's great,' Kimiko said. *Click, click, click.* 'Head to the left a bit.' *Click, click, click.* 'Rachel, can you just move that strand of hair from her face? Great, thanks.' *Click, click, click* and so on.

Legs sat sulking by the clothing rail. 'I promise we'll get her in Chanel at some stage,' I said to her. 'Let's just get the bath shots done and then we can have her in one of the dresses, juggling with the avocados or something.'

Legs rolled her eyes. 'Karl will not like eet, but OK.'

It took six hours in all. Six hours. Four different shots. Celestia in the bath covered with avocados; Celestia in the feathery Chanel dress holding two avocados in front of her breasts; Celestia in the avocado fancy-dress costume wearing several strands of Chanel pearls; Celestia in a bouclé Chanel suit with mashed avocado all over her face. A lump of avocado fell on the suit's collar which made Legs nearly explode in anger but I told her we'd dry-clean it and Chanel would never know.

'That was so fun,' said Celestia, standing in her knickers and a t-shirt by the clothes rail again.

'It looked great,' I said. 'Thanks for being such a good sport. Where are you off to now?'

'Oh, just going home and then I think I might go to yoga,' she said, 'I need to stretch.' She bent over and touched the floor with her fingertips. Jeffrey went puce at this and quickly turned to face the back of the studio.

'What are you doing tonight?' said Legs, looking at me while folding a dress over her arm. 'You seeing Jasper?'

'Is that your boyfriend?' said Celestia, standing up again and reaching her arms over her head.

'Well, I'm not sure about boyfriend. But someone I've been seeing. But he lives in Yorkshire so it's a bit, um, tricky during the week.'

Celestia frowned, her arms still stretched above her head in the air. 'You don't mean Jasper Milton?'

I look at her surprised. 'Yep, how come? I mean, do you know him?' 'Course she knew him, I then realized. All the aristocracy knew each other. They were basically all related to one another.

Celestia pulled her arms down again and shook her head. 'No. No, I don't actually know him but my brother went to Eton with him. And I've always had such a crush on him. So how long have you been going out?'

'Er, a couple of months,' I said. Standing in my saggy jeans and trainers beside a small, creamy-skinned nymph like Celestia while she asked about Jasper made me feel awkward. I felt like she was scrutinizing me, as if she was trying to work out why someone like Jasper would be dating me.

'God, I'm jealous,' she went on. 'He's dreamy. And funny. Jake always said he was funny.'

'Mmm, he is,' I said, quite wishing she'd get dressed and we could all go home. I was suddenly exhausted and wanted a bath. A hot bath filled with bubbles instead of avocados.

'Well done you!' she went on. 'Do you just feel like the luckiest girl in the world?'

'Sometimes,' I said, trying to find an excuse to change the subject.

'Legs,' I called out, 'do you know when the car is getting here?'

Legs looked up from layering Chanel dresses back into a gigantic trunk to cart back to the office. '*Oui*, I just got a message on my phone. Eet's just arrived,' she said.

'Great,' I replied. I didn't want to go back to the office, but I could pretend I had to leave with Legs to escape the studio.

'Hang on, let me just zip this up and we can go.'

'So lovely to meet you,' I said, turning to Celestia.

'You too!' she said, leaning forward and hugging me. 'Maybe see you with Jasper sometime?'

Not if I could help it, I thought.

★

Emails flooded in all week from Willow about the arrangements for Bill's surprise party. Finally, it was decided that everyone should be at his flat by 6.30 on Friday to hide themselves before Bill came home around seven o'clock.

'What if he gets stuck in the office?' someone had asked on an email chain of about forty people. I thought people who hit 'Reply all' on emails like this shouldn't be allowed access to technology. Willow had replied saying she'd 'made sure' he would be leaving on time.

Joe had begun a separate email chain with me and Lex.

I bet she's promised him a blow job when he gets home…

I replied, cautiously.

Guys, can we be suuuuuper careful none of us hits the wrong button and sends this back to Willow?

An email from Lex popped up.

What did you say, Joe?! It won't get through my email filter?

I wondered, as I did several times every day, how much more productive I'd be without the constant dribble of anatomical emails from them both.

Meanwhile, I was trying to write the Celestia interview. Peregrine had roared with delight at the photos that morning, saying how much he liked them. I sighed and looked at the blank Word document in front of me. I wasn't sure I could interview people about their dogs and their avocado cookery books much longer. All right, so I probably wasn't going to leapfrog into a newspaper job reporting about the Iranian nuclear crisis from *Posh!* But I felt like I needed to start thinking about a new writing job. A more serious job. Where was I going to find that?

11

ON FRIDAY EVENING, LEX, Hamish, Joe and I were lying on the carpet in Bill's bedroom, sardined between his bed and the wall. The rest of the surprise party were hiding in the kitchen, crouching behind various bits of furniture. Joe was balancing a bottle of beer on his stomach.

'Joe, hold your beer, you're going to spill it,' I said bossily.

'Can you relax?' he replied.

'What's the time?' asked Lex from his other side.

'Three minutes to seven,' said Hamish, craning his neck to look at the clock on Bill's bedside table.

'This is my sort of party,' said Joe, yawning. 'I might just stay here when he arrives.'

'He's going to know,' said Lex. 'Nobody in history has ever pulled off a successful surprise party.'

I could hear Willow hushing people in the kitchen and bridled slightly, but she had made a huge effort. Balloons all over the flat, birthday bunting strung across the kitchen, a bath full of Prosecco bottles and she'd shown us a Thomas the Tank Engine cake hidden on top of the fridge because Thomas was Bill's favourite cartoon when he was little.

'I've got a dead leg,' said Joe.

'I need a slash,' said Hamish.

'I want another drink,' said Lex.

'Guys, *shhh*, we've only got a few minutes. Lex, if you can't go a few minutes without another glass of wine you need to go and see a doctor. Or a therapist.'

'All right, all right.'

We lay in silence for a few minutes while there was more frantic hushing from the kitchen.

Then I heard Bill's voice.

'Hi, darling, I'm back.'

The clank of the front door closing.

'SURPRISE!' shouted everyone hidden in the kitchen.

'We should get up,' I said, as we remained motionless on the floor of his bedroom while more shouts of surprise and general celebrations went on in the rest of the flat.

'Finally,' said Lex, sitting up. 'Who wants a top up?'

'Me,' said Joe and Hamish in tandem.

'Yup,' I said, getting to my feet. 'Come on, let's go and be friendly.'

We shuffled out into the kitchen where Bill was standing in his suit, one arm over Willow's shoulder.

'You're brilliant,' he told her. 'I had no idea.'

'Really?' she squeaked, gazing up at him.

'Really,' he said, smiling and kissing her. He didn't mean it. I could tell from his face. It was a forced smile. The sort of rictus grin a small child might make in a school photo.

'Please, you guys, get a room,' said Joe, stepping forward and giving Bill a hug.

'Happy birthday, you,' I said, hugging Bill after Joe moved out the way. 'Mum sends her love.'

'How is she?'

'Fine, fine. Well, you know. Some hair's started to come out. But she's all right.'

He pulled me back in for a hug. 'Bloody hell, Pols.'

'It's OK, dude, it's your birthday. None of that.'

'Where's the Dark Lord?' he asked.

I rolled my eyes at him. 'Driving down from Yorkshire, so I'm not sure if he'll make it. He said it depends on traffic.'

'Excellent.'

'Bill,' I warned.

'What?'

'You know what.'

'I said "excellent".'

'Fine, come on, let's get a drink.'

Lex and I topped up our wine glasses, Hamish and Joe grabbed more beer from the fridge and we all went to sit outside at the table. It was one of those Friday evenings when you sense summer around the corner – sunny evening light, birds chirruping merrily to themselves, the air thick with the smell of a neighbour burning some sort of sausage on a barbecue. All was well. All was excellent. All was… *Oh, fuck.* I spotted Callum through the French windows in the kitchen.

'What's he doing here?' I whispered.

'Who?' they all asked.

'Callum.'

Hamish swung round in his seat to look at him.

'Hamish,' I hissed. 'Can you not? He'll see you.'

'He's my mate. What's wrong with him seeing me?'

'He's not my mate,' I said.

'Who's Callum?' said Joe.

'The one who came home that time a few months ago,' I said.

Joe looked blankly at me.

'You know, who left in the middle of the night?'

He still looked blank.

'You do know. The one who I gave a blow job to and who then got an Uber home because he had golf in the morning.'

Joe threw his head back and laughed. 'Oh, that guy. He's great. I miss that guy.'

'You didn't even meet him.'

'Yeah, but I liked the sound of him.'

'Classic Callum,' added Hamish. 'Such a lad.'

I rolled my eyes. 'Shall I go and say hello?'

'No,' said Lex. 'Stay right here. He can come out to you. Anyway, when's Jasper getting here?'

I looked at my phone. It was 8 p.m. 'Dunno. Depends on traffic, he said.'

I looked into the kitchen again and caught Callum's eye. Shit. I waved lamely. He grinned back and started moving towards the doors. Shit.

'Joe, you are not to say anything embarrassing.'

'Like what?'

But I didn't have time to reply because Callum was already by the table.

'Hello,' he said, bending down to kiss me on the cheek.

'Hi,' I said in an unnaturally high voice. What was that about? Why was I being so awkward? I'd already had his penis in my mouth. 'How are you?'

'Great,' he said, 'all the better for seeing you. And you, mate.' He reached over me to shake Hamish's hand and then kissed Lex. 'Hello, future Mrs Wellington.'

'Oh stop it,' said Lex, smiling at him. Traitor.

'Do you mind if I sit?'

'No. No, go for it,' she said, gesturing at the seat beside her.

'I'm Joe,' said Joe, from across the table, looking at Callum as if my stern, protective father. 'I live with Pols.'

'Oh, right,' said Callum, 'not far from me then. I'm Shepherd's Bush too.'

'Sure,' said Joe, still eyeballing him.

'So what have you been up to?' I asked Callum.

'How's your handicap?' chipped in Joe.

Callum laughed nervously. 'Ha. Well, yes, I haven't been playing much golf recently. I got a new job.'

'Nice one, mate,' said Hamish.

'Oh, congrats,' I added. 'In… I can't remember what you were looking for.'

'Sort of private security really. What they call K&R. Kidnap and ransom.'

'Ooh,' said Lex, sitting forwards. 'That sounds manly and exciting. What does that mean?'

'Mostly that I insure shipping companies and businesses

working abroad. But in security hotspots. Africa, bit of the Middle East, that sort of thing.'

'So you're in insurance?' said Joe, looking unimpressed. 'You're an insurance man.'

I tried to kick him and missed, thwacking my shin on the metal bar underneath the table instead.

'Basically yes,' said Callum, grinning at Joe.

'But what have you been up to?' said Callum, looking at me.

'She's got an incredibly rich and handsome boyfriend,' said Joe.

'Joe!'

'What? You have. Bangs like a soldier of Rome,' he went on.

'JOE!'

'Oh, come on, I can hear you. Those walls are like paper in our flat.'

'Sorry about him,' I said, turning towards Callum.

He looked uncomfortable, I was pleased to note. 'Oh yeah, I remember. From the engagement party. A society playboy, or something?'

I opened my mouth to reply, to start saying that, actually, he wasn't such a playboy as everyone made out. It was starting to annoy me, having to constantly defend Jasper. But Joe interrupted me.

'Who wants another wine?' he said, gesturing at our empty glasses. 'I'll go and get another bottle.'

'I'll come with you,' said Lex.

'No need. I can manage a bottle by myself.'

'No. No, I'll come inside with you,' said Lex again, making a face at Joe. 'And you, Hamish, come and help me open another bottle.'

'Lex, my darling, you of all people don't need help opening a wine bottle.'

'Come inside now,' she hissed at him.

'Oh, right,' said Hamish, getting to his feet. 'Cal, mate, see you in a bit.'

They went inside.

'So yes,' I continued. 'That guy… When I last saw you… He's called Jasper. He's coming in a bit actually. You'll meet him. He's better than people think.'

Callum had a swig from his beer bottle. 'Good, I'm glad,' he said after a moment. 'Would he beat me in a fight?'

I looked at his muscly arms. 'I'm not sure. Maybe, he's quite tall.'

'Oh, tall guys. I hate them.' He grinned at me.

'Ha. Anyway, what about you?'

'Me?'

'How's your love life?'

'Dreadful. The dating scene in London is like a warzone.'

'You seem to quite like warzones.'

'Sure, but they're not much good for romance.'

I laughed again, then looked into the kitchen where Joe and Lex were watching us.

'Do you mind if I just nip to the loo? Desperate to pee,' I said, standing up. 'You didn't need to know that, did you?'

'Hey, listen, we're friends now. And friends share. Come back out and find me though.'

'OK, will do.'

I dodged Lex and Joe and went straight to the loo because I was genuinely desperate to pee. I sat down and felt a bit dizzy. So, that was good. Callum and I were friends. Good friends. Pals. Pals who flirt a bit. But pals all the same.

I stood up and stepped outside the loo to wash my hands. Which is when I heard Willow next door in the bedroom.

'We should have them round for dinner soon, you know. Just us and them.'

'Maybe,' came Bill's voice in reply.

'I think we should. I think it'd be fun. Oh, come on, just because you don't like him.'

'I don't *dislike* him, I just don't want Pols to get hurt.'

I dropped the hand towel.

'You don't know that's going to happen,' she said.

'I'm not so sure. Men like him… Well, we'll see.'

I was torn between wanting to stand and hear them prophesy more about my love life, interrupting them and saying, 'Excuse me, can you let me worry about my own relationship?' and worrying about being caught, hovering outside their bedroom. The fear about hovering won, so I tiptoed back to the kitchen, where Joe and Lex had put on an old Britney song.

'Pols,' shouted Joe. 'Come on, join in.'

I smiled at them and nodded my head towards outside. 'I'm good, I'm going to sit out here for a bit.'

Callum was still there, and smoking. 'Oh perfect, can I have one?' I asked.

'Sure,' he said, tossing the packet on the table. 'Didn't know you smoked?'

'I don't really. Just... every now and then.' I knew I shouldn't, but I felt rocked.

'Help yourself.'

We sat smoking in silence for a few moments while I ran through the conversation in my head. So that was what everyone thought. That he'd get bored soon and that would be that. Not surprising, I supposed. Castle-owning future dukes weren't supposed to end up with girls from Battersea. Even though we'd all been indoctrinated with Disney cartoons to believe it could happen. Fucking *Cinderella*.

'What are you doing this weekend?' said Callum.

'Er, hanging out with my mum mostly, she's not very well at the moment.'

'Oh, I'm sorry. With what?'

I exhaled smoke slowly into the evening air. 'Breast cancer.'

'Oh fuck, sorry again.'

'Yeahhhhh. She's had an operation though, so it's just chemo now.'

'Brutal,' he replied. 'My dad had it. Chemo, I mean.'

'For what?'

'Liver, it was a few years ago.'

'And how is he now?'

'He is no longer with us.'

'Oh, I'm sorry.'

'No. No, don't be sorry. It was a while ago, it's OK.'

Sitting at Bill's garden table, talking about this in the dusk, made me realize Jasper and I had never talked properly about Mum. That he'd never really asked. That any time I'd even mentioned cancer or her treatment had been because I'd raised it first. Bill always asked about her, even Lex probed me about it if she'd run out of wedding chat. But Jasper... not so much. Although I supposed he had his own family problems.

My phone suddenly lit up on the table. It was him.

Do you mind if we meet at mine? The M1's been a nightmare.

I smiled quickly at Callum, then replied.

Course not. What ETA?

Half an hour or so. That OK?

I sent a smiley face emoji back.

'The playboy?' said Callum.

'Yep,' I said. 'But bad luck, he's not coming here. He's been driving all day so I'm going to his.' I'd never been to his house before. In two months of dating, he'd been weird about us ever staying there on the basis that Violet lived there and his parents stayed there when they were in London.

'That's a great tragedy,' he said.

'You guys are animals,' I joked.

'I don't disagree,' he said.

I went back into the kitchen, put my glass in the sink, and scanned the flat for Bill to say goodbye. I found him in the hall chatting to a girl I didn't recognize.

'Pols, this is Emma, one of Willow's workmates. Emma, this is Polly.'

'Emma, hi,' I said, 'so sorry, would love to stay and chat but I've got to run.'

'You're going? Already?' said Bill. 'I haven't even talked to you properly yet. And there's someone I want you to meet in the kitchen. Runs a news website. I thought you should chat to him. See if he needs any new writers?'

'Sorry,' I said coolly back, still raging about the conversation I'd overheard him having with Willow. 'But Jasper's just driven all the way down from Yorkshire so I said I'd go over to his.'

'You all right?'

'Yes, fine,' I said. 'He's just exhausted so I don't think he feels like a party.' I could hear Joe and Lex singing Rita Ora in the background.

'OK, go on then,' Bill said, reaching for a hug. 'But you owe me. Leaving your best friend's birthday to… actually, I don't want to think about what you're leaving to do. Just go.'

I hugged him back briefly and left.

★

Jasper's house was in South Kensington, one of those big London squares with private gardens surrounded by vast white houses with pillars outside. I squinted at my phone. He said forty-three. I hoped his parents weren't there. Or Violet. I couldn't face the Duchess walking in on me while I was on the loo. But I presumed that's why I could stay here for the first time ever, because they were elsewhere.

'It's number forty-three,' I told the driver, as we crawled along, looking at the odd numbers rising.

I got out and he drove off just as Jasper arrived in his Range Rover.

'How was the drive?' I asked, as he climbed out the car.

'Bloody awful, but I'm here now,' he said, kissing me.

'Hi,' I said, smiling at him when he pulled his head back.

'Hello, madam,' he said, his face still close to mine. 'How many bottles?'

'Not that many.'

''Course not. Let's go inside and I'll try and catch up.'

He fumbled in his jeans for his keys, then opened the door. The hall was bigger than my entire flat alone. White marble floor, black and white photographs, portraits of the family on the walls. And a lamp on a side table, switched on.

'You're sure your parents aren't here?' I checked.

'I just left them in Yorkshire, so unless they've magically teleported here then fairly sure, yes.'

'And your sister…'

'Is also at home in Yorkshire.'

'Can I wear my shoes?'

Jasper laughed. 'Yes, come on. Get inside.' I stepped onto the marble and he closed the door behind me. It even smelt expensive. Of silver polish and leather furniture.

I followed him along the marble and down a flight of stairs into the kitchen. It looked like the sort of kitchen you see in period dramas. Copper pans hanging along one stretch of wall above the oven. A huge fireplace. A long wooden table which would seat at least twenty footmen and twenty scullery maids.

Jasper swung open one of the cupboards to reveal a gigantic fridge.

'Glass of white?'

'Sure,' I said.

He closed the fridge again and opened another cupboard to retrieve two glasses.

'Have you ever actually lived here?' I said, gazing round at the room. I was in awe. It was one of those superhouses you read about in the *Evening Standard*. The sort of house that cost thirty million pounds and had seven floors, a cinema room, three basements, a nuclear bunker and a pool.

'London? No, not really. I stay here every now and then but I try to avoid it if anyone else is around,' he said.

'How many bedrooms are there?'

'I'm not honestly sure,' he said. 'Eight? Nine?'

'But it's too small for you to be here with another member of your family?' It felt odd that he wanted to avoid them given the size of this place. Unless, I suddenly thought... unless he didn't want them to bump into me? I thought back to the conversation I'd overheard earlier that night and felt a flutter of doubt knock inside my ribcage. Maybe Bill was right. Maybe it was just a matter of time.

'You have met my family,' he said, handing me a glass.

'Mmm.' Or was I just being paranoid?

'How was the party?' he asked.

'All right. Chatted to a few old friends. Left Joe singing

in the kitchen. You know, your average Friday night. How are you?'

'I am...' He paused as if to think while putting the bottle back in the fridge. 'I'm good. I missed you this week.'

It was the first time he'd said he missed me.

'Really?' I said, grinning at him. Pathetic, really, how quickly and easily this one line made my worries evaporate.

'Really,' Jasper said. He put his glass down on the counter and moved towards me, putting his hands around my face.

'I missed you too,' I said. And then I blushed.

'And I missed fucking you,' he said, putting his arms around me and pulling me into him.

'Did you now?'

He didn't reply. He just kissed me and ran a hand through my hair, holding the back of my head. 'Shall we go upstairs?'

'To one of your five hundred bedrooms?'

'Don't be a smart-arse.'

'All right, all right, but what about the wine?'

'The clever thing about wine glasses is that they're mobile,' he said.

There was a lift outside the kitchen. An actual lift with one of those metal grilles you have to close before it will move. Jasper hit the button for the fourth floor and we clanked slowly upwards, him pressing me against the wall, wine glass in one hand, wine bottle in the other. Then the lift jolted to a stop.

'Out you get,' he said, opening up the metal gates again. 'Second door on the right.'

His bedroom was at the front of the house, overlooking

the square. It had a four-poster bed on one side, facing an old wooden desk. He put the bottle and his glass down on the desk and drew the curtains. Various sporting photographs lined the walls.

'Cute. Baby Jasper,' I said, leaning in to look at them.

'A dangerous lunatic, armed with a cricket ball,' Jasper said, coming up behind me and moving my hair to one side so he could kiss my neck.

I tried to move around but he wouldn't let me. 'Stay there,' he whispered in my ear.

He put his hands underneath my t-shirt and ran them up my stomach, unhooking my bra and pulling my shirt off over my head. I reached my hands up behind me for his head.

'Put them down,' he said. 'Flat. On the desk.'

So I did. And then he ran his hands back down my body, to my flies, and undid them. Then he peeled my jeans and my knickers down my legs, so they were around my ankles. 'Step out of them,' he said, so I tried to do this in a faintly sexy manner instead of trampling all over the floor like a baby elephant. Quite hard to pull off skinny jeans seductively.

And there I was, naked, still facing away from him, while his hands ran up the outside of my legs again, over my hips, before he turned me around to face him. 'Lie on the bed,' he instructed.

'Can we turn the lights down a bit so it's less...'

'Lie on the bed,' he repeated. 'On your back.' He walked to the door, closed it and dimmed the lights. Then he walked towards the bed and lit a candle on his bedside table. 'Put your arms above your head and leave them there,' he said, pulling off his own shirt.

He knelt over me and started kissing my wrists, crossed over above my head. And down my left forearm, then my right forearm, then he kissed down my left bicep. Then my right bicep. I wondered for a moment if I'd put deodorant on. I thought so. The sex scene in *The Horse Whisperer* where Robert Redford licked Kristin Scott Thomas' underarm hair popped into my head. I'd watched the film as a teenager and worried for several years afterwards that being 'good' at sex meant licking underarm hair. But then I'd realized Kristin Scott Thomas lived in France for a long time and decided that explained it.

Jasper continued working down my body with his mouth, biting my nipples softly, kissing down in a line towards my hips. I sighed with pleasure at the thought of his tongue pushing its way inside me and put my hands down to his head to run them through his hair.

'Leave your hands above your head,' he said, 'otherwise I will tie them up.'

'All right, Christian Grey,' I said. Then he stopped and stood up.

I looked at him. 'What?'

He picked up the candle, knelt above me and tipped it so wax dripped down from the hollow between my breasts to my stomach. The wax drops burned for a second and then hardened.

'Do you like that?' he said.

'Yes...' I said, although I wasn't entirely convinced. Having hot wax dripped on me from a Jo Malone candle was about as Marquis de Sade as my sex life had ever been. But I was worried about the sheets. Wax was murder to wash out.

He tipped the candle again so it continued to drip towards my hips. I was quite nervous about this too. Hot wax on your clitoris is going to hurt, surely? And it was perfumed wax. And I was always mindful of the warning about perfumed bath oils and bubbles giving you thrush. Perfumed candle wax might have the same effect? But then Jasper stopped and put the candle back on the bedside table, before pulling off his jeans and boxer shorts and pushing his cock into me.

I exhaled and wrapped my arms around his back as he pushed into me again and again. Hard. And deep. So deep I felt like he might dislodge a kidney. But then he stopped again and pulled out, knelt between my legs, licked his finger and started softly circling my clitoris with it. My hips started rolling, and he pushed his finger inside me.

'No. No, do what you were doing, back, up,' I said between breaths. He started rubbing my clitoris again. Until the moment that I was about to explode when he moved his hand and pushed his cock inside me again. I came, clenching around him, and then he roared in my ear as he came too and we lay there, panting, damp from sweat.

'Jesus,' he said, breathing into my ear. 'I've been thinking about that all week.'

'Me too.'

'You liked it?' he said, picking his head up and looking at me. 'The wax?'

'Yep,' I said. 'Totally.' Although, I thought in my head, dripping hot wax over one another was definitely a Saturday evening activity and not a Tuesday night thing. I always get nervous with these conversations about what one is into versus what one is absolutely not into. Like when a man asks 'What's your fantasy?' and you want to say 'A film on the sofa and a grab bag of Maltesers,' but you have to think up some implausible position and say you like dressing up as a naughty optician because that's what you think they want to hear.

'Can I have a shower?' I said, as he rolled off me, looking down at the hardened wax on my stomach.

★

I left Jasper's the next morning and went home, ducking into Barbara's first to buy some milk.

'How is that boyfriend of yours, hmm?' she said.

'Good, thanks,' I said, absent-mindedly, while I was checking the dates on the semi-skimmed milk. Barbara always lined up the milk that was about to go off at the front, burying the fresh stuff at the back. I reached for the back of the shelf.

'And how is the sex?'

I cast a glance around the shop to make sure an unsuspecting customer who wanted a four-pack of loo roll wasn't overhearing.

'Er, also good, thanks.' I put the milk on the counter.

'You need a man, Polly, a real man. This is good.' She ignored the milk in front of her.

'Mmm.'

'When is his birthday?'

'End of November.' I'd been waiting for this question.

She nodded her head as if in approval. 'Adventurous.' She still hadn't picked up the milk. 'Although they can sometimes be impatient. Is he impatient, Polly?'

I reflected on the wax the night before.

'No, I don't think impatient exactly. I'm quite impatient actually,' I said, looking at the milk on the counter.

'Sagittarius and a Capricorn,' she said, finally picking it up. 'Hmm. That combination is unusual. Experimental.' She raised her eyebrows at me.

Why did I have to suffer this much for milk?

'Very passionate, Sagittarians,' she went on, before looking at the till. 'One pound twenty, please.'

'Thanks, Barbara, see you later,' I said, handing over the coins and grabbing the milk. 'Don't worry about a bag.'

'Keep me posted,' she shouted as the door jangled behind me.

12

PEREGRINE SWIRLED ROUND IN his chair and looked at me intently. Please, please, please don't ask me about my love life, I thought, as I sat down in front of his desk.

'Polly, good morning,' he said.

'Morning,' I said, cradling my coffee in my lap as if it was an amulet to ward off evil.

'Now,' Peregrine started, 'what I want to talk to you about is quite delicate.'

Oh God.

'But I think you're just the woman for the job.'

'Rrrright…' I said.

'I have discovered that there's an Italian woman in London who's organizing extraordinary parties.'

'What do you mean "extraordinary"?'

'Well,' Peregrine paused, 'I think, to be perfectly honest, the only way I can describe them is an orgy.'

I stared at him.

'Yes,' he went on, 'apparently her guest list is sensational. Cabinet ministers, high court judges, bankers, lawyers, former mayors of London, you name it. All beating one another with leather whips.'

'How do you know?'

'What?'

'I mean, how did you find out about these parties?'

'Oh, never mind that,' said Peregrine, flapping in the air with his hands. 'But listen, what I want you to do is go along to one, and then write about it. They take place at a private house in Mayfair every month... Apparently,' he added quickly.

'How am I going to get in though, if the guest list is so strict? Presumably there's a no-journalists policy. *Omertà* and all that?'

'Don't worry. It's run by this Italian called Ana, who I have already spoken to. She doesn't mind *Posh!* writing about it, it's the papers she wants to keep out.'

'OKKKK,' I ventured slowly. 'So I'm going to go to one of these parties and then... just write it up?'

'Yes, exactly,' he replied. 'Lots of colour, lots of detail, no names. Just hints perhaps. An MP here, a countess there. It'll practically write itself this piece, Polly, really colourful stuff. "The most exclusive party in the world", we'll call it.'

'Fine,' I said, standing up, 'will you send me the woman's email address?'

'What?' He'd already turned back to his computer on his desk.

'The woman who organizes these parties?'

'Oh, Ana. Yes, of course.'

I walked back to my desk and sat down. Could I convince

myself that going to some big posh house for a sex party was an intrepid bit of investigative reporting? The sort of thing that proper, real journalists get awards for? I wasn't sure.

'And where's Lala?' Peregrine said, sticking his head through his door again.

I shrugged.

'Doctor's,' said Enid. 'Women's troubles apparently.'

He shuddered. 'Don't be revolting.' Then he went back into his office and closed the door.

★

Later that evening, at Mum's flat, I picked up the shaver and looked at her tufty scalp. After two chemo sessions, we'd decided that I would shave her head to get rid of the fuzzy bits that were making her look like a barn owl chick. Sidney had lent us his electric shaver because I didn't trust myself with a razor.

'Come on, Mums, let's do this. You're going to look like a rock 'n' roll star,' I said, smiling encouragingly at her.

She grimaced. 'More like that man who used to present *The Crystal Maze*. What was he called?'

'Richard O'Brien. In which case, you'd need a long velvet frock coat and to be off your head on drugs.'

'I've probably got one of those in my cupboard and I wouldn't mind being off my head on drugs.'

'Let's not worry about Richard O'Brien for now,' I said. 'Are you comfortable?'

'Yes,' she replied.

'OK. Here goes.'

I flicked the shaver on, then realized I didn't know where to start. From the forehead back across the head and down towards the neck or vice versa? The shaver hovered above Mum's head. I gently put it down right on the top of it and slowly moved it backwards.

Mum stayed quiet.

'Is that all right?' I asked, as strands of hair started floating down on the towel, catching the evening light on their way. Bertie lay by the chair, his head resting on one of Mum's feet.

'Yes,' she said, in a small voice.

I carried on slowly, dragging the shaver down the back of her head, leaving a line of bright white scalp behind it.

'You still all right?'

'Yes I think so, it sort of tickles. What does it look like?'

'Er, great. Amazing. Much better. Everyone's going to want one of these by the time I've finished.' Making jokes seemed to be the only way I could handle this scenario. I wasn't trying to be insensitive, I just wasn't sure how I'd get through it otherwise.

'Do you think Sidney will mind it?'

'"Course he won't. He'll love it.' I wasn't convinced about this but we could worry about that later.

Mum had gone through one of her drawers and pulled out various old, creased silk scarves. Then she'd ironed them. A pile of scarves now sat on the kitchen table, neatly folded.

More hair floated down on to the towel, then Mum turned

and looked up at me, putting a hand up to her head to feel it. 'It's quite cold,' she said.

'That's what the scarves are for. You're going to channel the Queen.'

'She's not bald.'

'Well, I know,' I said, leaning forward to shave a tuft behind her left ear. 'But think how elegant she looks wearing those Hermès headscarves.'

I pulled the electric cord around the chair and moved to stand in front of her. 'Close your eyes, I need to do the front. Otherwise you'll end up looking like one of those monks.'

Mum closed her eyes, which were also now bald and unprotected, her eyelashes and eyebrows having fallen out a few days earlier. They'd grow back, the internet said. Possibly thinner than before. But they would grow back.

She'd lost weight too, I noticed, looking down at her legs. Her hands were clasped tightly between them and her jeans were loose. Her fridge was even emptier than usual. A pint of milk, a minute piece of Parmesan and an old, hardened lemon were its only occupants. I'd do a shop later.

'Don't worry, darling. I'm going to be fine,' said Mum, her eyes still shut, as if reading my mind.

'I know,' I said. 'I was just thinking about… work.' I wanted to distract her. And me.

'Why, what's up?'

I thought back to the scene in the office earlier that afternoon. 'Peregrine has got this mad new idea for a story. He wants me to go to a party.'

'What's wrong with that?'

'It's a sex party.'

'A *whattie*?' she asked, twisting her head to face me.

'Hold still and shut your eyes,' I said. 'Well, it's more of an orgy really. I think. I'm not sure.'

'What do you mean?' Mum frowned at me.

'Turn your head towards the fireplace,' I said. 'Basically, he's met some Italian woman who throws these risqué parties in a big house in Mayfair somewhere. Where you go. And you dress up. And then, well, God knows what happens.'

'Sex? Does sex happen at these parties?' said Mum.

'I think possibly yes. Stay still.'

'Golly! And you've got to go to one of these parties?'

'Peregrine wants me to, yes.'

'Golly! Will you have to have sex?'

'No. No, I'm not going to,' I said. 'I'm just going to go and sort of watch, I suppose. Turn your head the other way. I'm nearly done.'

She turned her head. 'Darling, you will be careful, won't you? All sorts of weirdos might be there.'

'I'm sure they will be.'

'Can you take Jasper?'

I hadn't mentioned it to Jasper. 'Er, maybe. Not sure it's his thing.'

'What does one wear to one of these parties? A pretty dress?'

'No, I don't think it's dress territory. I think we're talking leather. Some kind of leather outfit.'

'Golly!' She paused while the whirring of the electric

shaver continued. 'I've got that old leather jacket of your dad's somewhere if you like?'

I laughed. 'Thanks, Mum. But I'm not sure Eighties Hell's Angel is quite the look at these parties.'

'Well, it's there if you want it.'

'OK,' I said, brushing hair from her shoulders and turning the shaver off. 'Now, stand up, have a look in the mirror.'

She stood and looked above the fireplace into the mirror. 'Oh.' She clutched both hands to her mouth, and then lifted them to her head. 'It's sort of knobbly, isn't it?'

'Er, a bit yeah.' It made me tear up to see Mum looking at herself in the mirror. She looked even more vulnerable, as if shaving her head had made her regress sixty years and she was a newborn baby again. I blinked to try to stop myself from crying. Get a grip, I told myself, you're not the one who's ill.

'It looks weird. Don't you think I look weird?' She looked at me with her bald eyes.

'No,' I said firmly. 'I think you look great. Much better. Like a rock star. Like you're not going to let this get you down. Shall we try a headscarf?'

She nodded and retrieved one from the kitchen table. A red and yellow number with horses cantering across it. She folded it into a large triangle and put it over her head, tying it under her chin. Then she frowned at herself in the mirror.

'It doesn't look much like the Queen,' she said dubiously.

'No,' I agreed. 'Hang on, let's try it another way.' I untied the knot and moved behind her, putting the scarf back on and tying it with a knot at the back, in the manner of Steve Tyler.

'There,' I said. 'Better.'

Mum frowned again. 'Really?'

'Really. Honestly. Sidney's going to love it.'

'You don't think it says tragic cancer patient?'

'Nope,' I shook my head. 'Because you're not tragic and the chemo's getting rid of all that cancer. Shall we have a cup of tea and a biscuit?'

She nodded at me in the mirror.

*

I'd told Bill I'd go shopping with him later that week for a birthday present for Willow. It was her thirtieth, so he'd decided it had to be something 'significant', which I thought sounded ominous. Did 'significant' mean a diamond?

We had lunch first because Bill said he couldn't possibly go shopping on an empty stomach, so I met him around Old Street.

'You should just get a puppy,' I said, through a mouthful of ham sandwich. 'Good practice for when you guys have children.'

'Oh, right. Do small children pee and shit all over the floor too?'

'Yours probably will.'

'I'm not mature enough for children.Last night I got home at eleven and watched *Toy Story* with a beer and a pizza.'

'All right. If it's not a puppy then what do you want to get her?'

'I don't know. That's why you're here.'

'Jewellery? That's the obvious thing.'

'Like a ring?'

'No! Not a ring. That's too suggestive.'

'Of what?'

'What do you think?' Why are men so dense, is what I was thinking.

'A necklace?' he suggested.

'Mmm, maybe. How much do you want to spend?'

'Dunno. Three, four hundred quid maybe?'

'Blimey, William!'

'What?'

'Well, that's pretty serious. Puppies are actually cheaper than that.' I put down my sandwich. 'Or maybe they're about the same, actually.'

'I think we're getting stuck on this puppy thing, Pols. What about a bag? Or a pair of shoes? What are those ones with red soles?'

'Louboutins, and no. She's your girlfriend not your mistress. I think jewellery is probably better.'

'But not a ring?'

'No, not a ring.'

'Because she'll think I want to marry her?'

'Yes. Unless you do want to marry her?'

'What? Already? Come on, be sensible.'

'I dunno, she was talking about you guys and children the other day.'

'When?'

I burst out laughing. 'Lol, your face.'

'When were you guys discussing that?'

'At Mum's the other day. I mean, I don't think she meant tomorrow but she definitely meant at some point.'

Bill puffed out his cheeks. 'God, women! How's your mum, by the way?'

'All right. Well, a bit tired actually.'

'How many more chemo sessions has she got?'

'Just one. But her hair's all gone now. And she's not feeling great so not really eating. I just…' I trailed off. 'But she's got Sidney, which is something.'

'I liked him,' Bill said, dusting crumbs off his lap.

'Yeah, he's sweet, isn't he? A nice man, I think. I just worry that…'

'What?'

'Well, it's not worry as such. I just feel sad that in one sense she's found someone and seems happier than she has in years. But on the other she's…'

'Ill?'

'Yeah.' I clenched my jaw so I didn't cry.

'Hey.' Bill reached for my hand across the table. 'She's going to be fine.'

I nodded. 'Yup, she's got to be, right?' It felt more like I was reassuring myself though.

''Course.' He took his hand back. 'And I hope Jasper's looking after you?'

My mind flicked back to Callum asking about Mum instead of Jasper, but the last thing I wanted to do was admit as much to Bill. 'It looked like it physically pained you to ask that,' I said, narrowing my eyes at him.

He dropped his baguette and held his hands up in the air as if surrendering. 'I'm not saying anything. So long as you're happy, I'm happy.'

'Listen,' I started. I'd been worrying about the conversation I'd overheard between him and Willow at his party. I hadn't said anything because I hadn't seen Bill since. And because I would rather cut off my left foot than ever have any sort of awkward conversation with him. But I hated the idea that people were discussing my relationship behind my back. Or, more specifically, I hated the idea that Bill was discussing me behind my back.

'Listen,' I said again, 'I heard you and Willow.'

He looked confused. 'What do you mean? In bed?'

'No, gross! Stop it. I heard you guys talking about me and Jasper.'

He still looked blank.

'At your party. In your room. I wasn't eavesdropping. Well, I was. But I went to the loo and then I heard you guys. And I know what everyone thinks. I know it's wildly implausible that this will have a happy ending. I know he's been a jerk in the past, but he hasn't been a jerk to me.'

He held his hands up again. 'Sorry that you heard. Or sorry that we were discussing it is what I should say. Guilty.'

'It's all right,' I said, feeling relief at finally having talked to him about it.

'It's only that I don't want you to get hurt. And—'

'Me neither,' I said, interrupting. 'But so far it's been… fun. Am I going to end up with him? God knows. But I just want people to give him a break.'

'OK,' he said. 'I still don't think he's good enough. But OK.'

'Dude, I love you, but it's like having a watchful big brother, armed with a bit of lead piping, waiting to kick his head in.'

'OK,' he replied, 'I promise. I'll play nice.'

'Good.'

'By the way,' he went on, 'did something happen between you and Callum?'

I felt instantly guilty. 'Why?' I said slowly.

His eyes widened. 'Oh, so it did!'

'Ages ago,' I said, trying to play it down. 'How come?'

'Something Lex said at my party, after you'd left.'

'Ah, my secret's safe with Lex then.'

'Why's it a secret?'

'I was joking. It's not. It was just back in January. After your dinner. And it really wasn't a big deal. I didn't sleep with him.'

Bill screwed up his eyes and shook his head. 'I don't want to think about you and Callum. Bad enough that I have to hear about Lord Voldemort.'

'Jasper,' I said. 'And why is it bad?'

'What?'

'Thinking about me with Callum?'

'It's not Callum. It's just… It's you, Pols. It just feels… weird, you kissing my mate.'

'Well, I don't think it's going to happen again so don't worry.'

'All right,' he replied, before having a swig from his Coke can. 'A very confessional lunch this has been, hasn't it? How's work, by the way?'

I sighed, thinking about Peregrine's orgy story. 'All right. But I need to start looking for something else, I think. *Posh!* has been great but I feel like… I dunno… I feel like I'm in a bit of a rut, I suppose. And I don't know how to get out of it. I'm running out of adjectives for dogs.'

Bill laughed. 'I really want you to meet my friend Luke, the one I mentioned at my party? He's just launched a sort of news website.'

'How d'you know him?'

'Google.'

'And what do you mean "sort of news"?'

'It's called Nice News,' said Bill, brushing crumbs off his legs. 'Memes about kittens and puppies, admittedly, but they also interview sort of unsung heroes, I think. People working for NGOs in Africa. Or Syria or… wherever. I can intro you over email if you like? He's just raised a load of funding from an American firm.'

'Amazing,' I replied. 'Yeah, if you wouldn't mind, I'd love to at least speak to him.'

''Course. Done.'

'Thanks, love. How's your work anyway?'

'Good,' he said, grinning. 'The NHS has just confirmed they can launch it in October so I've got to hire, like, ten more people to work on it. All on track. I mean, it's going to be a hectic few months, but I'm loving it.'

I shook my head and smiled at him. 'A modern Aneurin Bevan.'

Bill frowned. 'Who was he?'

'Labour politician, you nerd. Founded the NHS.'

'All right, all right. Nerd yourself. But come on, let's go shopping. Can't sit around all day enjoying ourselves.'

We spent a fruitless hour traipsing around the shops, looking at necklaces in Links. Everything I liked, Bill would say 'wasn't Willow'. Everything he liked was the sort of necklace a middle-aged bra saleswoman in John Lewis might wear.

'Thanks, you've been a fat lot of good,' he said, hugging me when I said I had to go back to the office.

'You're welcome. When's her birthday anyway?'

'Next weekend. We're going away to Wiltshire. Posh hotel booked.'

'OK, you'll find something. A necklace, I reckon. But not some hideous gold number. Just think, would my own mother wear this? And if the answer is yes then don't buy it.'

He saluted me. 'Roger that.'

★

Friday was fairly typical at the *Posh!* office in that nobody was there. Not even Enid. Just me, a strong Americano and my to-do list. At the top of which I had written, 'Speak to Ana', the Italian lady, about this sex party. She'd been travelling all week but had said she would be available to discuss it today, so I sent her a quick email to check.

Morning, Ana. I'm around whenever this morning to chat so let me know when's good and I'll give you a bell.

Then I had to ring Mum. 'Morning,' I trilled when she picked up. But it wasn't Mum, it was Sidney.

'Oh, Sidney! Morning. How are you?'

'I'm very well, thank you. But… um… your mother is still in bed.'

I looked at the time on my computer. It was 10.45.

'We didn't have a terribly good night,' he explained. 'She was sick.'

'Oh God, is she all right?' I felt my heart speed up.

'She's asleep again now, but shall I let you know when she wakes up?'

'Could you? This is all right, isn't it? I mean, it's expected. The chemo does this? I read the chemo might do this.' I was gabbling.

'Yes,' said Sidney firmly. 'It accumulates so she's feeling pretty rotten now but it'll pass.'

'OK. I'm in the office all day so ring whenever.'

'Absolutely. And don't worry, I'm staying here to keep an eye on her. We're going to have a quiet day and watch something on the Netflix.'

'You're amazing. Honestly. I'm so grateful.'

Sidney laughed nervously. 'Righto.'

'Bye, and thank you. Again.'

I hung up. Fuck. Fuck, fuck, fuck. I couldn't google 'breast cancer' for the 2,374th time. And then the door slammed open and Lala appeared.

'Morning,' she said glumly.

Hi,' I said. 'You all right?'

'Suicidal. My friend Morwenna got engaged last night.'

'And that's… sad news?'

'Yes! Why is everyone married and I'm not?' she said, signing into her computer and tapping the keyboard so hard I thought she might do herself a finger injury.

'I'm not married.'

'Yeah, but you've got a boyfriend.'

Having just spoken to Sidney I wasn't much in the mood to have a long discussion about my love life with Lala so I stayed quiet.

'I'm going to have a fag,' she said, having been in the office for less than three minutes. 'Want anything?'

'No. No, I'm good, thanks.'

I turned back to my computer screen and decided I wouldn't google breast cancer because I felt like I'd read the whole internet on the topic and it was only ever depressing statistics. Instead, I typed 'Ana Aubin' into Google. Nothing came up. Not a website, not a link, not a picture of her. I checked her email again. That was definitely how you spelled her name.

With perfect timing, my phone rang and an Italian voice at the other end said, 'Hello, ees that Polly?'

'Yep. Ana?'

'Yes.'

'Morning, how are you?'

'I am very well, thank you. And you?'

'Great, thanks. I was just trying to do some… research on your parties.'

'You won't find anything online. You need to come to one of my parties instead, to see, to understand.'

She had a soft, seductive accent. I felt like I was talking to a Bond girl.

'Yes, that's why I wanted to speak. Peregrine is very keen that I come to one.'

'Yes, of course, you must. Are you single, Polly?'

'Er… no, for once in my life I'm not actually. But that's OK. I can come along and just… watch… right? For the article?'

'Of course you can. And anyway they are all very civilized to begin with, my soirées. It's only later that they get a bit more party.'

'A bit more party?'

'Yes. More sexy, you know.' She cackled down the phone.

'Right, sure. OK. So, when is your next party?'

The next party, said Ana, was in two weeks' time at a private house just off Mount Street. The dress code was 'noir'.

'Like the coffee?' I joked.

'Bring a friend if you like?' she said, ignoring the joke. 'Maybe bring your boyfriend?'

'Thanks. I'm not sure it's his kind of thing. Maybe another girl?'

'Of course,' said Ana, smoothly. 'There will be around ninety people.'

'La,' I said, minutes later when she sidled back into the office and sat down at her desk with a sigh, wafting about with the air of someone who'd just been committed to Death Row. 'Do you want to come to a party with me in a couple of weeks?'

'Whose party?'

'This one that Peregrine wants me to go to. The sex party.'

'When is it?'

'Two Fridays' time.'

She sighed heavily. 'I mean I'd rather kill myself, but maybe I should. I might get a husband there.'

'Exactly. That's the spirit. OK, I'm going to tell Ana there will be two of us. Fun. It'll be a laugh if nothing else.'

'We'll see,' said Lala.

*

Later that day, Lex emailed me about her hen. Sal had booked a cottage on the Norfolk coast for ten of us. But there were certain duties I still had to do. The Ocado delivery for the weekend was one of them. Sorting out a suitable 'activity' for the Saturday was another. As was booking a pub for lunch. But I didn't mind any of those, so long as I didn't have to buy any penis crap. Veiny penis straws, penis feather boas, penis necklaces and so on. A bit funny for the first hen you ever went to. Less funny by the seventeenth hen party. Anyway, Lex had instructed me that her mother was absolutely not to be invited.

I love her to death but she'll just get pissed and be embarrassing.

I emailed her back.

So will you.

Another email notification popped up from Lex.

Yeah, but it's my hen. I'm allowed.

I called Mum again to check how she was. She picked up this time.

'Mum, hi, you all right?'

'Hi, darling,' she said sounding weak. 'I'm fine. I'm on the sofa with Bertie and a cup of tea.'

'I'm so sorry. Did you have a horrible night?'

'It wasn't great, but they did say I'd feel a bit wiped out.'

'I'm sorry. Again. But one more to go. And then that's it. Finished. Done.'

'Exactly,' she said. 'Now, darling, I'm just at a good bit of this Agatha Christie, so let's speak tomorrow.'

I took it as a good sign that she felt cheery enough to watch her murder programmes.

★

Legs, as usual, came to my rescue with an outfit for the sex party by calling in a latex catsuit from a company called Bondinage in Hackney.

'You need talcum powder to get into eet, which is een

there, and there's a bottle of latex polish een there too,' she said, handing me a bag in the office that week. 'You need to buff yourself afterwards.'

'Great, you're the best, thank you,' I said. 'Shall I go and try it on in the loo?'

'*Oui*. Go and check eet fits.'

Have you ever tried to get into a latex catsuit? It requires the flexibility of a gymnast and the nimble fingers of a harpist. First, take all your clothes off. All of them. Including underwear because you don't want any lines underneath the catsuit. Next, coat your feet and calves with talcum powder, then step into the rubbery thing. Inch the latex up your legs with the pads of your fingers, not your nails, in case you tear it. Apply more talcum powder to your thighs and heave the catsuit over them. There, halfway in, well done. Rub some more talcum powder over your stomach, your tits, your shoulders and arms. Especially your arms. Then put one arm in, and another, before pulling the catsuit over your shoulders and doing up the zip at the front.

I say the front, but the navy catsuit Legs had found me had a zip that not only ran down the front, it went underneath my actual vagina and up my backside to the top of my bum. 'Easy access,' she said, when I stepped out of the bathroom to show her, leaving the loo cubicle looking like a Mexican drugs factory. 'You look great though, eet suits you. Pulls in here,' she said, her fingers around my waist, 'and makes you look all chesty. Perfect. You will 'ave to fight all those perverts off.'

13

ON FRIDAY EVENING, WHEN I arrived at the address Ana had sent over, there was no sign of Lala. She'd said she was already here but the only person I could see when I squinted along the dark street was an old man with a cane walking a large, fat spaniel. He definitely didn't look as if he was on his way to a sex party. Although animals do it for some people, don't they? I shivered in my catsuit.

'Evening,' I said, as he walked past me.

He nodded back.

'Boo,' said a voice in my ear.

It was Lala, but no wonder I hadn't seen her. She was wearing an extraordinary cloak. A hood pulled up over her head, folds of it billowing around her legs.

'Nice cape!'

'I know it's good, isn't it?' she said. 'I got it from Versace so I can't get anything on it.'

'No semen stains?'

'No, ideally not,' she laughed. 'Come on, let's go in, I'm freezing.'

As we walked into a marble hall lit with dozens of flickering candles, two men in suits offered to take our coats. They looked like David Gandy's twin brothers, with dark, slicked-back hair.

'Sure,' said Lala, slipping off her Little Red Riding Hood and immediately revealing the reason she had been so cold outside. Underneath, she was basically naked. Black lace bra, black lace knickers, suspenders running down from her thigh, black stilettos.

'You forgot your dress?' I said, raising my eyebrows.

'I saw *Eyes Wide Shut*, Pols,' she said, handing David Gandy 1 her cloak. 'This is the sort of thing you're supposed to wear.'

'Rrrrrright,' I said. 'Do you feel awkward? Being in your knickers at a party?'

She shrugged. 'Not really. It's like wearing a bikini to the beach. And anyway, I had a few shots of vodka before leaving home.'

She looked phenomenal. Blonde hair piled up on her head, thick winged eyeliner, a body as taut as a teenager's, which came pretty exclusively from a diet of black coffee, cigarettes and the odd packet of Jelly Babies.

'Fucking hell, Pols, that looks wild!' she said, her eyes widening at the catsuit as I handed my coat to David Gandy 2.

'In a… good way?'

'In a great way. I love it. Is it comfortable?'

'Nope, I'm either too cold or too hot and it took me half an hour to get into,' I said. 'So I quite need a drink.'

'Everyone is in the drawing room at present,' said one of the Gandys, indicating his head along the corridor. I could hear a general burble of noise.

'Here goes, La,' I said nervously, as we walked towards it.

I'm bad at guessing numbers. Like when someone tells you
there were 53,000 people at a gig and I'm like 'Oh, it looked
like a few hundred to me.' But I reckon inside this room were
a few dozen people. And Lala was right. Most were in their
underwear.

'Thank you so much,' she said, taking a champagne flute
from a waiter and passing it to me. Then she took another
one for herself.

'Can we go and stand in the corner and check everyone
out,' I said quietly to her.

'We don't need to hide, Pols.'

'No, but I just mean I don't go out in latex much and I
quite want to stand with my bum to the wall somewhere.'

'Your bottom looks delicious,' she said. 'But sure, let's go
hang over there and drink these. Then I might need to go
have a fag outside.'

'OK.'

We walked across the room, me, self-consciously holding
my stomach in; Lala as if parading the catwalk in a Victoria's
Secret show.

It looked like a rough balance of men and women. But, I
quickly realized, it was easier for women to dress up in fetish
kit than the guys. I glanced at a blonde in a cream camisole
and pair of French knickers, and another woman who was
wearing a pair of slinky pink pyjama trousers but nothing
up top apart from a couple of silver nipple tassels. Standing
on the edge of the room, I felt like a spectator at the circus.

The men looked less at ease. One, a short chap, was wearing a pair of leather trousers and a gimp mask. Another was wearing leather lederhosen and a military cap. A tall, dark man standing with his back to us was wearing a kilt, a pair of leather ankle boots and that was it. It was all very different to a Friday night in the pub. Could there really be cabinet ministers and judges underneath those masks?

'Fag?' said Lala.

'No, but I'll come stand with you, I'm not sure loitering on your own is a good idea in here.'

Outside, on a terrace, there were several heaters. They'd obviously planned ahead for the guests that evening who wouldn't be bothering with clothes.

'I'd better not sit directly under one, La, I might melt,' I said.

'When does this all go on till then?'

'Around six in the morning, Ana said in her email.'

'Is she here?'

'She said she would be somewhere. We should go and have a look when we're back inside.'

'Do you think we can snoop around the house?'

'Yes, definitely. Let's get another drink and go for a wander.'

'Are you going to… do anything?'

'No! La, this is work. Plus, I feel like "doing anything" at a fetish party would probably count as cheating.'

She smiled. 'How is he?'

'Fine, good. Down this weekend.'

'What's it been now?' she said, exhaling smoke into the air.

'What's what been?'

'You and Jaz.'

'Erm, three months or so.'

'Not bad for him.'

'Can we not?'

'What?'

'Talk about it right now.'

'Why?'

'I just always feel a bit awkward with you, talking about it, I mean. Especially dressed like two extras from a porn film.'

'Don't feel awkward, you muppet. It's fine. Weird at first, now fine. You just have to make me godmother to your firstborn. That's all I ask.'

'Fine. Done. Come on, let's go inside.'

It was the smell as we climbed the stairs that hit me at first. The hot smell of bodies, of sex, of rubber. And the noise, the odd thwack and the panting and the sound of doors closing and opening. It was dim, with the light from various candles flickering off the walls.

There were more David Gandys upstairs too, standing at strategic intervals along the corridor. The house was enormous. Bigger than Jasper's, if such a thing were possible.

'Don't leave me,' I whispered at Lala's back as she walked ahead of me and up another flight of stairs.

At the top of that was a big, open-plan room which spanned the entire floor, darkly lit with red velvet curtains pulled across the windows. And more candles. Also, it was filled with what looked like the kind of apparatus that was used in Fifties gymnasiums. Pommel horses, springboards, that sort of thing.

It definitely wasn't a gym lesson though. As Peregrine had implied, it was an orgy. With various figures writhing away. The room was surrounded by benches, so Lala and I took another champagne glass each from a side table and sat down on one of them.

'Are we allowed to just watch?' I said.

'I'm pretty sure it's encouraged,' she said, her eyes fixed on a table in front of us on which a woman lay on her back, legs open, a man in a pair of leather shorts licking up her thigh. Could that be an MP? Maybe they were both MPs? She was making an awful lot of noise.

On the other side of the room, I could vaguely make out a couple having sex, she sitting on top of him, rocking backwards and forwards.

'Jesus, the smell, La!' I said, wrinkling my nose. Hot wafts of bodies and hormones kept hitting me.

'Bit yeasty, isn't it?' she replied.

Then a man appeared in front of us. He had a studded collar around his neck, with a leather dog's lead that ran off it, clipped brown hair and he was wearing tight leather trousers.

'Hello, I'm Rupert and I'd like to be your slave tonight,' he said, handing me the lead.

'Oh, Rupert, that's so kind but actually I'm just having a drink with my…'

'Get down on your hands and knees, Rupert,' said Lala, snatching the lead from my hand.

I looked at her and my mouth fell open, but I couldn't think what exactly to say.

Rupert looked ecstatic. He instantly dropped to his knees.

'And your hands on the floor,' instructed Lala.

He put his hands down.

'Rupes, you're going to be our table,' said Lala, 'Come on, Pols, put your legs on Rupert's back.'

'La, I've got heels on, I'll hurt him.'

'Don't be so feeble, he wants to be hurt, don't you, Rupes?'

Rupert, on the floor, nodded his head. So, I lifted my legs and gently laid them on his back. Lala did the same, less gently.

A waiter appeared with another tray of champagne, so we each took another glass. 'I've taken one for you, Rupert, you can have it later,' said Lala, putting his glass on the floor underneath our legs.

The screaming woman in front of us had now finished and she and her friend had vacated the table. There was a man strapped to a bench on the other side of the room being given a blow job by another man, though, so we weren't short of things to watch.

'This is fun,' said Lala, leaning back against the wall. 'I never thought it would be this much fun.'

'We could always have more fun, girls,' said Rupert, from the floor.

'Oh, er, thanks, but I just want to watch for a bit,' I said quickly. 'So have you been to many of these then?' I didn't want this human table to touch me but I did quite need him to give me some details about the sort of people who went to these parties.

'A few,' came Rupert's muffled voice from the floor.

'And do you know many others here?'

Still on his hands and knees, he waggled his head up and down like a nodding dog. 'Some. But it's a circle of trust.'

'Should we let you get up?' I said, suddenly feeling him twitch underneath my feet. 'He's probably got sore knees, La, we should let him get up.'

Lala sighed. 'Go on then, Rupert, up you get, and here's your champagne.' He leant back on his knees and she handed him the glass.

'So what do you, er, do then?' I asked, as he stood up.

'I'm in shipping,' he said, sitting beside me, holding his champagne glass in one hand, his lead in the other.

'Oh, right,' I said politely. I felt like I was at some kind of extreme dinner party.

'What about you?'

'I'm a writer,' I said quickly. I thought the word 'journalist' might alarm him. But I needed Rupert to tell me more. 'So, I know you said it's a circle of trust, but I'm, intrigued. Do you get lots of... famous people here?'

He leant in conspiratorially towards me. 'Don't tell anyone I told you this, but rumours are one of the princes came once.'

'What? When? How did he not get spotted?'

'Wore a mask,' said Rupert. 'It was for a stag do, I think.'

'And did he... do anything?'

'Circle of trust,' he said again, tapping his nose.

'Yes, sorry, 'course,' I said.

'Pols, will you come with me outside? I need some fresh air and another fag,' said Lala, from the other side of me.

'Go on then.' We told Rupert we'd see him later and went back downstairs, past a couple fingering one another on the landing.

'I'm quite up for being spanked,' Lala said outside, exhaling smoke into the air.

'By a total stranger?'

'Yeah, why not?'

I shrugged. 'No. No, go for it. It's, you know, the right place for it. I'm sure Rupert would oblige.'

'Not by him.'

Which is how, half an hour later, we were back in the apparatus room, me sitting on the bench again, watching Lala approach a tall man wearing a balaclava and a pair of latex Y-fronts. He had a leather bag slung across his shoulder and looked like a member of the IRA who'd only bothered getting half-dressed that morning. She introduced herself and they started chatting. Then both of them nodded vigorously and he gestured at a bench in front of him.

Lala dropped to her knees on to the bench, but got her weight distribution wrong so the bench reared up in her face. A couple grinding into one another against the wall stopped to watch. Lala's friend in the balaclava pointed out that she should put her knees higher up and rest her arms down to steady the bench. In position, her bottom primed behind her, she turned to me and winked. Then she put her head back down on top of her forearms.

The man reached into his bag and pulled out a whip.

'That's called a flogger,' said Rupert, materializing beside me and sitting down. 'A leather one. Hurts less than rubber.'

'Oh,' I said. 'Do they leave marks?'

'No, not really,' he said, shaking his head. 'Not unless you use the one with wire in it.'

'*Wire?!*' I shuddered. How do you work out you're into being spanked with wire? I wondered to myself. Like, what's the process? Start with the damp corner of a tea towel at home? Work up from there?

'I'm not a fan myself,' said Rupert.

Lala's inquisitor stood behind her and started flicking the leather strands at her bottom. She wriggled it. He started flicking it a bit harder. Every time he struck her bottom, Lala would clench it. But he continued, flick, flick, flick. Until he stopped and leant forward, whispering something in her ear. She nodded.

He reached into his bag and pulled out a different whip.

'Ah, that's a rubber one,' said Rupert. 'This might sting a bit.'

He went at her bottom again, flicking the flogger backwards and forwards, brushing her with the tips of the rubber strands.

'Fuck,' I heard her exclaim through clenched teeth. I squinted at her bum. Red lines were starting to come up on her skin.

'Do you think she's all right?' I said to Rupert. I felt like I was losing control of the evening.

'Yes, don't worry. He's a pro.'

'You know him?'

'Not really. But I've seen him here before. I don't think he'll hurt her.'

Lala twisted her head over her shoulder to try to look at her bottom. The balaclava man said something to her and she nodded her head, then she put one leg down on the floor and stood up, rubbing one bum cheek with her hand. She was laughing with him, luckily, even though the welts on her arse cheeks looked like something you'd see in a medieval documentary on the History Channel.

Then he pulled off his balaclava and my stomach lurched. It was Hamish. Lala laughed again and turned to point at me. Then his face fell. And what is the right thing to do at this point? What does one do when you're at a fetish party and you realize your friend has just been spanked by another friend's fiancé? What do you say?

I stared at him as he walked towards me.

'Hi,' he said awkwardly.

'Hello,' I said.

'I'm Rupert,' said Rupert, twirling his lead in his hand.

'Rupert, er, hello,' said Hamish.

'So,' I said. 'You're… you're here? You come to these?'

'Sometimes,' replied Hamish. 'I haven't been to that many.'

'You were here just before Christmas, weren't you?' said Rupert.

Hamish looked at Rupert as if he'd rather he wasn't there.

'Has Lex been?' I asked.

'No,' he replied quickly. 'Not her thing.'

'Oh my God, you know each other?' said Lala, who'd been hovering on the sidelines of this conversation, still rubbing her bottom.

'He's my friend Lex's fiancé, so yes, I do,' I said.

'Listen,' Hamish started, 'can we not make a big deal about this? It's just a thing I do. Sometimes. Not often.'

'Where does she think you are?'

'Rugby night out,' he said, looking embarrassed. 'Please, Pols. Please don't say anything.'

I looked at him, standing in front of me, in his silly, shiny knickers. Rubber flogger still in his hand.

'Dude, I think honestly that's a conversation you need to have with her. Before you get married.'

He looked at the ground.

'Right, La, I think we should make a move,' I said. 'It's all got a bit weird.'

She nodded.

'Or we could all have another drink?' said Rupert, quite optimistically given the circumstances.

I shook my head. 'Home time,' I said. 'But lovely to meet you. And Hamish… I don't even want to look at you.'

And then, with as much dignity as one can muster in a latex catsuit accompanied by someone in their underwear, I turned and walked out with Lala, who was still massaging her bum. We left Hamish standing with his flogger in one hand and his balaclava in the other.

*

As luck would have it, or not, I was hanging out with Lex the following day. Quite literally hanging out actually as I was reviewing a new spa in Notting Hill for *Posh!*'s beauty pages and it required the wearing of my least favourite item of clothing: a bikini. Lex had said she'd come with me because she said she was up for anything that would help her lose ten or twenty stone before the wedding.

'What is this place and will it make me thin?' she said, when she met me outside the Tube station that afternoon.

'It's called a *banya*,' I said, 'a Russian thing. Did you bring your bikini?'

'Yes, it's in my bag.'

'OK, let's find it and then they can explain.'

The spa was in a mews house a few streets away from the station.

'What did you get up to last night?' she asked me, as we walked there. I hadn't mentioned that I was going to an orgy for work. And I certainly wasn't feeling like going into details now. So I lied.

'Stayed in, lay on the sofa. Watched *Real Housewives* with Joe. You?'

'Had a drink with a few girls from work then went home. Hamish was out.'

'Mmmm. Oh, look, I think this is the street.' I looked at Google Maps on my phone. 'Should be along here.' Thank God it was a short walk. I was a) hungover, b) still had no idea whether to say anything to Lex about Hamish or not. And c) I was a terrible liar. So I didn't want to spend any more time discussing the previous night than was absolutely necessary.

We wandered along until we reached a pink door. Number seventeen. I knocked on the door and a blonde woman in white uniform answered it.

'Hello, I'm Polly,' I said, 'from *Posh!* magazine. We've got an appointment.'

'Yes, hello,' said the blonde. 'Please come in.'

We went in.

'If you could both just read these forms and sign them, then we can get started,' she said, handing us both a pen and a clipboard. 'You're both having the *banya*, is that correct?'

I nodded. And then looked down at the form in front of me. It was the usual thing. Alarming small print about sudden death being your own responsibility and so on. I signed it and handed it back.

'Thank you,' she said. 'Do you know much about the treatment?'

'No,' we chorused.

'So the Russian *banya* treatment it is a detox process,' she said reverently. 'A treatment that incorporates extremes of heat and cold to remove toxins from your body.'

'How extreme?' said Lex.

'It will be hot,' she said, seriously. 'And then you will be brushed with some birch leaves to improve your circulation, before going into our *bochka*…'

'What's that?' I interrupted.

She smiled again. 'It is a plunge pool. Quite cold. Freezing. And then you will get out and go in the flotation tank for a few minutes. And then you will be wrapped and have some ginger tea.'

'Fuck,' said Lex.

'Lovely,' I said quickly.

'So if you would like to follow me.' She led us down a twisting staircase to a changing room. 'There are towels and dressing gowns. If you don't mind getting changed then I will be waiting outside.'

We stripped off and put our bikinis on. 'I'd quite like it if this got rid of my cellulite,' I said, looking over my shoulder at the backs of my thighs in a full-length mirror.

'I want to come out of this looking like I've survived an African famine, but only just,' said Lex, poking her stomach with a finger.

'Worth a shot, right?' I said. 'Come on, let's go and be beaten.'

We followed the spa lady back upstairs, along a corridor and into a darkened room with a hot tub in the middle of it.

'Please, if you will go in the steam first,' she said, opening a wooden door. 'There are hooks just here for the towels. And then your therapist, he will come and get you.'

We lay back on hot wooden benches, breathing in the eucalyptus steam.

I exhaled. 'This is just what I need with a hangover.'

'I thought you had a quiet night?' said Lex.

'All right, Miss Marple, I had a few glasses on the sofa,' I said, thinking as fast as I could.

'How's Jasper?' she said.

'Good. Fine. In Yorkshire this weekend.'

'I can't tell you how excited Mum is about him being at the wedding,' she went on. 'She asked if she'd have to curtsey to him the other day.'

The door opened and a bald man stuck his head into the steam room. 'Lex?'

'That's me,' said Lex, swinging her legs down on to the floor. 'See you in a bit, Pols. I'll be so thin you won't even recognize me.'

She went out, which allowed a welcome gust of cold air into the steam room. Sweat started trickling down my cheeks and neck. I felt like I was letting out the excesses of the night before. Releasing the champagne and the stench of bodies and latex. I stretched. My bikini was drenched already, and sweat had soaked my hairline. Water tonight, I told myself, no wine. Bath. Early bed.

Ten minutes later, just when I thought I might explode with heat, the Russian man stuck his head through the door again. 'Polly? You now.'

I stood up and almost immediately fell down again with dizziness but stumbled through the door into cold air. There was no sign of Lex. 'This way please,' said the bald chap, in Speedos and flip-flops. He had a thick accent and the hard, menacing look of a man who had killed people.

'Lie down here,' he said, in another hot room with a single wooden bench. 'Put your face on this.' He pointed at what looked like the small branch of a tree.

'On it?' I double-checked.

'Yes, your face, you put it on these oak leaves.'

I lay one cheek on the leaves and closed my eyes. They were damp, cold and smelt herby.

'And now I will brush you for good bloods.'

I opened one eye and looked behind me as the assassin started beating the backs of my calves with a handful of twigs. They were hot. Up and down he went with them, quickly, so just when you thought the pain was unbearable he would lift it off again, working his way up my calves, the backs of my thighs, my bottom, my back and my shoulders.

'Turn over, please,' he said after a few moments. 'And take off your bikini top.' My heart was racing as if I'd just run a marathon. In the desert. At midday. More sweat was running down my face. Given the choice between this and being flogged by Hamish, I might even have plumped for the latter.

'Now, I will do your front,' he said, brushing the front of my legs with the twigs and working up my body again. I almost laughed when he got to my chest at the thought of a bald Russian man standing solemnly over me, flicking my nipples with bits of tree.

'Up, please,' he said, handing me back my bikini top, which I slid on and tied at the back again before he ushered me out. 'Now get in here.'

He pointed up some stone steps to a large wooden barrel filled with water. 'Get in.'

I jumped in and squealed. It was freezing. Colder than any sea I could remember.

'And your head,' said the man, putting his hand on the top

of my head and pushing it down. I came up again gasping for air. That was it. It had to be over now, right?

'Out, please,' he said, so I climbed out and he pointed at the hot tub in the middle of the room.

'Get in and lie down.'

I went up more stone steps and clambered in. I felt like a toddler, willingly being ordered around.

'Lie,' the Russian instructed again, 'put your head in my hands and totally relax.'

I tried to 'totally relax', him cradling my head while the bubbles held the rest of my body up. It was like floating. I lay like this for several moments, then it was out again and he draped two towels around me and rubbed my shoulders and back.

'Now, tea,' he said, 'this way.'

I followed him, shuffling like a penguin because I was encased in towelling, to a dimly lit room with white daybeds.

He pointed at one next to Lex, who was lying almost flat, wrapped in towels like an Egyptian mummy, her eyes closed.

'Pols, I don't know what just happened but I feel amazing,' she said. 'Do I look thinner?'

'I don't know, Lex, I need to lie down immediately.'

The man tucked me in with towels, went out and came back in several minutes later with a small metal teapot, slices of lemon and a small saucer of honey. 'You drink this, and then you drink water. And in twenty minutes you will be totally recovered,' he said.

'Thank you,' I said, smiling up at him from my towel sarcophagus. He nodded and went out again.

'Honestly,' she mumbled, 'I've never felt better. My whole body is vibrating. I think that was better than sex. I quite want to marry that man instead of Hamish.'

'Mmm,' I said. I was going to lie here, feigning bliss, for as long as I could. Which was about three minutes before Lex said she wanted some tea – 'Don't you want some tea?'– and sat up to make it. 'Do we put the lemon and the honey in, do you think? Just a slice of lemon? And how much honey?'

It would have been more relaxing to have come to the spa with Bertie.

Obviously, I wimped out of saying anything about Hamish. I wasn't sure if it was my place. I tried to imagine if the situation was reversed, if she'd caught Jasper there, would I rather know? The answer was yes, of course. But it was different with Lex. She was engaged to him. All the more reason to tell her, on the one hand, but on the other, did I want to be responsible for ruining everything? Not today, I decided. Not after being beaten with twigs by a Russian hitman. I didn't feel up to it.

★

Sidney called on Sunday evening. Mum had become so feverish that he'd taken her into hospital. Her white blood count was very low, he explained slowly on the phone from St Thomas'.

'The chemo's really taken it out of her a bit,' he said. 'So they might have to delay the last bout of it.'

'What does that mean?' I said, panicked, sitting on the sofa in my flat, fumbling for the remote control to turn *Antiques Roadshow* down.

'It seems they might have to delay the next chemo until she's fit enough. Until her body is strong enough for it. Her immune system is basically very low, not strong enough to handle chemo again at the moment,' he said.

'Can I speak to her?'

'She's just having a little sleep in a chair on the ward,' he said, 'but as soon as she wakes up I'll let you know.'

'OK, thanks, Sidney.' I hung up and burst into tears, giving in and letting myself fear the worst. Can you physically process the idea of someone you love not being there? Of someone you love simply disappearing? I wasn't sure I could. That was what grief was, surely? The process you had to go through to understand and make sense of someone being there one day and not the next. I literally couldn't imagine life without Mum. I'd refused to even think about it throughout this whole process. But if this treatment didn't work and she couldn't get better, then… what?

I sat on my sofa, tears falling into my lap, and decided to call Jasper at home in Yorkshire.

'Hello you, what's up?' he said. I cried down the phone about blood cells and chemo.

'Right,' he said, after a few minutes. 'Are you at home?'

'Yes,' I sniffed.

'On your own?'

'Yes.'

'OK. I'm getting in the car now. I should be there in…' He paused. 'Three hours if I put my foot down.'

'From Yorkshire? No, Jasper, it's too far, you're mad, it's...'

'I'm not mad, I want to see you. So, stay put. I'm literally walking out the door now. Listen.' He jangled something against the phone. 'Keys, see? On my way.'

I laughed and snot bubbled out of my nose. And then I felt a wave of relief. All right so Jasper might not have asked much about Mum's treatment, but he was coming now.

Ten minutes later, I went down to Barbara's to buy a bottle of red wine. She frowned when I put it on the counter and then squinted at my puffy face.

'Are you drinking on your own?'

'No, Jasper is on his way.' I fumbled in my hoody for my card.

'Good.' She nodded. 'I am glad. You should cook him something to go with it. Men like a woman who can cook. Something strong. Something proper. Not something like pizza. That is not real man food.'

I wasn't in the mood for domestic tips from Barbara, so I said thank you in a weak way and went back upstairs. It was one of those moments when I felt like this flat should come with reduced rent, given the emotional trauma I had to undergo every time I needed more loo paper.

Jasper arrived about three hours later.

'Hi,' I mumbled, into his shoulder, standing in my open doorway. 'You'll be done for speeding.'

'I don't care,' he said, 'I want to look after you.'

It was the kindest thing I could remember any man saying to me. We stood there silently, hugging for a few moments. Then he mumbled something I didn't hear.

'Huh?' I said.

He lifted his head up and looked at me. 'I said, I love you.'

I burst out laughing. 'Really?' I said. It was the only reply I could come up with.

Jasper sighed. 'Yes, really, even though you're completely impossible and you laugh when someone's trying to be serious.'

'Sorry.'

I'd only ever told my university boyfriend Harry that I loved him. Oh, and I'd also told an Australian I'd been seeing for about two seconds that I loved him when I was drunk and all he'd replied was 'That's a real honour.' He went back to Darwin shortly after that.

Did I love him? Jasper, I mean, not the Australian. You sort of have to say it back, don't you? Rude not to. And I think I do, anyway. I thought about him approximately every other second. He was never not in my head and I missed him when I wasn't with him.

I suddenly felt nervous.

'Do you know what?' I said.

'Mmm,' he murmured back.

'I *think* I love you too.'

'You think you love me?'

'No, no. I know I do.'

'You know what?'

'Are you going to make me say it again?'

'Yes.'

I paused. And then I said it, quietly. 'I love you too.'

'Good,' he replied. 'And I'm sorry about your mother.'

'It's OK. It'll be OK, it has to be.' I said it as firmly as I could.

''Course it will,' he said. 'I told you, I'm going to look after you.'

★

I woke up just after three in the morning that night and listened to Jasper breathing beside me. The Marquess of Milton, playboy of Britain, seducer of princesses, had told me he loved me. And I had said it back. Because I did. Even though it felt too obvious. Too much of a cliché: woman falls for handsome rich man. But I had fallen for Jasper – despite the stories, despite the reputation. Had he told all those women before that he loved them too? A splinter of insecurity pierced me. Maybe it would all still end in tears? But then I thought back to the first time we met at Castle Montgomery, when I'd realized he was more complex than his reputation suggested. When he told me he didn't know what he wanted either. When he said he was trying to work out life, just like the rest of us.

I turned my head to look at him sleeping, his face towards mine, as if I was trying to look into his brain and read his dreams. I mouthed the words again at him silently – 'I love you.' They felt unfamiliar on my lips. As if I was playing at being a grown-up. He'd said he wanted to look after me so maybe we really would end up together? Maybe he was The One?

I yawned and swivelled my head to the ceiling again,

worried that Jasper would wake and find me staring at him, a whisper from his face, like something from a horror film. Go to sleep, Polly, you maddo. No good ever came of obsessing about things in deepest night.

14

IT WAS THE DAY before Lex's hen weekend and I was in the flat, drinking a cup of tea and squinting at Google Maps on my laptop. Fuck's sake. It was going to take me four hours to drive to Norfolk to start setting everything up. I'd taken the day off, much to Peregrine's chagrin, who'd said charmingly that he wasn't running a holiday camp. But I had to get there early to unload the 472 Ocado bags I'd ordered before everyone arrived.

I looked at the time – 11 a.m. I needed to call Mum. Her white blood cell count had finally gone up enough for the doctors to approve her last session of chemo. Sidney was taking her. I felt guilty but she'd told me not to be so daft.

'Morning, Mum,' I said, when she picked up.

'Hi, darling, you off yet?'

'In a tick. How you feeling?'

'Oh, all right. I'll be glad when it's done.' She sounded weary. Tired. I was worried about leaving her for the weekend.

'Mum, are you sure you don't want me to stay? I can. Lex would totally understand.'

'Oh, don't worry about me, you daft girl. Go and have fun. Go and have a big glass of wine for me.'

'I will. Several glasses I would think this weekend.'

'All right, darling. Well, Sidney and I are about to leave for hospital so speak later.'

'Yep, I'll ring once I'm there.'

'Drive safely, darling.'

★

Five hours later I finally reached the Norfolk barn where we would all be staying for the weekend. The Ocado bags had been left stacked on top of one another in the porch. If I never have to go on another hen party, I thought, looking at them, I wouldn't be sad.

I was hungry, inevitably, so I rifled through the bags until I found a pack of chocolate digestives. There were nine of us on this hen for two nights. Two nights. Just two. Friday night. Saturday night. But I'd provisioned as if catering for the apocalypse. Fish pies, lasagne, which I'd bought because, really, who has the time to make lasagne and dick about with white sauce? Sliced ham, half a dozen baguettes, several loaves of sliced bread, enough salad to keep the fussy ones happy, crisps, dips, biscuits, Diet Coke, giant bags of Minstrels, chocolate cake, several cartons of eggs, muesli and soya milk because there was bound to be someone who claimed to be lactose intolerant. Then the bottles: ten bottles of Prosecco, fifteen bottles of white, fifteen bottles of rosé, two bottles of vodka, one bottle of gin, five bottles of tonic.

I'd also rather have multiple smear tests than have to round up the cash for another hen party. There was always at least one person who wasn't drinking – pregnancy or just sheer tiresomeness – and so they sent the inevitable email going, 'Oh, I'm not drinking so can I pay twenty pounds less?' And I would have to reply and say 'Of course, not a problem,' when I actually wanted to say 'Please don't come if you're going to be such a drip.'

I flicked the kettle on and wandered around the house. The vibe was yuppy cool: whitewashed farmhouse outside, New York loft inside. Lots of exposed brick walls, wooden floors and minimalist beige sofas. There goes my deposit, I thought, imagining the wine that would be dribbled all over the sofas by Sunday. Ah well. So long as the life drawing model didn't wipe his balls on them.

Gavin, the IT worker from Norwich and part-time life model, was booked for the following morning. Hen activities are hellish too. The worst ones are the twee, Fifties housewife classes – macaroon-making, cocktail-making, fascinator-making. I hated macaroons. Silly dainty little almond pastries. Not a proper snack. They wouldn't fill an anorexic mouse. So, if we had to do activities for Lex, I'd decided it would be a rude activity. Gavin was coming at 10 a.m. the following morning for two hours. A bit rude because it involved a penis, but also a bit cultural because we would be sitting drawing pictures with charcoal.

I unpacked the Ocado bags while mulling this all over, and decided to go and pick my bed before everyone else arrived. There were four bedrooms, all doubles, and Cathy from the lettings agency had said she'd put up a camp bed to make nine. I absolutely was not going to end up in that camp bed, so I slung my bag on one side of a big double bed and looked out over the shoreline. It was gloomy outside. Grey clouds were squatting over the sea.

I had another biscuit with a cup of tea downstairs and plotted. It was nearly six but I had ages because everyone else was getting the train from Liverpool Street and wouldn't arrive for a couple of hours. I needed some fresh air, so decided to walk down to the shoreline and dip my toes in.

It was a few hundred metres across the lawn and down a shingly bank covered in clumps of dried seaweed to the beach. Not a white sand, blue sea sort of beach. The sand was dark brown, the sea sludgy green. I took a photo anyway and sent it to Jasper. *Brrrrrrrr*, I wrote underneath the picture. I then threw my shoes up onto the shingle, rolled up my jeans, walked in up to my ankles and immediately lost all sensation in my feet. I'd never been one of those people who could jump into cold water. I took circa fifteen minutes to get into any swimming pool on holiday. First my feet, then my knees, then halfway up my thighs, then I'd put my hands in and wet my face, then I'd wade in until the water was around my bottom and my ovaries were leaping about inside me in horror at the cold, then to my belly button when, finally, I'd take a big breath and push the rest of myself underwater. Pathetic.

I felt my phone buzz in my back pocket. Jasper. 'Hello,' I said, smiling into it.

'You made it,' he said.

I looked out across the sea, my feet still stinging from the cold. 'Yup, just about. Unloaded four million shopping bags. Got the wine in the fridge. Just tried to put my feet in the sea but it's so cold I might have given myself frostbite.'

'Don't be a wimp. You wait until I push you into the lake at home.'

'Urgh. Not a massive wild swimmer.'

'Then we've found it.'

'Found what?'

'A reason I can't possibly marry you.'

'Ah. Sorry.' I smiled into the phone again. 'I don't mind nice pools and nice seas. Nice, clear blue water where you can see your feet and nothing can attack you.'

'Noted.'

'Where are you anyway?' I asked.

'In the car. On my way home with Bovril sitting beside me. We'll miss you this weekend.'

'I'll miss you too. I hope home's OK.'

'Oh, it'll be fine. Bovril and I will amuse ourselves, won't we, boy? Right, was just calling to check in, so you go and warm up and I'm going to put my foot down.'

'OK. Drive safe. Love you.'

'Love you back.'

I hung up and slid my phone back in my pocket so I didn't fumble and drop it in the sea. Then I looked out at the horizon again. I was still torn about whether or not to talk to Lex about Hamish. About the party. About the spanking. I hadn't told anyone. Not even Joe. On the one hand, I was possibly the worst friend in the world if I didn't mention it. On the other, how could I break it to her on her hen? But if not this weekend then when? It was getting closer and closer to the wedding.

I went inside for a bath and an hour or so later was still thinking about the Hamish situation, but two glasses of wine down. I'd also called Mums, who was watching an old episode of *Taggart* with Sidney, spent half an hour trying to work out how to use the oven, kicked the oven, put the fish pies into the oven once I'd calmed down again and spoken to Sal, who said they were all in taxis from the station. I could hear them singing 'Girls Just Wanna Have Fun' in the background.

I was pouring a third glass of wine when headlights flashed through the kitchen window. The door banged open. Lex came through it first draped with a 'bride-to-be' sash and a pink tiara. She hugged me and hiccupped in my ear.

'It's worth getting married just for the hen.' She hiccupped again as others appeared behind her.

I knew Sal, obviously. I'd met two of Lex's former work colleagues, Rachel and Laura. And I knew Lex's lesbian cousin, Hattie. I'd first met Hattie when we were both seventeen and I'd been vaguely wondering if I was a lesbian too because I still hadn't had sex with a boy, but then Hattie had explained what 'scissoring' was and I'd decided I definitely wasn't.

I'd met the others from time to time with Lex, they were mostly friends from her primary school. I'd been sending them increasingly threatening emails in the preceding weeks asking for their money. 'Hi, guys.' I lamely waved at them. One was called Alice, another was Beatrice. This left the one with pink hair, who I guessed was Lex's pal from art college. Elisa.

'Anyone want a glass of wine?' I said.

'Oh no, not for me, thanks,' said the one I took to be Beatrice, patting her stomach. Oh yes, I remembered, Beatrice was pregnant. 'Have you got any elderflower cordial?'

'Ah, shit! No, sorry I don't. But there's Diet Coke?'

Beatrice looked at me as if I'd just suggested eating her baby.

'Oh no. No, thanks. I'll just have water then.'

'Okey-dokes,' I replied cheerfully, 'tap's there. Go grab rooms, everyone, dinner's nearly ready. Fish pie and peas.'

'What kind of fish is in it?' asked Beatrice. 'I need to be careful about mercury poisoning.'

★

Obviously, everyone was still in bed at ten o'clock the next morning when Gavin – the sometime IT worker, sometime life model – rang the doorbell. I pulled on a pair of tracksuit bottoms and ran downstairs.

'You must be Gavin,' I said, opening the door.

Gavin was presumably a life model because he would never have made it as any other sort of model. He was small and thin, with a shaved head and thick glasses behind which he was squinting.

'Come in, come in,' I said. 'Bit of a slow morning. Let me just go and hurry everyone up. Can I get you a coffee?'

'Yeah, please. I'd love one. Black, two sugars. And where shall I go and get freshened up?'

'Ah, 'course, go through the kitchen and the bathroom's at the end.'

I bolted upstairs and stuck my head into multiple bedrooms. 'Get up, you lazy toads, the activity is kicking off. I'm making coffee.'

Ten minutes later, everyone was more or less assembled on the sofas in the sitting room with coffee in one hand, croissants in the other. Apart from Alice, who had said she was so hungover she might die if she had to get out of bed. So I left a packet of Nurofen and another bottle of water on her bedside table.

'Right then, ladies, where do you want me?' Gavin appeared from the bathroom in a dressing gown. Coffee cups froze in mid-air. Sal sniggered.

'Well, we thought in the middle might work,' I said, gesturing at a chair in between the two sofas. I'd put a towel on the chair. I really couldn't face any smearing on the upholstery.

'Terrific,' said Gavin, stepping carefully between the sofas, wafting a strong smell of Lynx as he went, which caught me right in the back of the throat and made Elisa cough.

Chair reached, he undid his dressing gown cord. I glanced across the room at Beatrice, who was looking down determinedly and inspecting her nails. Lex and Sal were on the same sofa, but their eyes were focused on Gavin like lions at feeding time.

The dressing gown fell to the floor and another wave of

Lynx drifted across the room. 'Oh goodness,' said Rachel, to my left, then, 'Sorry. It's just… quite early.'

Gavin didn't appear to notice because he was busy positioning himself. Quite odd to find yourself in a seaside cottage on a Saturday morning in June, eyeballing the freshly shaved scrotum of a stranger from Norwich.

'Does this work for you, ladies?' He was standing with one leg on the floor, one leg on the chair, arms suspended in the air as if he was pulling on a bow. He had a tattoo of an Alsatian on his left shoulder blade.

'Mmm,' murmured everyone vaguely. Lex and Sal were shaking with silent laughter.

'Great, I'll hold this for ten minutes and then I'll do another one. Ready, steady, go.'

Heads bowed down, everyone started sketching. I was crap at art at school. Mr Robertson, the art teacher, had once complimented me on my 'excellent' drawing of a rabbit.

I'd looked at him coldly and replied: 'It's a horse.'

Still, I thought, looking at the charcoal in my hand, how hard can a bottom be?

'Time's up,' said Gavin ten minutes later, putting his leg down from the chair and stretching his arms into the air. 'Show and tell. Everyone hold up their drawings so we can see.'

'Here you go, Gavin,' said Sal, holding her drawing in the air. It was a stick man with an enormous penis.

'Very flattering,' said Gavin. 'I think you've captured me perfectly.'

'Pols, what on earth is that?' asked Sal.

'Well,' I said, peering over the top of my pad at the drawing, 'I thought drawing a bottom would be relatively easy. Turns out it's not.' I'd seen finger-paintings stuck on fridges that were more accomplished than my study of Gavin's bottom.

★

After nearly two hours of drawing Gavin and several glasses of Buck's Fizz, everyone had become friendly enough to take selfies with him. Then he put his clothes back on, wished Lex good luck and got back into his Corsa, tooting his horn as he drove back down the drive.

'I thought he had quite a nice penis,' said Rachel.

'A bit squat,' said Sal.

'Blimey, Sal,' I said. 'If that's squat then I'm terrified to know what your fiancé's penis is like.'

'I don't like them shaved,' announced Elisa.

Alice appeared from upstairs.

'Morning, babe. How you feeling?' asked Lex.

'Great,' she said. 'Completely fine. A few of those Nurofen and a couple of extra hours in bed and I'm mended.'

'Good,' I said. 'Because we need to be in the pub for lunch in just under an hour.'

The Cow and Fiddle was in the next-door village, a short but bracing walk along the beach. It was Jasper who'd told me to book it. His knowledge of country pubs was encyclopaedic. While everyone else murmured about showers and getting dressed, I texted him a photo of my best Gavin drawing, one where he'd been lying on the floor, head resting on his right hand, one knee bent in the air, his penis falling over his other thigh, dangling towards the carpet.

'Not sure I'm ready for a walk,' said Alice, peering through the windows just as it started raining.

*

The Cow and Fiddle was the sort of pub that existed in Twenties Ireland. It was thatched on the outside and inside it smelled of old beer and stale cigarettes. Men who looked like they'd been alive since the Renaissance sat at the bar; a dog of indiscernible breed lay like a corpse underneath a stool beside it.

Our table was in a corner, beside a window which looked out over the sea. 'Everyone has to wear these,' said Sal, handing out headbands which each had two small pink penises on springs attached to them. I put mine on and squinted at a cloudy Guinness mirror next to the window. The penises waggled when I moved my head.

'No excuses, Bea, it's like Christmas hats. Everyone has to wear them. And drink out of these.' Sal reached back into her bag and pulled out a fistful of neon straws with a small plastic penis attached to the top, so you had to drink through a veiny plastic knob.

'Happy hen, Lex,' I said, waggling my head at her.

'And, you have to put on this…' Sal leant over the table and handed Lex an L-plate badge.

'Can we start with three bottles of Prosecco?' said Sal, to a waiter who'd appeared at the table.

'And a big jug of tap water please,' said Alice. 'And some bread?'

'Guys,' said Lex, at the head of the table, 'can I just say before we all get too pissed...'

'Again,' said Laura.

'Yes, again,' said Lex. 'But I just want to say how happy it makes me that you're all here. Honestly, if you'd said to me a year ago that we'd be sitting in a pub in Norfolk on my hen because I was getting married to Hamish I would have suggested you need sectioning. And yet here we are, doing exactly that. And I'm just so, so happy.'

'You next, Pols,' said Sal, digging an elbow into my side.

'Yes, Polly Spencer,' said Lex, loudly. 'This time next year I want to be on your hen.'

I rolled my eyes. 'Guys.'

'Or even earlier, to be honest,' Lex ploughed on. 'How long have you been going out now?'

'Erm, about four months,' I said, aware that everyone around the table was listening. 'So I think we're possibly getting a bit ahead of ourselves.'

'A September wedding at Castle Montgomery would be amazing,' said Lex.

'Sure, no problem,' I said, fumbling to check my phone in case it had somehow accidentally dialled Jasper in my bag and he was overhearing this.

'Would you get married at Castle Montgomery then, not where you grew up?' said Sal.

'Guys, honestly, this is a bit mad. I don't know. Where are our drinks?'

'You're going to marry Jasper and you're going to be a duchess,' said Lex. 'Can I please come and stay when you live in a castle? For weekends?'

'Sure, and we should get Gavin around,' I said, waving at the waiter.

'Well, all I'm saying is I'm keeping my fingers firmly crossed,' said Lex, holding out an empty glass for the waiter. She smiled at me and made an excited squeal.

We managed to drink seven bottles of Prosecco at the pub, which was when Lex started demanding Espresso Martinis.

'Is that like a coffee? Like a white coffee?' the waiter asked, looking confused, so we decided to get the bill and go back to the house before it was dark and someone drowned in the sea on the walk home.

Not that the walk did much to sober anyone up. Sal and I walked into the kitchen singing 'It's Raining Men' and immediately ransacked the cupboards, hunting for the crisps.

'What time is it?' I asked, squinting at the kitchen clock. 'Five-thirty. And let's say we want to sit for supper at eight-thirty. Which means putting the lasagne in at eight, which means starting Mr and Mrs at about seven-ish, right?'

'Mmmm.' Sal nodded her head through a mouthful of crisps.

'Everyone back downstairs at seven for drinks and games,' I bellowed through the house, reflecting, for the 392nd time, how exhausting hen weekends were. *If* I ever got married, I wanted it to be a piss-up in the Italian in Battersea.

I checked my phone. No word from Jasper, which was fine, I told myself, because I wasn't becoming *that* kind of girlfriend. I was on a hen, having a good time without him. No need for us to be in constant communication. Although I'd sent him a picture of my drawing earlier and he'd definitely seen it because the WhatsApp ticks had gone blue.

★

Mr and Mrs has got high-tech in recent years. It is no longer acceptable to send the groom a few questions which he can reply to on email. Instead, one or more of the hens must find a mutually convenient time with the groom and film his answers on camera. Sometimes the groom will be forced to wear fancy dress for this ordeal. Sometimes he will be made to drink shots while he answers. No one seems to think it odd that a friend of the bride has met up with her groom to ask him about the couple's sexual preferences.

Sal filmed Hamish in his office a couple of weeks before the hen. She'd then done some fancy editing so that, by the time everyone was on the sofas, Moscow Mules in hand, we were gazing at a TV screen which said: 'Mr and Mrs Wellington'.

'Ready?' said Sal.

Everyone cheered. Hamish appeared on the screen behind what I assumed was his desk. No fancy dress, he was wearing a suit. He waved nervously at the camera. 'Hi, girls.'

'Hi, Hamish,' chorused everyone back.

The first question appeared on the screen, underneath

Hamish. 'What did Lex wear on your first date?' Sal paused the video.

'Easy,' said Lex. 'Black Maje dress with my leather jacket and silver espadrilles. It was summer. We went to a pub by the river.'

Sal pressed play again. 'Oh God,' said Hamish, frowning back at us. 'I know it was at the Blue Anchor in Hammersmith.' He sat back in his chair and looked stricken. 'Christ... Was it... erm... I'm going to guess jeans and a pair of heels. And maybe some sort of top?'

'Pathetic,' said Lex, shaking her head.

'First shot then, Lex,' said Sal, pushing a small glass of vodka towards her.

The second question appeared on the screen: 'When did you and Lex first say you loved one another?'

'Oh, that's easy too,' said Lex. 'We went away after we'd been going out for about a month, to the New Forest.'

Sal pressed play. 'Erm. God. Erm.' Hamish looked panicked again. 'Erm.' He scratched his chin. 'I remember. It was a Sunday morning, and we were in bed at home and she brought me a coffee in bed. And I just thought, Yeah, I can do this.' Sal pressed pause again.

'Total crap,' said Lex. 'It was at The Pig. A hundred per cent. We were lying in bed there. He's an idiot.'

'OK, OK, next one,' said Sal. The question appeared on the screen: 'Where is the weirdest place you've had sex?'

Lex laughed. 'My parents' bed. One hundred per cent. They were away. It was Hamish's idea, it seemed kind of funny at the time.'

'Course it was his idea, I thought to myself.

Sal pressed play again and Hamish's face brightened at the question. 'On the highest road in the world. In the Himalayas. Well, not actually on the road... more like on the side of it. In a tent.'

'Lex!' I turned to look at her. 'When did you guys do that?'

'We didn't.'

'What?'

She frowned. 'He's talking about another girl. This girl he met on his gap year.'

I looked at Sal. Then back to Lex. 'Huh?' I said. 'Surely the question was the weirdest place you *both* had sex? Together?'

'That was the question,' Sal replied. 'I just thought it was funny to include this.' She paused and squinted at Lex. 'Not funny?'

'Not that funny,' she replied, quietly. 'It would be nice if he got one question right.'

'OK, let's forget that one and carry on.' Sal pressed play again.

The next question was 'When did you know you wanted to marry Lex?' Hamish, luckily, managed to claw a few points back with his answer. 'It was Christmas, after we'd been going out for four months. And I was at my home, she was with her parents. But all I wanted was to be with her. And I knew that I wanted that for all my Christmases after that too. In our own house, with our own kids. So I told my parents that day.'

'Awwwwww,' cooed everyone.

'Stop it,' said Lex, blushing.

Then there was the favourite position question, an old favourite, which Hamish claimed was 'reverse cowgirl'. Men often pick reverse cowgirl in this game, I'd noticed. They can't say missionary because they worry that makes them like the local vicar who does it with the lights off. A few men go for 'doggy', but that often goes down badly because it gives off a get-in-the-kitchen-and-fetch-me-another-beer vibe. Reverse cowgirl suggests a more democratic process. She's on top, so, you know, three cheers for feminism, but she's facing away from him so it's slightly spicier than normal. Personally, it was the climbing on bit of reverse cowgirl that I found off-putting because it involved waving your bottom right in their face like a reversing dumper truck. And surely that is nobody's best angle? Certainly wasn't mine.

And so it went on. What was Lex's best body part? (He said eyes when he really wanted to say tits because Lex has great tits but he wimped out and went for the 'sensitive' option.) What would she save in a fire? (He said himself; she said her vintage McQueen jacket.)

I wondered briefly whether Jasper would get any of these questions right. Would he be able to recall what I wore on our dinner at the Italian? What bit of my body did he like best? And did he know that my worst, absolutely pathological fear was about swallowing spiders in my sleep? I doubted it. The only person who knew that was Mum. And Bill, actually. Not that either of them would be able to answer the favourite position question. Thank GOD. Once, ages ago in the pub, Lex said hers was on the kitchen table in her flat, which always made me feel alarmed when I went for dinner there. I briefly wondered what Bill's was and then felt embarrassed.

'You all right, Pol?' said Sal.

'Mmm, yep totally,' I replied.

'I can't believe he talked about where he had sex with someone else,' said Lex, shaking her head.

Sal shot me a look. 'Oh, he just wasn't concentrating. You know what boys are like. Morons. They just say the first thing that comes into their heads.'

'Especially if it's about sex,' I said.

'*Especially* that,' added Sal.

'Yeah, but he didn't get the one about when we said we loved each other either.'

'He was just confusing it with another time,' said Sal. 'Shall we open another bottle?' She stood up and went to the fridge.

Lex looked like she was close to tears. 'I just wish he'd thought harder about it.'

'Anyone for a crisp?' said Rachel loudly, holding a bowl in the air.

'But how difficult is it to remember when you first said you love someone?' said Lex.

'I wonder if I should put the lasagne in?' I said. 'How hungry is everyone?'

Everyone murmured back that they were, indeed, hungry. 'And let's have some music,' I added.

'Lex,' said Sal seriously, leaning towards her on the sofa. 'He said that sweet thing about knowing he wanted to marry you on Christmas Day.'

'He was probably just drunk,' she replied, throwing her hands up in the air. I winced as Prosecco sloshed over the side of her glass and dangerously close to the beige sofas.

'He was very nice about your eyes,' ventured Beatrice.

'Bollocks,' said Lex. 'He only said eyes because he was too embarrassed to say my tits.' She closed her eyes as her lip started wobbling. I looked at the kitchen clock. It was just after eight and we'd been drinking since midday so tears were probably inevitable. Just, ideally, not from the bride.

'Look,' said Beatrice. 'Have a crisp and some hummus. And a glass of water.'

Lex shook her head and sniffed. 'Is he even going to remember my middle name at the top of the aisle? Probably not. He's such a moron. Why am I marrying such a moron?' We were getting close to hysterical. She picked up a cushion and wailed into it. Everyone made faces silently at one another across the room. I carried on chopping up cucumber for the salad.

'Lex,' said Sal, squatting on the carpet in front of her. 'It was just a game. A silly game.'

'You're like him, you never take anything seriously,' said Lex. It was muffled because she was still holding the cushion to her face. My knife paused in mid-air as I wondered if her mascara would stain the cushion.

'All right, you don't need to have a go at me,' replied Sal. 'I was only trying to help.' And then she started crying too. I stopped chopping cucumber and stared at them both. For God's sake. Now we had two sobbing 31-year-olds. I was quite literally never, ever, *ever* going on a hen again. Even if it was my own.

'Well, it's not a help,' said Lex. 'I'm marrying a man who is so stupid he practically has to be watered twice a day...' she stopped to sniff loudly. 'And you're egging him on.'

'I wasn't egging him on,' said Sal, through her tears, still squatting on the floor. 'I thought you knew about the sex on Machu Picchu.'

'Himalayas,' said Lex.

'I don't care if it was in the fucking Cairngorms. I just thought you'd find it funny.'

Lex opened her mouth to say something and then started laughing. She fell onto her side on the sofa shaking with laughter. Oh good, now she'd get mascara on the sofa as well as the cushions.

'Sal, I'm sorry,' said Lex, sitting up again. 'I didn't mean any of it. I'm just being drunk and emotional and look at me. And look at you. You never cry.' She reached her arms down from the sofa and awkwardly hung them around Sal's shoulders in an attempt to hug her.

'It's all right,' said Sal, wiping her nose with the back of her hand.

'Right, everyone,' I said loudly from the kitchen. 'The salad's nearly done. Laura and Rachel, can you guys lay the table. I think lasagne and garlic bread is the answer to all this.'

'What are we supposed to be doing after supper?' said Rachel, quietly, as she opened the cutlery drawer.

'Well, technically more drinking,' I said, opening the fridge and looking into it. We still had eight bottles of rosé to get through. And a litre of vodka. 'But I'm not sure that's a good idea.'

'We could just watch a film or something?' she suggested.

So, in the end, although there was a monumental bickering match about which film to watch (someone wanted *Bridget Jones*, someone else wanted *The Notebook*), we settled on *Notting Hill* and everyone, finally, stopped crying.

★

You know in American high school movies when they hire a white clapboard house near a beach for 'vacation' and proceed to trash this house with a party involving kegs of beer and red plastic cups and thousands of other students who all take it in turns to shag one another in the bedrooms upstairs? The house looked like that the next morning. Dirty glasses, dirty plates, dirty napkins, dirty jugs, empty bottles of wine, overflowing ashtrays and shoes everywhere. *So* many shoes. Why were there so many shoes? Had the shoes had sex with one other and reproduced in the night? I tiptoed over the sticky floor like I was crossing a minefield to flick the kettle on and reached for the window behind the sink to open it.

If I was feeling kind and generous, I would start clearing this all up now. On my own. So that I could get breakfast going and everyone upstairs would be enticed by the smell of bacon and coffee. But I wasn't feeling that way and, anyway, if I cleared the whole thing up and put breakfast on nobody would realize I'd done it and I wouldn't get the brownie points. So, I'd make a coffee and watch telly until someone else woke up.

I scrolled through Instagram while the kettle boiled. The usual Sunday morning stuff. Pictures of some fried eggs beside the *Sunday Times*, pictures of someone pretending to be still asleep in bed, pictures of someone's dog actually in bed, under the duvet, a picture of Lala's toes, which she'd Instagrammed in the bath and a few memes about hangovers. I sighed and slipped my phone back on the counter beside a penis straw. Still no word from Jasper, which was weird. Or was it weird? Maybe I was just being hungover and needy.

By the time Sal came downstairs, I was lying horizontal on the sofa on my third cup of lukewarm coffee watching *Hollyoaks*, a show which never gets less depressing. 'Morning,' she said. 'Jesus, look at this place.'

'I know, I couldn't face doing it on my own. Sorry.' I looked up from the sofa. 'There's warm-ish coffee on the Aga.'

'Cool.' She reached for a mug. 'Lex all right this morning?'

'She's still asleep. I think she'll be fine. Just tired and over-emotional. And we'd been drinking since lunch.'

Sal poured herself a coffee and lay down on the sofa opposite me. We watched *Hollyoaks* in silence for a few minutes.

'Sal,' I said, deciding I needed to get the Hamish thing off my chest, given the scene the night before, 'if I tell you something, you promise you won't talk to Lex about it?'

'What?' she said, looking nervous. So, I explained about the party. About seeing Hamish there. About him asking me not to say anything to Lex. 'So I haven't said anything,' I said finally. 'But I feel like I'm carrying this great secret. I feel like if it was me I'd want to know. Right?'

She nodded. 'You've got to tell her. She needs to know. Honestly, Pols. I know it's an impossible thing, but you can't just leave it. Imagine if she finds out you knew later on?'

'I know, I know. OK, I'll tell her. Thing is, he wasn't technically cheating. He was just... spanking. I don't know if he, you know, goes any further.'

'Oh please,' she said. 'The guy's a psycho. She needs to know.'

'OK, I'll tell her,' I said again, feeling sick about it. 'I'm just not sure when. Now, shall we cheer ourselves up with a bit of cleaning?' I looked over at the kitchen sink, piled with smeary glasses and plates. A half-eaten bowl of hummus was crusting next to it. 'I'll wash, you dry?'

*

'Lex, why don't you go with Pols in the car and keep her company?' said Sal, when we'd packed up the house a few hours later. Everyone else was getting the train.

'I don't live anywhere near her,' said Lex.

'Never mind that,' said Sal, looking pointedly at me. 'You can talk about wedding stuff.'

Thanks, Sal, I thought, getting into the car, so hungover I felt brainless. Like a jellyfish. Just the time to have a stupendously awkward conversation. Lex and I would probably both cry and driving back from Norfolk is like returning from Middle Earth. It takes fucking hours. So we'd be crying for ages. Perfect. The perfect end to a hen weekend. The perfect Sunday evening. Crying on the M11. Ideal.

Lex got in and wound the passenger seat back, then put her 'bride-in-waiting' eye mask over her face as I pulled out of the drive.

'I might just have a snooze, Pols, do you mind?'

'Actually,' I said, feeling like I might be sick. I might actually throw up all over the steering wheel. 'Can I talk to you about... something?'

'Sure, what's up?' She frowned at me and pulled her eye mask on top of her head.

'Oh God, I don't even really know how to say this, so I'm just going to come out with it. I'm just going to tell you, just say it, just...'

'OK, Pols. Can you just tell me? You're freaking me out.'

I took a deep breath. 'OK, so the other day I had to go to a party for work. A sort of fetish party, I suppose. Run by some Italian woman. Peregrine wanted me to cover it so I said I'd go. And I went with Lala. It was in this big house in Mayfair with various people in frankly quite undignified outfits and...'

Lex interrupted me. 'I know what you're going to say. You saw him. Hamish. Right?'

I was stunned. 'What? Yes. But what? You know? How do you know? He said you didn't know he went to them.'

'Pols, can you concentrate on the road? I'm a bit worried about that wall.'

'Sure, sorry,' I said, straightening up. 'But I'm really confused. I was psyching myself up to tell you, but you know? You *know*?'

She sighed. 'I've known for a while. He's been going to them for a while.'

'But he said you don't know about them?'

'I do know. We've talked about it. I don't know why he told you that. He was probably just protecting me.'

'But why? Like, don't you mind? Isn't it a bit weird, Lex, that your fiancé goes off to these parties by himself?' I couldn't get my head round it.

She looked out of her window. 'I know it seems weird,' she said finally. 'And it was weird when I found out. But then we talked about it and I decided if that was his thing, if he wants to go off to these parties then fine, he can do that. He doesn't actually sleep with anyone at them. And if it means he still comes home to me afterwards.'

I frowned. 'Lex, you can't seriously marry…'

'Pols,' she said, turning to face me, 'I get it. You're all independent. You don't feel like you have to get married. You haven't thought about the big day and the dress and you hate all that stuff. I get it. I know you. I know you're not into it. I know you probably don't even want to be my maid of honour. But do you know what? I do want the big day. I do want the dress. And I'm sorry if you disapprove and it's not modern enough for you. But I do want that and I do want to marry Hamish. And I do want you to be maid of honour because you're my best friend, so can you please just be happy. Try and support me?'

I didn't think I'd be the one to cry, but I broke and a tear rolled down my face.

'I'm sorry,' I said. 'I don't know what to say. I guess I just wanted to make sure that you're all right.' I wiped my face with a hand.

'I'm all right,' she said. 'I promise. So he goes to these parties. And he's totally fucking useless because he can't remember when we said "I love you" to one another and I lost my shit last night because I was drunk. But he's honest with me. We're probably more honest with one another than a load of other couples I can think of.'

'OK,' I said, wiping my face again. 'OK. I'm sorry.'

'Don't be sorry, you idiot,' she said, laughing. 'I'm sorry I've made you cry. But at least we've both now cried this weekend, right?'

I laughed and reached into my bag for a tissue to wipe my nose. 'Can I just ask one thing?' I said, a few minutes later, still confused.

'Sure.'

'How did you find out? About the parties, I mean.'

'I found a pair of leather Y-fronts in his chest of drawers,' she said, and then we both burst out laughing. We laughed so hard that tears ran down Lex's cheeks too. So, actually, in the end, it was quite a bonding car journey. I still thought Lex was mad to be marrying Hamish, but if she said she was happy then that had to be that.

Three hours later, I dropped her at Notting Hill Gate Tube station. 'Thank you for the best hen ever,' said Lex, leaning over to hug me.

'Don't be silly. Get home safely.'

'I will. Are you seeing Jasper tonight?'

'Err, not sure,' I said.

'OK, well, send my love if you do.'

''Course.' I waved at her through the car window and drove back down towards Shepherd's Bush roundabout. I needed a bath and maybe a tiny glass of wine after that drive, and then I'd ring Jasper. And Mums. Crap. Must ring her too.

★

The flat was dark and freezing which meant Joe was out. I threw my bag on my bed, flicked the heating on and started running a bath.

I called Mums but got her voicemail. Where was everyone? Had there been some sort of apocalypse?

'Hi, Mums. Just back from Norfolk. Fun weekend. Well, mad weekend. But will tell you later. Am having a bath now so if you ring back and I don't answer, I'm cleansing myself from all the vodka. Hope you're feeling all right. Love you.'

Jasper. Should I ring him? I checked the time – 7.02 p.m. on a Sunday. Fuck it, I'd ring him. Silence all weekend was weird.

It rang and rang and rang and then went to voicemail so I hung up.

Neither Jasper nor Mums had called back by the time I slithered, still steaming from the bath, directly into bed an hour or so later. At which point I started worrying. Not so much about Mums, who would probably be watching

Midsomer Murders with Sidney and a can of chickpeas which the Vikings had brought over with them. I was obsessing more about Jasper. I couldn't help it. What if something had happened to him? What if he'd had a car crash? Or had been shot in a shooting accident? My head was full of possibilities: a freak lightning bolt in Yorkshire? A fall off one of the castle ramparts? I turned my lamp on again and sent him a message.

Hi, you, hope all OK?? Am home so ring me when you get this. I miss you X

I switched the light off and lay my mobile on my pillow on vibrate mode, so I'd know when he replied. *If* he replied. If he hadn't been savaged to death by Bovril or something. I fell asleep and dreamed that a Labrador with big teeth was chasing me.

I woke in the middle of the night and checked my phone. And felt a wave of relief when I saw a WhatsApp from him.

Am so sorry, my darling. Don't want to ring and wake you, but just a difficult weekend at home. Can I sweep you out for dinner tomorrow night?

It was followed by three little emoji faces with hearts for eyes. Ha, I thought, he felt guilty. Good. I drifted back to sleep, my dreams troubled no further by Labradors.

15

AT WORK THE NEXT day I still felt a bit unsettled, and tired, unable to concentrate on anything more taxing than a piece about Britain's fattest cat on *MailOnline*.

Peregrine interrupted my thoughts. 'Polly,' he barked from his office, 'I want you to write a piece about how whippets are the new black.'

'What?' I got up and stuck my head around his office door.

'I was with the Wolverhamptons on Saturday and they've just got a new whippet. So, I thought it would make a good story. The hottest dog breed right now. Eight hundred words by teatime. All right?'

I wasn't feeling strong enough to argue. 'Sure. Will do.'

I sat back down at my computer. By this time next year, I thought, as I opened a new Word document, I would no longer be writing about dogs. I probably wouldn't be writing about Syria or the Gaza Strip either, but I would have a new job. Surely there was a middle ground between dogs and the Middle East, journalistically speaking? Travel pieces, perhaps. I definitely wanted to travel more. Where did I want to go? I opened a map on my computer and scrutinized it. Burma? Colombia? Sri Lanka? Perhaps I could be one of those intrepid journalists who went abroad with a small rucksack for several weeks and sent stories back about their adventures with criminal outlaws and remote tribes. I wondered what Jasper would think if I said I was off to hang out with a drug cartel in Colombia for few weeks. Then I closed the map and typed 'whippet type of dog' into Google.

Lala arrived a few hours later, bringing with her the fragrant aroma of cigarettes.

'Pols, how was it?' she asked.

'How was what?'

'The hen obviously.'

'Oh yes, sorry.' I sat back in my seat. 'It was good, I think. The usual. Tears, bickering, willy straws, 593 bottles of rosé, drawing a naked man. How was yours?'

'My what?'

'Weekend.'

'Oh, it was all right. I went on a yoga retreat.'

'What?' I sat back in my chair and looked at her again. Lala on a yoga retreat seemed about as likely as the Dalai Lama taking pills and getting smashed at a rave.

'Yeah,' she carried on, signing into her computer. 'I just needed a weekend of chilling out, of being Zen. Dogging and that sort of thing.'

'Downward dogging?'

'That's what I mean. Anyway, any word from himself this morning?' Lala inclined her head towards Peregrine's office.

'Yes, he's got me writing a piece about whippets.'

'The ice cream?'

'That's Mr Whippy. The dog, I mean, the thin breed of dog. They're in apparently.'

'In where?'

I sighed. 'Do you need a coffee, La?'

'YES,' she said emphatically. 'And then I've got to finish off all the things I said I would on Friday and obviously didn't. Do you want a coffee too?'

'Yes please. Strong one.'

Lala nodded and, having done not a second's work yet that morning, wandered off to get us both coffees.

She came back forty-five minutes later without any coffee.

Bill emailed me later that day.

> How was the hen? I bought Willow a Scottie dog,
> we went to see it yesterday. She's called Crumpet.
> The dog I mean, not Willow. Obviously. So, my life
> is ruined. Thanks for all your help. X

Buying a dog with someone basically meant you were going to marry them, didn't it? Which means Bill was going to marry Willow. The thought depressed me. Yet another ring to coo over, as if having a diamond on your finger was the pinnacle of human achievement. Yet another wedding list to scroll through (let me think, the hand towels or the glass vase?). Yet another friend paired off. I turned back to my research on whippets.

★

Jasper was already upstairs at the bar of The Electric when I arrived that evening. 'There she is,' he said, standing up and holding his arms out.

'Hi, you,' I said, kissing him.

'I missed you,' he said, pulling a bar stool out for me.

'Missed you back. And I want to hear about your weekend.'

'Oh that,' he said, waving his hand in the air. 'No big deal.' He reached for the ice bucket beside him and pulled out a bottle of champagne. 'Anyway, I thought we should relax with this.'

He poured me a glass as I frowned at him.

'What?' he said.

'Nothing,' I replied, and then after a pause, 'Well, something.'

'OK,' he said slowly. 'What is it?'

'You were just… well, it's a bit embarrassing to say out loud like a 3-year-old. You were just a bit quiet all weekend.'

He ran a hand through his hair and laughed. 'That's why you're looking at me like you are now? All pouty and sweetly cross?'

'Don't laugh at me. I was just… a bit… I don't know. Sad maybe. And worried.'

He laughed again and leant forward, taking my hands in his. 'I'm sorry, my darling. It was just home. Just fucking home. My father shouting at my mother, who didn't come home on Saturday night. So, he sat up drinking all night and I had to talk to Vi and make sure she was all right and… it was a bloody awful weekend, if I'm honest.'

'Oh.' I felt silly. And sorry for him. 'I'm sorry. Was it really bad?'

'As bad as I've seen it. Dad threatening divorce. Mum saying he never would because he didn't even have the guts to do that. Vi in tears in her room. Ian opening bottle after bottle of wine for my father. Not great.' He stopped. 'But I'm sorry for worrying you. I'm sorry for being selfish. I suppose…' He stopped.

'What?' I said.

'I suppose… the thing is… I'm still getting used to being in a relationship. As you know, I haven't ever been very good at them. But I want to be good at them. You make me want to be good at this.'

My eyes welled up at this so I quickly blinked and shook my head at him. 'No, no. The last thing you need is to worry about me.'

'I was just a bit out of it. Anyway…' He picked up his glass again. 'Here's to… us. Thank you for putting up with me. I don't deserve you.'

'OK,' I said, raising my glass to his. 'And no more sorrys. Let's talk about something else.'

'Yes, I want you to tell me all about your weekend. Apart from the bit about any naked men. I don't want to hear anything about them.'

'There weren't any. Well, not totally true. There was Gavin from Norwich. But none apart from that.'

'Gavin is a frightful name,' said Jasper, picking up a menu. 'Now, my darling, what are we going to eat?' He looked across his menu at me. 'Apart from you later, obviously.'

'Oh. We're in that sort of mood, are we?'

'Yes. I am incredibly hungry,' he said, leaning in to kiss me again.

★

'No time for pudding,' Jasper said, a couple of hours and a bottle of red wine later. 'I want to take you home.'

'Your home or my home?'

'Either.' He shrugged, gesturing across The Electric at the waitress for the bill. 'I just need to nip to the bathroom, you're in charge.' He threw his wallet across the table at me. 'Use the silver card, 4721.'

'OK, cool,' I said, catching the wallet. 'I can run away and steal all your money.'

'I would chase you,' he said, leaning down to kiss me. 'And then I would spank you very, very hard.'

The waitress put the bill down and said she'd be back with the machine, so I opened his wallet. Not his gold American Express card. Not his gold Visa card. Not his dark blue Coutts card. He had more cards than a stationer's in there. I retrieved the silver card sandwiched between several fifty pound notes and a receipt and ran my finger across his name on it – JRT Milton. Jasper Ralph Thomas. Montgomery men always had to have Ralph as a middle name, he'd told me. So presumably if we had a son he would have the same... *STOP it, Polly.* I looked at the bill.

It was £144. Madly expensive for a quiet Monday night

supper but Jasper was the one who'd bought a bottle of champagne, I told myself, handing the waitress the silver card. I absentmindedly opened the receipt from his wallet as the waitress tapped at the machine. Blimey. I didn't have to feel bad about dinner because this was even more expensive. It was a hotel bill for £850.

And then, and I still don't know why I did this, what impulse made me do this, but I checked the date. It was from this weekend. A hotel in the Cotswolds called The Olde Bell. But. Weird. He'd been at home this weekend. So why did he have a receipt from a hotel in the Cotswolds in his wallet? My mind seemed to slow as I stared at the receipt. The bill was for two nights, two dinners and… five bottles of champagne. Plus a packet of Marlboro Lights. This weekend. I triple-checked the date. When he said he'd been at home, when he'd literally just told me he'd been at home trying to sort out his dysfunctional family. When he'd been oddly quiet all weekend.

My head felt foggy.

'Sorry, madam, your PIN?' said a voice at my shoulder. I reached for the machine. But I couldn't remember what his PIN was.

'All settled?' said Jasper, appearing at the table again.

'I can't remember the PIN,' I said woodenly, handing him the machine.

'Polly, darling,' he said, taking the machine and smiling at the waitress. 'I don't know. I tell you four little numbers and you forget in a matter of seconds. Here you go.' He handed it back to the waitress. 'And thank you very much, that was delicious.'

'No problem. See you again soon.'

'I hope so,' said Jasper, reaching across the table for his jacket. 'Right you, let's go home immediately.'

'I don't think I can,' I said, frozen in my seat.

'What? What's happened? I was only joking about the PIN.'

'No, it's not that,' I said, fingering the receipt in my lap. 'It's just... Where were you this weekend?'

'Oh, Pols. Come on. Can we not talk about my weekend again? Putting up with my decrepit father bellowing at my mad mother. I told you. Come on, let's go home.'

'Hang on,' I said, placing the receipt on the table in front of him and smoothing it out with the side of my hand. 'Talk me through this.'

He reached down, picked it up and frowned at it.

'Presumably you know what it says on it,' I went on, 'because you were there this weekend. Drinking champagne. A lot of champagne. Like some sort of... some sort of... rapper in a music video.'

'Ah,' Jasper said, looking down at the receipt. He paused, then moved to crouch down beside me and sighed. 'OK, OK, OK. I wasn't at home. I was in Burford. At a hotel. But the reason I was there, which I couldn't tell you before, is that Barny called me and he needed me to go and look after him. He and Willy are getting a divorce.'

'What?'

'The whole thing's a bloody mess,' he said, still crouching beside me. 'She caught him cheating on her.'

'With *whom*?' The thought that Barny could persuade not one but two women to sleep with him was genuinely astounding.

'*Shh*,' he said, glancing over his shoulder. 'Some woman he met in London. She went through his phone.'

'But why didn't you just tell me?' I was close to tears. I couldn't cry in The Electric.

'Budge up,' he said, standing up and sitting beside me. He took my hands in his. 'I promised him. And I didn't want to lie to you. So I thought the simplest thing was to get him drunk all weekend. And then I'd tell you in due course.'

A tear rolled down my cheek. I was now crying in The Electric. I was one of those women you see crying in public and feel sorry for.

Jasper wiped a tear away with a thumb and took my face in his hands. 'I'm so sorry. I'm sorry for not telling you. I'm sorry for being evasive. But he's one of my oldest friends and… and…' He stopped. 'Well, he needed me not to tell anyone.'

More tears rolled down my face.

'Come here.' He pulled my chin towards his face and kissed me, the salt of the tears mingling between our lips. 'Now, let's go home. Your home.'

I sniffed and picked my coat up. I felt relieved but still uncertain and confused all at the same time. And I had more questions but I felt afraid to ask them. We caught a black cab home but didn't even make it to my bedroom. Instead, he sat down on the sofa while I stood in front of him, then he reached his hands underneath my skirt and rolled my knickers down my legs, pulled me on top of him and we rocked together until we both came, my arms around his neck, Jasper biting into my shoulder. I felt a bit bad about doing this on Joe's sofa, but not that bad.

★

It was the next day that it all changed, although it started like any other in the office. Coffee, 430-calorie muffin when I told myself I was going to have a 200-calorie porridge, faff about on the internet for half an hour and try to think of a joke to post on Twitter, wonder where Lala is. I checked my phone. Nope. No message from her. Presumably her alarm hadn't gone off or she had a sore ear lobe or something.

A summons floated out from Peregrine's office: 'Polly, can you step inside my office for a moment?'

I shut down Twitter, wiped crumbs from around my mouth and went in. 'What's up?'

Peregrine looked up from his computer. 'Ah, Polly, morning.' He sounded oddly formal.

'What is it?' I said, feeling nervous. Had we got into some sort of legal trouble? Had my piece about the most handsome gynaecologist in Britain caused a letter from his lawyer?

Peregrine opened his mouth. Then closed it. Then opened it again. 'Well, the thing is, I mean...'

Oh, shit. I envisaged *Posh!* being sued by a strong-jawed

gynaecologist in a white coat. I'd be out of a job. Although at least it would force me to finally look for another one.

'What I'm trying to say,' he went on, 'is that I've been sent some pictures. Some paparazzi pictures. From the weekend, apparently. And, well…' He stopped.

'What?' I said. 'What are they?'

Peregrine turned his computer screen to face me and I leaned in towards it.

They had been taken in the dark and clearly from some distance, so it was quite hard to make them out. There was a figure, a tall man, and a woman with brunette hair in some sort of clinch outside a country pub. And the thing is, I don't know if you've ever discovered that someone you're in love with has been cheating on you. It only takes seconds to work it out when you find something – a pair of foreign knickers at the end of your bed, a text message that you 'accidentally' find on their phone, a grainy photograph of them kissing someone else – but everything slows down in those early seconds. Or stops, even. You can't compute it. It's like your brain is going on strike.

Me: *He wouldn't do this to me. He couldn't.*

My brain: *This is fairly conclusive evidence.*

Me: *But I was with him just last night. He told me he loved me when I left this morning. His sperm was actually still inside me. Some of it's probably still inside me now.*

Brain: *I know. Brutal. But you did know he was trouble. You knew that from the very start. You just forgot.*

Me: *Yes, but how could he do this? How could he physically actually do this? When he said he loved me?*

Brain: *He's a bastard.*

Me: *No, he's not, I love him.*

Brain: *Even though he's kissing someone else? That's quite a kiss, by the looks of things.*

Me: *Yes. No. I don't know. Fuck off.*

It sort of went a bit like that in my head. It was Jasper in the photos, no doubt. It was his hair and his tweed coat. But who was the woman? I leant in closer. Oh my God! I suddenly realized. Of course it was. It was Celestia from the photo shoot. Five-hundred-avocados-Celestia-Smythe, who wasn't Honourable at all, it turned out. Jasper had been away with Celestia this weekend. In Burford. Drinking all that champagne.

I stood up and felt dizzy.

Peregrine cleared his throat. 'So I've said we're not interested in the pictures.'

I stayed quiet.

'And, er, would you like to take the rest of the day off?'

I remained quiet.

'The thing is, that family, you know. Barking, I always thought...' He tailed off. 'Right, well, I'm just going to nip out for a second,' he added. 'You stay here for as long as you like.' He glanced up at his clock. 'Although I have got a meeting in an hour or so, but that can always be moved.'

Peregrine disappeared and I stood staring down at his computer screen. Then tears started rolling down my face. *Of course.* Of course this was going to happen. Of course I was never going to marry him. Of course there wasn't going to be a happy ending. There was never going to be a happy ending. I thought about Lala's warnings. I thought about Bill's warnings. I thought of Barny's snideness about Jasper's girlfriends and felt great waves of sadness fight with sheer disbelief inside my chest.

I had competing voices in my head. If I was really, truly, honest, hadn't I always felt like a fling for him? He was always going to end up with someone glossy and shiny like Celestia, wasn't he? Except he'd told me he loved me and he'd told me how different I was to the other women he'd ever dated. And then I thought back to my visit to Castle Montgomery four months ago, when I arrived a sceptic, assuming he'd be a bastard. A handsome bastard. But a bastard all the same. Except then he'd managed to lower my defences. So maybe I'd been nothing but a challenge for him all along? And once he'd proved he could win me over, the hunt was up. They loved fucking hunting, didn't they, the aristocracy? Jasper was the hound and I was the fox. The poor old fox. And now he'd caught me.

I suddenly had to get out of that office. I knew where I wanted to be, so I quickly went back to my desk, grabbed my bag and my coat and went. 'I've gotta go,' I said, over my shoulder to Enid as I left.

I wrote a text message to Jasper in my Uber.

I never want to see or hear from you again.

There. Not a complicated message to understand. Then I sat back and started crying. Nina Simone was warbling away on the radio, which made me cry harder. My phone started buzzing in my hand. But I didn't want to talk. There was literally nothing to say. I was going to have my dramatic moment of crying in the back of this Uber to Nina Simone. It was like that *Sense and Sensibility* scene where Marianne finds out Willoughby has become engaged to that rich woman because he's been cut off from his own fortune. I just wanted to lie on my bed and cry. I caught the eye of the Uber driver in his mirror, who looked away quickly. A modern version of that scene anyway.

Twenty minutes later, I rang the doorbell and Sidney answered, looking immediately panicked at my face. 'Oh, Polly, dear me, are you all right?'

'No,' I said, through a thick nose. 'I've broken up with Jasper.'

'Oh, poor you,' said Sidney, ever the master of understatement. 'Well, your mother's upstairs.'

'Thank you,' I said, wiping my nose with the back of my hand and climbing the stairs.

Upstairs, Mum was peering into the fridge, her back to me. She wasn't wearing a headscarf so it looked like a small bald burglar was seeing what he could scavenge.

'Hi, Mum,' I said, through a blocked nose.

Mum whirled around, hand still on the fridge door. 'Polly, what are you doing here? What on earth's the matter?'

'Jasper's cheated on me.' As I said it, my voice broke again and a fresh wave of tears sprang up.

'Oh, darling, come here.' Mum opened her arms. Her head smelt of talcum powder.

I sobbed into her shoulder, mumbling words, trying to explain.

'Lied... weekend... Celestia,' I burbled into her shoulder. I heard the flick of a kettle in the background.

'Big cup of sugary tea,' Mum said. 'And come and sit here.' She sat down and patted the space on the sofa next to her.

'I think I'm going to take Bertie for his constitutional,' said Sidney.

'Oh, would you?' said Mum. 'And take some plastic bags with you. He's got into an awful habit of going on the pavement outside Costa.'

'I should have known,' I said, Mum turning back to me. 'Everyone said so, didn't they? "He's so complicated", "he's got issues", "he's bad news".'

'I'm a bit lost, Polly, my love. I need you to tell me the whole story.'

Half an hour later, Mum was standing at the hob making lunch: her version of paella (to which she had added a tin of palm hearts) and I had finished updating her.

'Well,' she said, squinting at a packet of Knorr beef stock cubes. 'I think he's a cad and you're better off without him.'

'How do I not be in love with him though?'

'Oh, darling. Have you spoken to him?'

'No. I don't really want to. No point, is there?'

Mum shrugged and I reached into my bag for my phone. Fourteen missed calls from Jasper, one message saying *Ring me*, another one, ten minutes later, which just said *I'm so sorry*. Bastard.

There was also an email from Peregrine, offering me a few days off from the office.

> Polly, there's a new spa in Spain which I want some-
> one to review. Massages, yoga, coffee enemas, and
> that sort of thing. It's called The Olive Retreat, let
> me know and we'll arrange from here.

'Mum,' I said, looking up, 'how do you feel about a few days in Spain?'

16

A FEW DAYS LATER, after Mum was granted permission to fly by Dr Ross, we arrived in the arrivals hall of Malaga, where I spotted a thin man with a droopy moustache holding up a sign that read 'The Olive Retreat' with a picture of an olive tree on it.

'Mum, over there, that's us,' I said, nodding in his direction and pushing the trolley as Mum – floppy sun hat already on to protect her scalp – walked behind me.

'Hi there,' I said, approaching him.

'Welcome, welcome,' he said, with a thick Spanish accent. 'Miss Polly?'

'*Si*,' I replied. My GCSE Spanish could just about manage that one.

'And Miss Susan?' he said.

'"Miss Susan", I like very much,' said Mum. 'And you are?'

'I am Alejandro,' he said, doing a little bow and taking the trolley. 'We go now to The Olive Retreat. This way please. Follow me, follow me.' He whirled the trolley around as if driving a rally car and set off for the exit at a brisk pace, parting people like Moses.

'How long is it to the retreat?' asked Mum, in a hopeful

tone, half an hour later from the back of his taxi. We had climbed high into a range of hills covered with pine trees and Alejandro was taking bends with the confidence of an Olympic bobsleigh champion.

'Not far, Miss Susan. It's just down this hill and then through the town and up another hill.'

'We'll need a retreat after this,' Mum muttered, before closing her eyes. I looked at my phone. Three messages from EE welcoming me to Spain. Nothing else. Great. There was no reception and no Wi-Fi at the retreat anyway. I'd read the introduction pack on the flight. No reception, no Wi-Fi, no caffeine, no alcohol, no sugar, no wheat, no dairy, no meat. 'Just natural peace and tranquillity to help you shake off the pressures of everyday life,' it said. Although on the 'How to Reach Us' page, the retreat had given its helicopter coordinates. So presumably sometimes the natural peace and tranquillity was disturbed by bankers flying in to give their livers a break.

It would do me good to be phone-free for a few days anyway. The photos of Jasper had appeared on *MailOnline* two days earlier, I knew, because I'd had 2,810 messages from Lala, several from Lex and a message from Bill saying he knew I might not want to chat but I could call him whenever I wanted. I'd avoided the story myself, not wanting to relive the humiliation, the torturous sadness of seeing them again. Of knowing that they were taken when I was in Norfolk on Lex's hen, thinking about Jasper answering Mr and Mrs questions, listening to Lex bang on about my wedding at Castle

Montgomery. Why did I fall for it? Why did I let myself fall for Jasper's act, I thought, for the ninety billionth time since standing in Peregrine's office, looking at his computer screen.

I was jolted from my black reverie by Alejandro, who pulled right suddenly on to a dirt track. 'Up there, you see?' he said, pointing ahead into the hills. 'You can see the house.' His finger bumped up and down as we lurched along the track. 'We'll be there in five minutes,' he added.

He stopped, five minutes later, in front of a solid metal gate. Then he wound down his window, leant out and tapped in a few numbers, whereupon the gate gave a jolt and started slowly sliding open. Once he deemed it far enough, Alejandro drove us through it and, with expert precision, missed the gate with his wing mirror by a few millimetres.

'*Bienvenido* and welcome to The Olive Retreat,' he said, driving along a track and turning the engine off beside a cluster of stone houses.

Relieved to have made it, I opened my door and stood up in the afternoon sunshine. We were surrounded by dozens of olive trees that sloped down to an infinity pool halfway at the bottom of the garden. Cicadas croaked noisily around us while Alejandro, breathing heavily, hauled our bags out of the car.

A large woman appeared at the door of one of the cottages. She was dressed entirely in white. A white cotton tunic over white trousers and white espadrilles. Also, a white turban, with thick gold hoops hanging from each ear. Gold bangles clanked on each wrist as she hurried over.

'Darlings, my darlings, welcome to paradise!' she said,

holding her arms out and crushing me to her chest. 'Did you have an awful journey? You poor darlings, you must be frazzled.'

She released me and reached her arms out for Mum, who firmly stuck her hand out for the woman to shake.

'I'm Susan,' said Mum.

'Susan, you are so welcome, we are thrilled to have you here at The Olive Retreat,' said the woman, shaking Mum's hand. But it was a trick, because then she simply used her hand as leverage and pulled her into another vice-like hug.

'I'm Mary,' said the woman, letting go of Mum. 'Now, follow me, let me show you to your rooms. You're both in this cottage, the Rose Quartz cottage, rose quartz of course being the crystal for relationships, for divine love, for nourishment and healing. Very important, rose quartz.'

'What are the other cottages called?' I asked.

'Well, next door is Amethyst, for spiritual development, and also for the menopause.' Mary looked pointedly at Mum. 'Then Hematite along from that, which is marvellous for deflecting negative energies. And for your kidneys. And then there's Blue Moonstone on the end, which is all about inner growth and hormone balancing. We can have eight altogether on our little retreats, but we're just five this week. You two and three other detoxers, who are just finishing their afternoon meditation session.'

We followed Mary into the Rose Quartz cottage, into a small sitting room area with salmon-coloured walls, a big, pale pink sofa and a leather armchair underneath a bookcase. There was a wood stove in the corner.

'So, this is where you can sit and relax in the evenings if you like, after your massages. Read from our library, have a cup of ginger tea.'

'Lovely,' said Mum.

'And there's no Wi-Fi?' I thought I might as well check.

Mary threw her hands in the air, gold bracelets clanking. 'No, my love. No Wi-Fi here. No screens of any sort. If you've brought your laptops, then please leave them in your rooms. Ditto your phones. Emails interfere with the detox process. Now,' she went on, walking into a bedroom, 'Susan, I thought you might like this room because it has a bath.'

It was a white bedroom, with a pair of open pink shuttered doors leading out to the olive grove. A mosquito net hung over the bed, pinned back either side of the pale pink headboard.

'There is air conditioning if you like but you may prefer the fan,' she said, pointing upwards to the ceiling. 'Air conditioning interferes with the detox process but some people struggle with the heat here.'

She walked to the doors and pushed them wider to let more sunlight in. 'I tend to sleep with them open in the summer myself. Now, Polly...' She walked out of Mum's room and into another one on the other side of the sitting room. 'This is your room.'

'Great,' I said, my eye falling on a book called *Detox your Soul* on the bedside table.

'So,' said Mary, 'if you want to make yourselves comfortable, then come down to the main house in ten minutes. I'll introduce you to everyone then we have a gong bath.'

'A what?' I asked.

'All will be revealed,' said Mary, waggling an index finger at me.

Exactly nine minutes later, in case she waggled her finger at me again, Mum and I walked down the path through the olive grove towards the main building.

'It's an old farmhouse apparently,' I said to Mums.

'How did it all start? What's Mother Superior's story?'

'Mary's? No idea. I meant to google it on the way here. And obviously, I can't now.'

'No,' said Mum. 'I haven't got any bars on my phone and I told Sidney I'd text him when we arrived.'

Outside the house's main door was a courtyard with a small pond in it and the faint tinkling of a wind chime.

'Hello?' I said, down a long white corridor. '*Hellooooo*?'

'Shoes off, shoes off,' said Mary, suddenly appearing behind us. 'We operate a barefoot policy in this retreat.'

We slipped off our shoes and left them by the door, where there was a sign of a smiling Buddha above a picture of a flip-flop with a thick red line through it.

'I'll give you a quick tour, and then introduce you to everyone. That's the kitchen up there. That is where you will eat all your meals. Follow me, I'll just quickly show you the tea station outside it.'

She walked down the corridor and pointed through an archway. There, an electric urn sat on a huge dresser. The shelves were crammed with boxes of tea. I squinted at them. Mint tea, camomile tea, rhubarb and ginger tea, various detox teas, various 'night-time teas'. Even a pink box of 'women's tea'. I picked it up and looked at the contents.

'It's ayurvedic, that one,' said Mary. 'Ginger, orange peel, dandelion and camomile. Bit of fennel. Delicious. Very good for balancing your hormones, Polly.'

'And then through here,' she went on, going back down the corridor and turning right, 'is our classroom, where you'll have nutritional lectures tomorrow afternoon. And then beyond that are the massage rooms. You'll have one every night, different sorts. Sometimes deep tissue, sometimes Thai, sometimes shiatsu.' She looked at Mum's stomach. 'Have you ever thought about shiatsu, Susan?'

'Err, no, I don't believe I have,' said Mum.

'It's terribly good for getting sluggish systems moving a bit. Moving our energies around, you know, making us...' she dropped her voice to a loud whisper '... regular'.

'Oh, I see,' said Mum, putting a hand on her stomach.

'Now, no time for chit-chat. We must get to the studio. Just across the courtyard. This way.' She swept outside again, jewellery clanking over the wind chime, and into a converted barn, one wall of which was sheet glass and looked out to the swimming pool. Five mats lay on the floor and, at the front, a woman with dreadlocks and a pink leotard sat cross-legged on the floor beside what looked like an enormous dinner gong, at least a metre across.

'This is our studio,' said Mary, 'where you will do all yoga, meditation and possibly one or two other surprises we have for you. Like the gong bath. And this is Delilah, our gong expert.'

Delilah beamed at us from the floor. 'Welcome.'

'Hi,' I said, unsure of whether it was terribly London to offer out my hand. 'I'm Polly.'

'And I'm Susan,' said Mum, hands also hovering by her side.

'*Namaste*,' said Delilah, putting her hands together in prayer position and bowing her head.

The door behind us opened. First in was a young, thin blonde woman with thick black eyebrows that looked like they'd been drawn on by a marker pen. Then, a middle-aged Asian man, followed by a large, middle-aged woman with an unfortunate pixie haircut.

'Polly and Susan, this is Jane,' said Mary, pointing at the blonde one with eyebrows. 'Then that's Aidar, from Kazakhstan. And Alison bringing up the rear. Everyone, this is Polly and her mother Susan.' We smiled shyly at one another, apart from Aidar, who walked to a mat and sat down.

'*Shhhhh* now, everyone, settle yourselves,' said Delilah, tiptoeing around, handing out blankets and small bean bags. 'Lie on your backs and breathe. Just deep breaths in, deep breaths out.' She demonstrated in case we didn't know how to breathe, inhaling loudly through her nostrils and out again through her mouth.

I lay back, propping my head up with a cushion, and kicked the blanket so it covered my feet. I lay my arms over the top of it and put the bean bag over my eyes. It smelt of lavender. I breathed deeply. I was going to concentrate really hard on this. I was not going to let thoughts of Jasper or anyone else infiltrate my mind. I was just going to breathe and relax. I inhaled again as deeply as I could and was about to exhale when…

GONGGGGGGGGG. I opened one eye and squinted at the front, where Delilah was standing beside the gong, a stick in her hand. 'Eyes closed please,' she said, spotting me. 'Just breathe in, and breathe out, and let the vibration therapy still your mind.'

GONGGGGGGGGGGGGGGG, it went again. And again, and again. Sometimes softly, sometimes building into a crescendo. It was quite hard to still your mind while the Battle of Britain was going off metres from your ears. But I lay still, breathing in and breathing out. In and out. In and out. Letting the mad hippy play her musical instrument over us.

Within minutes, I was even less soothed by the sound of snoring to my left. It was Aidar, who'd apparently managed to still his mind so much he'd gone to sleep. And as his snores increased in volume, so did Delilah's gonging. It was, I thought on balance, probably the least relaxed I had ever been.

It finally came to a stop and I looked at the clock through one eye: forty-five minutes of din.

'Take your time to come up, everyone,' instructed Delilah, sitting cross-legged beside her instrument again. 'The gong bath can be quite intense for some people.'

I sat up immediately. Mum removed the bean bag from her eyes. 'Wasn't that good?' she said.

*

At supper, we were each given a quarter of an aubergine and a few leaves of kale drizzled with tahini sauce. Aidar poked suspiciously at his kale with a knife. Celestia would have liked this, I thought, before quickly trying to push her out of my head.

'I'll have yours, Aidar, if you don't want it?' said Alison. He passed over his plate.

'So what brings you two here?' she said, scraping the kale on to her own plate and handing Aidar's back.

'It's for work, technically. I work for a magazine and we get to review places like this,' I said. 'But I sort of needed a break too.'

'I'm not being funny,' interjected Jane. 'But this is one of the best places for that. And I've done 'em all.'

'All?'

'Aye. I've done the Mayr clinic; you know the one in Austria where you must chew all your food fifty times. And I've done Green Pastures in Arizona, where you only eat grass for ten days.'

'Actual grass?'

'Actual grass,' she said, nodding. 'It were hell. And colonics every day. But I've never felt so clean in all my life.'

'Have a look on the board and see when your massages are,' said Jane, waving her fork at a pinboard behind us.

The pinboard had postcards pinned to it with slogans like 'Be grateful to everyone' and 'No matter how hard the past, you can always begin again'. In the middle of the pinboard was a sheet of paper with our names next to times and massage rooms. I was due to have a shiatsu massage at seven. 'Mum, you're at seven this evening too. Deep tissue in room three.'

'Lovely,' said Mum. 'Massage then bath and bed. No chance of a nice glass of wine, I suppose?'

Jane shook her head.

★

'You have a lot of anger in your stomach,' said Isabel, my masseuse, an hour later. I was lying on blankets on the floor of the massage room in a t-shirt and tracksuit bottoms while she prodded my stomach with her hands. 'I just need to get a bit…' She pushed her hands deeper, as if she was trying to get them underneath my ribcage. 'There, that's it. That's releasing your liver a bit. Feel that?'

'Erm…'

'If you don't mind me asking, do you drink a lot, Polly?'

'No. Not really. I mean I've probably been overdoing it a bit recently because I broke up with someone but…'

'Ah, that explains all the anger then. It's very angry, your whole system,' she said, circling her hands on my stomach again before it bubbled. We both heard it. 'There!' said Isabel, like a delighted midwife. 'You see? That's energy shifting about.'

'Mmm,' I said, 'terrific.'

She prodded and pushed and poked – sometimes with her elbows – for the next half an hour while my stomach made more embarrassing noises.

'Sorry,' I said every time, while Isabel reorganized my internal organs.

'There,' she said, finally, cradling my head with her hands. 'You have much better energies now, Polly. Would you like a glass of water?'

'No, no, don't worry. I think I'm going to go back to my room and have a shower, but thank you very much. That was—' what was the right word? '—extraordinary.'

'You are most welcome. *Namaste*,' said Isabel, putting her hands together in prayer position and bowing.

'Goodnight,' I said solemnly, putting my hands together and bowing back.

Mum wasn't in her room when I got back to the cottage so I ran a bath in her bathroom. There was a Kilner jar of bath salts next to it, so I chucked in several handfuls for good measure. Bit more purging couldn't hurt. I'd run it too hot so I pushed the cold tap on again and slowly lay down, squeaking as the hot water scalded my back.

'Polly, are you all right? What on earth are you doing?' came Mum's voice from her room.

'Oh, sorry, Mum, I thought I'd grab the first bath. How was your massage?' I shouted back.

'Blissful. He had a good go at the knots in my shoulder and neck.'

'He?'

'Yes, an Australian. Long hair. If you're doing that I'm going to walk down the hill a bit and see if I can get any reception.'

'OK, cool, won't be long. I'm just going to flay myself for another ten minutes or so.'

I heard the door close behind her and lifted my leg out of the water to turn the cold tap off with my foot. I would not be walking anywhere to check my phone. I would read the book about detoxing my soul on the bedside table and fall asleep. Although in the end I didn't even get that far. I climbed into bed and fell asleep before 9 p.m. Must have been something in the bath salts.

★

The next morning started with an early yoga session at 7.15 a.m. Mum stood in the studio trying to touch her toes. She got to just below her knees and stood up again.

Aidar was sitting on his mat in the corner, rubbing his eyes. Jane was lying on her back, eyes closed, inhaling and exhaling like a twenty-a-day smoker. Alison hadn't appeared. I sat down on my mat. I'd never been very sure about yoga. All those weird positions like Barking Dragon done by people with t-shirts that say things like 'Love' and 'Joy'.

'Right then,' said a blond man with an Australian accent, walking through the door in a vest that said 'Breathe'. 'Morning, everyone, let's get started with a few breathing exercises. Legs crossed, on the mat.'

'Morning, Simon,' said Jane, sitting up and beaming at him in, I noticed, a fairly low-cut gym top.

'Good morning, Jane, how are you?'

'I'm wonderful, thank you. I'm not sure we've got Alison today. I don't think she's a morning person.'

'Not to worry,' said Simon. 'Morning, Susan.'

'Morning, Simon,' said Mum. 'I feel ever so good after last night.'

'That's what all the girls tell me.' He winked at her. Please.

'Sorry, we haven't met,' he said, holding his hand out to me.

'Hi, I'm Polly.'

It was like shaking hands with Samson.

'Polly, lovely name.'

'Thank you,' I mumbled.

'Right then, everyone else on your butts. Legs crossed, eyes closed. Deep breaths in for five. One, two, three, four, five. Then out for five. Five, four, three, two, one.'

We made a stiff bunch of four. Mum and I burst into laughter every few minutes, failing to stand on one leg for more than three seconds.

'Doesn't matter, girls,' said Simon, 'You're trying.'

He had the thick arms of a lumberjack, I thought, pulling my knees to my chest. My stomach rumbled and I twisted my head to the side to see if anyone heard.

After an hour, Simon told us to lie flat on our backs. 'One leg in the air, please, another quick stretch of your hamstrings before breakfast.'

I put my right leg in the air. Simon walked across, knelt down and pushed his shoulder into the back of my thigh, stretching it further. 'Let's get a bit deeper with that,' he said.

Given that I was wearing old Lycra running leggings with a

crotch that had, over the years, developed that smell of musty, dead mouse, I found this disconcerting. But, obviously, I didn't say anything. I just tried to concentrate on not farting. He had a tattoo on his bicep, some sort of Hindi, I thought.

'What does that mean?' I asked, nodding towards his arm, trying to break the quiet awkwardness of this man being within sniffing distance of my vagina.

'The tat? It's a Sanskrit mantra,' he said. 'Change legs.' He put my right leg down and I swung my left one into the air.

'What does it mean?'

'May all beings everywhere be happy and free,' said Simon.

Ha, fat chance, I thought, as he pushed into my left leg with his shoulder. Quite hard to feel happy and free when you felt so sad you'd recently considered googling 'has anyone ever actually died of a broken heart?'

'Right, you lot,' he said after a few seconds, lowering my leg down and winking again. 'Breakfast time.'

★

The following two days were more of the same. Up at 7 a.m. for yoga, a breakfast that involved several kinds of nut, a hike into the hills, more nuts, more yoga, more discussion of bowel movements, more meditation, more massages. On the final afternoon, Mum and I walked up to the cottage and sat in deckchairs outside it. Well, I sat in the sun, Mum sat in the shade underneath an umbrella, fanning herself with her copy of *The Lady*.

'How you feeling, love?' she said.

'All right, but I think my shoulders are burning,' I said, opening one eye to squint at my right arm.

'I meant about Jasper.'

'Oh.' I paused for a moment to think. The truth was I didn't really know. My brain was still churning through it all. 'All right. I mean, I hate him. But I think a bit of me is still in love with him at the same time.'

'Oh, darling, that won't change overnight.'

'What I still don't get though is how he can have said all that stuff, have told me he loved me and so on, and then did that. How can anyone do that? I keep going over it again and again in my head. I just can't imagine it. I can't imagine having gone away with someone else. How does that even work?'

'They're just so different. To us, I mean. You're a brilliant, talented, beautiful girl. And he's just a… silly, silly boy.'

'He's a fucking moron.'

'Well, let's not lower ourselves to vulgarities, Polly darling,' she said.

'Anyway, Mum, I'm sorry. More importantly, how are you?'

'I'm all right, darling,' she said, resting her copy of *The Lady* in her lap. 'It's been a funny few months, hasn't it?'

'Yeah,' I said. 'But you're feeling…'

'I'm feeling all right,' she replied firmly. 'I'm starting to feel much better. Less tired.'

'Good,' I said, feeling guilty that I'd been as wet as a flannel over Jasper, when Mum had been so stoic about cancer.

'It's hard being on your own sometimes, Polly love,' Mum

went on, as if psychic. 'And it's brutal having your heart broken, but it's better than being with the wrong person. You don't want to marry the wrong person.'

'But you and Dad weren't wrong...'

'No, no! He was the right person for me,' she said, 'he just had to leave us a bit early, that's all. And until Sidney came along, there wasn't anyone else I wanted to sacrifice my life for. Never sacrifice anything. The right person will only add to your life, he won't take anything away from it.'

I leant back in my deckchair, wondering whether I'd ever be as wise about men as my mother. Was it being in your sixties? Maybe it was.

'Do you know what I always thought?' she went on, fanning her face again with the magazine.

'Mmm?'

'I always imagined Bill might be the right person for you. Eventually.'

I opened my eyes again. 'What? Bill? Mum, come on. No. Gross. Absolutely *not*. And anyway, he's with Willow.'

'Oh, she's not right,' Mum said. 'Terribly sweet but not... Well... I'm not sure she's challenging enough for him.'

'Well, they've bought a dog so I feel like they're as good as married,' I said. Bill, I mean honestly. Perhaps the sun had made her temporarily mad. I loved him but not like THAT. I'd known that ever since we were teenagers. Bill was the friend who bought your mum flowers and always called when he said he would. One of the nice guys, which was all very well for some. Like Willow, for instance. But

I'd always wanted more than that. I'd always wanted to be shaken by love, consumed by it, inflated with passion and longing and with someone I ached for when we were apart. That was real love, right? Although, I reflected, reaching for the sun lotion, that was before I met Jasper and had actually been rocked by love. Perhaps I should dial my expectations down a fraction for whenever I next had a boyfriend, in five hundred years' time. In real life, all that emotional turbulence was quite trying.

I was off men for the time being anyway. I was going to take a break from worrying about being single and not having a plus one at Lex's wedding. Maybe it was the Spanish air making me feel stronger. When I got home, I was going to concentrate on finding a new job and potentially try to drink a bit less wine. Be healthier. Start taking vitamins. Eat five a day, or was it ten a day now?

'Buying a dog doesn't mean you have to get married, Polly darling,' Mum continued from her chair. 'Which reminds me, I wonder how Bertie's stomach is?'

I closed my eyes again at the prospect of a conversation about Bertie's movements.

'Anyway, there might be a nice chap at Lex's wedding,' she went on. 'A friend of Hamish's you haven't met.'

That seemed unlikely.

'You never know,' she added.

People always say that. 'You never know.' As if you're going to meet someone when you pop to the shops for a loaf of bread. Or on the bus. I never saw anyone promising on the bus. It was usually teenagers sexting one another or mothers ramming everybody's ankles with their buggies.

'Nope, no more men,' I said, my eyes still shut.

Later that night, I got out of the bath and brushed my teeth, wiping a circle in the steamed-up mirror. Four days of eating like a creature from Farthing Wood had at least perked up my skin, I noticed. And the dark circles under my eyes had gone. Plus, when I looked down at my belly, that was a bit flatter. Which would help with that blood clot of a dress that I had to wear at Lex's wedding.

*

'Did you have a nice time?' said Alejandro, putting my bag into the boot of his car the next morning.

'Yes, thank you,' I said primly, climbing into the back, where Mum was already sitting, headscarf in her hands, rubbing her head.

'I feel ever so much better, Polly darling,' she said. 'Do I look better?'

I nodded because she did. She looked less tired. 'Yup, Mum, you look like a total babe. Like Sinead O'Connor.'

'Who's that?'

'An Irish singer.'

'I don't know him. But look, here, can you hold my phone and take one of those, what are they called? Belfies? For Sidney?'

*

At the airport, I turned my phone on for the first time in five days and it started vibrating instantly. Dozens of boring work emails, a message from Lex asking if I'd died, a message from Bill saying could I ring him, five million more misspelt messages from Lala.

'Sidney says he and Bertie have had a lovely time together,' said Mum in the lounge. 'I'm going to get a *Daily Mail*. Do you want anything?'

'I'll come with you. I need some paper and a pen.'

I'd decided I was going to spend the flight back writing a to-do list. Top of which was to get a new job. But what?

It was in the airport shop that I saw it, the *Posh!* cover with Celestia grinning out from it, lying in a bath of avocados. I felt another wave of humiliation and quite sick at the sight of her face. I was never going to eat another avocado again.

★

I didn't exactly bounce out of bed with glee at the thought of returning to *Posh!* the next morning.

'Morning,' I said, sticking my head around Peregrine's door when I got in, wondering if he'd mention Jasper.

'Ah, Polly,' he said, 'good to have you back. Now, I've had an idea. Can you make a start on a piece about the Countess of Basingstoke's new guinea pig?'

Lala appeared in the office an hour or so later. 'Oh, Pols,' she said, giving me a huge, cigarette-infused hug. 'I've missed you. I'm sorry about Jaz. He's not good enough, that's the thing. And if he wants to date boring old Celestia Smythe then good luck to him, I say. Honestly, if I see him at the Fotheringham-Montagues' drinks party this weekend I will...'

She rattled on while I winced internally a bit at the word 'date'. Part of me wanted to quiz Lala on what she knew about Jasper and Celestia, but I knew it wouldn't help. That probing her for information was essentially mental self-harm.

So, instead of discussing Jasper or thinking up interview questions for a guinea pig, I spent most of the morning in the fashion cupboard with Legs, who had called in several pairs of shoes for me to wear to Lex's wedding.

'It is like trying to work with that monster who lives in the hills,' said Legs, kneeling in front of me, a pile of discarded shoes lying around us like fallen soldiers.

'What monster?' I asked.

'You know, that one who has all those hairs and leaves feet marks in the snow.'

'Bigfoot?'

'Yes. You are him.'

'Thanks. What about those ones?' I pointed at a Valentino box which contained a pair of black silk heels.

Legs sighed and reached for the box. 'They might work. Now, do we want to talk about Jasper or maybe we don't talk about him?'

'I don't think there's much to say, Legs. We've broken up and...'

'OK, we don't talk about him,' she said. 'Bastard man.'

'He is a bastard man,' I replied as she held out one of the shoes for me to try.

'Polly, you need to wax your giant toes.'

'Big toes, they're called. Not giant toes.'

They fitted. Just about. Obviously they cut off all circulation to my giant toes and they would give me blisters within five minutes of arriving at church, but I'd just lob a few Compeed plasters in my bag.

★

'Joe told me your sad news,' said Barbara as she scanned my solitary carton of soup that evening with disapproval.

'Did he now?'

'You should try and get him back.'

I ignored this and fished in my purse for some coins.

'A woman needs a man, Polly. And this man was a good man. He had a castle.'

'A woman doesn't need a man, Barbara,' I said firmly, 'and he wasn't *that* good anyway. He cheated on me with someone else.'

'Ah,' she said, throwing her hands in the air. 'This is just sex, Polly. It doesn't matter. Men need sex all the time. This is how it is. When Albert was alive he…'

I absolutely didn't need to hear about Albert and Barbara's sex life. 'I've got to run, Barbara. I need to pack for my friend's wedding.'

'It should be your wedding,' she shouted at me as I left.

★

'Thanks for sharing the news with Barbara,' I said upstairs to Joe, who was lying on his sofa with a plate of toast balanced on his chest.

'She was asking all sorts of indelicate questions about when you were getting engaged, so I wanted to shut the old harridan up before you came back.'

'Hasn't worked,' I said, emptying my pea soup into a saucepan.

'Any word from him?' he went on.

'Nope. I think he's given up.'

'You couldn't have married a toff,' he said a few minutes later, through a mouthful of toast. His eyes remained on *EastEnders*.

'Really?'

'No. It may be the twenty-first century but the aristocracy is still insane. Bad genes, bad breath, terrible taste in clothes.' He swallowed his toast and brushed crumbs off his chest on to the carpet. 'This just confirms my belief that we should have had a revolution and lopped all their heads off.'

'Maybe.'

'No maybe about it, he wasn't nearly good enough for you, Pols. I mean it.'

'Thanks, love.' I poured my soup into a bowl and sat on the sofa, balancing the bowl on my knees. 'Anyway, catch me up with *EastEnders*, will you?'

★

Later that night I was lying in bed, scrolling through all of Lala's Instagram pictures, when my phone buzzed with a WhatsApp from Bill.

I am about to send a carrier pigeon, as I can only assume my messages of concern aren't getting through. You around for dinner this week?

I realized I still hadn't replied to him.

SORRY, but yes. Thursday? And I'll probably live. X

Bill's reply popped up on the screen.

Perfect. Our usual. Will book a table for 7. Lots of wine. What a tosser. X

I put my phone on my bedside table and told myself to go to sleep. At least Bill hadn't said 'I told you so'. Although he was probably saving that for Thursday.

★

'I've ordered a bottle of red,' said Bill, when I arrived at the Italian later that week.

'Good,' I said, sitting down and reaching for a packet of breadsticks.

'How you doing?'

'Don't look at me like that.'

'Like what?'

'Like I'm a wounded animal,' I said, crunching a breadstick. 'I'm fine. I should have known. Everybody warned me and so on and so on.'

'Did I say a thing?'

'No, I could just tell. From your expression.'

'For what it's worth,' said Bill, 'I'm sorry for you but relieved. He wasn't the one for you. I don't care if the guy owned a hundred castles. You don't want to live in a castle anyway. In Yorkshire. It's very cold in Yorkshire.'

'Thanks,' I said. 'That's what Joe said. But I'm still a bit confused. How we went from full on, saying I love you, to him going away for a weekend with someone. But I guess...' I trailed off.

'Listen,' he said, 'men are strange. People are pretty strange. But men are even stranger. Who knows why he did it. But don't drive yourself mad by wondering. Although easier said than done, I know.'

'When did you become such a relationship guru?'

'I'm not,' he said. 'I just know you. I know you'll say you're fine but you'll go round and round in your head about it. But... fuck him.'

'Cheers to that,' I said, raising my glass to him. We clinked and a waiter came over to take our order. Bill had his usual (American Hot extra hot); I had mine (spaghetti carbonara).

'How are you anyway?' I said.

'I am good,' he said slowly.

'What?' I said, sensing something.

'I've got some news actually.'

'Which is... ?'

'I've asked Willow to move in with me.'

'Oh my God! Are you serious?'

'Yes!' He burst out laughing. 'Why would I joke about that?'

'I just… It's just… you've only been going out for what…
six months?'

He shook his head. 'Eight or so. And I know. That's still
quick. But she's been staying there anyway, and she makes
me happy. And I just think why not? Especially at our age.'

I blinked at him. Firstly, 'at our age' indeed. Bill was thirty.
He wasn't ninety. And secondly, just, well, blimey.

'She's just not totally who I thought you'd end up with,' I
said, trying to sound cheery.

'Me neither,' he said, through another mouthful of breadstick. 'But the more I thought about it, the more it seemed
to make sense. We've got Crumpet now. And I didn't want
to tell you so soon after, well, Jasper and everything,' he
continued. 'But then I thought you'd see us at Lex's wedding
next weekend anyway, so…'

'Dude, congratulations,' I said, raising my glass again. But
then I suddenly felt a wave of tears. Oh, Christ, not again,
Polly. You cannot cry in a restaurant again, I told myself.
Are you trying to clock up some sort of record for number of
London restaurants you can cause a scene in? But it was too
late. My eyes welled up and spilled over. Tears all down my
cheeks again. Fucking hell.

'Pols?' said Bill. 'What's up?'

'I don't know,' I said, my voice all thick. 'I'm sorry. I'm
happy for you, I promise. I'm just tired, I think. And emotional
at the moment. And just… oh God, I don't know. I'm sorry.'

A waiter appeared at our table and put our plates down.

'Would you like some Parmesan?' he said chirpily.

'I think we're good for the moment, thanks, mate,' said Bill to the waiter, as a tear fell into my carbonara. He handed me his napkin then put his hand over mine on the table.

'Maybe you need some time off work?' he said. 'Everything with Jasper. And your mum…'

'I've just had some time off,' I said, blowing my nose on a napkin. 'I think I need a new job.'

'Did you ever email my mate Luke? About that website?'

I shook my head. 'Sorry, I totally forgot.' I'd meant to and then I'd got distracted by Jasper. I welled up again. How was I ever going to get a new job if I was so useless?

'Why don't you do that tomorrow?' said Bill. 'I mentioned you to him and he was keen to meet. They need a ton of new writers apparently.'

I sniffed. *Come on, Polly, get your shit together.* 'Yep, good plan. And thank you.'

''Course,' he said. 'I'd do anything for you. You know that. Or you should know that. How's your mum by the way?'

'Good,' I said, blowing my nose again. 'I think so, anyway. Last chemo done. Feeling better. So, we just need to keep an eye on her bloods now and make sure everything's gone.'

'Phew,' he said. 'I mean you're my favourite Spencer but Susan comes in a pretty close second.'

I smiled at him through my puffy eyes. 'Thanks.'

17

ON THE BUS HOME that evening after dinner with Bill I mulled everything over. Mum had been on her own for years. I was perfectly capable of doing the same thing. I didn't need to be with anyone. I was going to concentrate on my career and Bill was going to introduce me to his news website mate. But I still felt a tiny slither of unease in my chest about Bill moving in with Willow. And I wasn't sure whether that was because my friends were all growing up and several stages ahead of me in life. Or because it felt like I was losing Bill.

By Saturday morning, the day of Lex and Hamish's wedding, I hadn't resolved it. And I woke at Lex's parents' house in a funny mood. Funny as in contemplative, not as in 'ha ha'. My best friend was getting married, I didn't even have a plus one. But my best friend was getting married to the wrong person. At least to someone who I still worried was the wrong person, for all Lex's assurances that she loved him. It was never like this in *Sense and Sensibility*. Eleanor and Marianne married their right men in the end, although Marianne was still a bit sad about Willoughby. But she'd definitely picked the right one in the end. Good old Colonel Brandon. Where was my Colonel Brandon? I wondered. Safe, dependable Colonel

Brandon with a nice big house. There didn't seem to be many of them lurking in the pubs of West London.

I got out of bed and looked through the window at the lawn. Or where the lawn would be if it wasn't covered with a marquee the size of a circus tent. Lex's parents, Pete and Karen, lived in a big, yellowstone house twenty minutes from the centre of Oxford. Pete had 'done very well' (the polite way of saying 'made out like a bandit') in the City in the early 2000s and retired just before everything went wrong in 2008. These days he had the relaxed air of a man who had nothing more strenuous to worry about than his golf handicap. Lex was their only daughter, so they were going all out on this wedding.

I went next door to Lex's room and pushed the door open. She was lying on her back, staring at the ceiling.

'Morning.'

She looked at me and sat up in bed. 'Pols, it's my wedding day,' she said slowly.

'I know. Good thing you remembered.'

'I mean…' She stopped.

'What?'

'No, it's just, it's my *wedding* day. How weird is that?'

'A bit weird, I guess. On the one hand, I'm still quite surprised that we're old enough to be allowed to drive. I'm basically still about fifteen in my head.' I paused. 'On the other, we've been talking about your wedding for the past six months and there's a bloody enormous marquee downstairs.'

She looked at her hands. 'Yeah. I think… it's probably

normal, right? To wake up on your wedding day and feel weird?'

'I'm not really the one to ask, but I'm sure it probably is. Come on, let's go downstairs and have a coffee.'

Lex climbed wordlessly out of bed and picked her phone up from her bedside table. 'Should I text him?'

'Who?'

'Hammy.'

'Why?'

'Well, you know, just to see if he's feeling… weird.'

'Nope,' I said firmly. 'I'm sure that's bad luck. Honestly, let's go downstairs and have breakfast and get the day started. It's the anticipation of it all probably.' Was it? Who knows, but I wanted a coffee and I felt this sort of pre-wedding jitter was more Karen's department than mine.

★

Downstairs, Karen and Pete's brother, known to everyone as Uncle Nick, were both sitting at the kitchen table in their dressing gowns. Karen was eating a kiwi and there was an enormous plate of croissants in the middle of the table.

'Darling!' she said, jumping up as we walked through the door. 'Come here and give your ancient mother a hug. My daughter's wedding day. What a thing!'

I put the kettle on the Aga while Karen enveloped a silent Lex.

'Did we all sleep well?' said Uncle Nick, picking up a

croissant. He was a banker who had no hair and a fantastically fat stomach. He'd never married, but was adored by everyone because he was the kindest man in Britain.

'Kind of,' said Lex. She looked at Karen. 'Mum, I think I'm a bit nervous.'

''Course you are, my love, it's your wedding day. I was terrified on mine.'

'Really?'

'Yesssss, darling. I ran along to my mother's bedroom at 7 a.m. on the day itself and told her I couldn't go through with it.'

'I didn't know that,' said Lex. 'And then what?'

'My mother took one look at me and said, "Darling, the women in the village have been doing the flowers for three days." And that was that.'

'So you married Dad to avoid disappointing the women in the village and their marigolds?'

'Roses actually, Alexa. But yes. Exactly. And look at us, thirty-five years on and I still love the daft prat.'

Pete chose that moment to make his entrance into the kitchen. He had a dog lead in his hand and a maroon JP Morgan baseball hat on his head.

'I'm going to take Daisy for a walk,' he said. 'Does my only daughter want to come on a last walk with her father?'

'I'm not dying, Dad,' she said, but she was smiling, which I took as a positive sign given the look of terror she'd been sporting in bed minutes earlier. ''Course I will. Let me just go and put some clothes on.'

'I'll leave you to it, I think,' said Uncle Nick from the kitchen table. 'Very dangerous thing, walking.' He reached for another croissant.

'I need to do my nails,' said Karen. 'Polly, are you all right? Help yourself to breakfast, you know the score. I'll be upstairs.'

''Course,' I said.

'And Her Majesty will appear in an hour or so, I imagine, demanding half a grapefruit, but she'll have to look after herself.'

Karen meant her mother-in-law, Fiona, who had been a model in the Forties, photographed by Cecil Beaton, Cartier-Bresson and Man Ray. She'd married Pete's father, a diplomat, aged twenty-one and gave up modelling to have children. But she still prepared for every act of her life since as if she might be called for a photo shoot at any minute. Karen was always exasperated by Fiona's grandness but I liked her because she was prone to telling stories about the time she and Audrey Hepburn had gone to a party in Switzerland together. Or another time when a 'little man in the movies', who transpired to be Steve McQueen, had chatted her up at a dinner in LA.

'I'll be here, soldiering through these croissants. Don't worry,' said Uncle Nick, remaining at the kitchen table.

Minutes later, Lex reappeared in her gym kit. 'Right, Dad, let's go.' They walked out, Karen disappeared upstairs and I sat at the kitchen table and sighed.

Uncle Nick raised his eyebrows at me.

'What?'

'That was a very heavy sigh.'

I smiled at him and reached for the coffee. 'Wasn't meant to be, promise.'

He pushed the plate of croissants towards me. 'Not everyone has to get married at the same time, you know. It might feel like the world is merrily skipping down the aisle, but some people manage perfectly well without. Better, even, dare I say it.' He winked at me. 'But don't tell anyone I told you that.'

I smiled at him and reached for the raspberry jam. 'Thanks, Uncle Nick. You're a dude. If only we could get married.'

'Nonsense, darling. I'm much too fat for you, it would be like marrying Henry VIII in his twilight years. Disgusting. Pass the butter.'

*

By 2.30 p.m., Orsino, one of the two small page boys I was in charge of, had been sick on one of his patent shoes. So I carefully slipped it off his foot and stood at the kitchen sink, trying to remove small globules of vomit from around the silver buckle with a piece of kitchen roll. I told 4-year-old Orsino and his 3-year-old accomplice, Wolf, to sit quietly on a sofa in the corner and watch *Peppa Pig* on my phone.

Orsino was Hamish's godson, Wolf was his nephew. They were dressed like miniature eighteenth-century footmen. Beige knickerbockers, white tights, white shirts with frilly lace collars, long blue frock coats over that.

Outside, a Rolls-Royce had pulled up by the front door and the chauffeur was walking around it, polishing it with a cloth.

Pete appeared in the kitchen. 'I think we should get going, don't you, Pols?'

I looked at the kitchen clock. 'Don't panic, we've got twenty minutes or so. And the others haven't even left yet.'

By others, I meant Karen, Fiona and Uncle Nick, the latter of whom was sitting on a bench outside the front door having his first cigar of the day. Karen was upstairs with Lex, who had recovered her spirits and was drinking champagne in her mother's bedroom, having her veil pinned on.

'You're right,' said Pete. 'I'll have a sandwich instead. And how are you two?' he said, looking down at the small heads of Orsino and Wolf, who ignored him and continued staring at my mobile phone.

'Righto,' said Pete, to no one in particular. 'Think I'll just go and check Nick knows where he's going.'

I squinted at the small patent shoe in my hand. Looked all right. Smelled terrible.

'Here you go, Orsino,' I said, 'let's get this back on so we're ready.' Orsino wordlessly lifted his left foot up for me to put the shoe back on.

'No, other foot,' I said. He lifted the other one, keeping his gaze on *Peppa Pig*.

I stood and caught a glimpse of myself in the kitchen mirror. My hair had started to go frizzy, my purple dress was too tight around the waist, which was creating an unfortunate tyre above it whenever I sat down, and I suspected that Michelle, the make-up artist, had honed her talents in local pantomime. My cheeks were a luminous shade of pink, but when I'd tried to rub it off, I'd flushed even more. I looked like a Geisha girl, not a maid of honour.

Then I heard floorboards creak above me which meant the bridal party were on the move. Karen bowled into the kitchen first. In the end, she'd decided on a pale blue dress and jacket from Caroline Charles. 'A bit of cleavage, but not so much that everyone goes on about what a slapper the mother of the bride is,' she said, putting two empty champagne flutes in the sink. 'Where's Pete?'

'Outside with Uncle Nick, checking he knows where he's going.'

'Oh, for fuck's sake! The church is only five minutes away. And I'm going to be in the bloody car with him anyway.' She stuck her head through the kitchen window. 'Pete, Nick, in the kitchen please immediately. Lex is on her way down.'

'And where's Fiona?' she said, pulling the window closed and locking it.

'Haven't seen her.'

'I'm going to fucking murder that fucking woman,' said Karen, walking back towards the stairs.

★

It was the moment Pete saw Lex that got me. She came downstairs, her dress rustling against the banisters, then stopped at the bottom of them.

'Well…' said Pete, standing in the kitchen doorway, fiddling with his cufflinks. His eyes welled up and he couldn't say anything else. Then my eyes welled up.

Her dress was from a bridal boutique in Wimbledon. White, with little capped sleeves and a fitted lace bodice which was gathered with a thin band at the waist, before it fell into a long silk skirt. Her veil, the same lace as her bodice, trailed out behind her. I thought back to the mornings when we'd both woken up at university, eyeliner smeared down our faces, knickers on inside out, hair as if we were auditioning for the Sex Pistols.

'I can't get make-up on your suit,' said Lex, hugging Pete.

'Oh, don't worry about that, my darling. But we need to get going. Your mother will have hysterics if we're not at the church in ten minutes.'

'Have they already gone?'

'Yes,' said Pete. 'Thank God!'

'I'll get these two organized,' I said, looking at Orsino and Wolf, still engrossed in *Peppa Pig* on the sofa. 'Boys, up we get, time to go to church.'

Outside, in the drive, the chauffeur stood waiting by the Rolls-Royce. A big black Mercedes was behind it for the pageboys and me. I'd retrieved a plastic M&S Bag for Life from under the kitchen sink for the journey in case Orsino decided to be sick over his other shoe.

'In you get,' I said, bundling them into the car.

Beside us, Pete was lifting Lex's train into the Rolls-Royce as carefully as if he was handling a grenade. Then he climbed in and the Rolls moved sedately off. We followed.

'Can we watch *Peppa Pig*?' asked Orsino.

'No, it might make you sick again,' I said crisply.

Orsino and Wolf were supposed to go down the aisle first, but there was an attack of stage fright just outside the church, so I ended up walking down with one small boy either side of me, little clammy hands in mine, the smell of sick wafting behind us. Nobody was looking at us though, because Lex and Pete were following.

I looked at Hamish standing at the front, who didn't turn around until the boys and I had reached their pew. He smiled nervously at me, then turned to look at Lex and his eyes started watering. At least I think they did, but that was the moment that Wolf decided to tug on my sash. 'I need a wee,' he said.

'Oh, Wolfie, you'll have to hold it in. Look, here comes Lex. Doesn't she look pretty?'

'But I really need a wee.'

'Look at her flowers! Aren't they lovely? Here, play with this.' I handed him an Order of Service, hoping that a 4-year-old would be interested in reading hymns.

'Dearly beloved,' boomed Vicar John, who looked 600 years old and had hair sprouting from his ears. The Swifts had been coming to this church on Christmas Day and Easter for years. Although Vicar John had shocked Lex recently in her wedding class with Hamish by suggesting that if she wasn't sure about her fiancé then he remained available. 'I think he was joking,' she told me afterwards. 'But I can't be sure.'

And then we were into 'I Vow to Thee My Country', Pete rumbling out the words behind us like a Welsh chorister.

'I still need a wee,' said Wolf, when we sat down and Uncle Nick stood to do a reading.

'Can you hold it? Just for a bit? Look, it's Uncle Nick, he's going to tell us a story,' I said, nodding towards the lectern.

'And the greatest of these is love,' intoned Uncle Nick, a few moments later, looking gravely at Lex and Hamish over his glasses.

'Bloody isn't,' I muttered to myself.

'What?' whispered Wolf, looking up.

'Nothing, don't worry. Nearly there, then we can go home and have a drink,' I whispered to him.

Next, Vicar John stood to make the address, which I only half listened to because I was wondering what canapés there would be at the reception. A smoked salmon one, inevitably. Hopefully mini beef Yorkshire puddings. Maybe some sort of cheese tartlet?

A small hand tapped me on the knee, and I looked down at Wolf again. 'I really have to do a wee,' he said. A small tear trickled down his cheek.

Oh, God. I looked up at Vicar John and then to the end of our pew. I could sneak out the side of the pew, I realized, and along the side of the church to the doors at the back. Was weeing allowed in a graveyard?

'Orsino,' I whispered, handing him my phone. 'You stay here and watch *Peppa Pig* quietly. Wolf and I will be back in a minute.'

I took Wolf's little hand in mine and, crouching down, led him to the end of the pew. Then I tiptoed as quietly as possible towards the door, sensing everybody's eyes on us. The door clanked and creaked as I opened it. Fuck. I was starting to sweat into my purple dress at the stress of it all. My biological clock had never been more silent.

'Quick, Wolfie, trousers down, just wee here,' I said, crouching behind an old gravestone. Which is when I heard a familiar voice behind me.

'Pols,' it said, so I turned around.

It was Jasper.

'*Jasper!* What… Why are you… ?' I was so surprised to see him here, at Lex's wedding, that I couldn't think of anything else to say.

'Jasper, seriously, what are you doing here?' I asked, louder, still crouching by Wolf as he peed all over the gravestone.

'Polly, I'm so sorry. So, so, sorry, I just need to explain,' he started. He was wearing a morning suit, albeit without a tie. And he was slurring his words.

'Are you drunk? And why are you in a suit? You're not invited any more, Jasper. What are you doing? Why are you here?'

He looked down at his clothes in surprise. 'Don't worry about my suit,' he said. 'I've missed you.'

'How did you get down here? Did you drive?'

'No, I got an Uber. Nice chap called… Well, I can't quite remember what he was called but he drove me.'

'From London? Jesus.'

Jasper shook his head. 'Polly, my darling, you're getting hung up on all the wrong things. Look, I'm here. I'm supposed to be here. I'm your plus one. So, can we talk? We haven't even spoken and I need…'

What happened next was so quick that it took me several seconds to realize what was going on. A rocket seemed to appear from behind me and suddenly Jasper was on the grass, wrestling. There was grunting. And then I realized it wasn't a rocket. It was Bill.

'YOU ARE AN ABSOLUTE WANKER,' he roared.

'What are you doing? Get off me,' shrieked Jasper.

Bill grabbed a fistful of his hair.

'Don't touch my hair!' shouted Jasper, who yanked Bill's tie.

'He's trying to strangle me!' shouted Bill.

I stood motionless, unsure of what to do. Alert anyone and risk ruining the wedding service? Let them slog it out? 'Don't worry, Wolfie,' I said, helping him pull his trousers up and taking his hand again. 'They're just… wrestling.'

Wolf and I stood silently watching the pair of them grappling on the grass between gravestones. Jasper tried to punch Bill, but missed and pummelled his fist into the ground. Bill reached for Jasper's collar and ripped his shirt.

'This is a very expensive shirt!' screamed Jasper.

'GOOD,' roared Bill.

'That is ENOUGH,' I said. 'Both of you get up.'

They ignored me and continued fighting. Then Jasper managed to land a blow on Bill's face. 'You asked for that,' he said.

And then Uncle Nick suddenly appeared from the church, stepping into the fray and pulling Bill away from Jasper.

'This is a disgrace,' he said to them. 'Look at the pair of you.'

'Sorry,' Bill said, dusting his trousers down. His lip was bleeding.

'Sorry, sir,' added Jasper. 'But, Pols…'

'I don't want to hear it.'

'I need to talk to you,' Jasper said, feebly.

'No, you don't,' I said. 'Go home. You shouldn't even be here.'

Jasper looked at me in surprise. 'You're picking him? Over me?'

'I'm not picking anyone. Both of you are mad, but you need to go home before you totally ruin this wedding. Now.'

'How do I get home?' he said. 'I let the driver go and we're in the middle of the country. Pols, come on.'

'Don't "Pols, come on" me. I don't care.'

'Bill, you go back inside the church. And you, Polly. I'll call you a taxi,' said Uncle Nick, looking at Jasper.

Jasper looked at me once more, so I looked in the opposite direction.

'Pols,' said Bill.

'Bill, I don't want to hear it from you either. This whole thing is…' I was going to say crazy, but it was beyond that. I looked at Bill. His lip was still bleeding. 'You need to go sort your face out.'

'Oh, thanks very much. I come out to check you're OK, then I defend your honour and…'

'Bill,' said Uncle Nick, handing him a handkerchief. 'Take this and go inside.'

Bill sighed. 'All right.' He raised his fingers to his lip. 'It really hurts. That guy's a psycho.'

'And you,' Uncle Nick said, looking at Jasper, 'you can follow me and we will wait out here until your taxi arrives.'

'Pols…' Jasper said once more. But I took Wolf's hand and walked back into the church.

Wolf and I tiptoed down the side of the pews again and back into our row, where Orsino was still transfixed to my phone. As I sat down as quietly as possible, Lex looked at me questioningly from her seat while Vicar John – apparently undisturbed – carried on with his address. 'All good,' I mouthed back at her.

I sat and tried to process the scene outside. It was too bad if he missed me, I told myself. He was trouble. My plus one indeed. Jesus, as if. He was delusional if he thought I still wanted him here.

Lex and Hamish stood to do the love and honour bit. She then tried to wedge his ring on, and giggled. The congregation laughed back in a polite sort of way that suggested '*This isn't the best joke in the world, but we're laughing to be polite and because we're British and we don't know how else to alleviate the social tension of a wedding ring not fitting properly*'.

'Now, Alexa, repeat after me. I, Alexa Jennifer Swift, take Hamish James Thomas Wellington to be my husband.'

Lex did her lines, Hamish took her hand and slid the ring on, then she took it off again and held out her left hand, because he'd put it on the right. The congregation laughed in the same way again.

'Wonderful,' said Vicar John. 'I now pronounce you man and wife; you may kiss the bride.'

Clapping and whoops rippled across the church as they shyly kissed one another.

'Now let us all stand for the final hymn,' said Vicar John, as the organist struck up the opening chords of 'Jerusalem'. God, I want a glass of champagne, I thought. A really big glass. One of those champagne glasses that was actually more like a wine glass. The sort of wine glass that Dita Von Teese liked writhing around in.

They sat for the final prayers and blessing and I glanced sideways at the boys, still watching my phone screen.

'Come on,' I said, taking my phone and dropping it into my clutch bag.

'Why?' said Orsino.

'Because it's time to go back to the house for the party and a big drink.'

Half an hour later it was chaos at the house. Cars were blocking the drive, waiters were carrying tray after tray of champagne flutes through to the marquee and I was still trying to hand over Wolf to his mother.

'Photos, Polly, photos,' said Karen. 'Come on, chop, chop, in the drawing room.' She had gone full Stalin.

Pierre, the photographer, was standing on a chair in the drawing room directing everyone.

'You, darling,' he said, pointing at Uncle Nick, 'you need to go to the back.'

'Ah, the small boys,' he said, looking at Wolf and Orsino. 'They must be here. In the front.' He gestured on the carpet in front of Lex and Hamish, so I shepherded my flock to the floor.

I smiled at Lex. 'Look at you all radiant, Mrs Wellington.'

She frowned at me. 'What happened outside? What's up with Bill? Have you seen him today?'

'Err, yes, briefly.' I didn't think I needed to go into the full story right now. 'Why?'

'Well, Mum says he's on his own.'

'On his own?'

'Without Willow,' added Hamish.

'I don't know what's going on but it completely screws the table plan,' said Lex, smoothing a strand of hair behind her ear.

'It'll be fine, your mother's on it. Let's not have hysterics,' said Hamish.

'EVERYONE GET INTO THEIR PLACES PLEASE,' shouted Pierre, still standing on his chair.

'You,' he added, looking at me. 'You are, how you say it, the virgin one?'

'What?' I replied.

'The virgin one. You know, the virgin friend of Alexa,' said Pierre.

'He means the maid of honour,' hissed Uncle Nick behind me.

'Yes, the maiden. That's what I meant. Stand beside Alexa please.'

I tucked in behind Lex.

'Beautiful, beautiful. Now, everyone, look right at my lens and say cheese,' said Pierre.

'CHEEEEEESE,' shouted Orsino and Wolf, before rolling on to their sides and giggling together.

★

I needed three things after the photographs, in this order:

1) *To return Wolf to his mother.*
2) *A drink.*
3) *To find Bill.*

Wolf's mother was lurking in the kitchen so I quickly palmed him off on her, wondering if the canapés had run out yet. 'See you in the marquee,' I said.

Then I ducked through the main entrance to the marquee and scanned it from just inside. Two hundred heads throwing back champagne flutes and eyeballing the room for waiters carrying trays. I watched one waiter appear in the corner with a tray of something – I squinted at it, tuna tartare maybe? – and a cluster of people moved in on him like hyenas. When the waiter came back into view, he looked like he'd been at war and the tray was empty.

'Polly!' said a voice on my other side. I turned. It was Mrs Maloney, our old secondary school teacher.

'Mrs Maloney!' I said, as she pulled me towards her for a hug. She looked like Queen Victoria – short, with a bun pinned up on the very top of her head, and a majestic bosom that, in its younger days, could have graced the front of a ship.

'I've missed you girls. Didn't she look superb? And you, my darling, when's your big day?'

'No time soon, I'm afraid,' I said, desperately looking around for a tray of champagne.

'No man on the scene? You look ever so lovely. You've lost all that puppy fat!'

'That's so kind of you. It's all the sex I've been having. I don't want to marry any of them though…'

The bun on Mrs Maloney's head quivered.

'Do you mind if I go and find a drink? Desperate for a glass of champagne! See you at dinner,' I said. Bad, I know, but I had low blood sugar levels and it wasn't the moment to reminisce with my old teacher.

'Polly, there you are,' said Karen, as I turned around.

'Now, we've got to jiggle the seating plan a bit because Bill's Willow hasn't come and Cousin Mabel had a funny turn this morning and hasn't made it down from Birmingham. So, do you mind finding the wedding planner, the one with the clipboard and the very severe haircut, and telling her to rearrange those two tables. Fucked if I can remember which ones they were on. Just get her to take them off and move the knives and everything around. Sorry to ask you but I've got to introduce Vicar John to Pete's mother.'

''Course,' I said, that glass of champagne looking ever more like some sort of desert mirage.

I stalked out of the marquee and walked around the back. There was an extension off the side where the ovens and staff were preparing dinner. I spotted Janie, the wedding planner, standing in the corner, talking to a handful of waiters.

'Sorry to disturb,' I said, standing beside her. 'Karen sent me. It's just that we need to take two people out of the seating plan.'

'No problem,' she snapped. 'Have they died? We always have that. Deaths overnight of Great-Aunt Agatha or Great-Uncle Henry.'

'Erm, no. No deaths. Not that I know of. It's Willow

Maldon. On Polzeath. And Mabel, er, not sure about her surname. On Lisbon.' Lex had named the tables after the places she and Hamish had been on holiday.

'You,' said Janie, clicking her fingers at a nearby waiter, 'listen to me. Can you go and remove two places from the tables?'

'Yes,' he said decisively, and then a bit less decisively, 'Which places?'

'One from Lisbon, one from… Oh never mind, I'll do it. Otherwise it'll get messed up. You get back to pouring champagne. Speeches are in…' she squinted at her watch '… twenty minutes and everyone's glasses need to be full.'

'Ah, talking of which, can I grab a glass while I'm back here? Haven't had one yet and I'm desperate,' I said.

''Course you can. You, anonymous waiter, take this lady and give her a large glass of champagne. Then get back out there with the bottle. I'll go and sort these tables. Willow and Mabel, Willow and Mabel…' She hurried off, muttering to herself with her clipboard.

'Hang on,' said the waiter, walking towards the fridges. He came back with a bottle and a glass. He handed me the glass, then opened the bottle with a loud bang.

'Keep the bottle,' he said, pouring me a glass. 'There's loads of them in the fridge. I'll just take another one.' He handed me the bottle and went back to the fridge, opened another bottle, spilled half of it onto his shoes, and hurried back out towards the fray.

I took a big gulp, then another, then a few more. Then I

topped up the glass again. I couldn't go wandering back out with a bottle in my hand. Looked bad. I'd just have to drink the whole thing. I needed ten minutes of calm. On my own. Having a drink. There was a chair in the corner of the catering tent. So, I sat down, topped up my glass and had a quick read of a text from Mum.

Send us some pictures Xxxx

I worked my way through three glasses, which gave me a few minutes to have a wee and get back into the marquee for the speeches. Perfect. Also, Bill. Must find Bill and talk to him about earlier.

Trouble was, back in the marquee, people were starting to sit down at their tables. Fuck. I still hadn't found him and it would now have to wait. I was on a table called Ben Nevis, with Hamish's best man, a character called Ed, on one side and Pete on the other.

'You nervous?' I said to Ed when he appeared at the table.

'Nah,' he said. 'Nothing to it. A few gags about anal sex and we're away.'

I looked at Pete on my other side and smiled weakly at him.

Pete was up first, although he was crying, so he struggled to get the words out. 'Come on, Pete, pull yourself together, love,' said Karen from across the table, as he tried to tell a story about Lex falling off her first bicycle. When he sat down, he reached for his napkin and blew his nose into it so loudly I feared bits of his brain would come out.

Then it was Hamish, who stood and dutifully read through his list of 'thank yous'. To Pete and Karen, to his own parents, to his best man and ushers, to the caterers and to the flower ladies, to the 'adorable' pageboys. To his 'new wife' – cue cheers from around the marquee – and he also thanked me. 'I know Lex couldn't have done it without you, Pols, so thank you.' And then he added: 'And she's newly single, chaps, so form an orderly queue!'

At this, there was another ripple of laughter and various laddy cheers. I wanted to crawl underneath the table and die. Here I was, trussed up like Widow Twankey, essentially being tendered for market.

Finally, Ed stood to make his speech. I squinted up at him. Could I snog him? It was sort of traditional, the maid of honour getting it on with the best man. But Ed was a bit short for me.

I looked across the marquee and spotted Joe in animated conversation with Laura from the hen. Then I saw Bill on her other side and gazed at him, trying to catch his eye, but he was talking to Lex's cousin Hattie. At least his lip had stopped bleeding.

Then I also spotted Callum on another table. He winked at me, so I obviously immediately blushed. Really cool, Polly, well done.

'And Hamish said, "I'm more of a breast man myself!"', said Ed, to raucous laughter. 'But then, suddenly, those days were over when he found Lex. So, ladies and gentlemen, once more can we please all be upstanding for Mr and Mrs Wellington.'

Everyone duly stood, starving by this point, raised their glasses for the 234th time and sat back down. I was so hungry I could eat my own head.

'So, newly single, eh?' said Ed, leaning towards me.

I reached for a bread roll.

★

Pudding was mini brownies and shots of Espresso Martini. 'See it off,' said Ed, an expression I loathed, but I picked up the shot glass and knocked it back with him. I was definitely not snogging him. Then, from behind us, the music started. We craned our necks to see Hamish lead Lex on to the dance floor. 'You give me fever,' trilled Peggy Lee, as Hamish lifted his arm for Lex to twirl underneath.

A minute or so later, Lex made a face at me from the dance floor, which I knew was the cue. 'Everyone on,' I said, encouraging those around me on to the dance floor. 'Come on.' I found Joe in the throng, took his hand and he led me into the middle of the dance floor and started rolling me around.

'Have you spoken to Bill?' he shouted over the music.

I shook my head. 'Not really. Is he all right?'

'Yeah. Think so. It's for the best,' said Joe, throwing me out with one arm.

'But I'm confused, what's actually happened? Last time I spoke to him they were moving in together?'

'Not sure really, I think he just freaked out,' said Joe.

'And you're all right?' he said, as I twirled under his arm.

'Yeah, why wouldn't I be?'

'Just checking,' said Joe. 'Bill mentioned Jasper was here so I thought I should ask and—'

'Can we not talk about him right now?' I said. 'Let's just get drunk.'

Around us, Hamish was dancing with his mother, Lex was jumping on the spot, holding up her skirt, while various hens danced in a circle around her and Karen was doing something extraordinary with one of her nephews. Poor boy. Imagine having to slut-drop with your aunt.

'Who've you got your eye on anyway?' I asked Joe. I knew there would be someone.

'Narrow field tonight. But there was a cute waiter around earlier so I might nip behind the scenes in a bit.'

I rolled my eyes. ''Course you will. Right, that's probably enough of this for a bit. Shall we get a drink?'

'Yup,' said Joe, so we headed for the bar, where barmen were doling out Espresso Martinis as fast as they could make them. Weddings are bizarre. One minute everyone's in the church, whispering their prayers on their knees like a devout bunch of Quakers, the next they're elbowing one another out of the way for a cocktail.

Joe passed me a Martini and we moved out of the way. 'Where's Bill gone?' I said, scanning the dance floor. 'I keep trying to find him.'

'Dunno,' said Joe, then he squinted at me. 'But what's wrong with your face?'

I lifted a hand to my cheek. 'Nothing, what do you mean?'

'Your eyeliner's gone a bit… off-piste,' he said.

'Oh, probably the dancing. I'll go sort it out. But if you see Bill, will you tell him not to move because I want to talk to him.'

'Sure,' said Joe.

My make-up bag was in the house so I dodged various dancing bodies, the floor sticky with spilled Espresso Martinis, and left the marquee. As I walked across the lawn I saw Uncle Nick, puffing on a cigar coming towards me. 'Oh, Uncle Nick, thank you for earlier. And sorry.'

'Not at all,' he said. 'I put him in a taxi and that was that.'

I half smiled, half grimaced at him.

'And you're OK?' he asked.

'Fine,' I said. 'Just need to go and sort my face out.'

'You go and do that,' he said. 'And when you come back, we're hitting the dance floor.'

'Sure,' I said. 'See you in a sec.'

'It might give me a heart attack but we're hitting the dance floor,' he repeated, over his shoulder, as he walked back towards the marquee, a trail of cigar smoke in his wake.

Inside the house, I went up to my attic room to find my make-up bag. I could feel the thumping of the music from the marquee. *Doof, doof, doof,* reverberating through the floor.

I looked in the mirror. It was like Marilyn Manson was staring back at me. And I'd got some sort of oily stain on the maroon dress just under my chin; it was shaped like Wales, I thought, scratching at it. Not that I was wearing this dress ever again anyway. Straight to the charity shop. Although even they might baulk at it.

I tore a strip of loo roll and started wiping underneath my eyes. What was Jasper even thinking, turning up drunk and crashing the wedding? What a scene. I still couldn't process it. Was there a tiny bit of me that was pleased to see him? I looked at myself in the mirror. 'Course there was. But, I told myself sternly, as I reached into my make-up bag, there was more of me that didn't want to see him.

I jumped as a floorboard creaked behind me.

'Can I come in? Joe said I'd find you up here.'

It was Bill.

'Jesus, you gave me a fright.'

'Yeah, I can see that from your face.' He smiled and then winced and put his hand to his mouth.

'Serves you right,' I said, slowly running my kohl along one eye. 'I'm sorry though. Is it very sore?'

'Yes, it bloody hurts. All for defending you and for absolutely no thanks.' He sat on the end of my bed and fell backwards on to it.

'I didn't ask you to behave like you were some sort of extra in a Guy Ritchie film. To get into a fight. But thank you, very chivalrous.'

Bill didn't say anything.

'Anyway,' I went on, leaning into the mirror to dust some powder under my puffy eyes. 'Can we talk about Willow? What's happened? You all right?'

'I'm fine,' he said. 'It wasn't right, it turns out.'

'What do you mean?' I looked at him through the bathroom door.

'Well, I think I was trying to force it. Trying to make it right. Trying to imagine our life and I guess I thought that settling down with Willow was what I wanted.'

'But you didn't?' I was confused. 'So why did you ask her to move in?'

'Oh God, I dunno. It felt like I should,' he said. 'And she was dropping hints.'

'How's she now?'

He shrugged. 'All right. Moved out. I think she knew too, deep down. And I've told her she can keep Crumpet.'

'Why did you suddenly realize it wasn't right though?' I went on. 'Or did you know that from the beginning? I sometimes think you know. If I'm honest, looking back to when I first met Jasper, there is no way that was—'

'*For God's sake, Polly!*' said Bill, loudly.

'What?'

'That guy is such a fucking bell—'

'I *know*, that's what I'm saying. You never listen to me. I just fell for the whole thing. The whole being swept off my feet by someone who owns a castle like it was some sort of fucking film. I mean, what a cliché…'

'Pols,' said Bill.

I carried on, I was warming to my theme. 'I mean, no wonder you all knew it would go wrong. No wonder you were all talking about it behind my back—'

'Polly…'

'I mean, what on earth did I think was going to happen? That we were going to get fucking married and I'd spend the rest of my life hanging out with people like… like… Barny Kitchener? I mean—'

'POLLY!' yelled Bill, sitting up on the bed.

I fell silent, staring at him.

'Can you… just… stop talking. Just *stop*. For one second. Just stop. I don't want to hear another word about people called things like Barny. Can we have one moment of peace where your mad, exhausting, unbelievably overanalysing brain just shuts up?'

I frowned at him, make-up brush frozen in mid-air. 'Why are you being so mean? What is wrong with everyone today?'

'I'm not being mean, I just need you to be quiet.' He stood up.

'Oh, hang on, wait for me. I just need to do my bronzer.'

'I'm not going anywhere,' he said.

'Two ticks,' I said, brushing my nose with powder. *Why was it always so shiny?* There were wells in the Middle East that produced less oil than my nose.

'I'm not going yet because I want to do this,' said Bill. He was suddenly beside me in the bathroom. And then he moved my make-up brush out of the way and kissed me. On the mouth. Not a friend kiss, a *man* kiss.

I dropped the brush in surprise.

'Bill, what are you… ?' I said, pulling back from him. 'I mean… you've got a split lip…'

'Polly Spencer,' he said, 'can you just be quiet for two seconds?'

And I was about to ask him if he'd gone mad but I didn't have the chance because he kissed me again. And I didn't pull away this time or interrupt him because I realized it felt kind of right. Better than right. Maybe a bit like when Marianne kissed Colonel Brandon for the first time. Strange, but sort of familiar. Weird, but kind of great. I felt goosebumps along my arms as Bill put his hand on the back of my head to pull me closer to him. I wanted to laugh – I was snogging Bill! – but I thought now was probably the time to be serious. And suddenly I knew, standing there in that hideous dress, kissing my best friend, it was him. It had always been him.

SIX MONTHS LATER...

'MUM, COME ON, WE'RE going to be late. Don't worry about Bertie, he's fine. Let's get going.'

'Darling,' she said, kneeling in front of me, tying a polka-dot bow tie around Bertie's neck, 'it doesn't matter if we're late. It is tradition for a bride to be late.'

There had been much discussion about Bertie's bow tie. More discussion about the bow tie than anything the rest of us were wearing. Mum found the bow tie on Etsy, which had warranted a phone call to my new office, a shiny glass building just off Tower Bridge where Nice News was based. 'Mum, I can't talk now,' I'd hissed down the phone when she'd called me to discuss it. 'I'm writing a story about a human rights lawyer.'

Bill's friend Luke had offered me a job as a writer for his website two months before, so I'd left *Posh!* and started a more serious job where I didn't need to know who the heir to the Duke of Portsmouth was or what kind of dog breed was the most fashionable. Now I spent my days researching and interviewing stories for the site – some serious ('Meet the Headmistress Who's Turned Around This Struggling Academy'), some less serious ('What Flavour Hummus Are

You?'). Last week I'd had a viral hit with a piece headlined 'How Posh Is Your Bathroom?', so my time working for Peregrine hadn't been entirely wasted.

Finally, Mum stood up again, Bertie's bow tie attached. 'There,' she said, smiling down at him. 'Very smart.' Bertie looked embarrassed.

'Seriously, come on. We've got to get going,' I said, looking at the kitchen clock. 'The car's been waiting for ages.'

'Let me just check my lipstick.' She glanced in the mirror at herself. Her hair had nearly all grown back so she looked like she did before being ill. She looked like Mum.

'Your lipstick is fine. Come on. Seriously.'

'Darling, you're very tense.'

'I know, I'm tense because we're going to be extremely late and the congregation will all die of old age. *Come on.*' I made a chivvying gesture with my arms at her and nodded towards the front door. 'Let's go, let's go, time waits for no man. Or woman, in this instance.'

'OK,' Mum said. 'Honestly, Bertie, she's being very grouchy today, isn't she? And today of all days. Right then…' She made for the stairs humming 'Here Comes the Bride', Bertie trotting behind her, then turned around at the top of them to face me.

'Oh lord, what now?' I said.

She smiled. 'Nothing. I just wanted to say I never thought this day would come and…' Her voice started wobbling.

'Mums, don't cry, you'll get it all over…'

She held a hand up. 'Polly, please let me have this moment. Everyone can wait.'

402   SOPHIA MONEY-COUTTS

'All right.' I bit my lip.

'All I want to say is, well, life can feel difficult at times, can't it? Jolly difficult. But we're all right now, aren't we? And I've never been so proud of you and I can't remember a time I felt this happy and...' Her voice cracked.

'Mums, come here.' I reached my arms out for her at the exact moment she lost it. She'd only cried openly with me once since her diagnosis, the day she'd called me at *Posh!* with her results. It felt like she'd been storing it all up for now, I thought, hugging her. I wanted to fully share this emotional moment, but, also, a little bit of me was worrying that she was getting lipstick on my dress.

'That's enough,' she said, pulling back a few moments later. 'We should be going, come on. Oh, Polly, love, look at the time! You should have told me. We're going to be awfully late.'

It was the perfect December day. Freezing but clear, the air so crisp your breath hung in it. Reverend Housley was standing outside the church. She beamed as our car pulled up and reached for the passenger door to let us out: Mum first, then Bertie, then me.

'Susan! Polly! Well, this is a happy day, what a happy day. You look sensational, both of you. Oh, such a happy, happy day!' If a human being was ever to explode with excitement, I mused, looking at the vicar bounce from one foot to the next in her cassock, it would be her.

'Don't start, Vicar, we've already had a little cry this morning,' said Mum.

'Of course, of course,' said Reverend Housley, still smiling.

'Now,' she forged on, 'everyone's sitting inside and waiting. So, if you're ready, then let's get cracking.'

We nodded.

'Ready, Bertie?' said Mum, looking down at him. He still looked embarrassed about the bow tie.

'Terrific. I'm going to go inside and you wait here until the music starts. Then, show time.' Reverend Housley beamed again then hurried inside.

'Right,' I said, smiling at Mum and offering her my arm. 'Let's get you married.'

'Yes,' she said. 'Come on, Bertie, off we go.'

So, with Mum on my right arm and Bertie on his lead walking beside her, we walked into St Saviour's as the organist, a friend of Joe's from the academy, started playing Handel. There had been weeks of deliberation over the music, Joe patiently scrolling through Spotify at Mum's flat, playing different pieces again and again as she declared they were 'too quick', 'too slow', 'too dramatic', 'not dramatic enough', 'too sad', 'too jaunty', and so on.

'This isn't a barn dance, Joseph,' she told him at one juncture, whereupon Joe said Bertie needed a walk in Battersea Park and took him out for half an hour of solitude.

As I walked down the aisle, I caught various people's eyes. It wasn't a big crowd. Mum and Sidney had only invited their 'closest people' to the blessing. But they were mostly my closest people too.

In a pew on the left stood Hamish with a protective arm around Lex, enormous already even though she was only five months pregnant. (*The only way we can have sex these days is doggy style and nobody tells you that, do they? It's not in any of the books*, she'd emailed me earlier that week.)

Up ahead was Sidney, smiling shyly from behind his spectacles at the top of the aisle.

As we neared him, I saw Joe, sitting in a pew on our right, smiling, eyes closed, swaying theatrically to the music.

And then, along from Joe, in the same pew, was Bill. My plus one. An actual, real-life plus one. He wasn't swaying. He was looking at me, grinning. I'd heard people before say, 'One day I woke up and realized I was in love with my best friend,' and I'd always thought, what a total moron, how did you not realize that years earlier? And yet, here Bill and I were, grinning at one another like teenagers. And I thought back to what Mum had said earlier in her flat and decided I'd never been this happy either. Then Bill winked at me, which very nearly ruined the moment. Idiot. But at least he was *my* idiot.

My Colonel Brandon, it turned out.

ACKNOWLEDGMENTS

I'm sitting in the Lake District as I write this, staring at a blank word document on my laptop with the word 'Acknowledgments' written at the top of it. I feel like I've got to make an Oscar speech and I'm about to forget someone. I'm so sorry if it's *you* I forget. I didn't mean it. Honest. You were also very important. Perhaps just slightly less important than the people I've managed to remember below.

Firstly, an enormous thank you to my agent, Rebecca Ritchie, who emailed me some time ago saying had I ever thought about writing a book. I remember walking down the Earl's Court Road when I got the email on my phone and I didn't sleep that night because I was so excited. Well, she's been incredibly patient because a mere 37,282 years on, here we are. A book! Becky, to borrow a phrase from Paul Burrell, you've been my rock. And my sounding-board. I'm stupendously grateful.

Secondly, to editor extraordinaire Charlotte Mursell, Lisa Milton and the team at HQ for publishing *The Plus One*. For loving it and for looking after it and being such immensely supportive champions. I'm still thrilled that you didn't just cackle with laughter at the sex scenes when you first read the manuscript and immediately turn it down. GENUINELY, THANK YOU FOR NOT DOING THAT. I can't wait to work with you on the next book and really try to shock you.

I also owe huge thanks to, well, anyone I've ever worked with on a newspaper or a magazine for putting up with me, but especially to Kate Reardon, Gavanndra Hodge, Annabel Rivkin and Clare Bennett for their friendship and encouragement while I worked at *Tatler*. I want to mention everyone I worked with at *Tatler* here because I love them all, but the list would go on for pages because of the double-barrelled names so I can't, sorry.

To my *Telegraph* supporters – notably Paul Davies, Jane Bruton and Hattie Brett. You have given me the opportunity to write columns about important issues like marmalade and the trouble with having large feet and I am very thankful.

Friends. So many of you to thank for chivvying me along with the book. For encouraging me. For asking if I'd named any of the characters after you. While I was doing the final edits on this book, it struck me that there's a good deal of wine drinking in it. This is inspired by you all and I look forward to many more bottles together.

Mostly, thank you to my family. I can't single anyone out because, again, there are millions of you and we'll be here for days. But you are my world and I owe you everything.

Finally, a nod to Pret A Manger because this book was mostly written in Prets across London while drinking strong white Americanos. I couldn't have done this without your coffee and your egg and sundried-tomato baguettes. Thanks, guys.

ONE PLACE. MANY STORIES

Bold, innovative and
empowering publishing.

FOLLOW US ON:

@HQStories